CRITICAL PRAISE FOR
THE LUSH ROMANTIC NOVELS
OF BRONWYN WILLIAMS

Seaspell

"THE WIT AND WISDOM OF BRONWYN WILLIAMS is unmatched. A tremendous talent writes another great read."

—Pamela Morsi

Halfway Home

"*HALFWAY HOME* IS PURE READING ENJOYMENT, AS SPLENDID AND SATISFYING AS SOUTHERN PECAN PIE. Bronwyn Williams's lively characters leap off the page and lodge in the heart."

—Curtis Ann Matlock

"*HALFWAY HOME* IS FILLED WITH SEXUAL TENSION AND HUMOR. The characters' search for love triumphs in the end to the reader's satisfaction."

—*Romantic Times*

Slow Surrender

"SIMPLY WONDERFUL. Don't miss this novel or you'll be unfulfilled."

—Catherine Coulter

BEHOLDEN

Bronwyn Williams

A TOPAZ BOOK

TOPAZ
Published by the Penguin Group
Penguin Putnam Inc., 375 Hudson Street,
New York, New York 10014, U.S.A.
Penguin Books Ltd, 27 Wrights Lane,
London W8 5TZ, England
Penguin Books Australia Ltd,
Ringwood, Victoria, Australia
Penguin Books Canada Ltd, 10 Alcorn Avenue,
Toronto, Ontario, Canada M4V 3B2
Penguin Books (N.Z.) Ltd, 182–190 Wairau Road,
Auckland 10, New Zealand

Penguin Books Ltd, Registered Offices:
Harmondsworth, Middlesex, England

First published by Topaz, an imprint of Dutton NAL,
a member of Penguin Putnam Inc.

First Printing, September, 1998
10 9 7 6 5 4 3 2 1

 REGISTERED TRADEMARK—MARCA REGISTRADA

Printed in the United States of America

BOOKS ARE AVAILABLE AT QUANTITY DISCOUNTS WHEN USED TO
PROMOTE PRODUCTS OR SERVICES. FOR INFORMATION PLEASE WRITE
TO PREMIUM MARKETING DIVISION, PENGUIN PUTNAM INC.,
375 HUDSON STREET, NEW YORK, NY 10014.

Chapter One

~

Galen tipped his deck chair, propped his feet on the railing, crossed his arms behind his head, and concluded that life, on the whole, was good. Not a single cloud marred the sky. Going to be a scorcher, all right. He liked it hot. The hotter, the better.

Out on the street a mule clopped past, pulling an ice wagon. "Fre-esh ice, nickel a block, git it while it's cold."

Three ragged, yelping boys raced along the wharf, chasing a dog. The dog paused to sniff at a drunk sleeping off the night's revelry. The boys dutifully waited to see if the mutt would cock a leg. When he didn't, the parade continued along the waterfront, ignoring a whore who sat morosely on a bench sipping coffee from a chipped enamelware mug. Ignoring the two gambling boats moored bow to bow, their decks largely empty at this early hour.

From the vantage point of his private balcony on the top deck of the *Pasquotank Queen,* Galen surveyed his world with a degree of satisfaction. Growing up in Connecticut, he'd never expected to end up owning a gambling boat in a small southern town.

But then, he'd never expected to end up drifting for two days with a hole in his head and a broken leg in the icy waters off the west coast of Ireland a couple of years ago, either. If it hadn't been for Declan O'Sullivan, a fisherman with more pluck than luck, he might still be there, six fathoms under.

Yes indeed, life was good. Not perfect, but pretty damned good, considering the alternatives.

Two decks below, he could hear the sounds of another day getting under way. The dry rattle of dice. The clatter of the roulette wheel. A gasp and giggle from one of the girls.

The girls were a compromise, one of several he'd made since he'd parlayed a small stake into fifty-one percent ownership of the *Pasquotank Queen*. He still wasn't certain Elsworth Tyler hadn't lost that hand deliberately as an excuse to ease out from under his daughter's thumb. Ever since then, that gentleman had traveled from one resort to another, reveling in his newfound freedom and spending his cut of the profits as fast as he received his quarterly checks.

And profits were up. It riled the devil out of Tyler's daughter, Aster, who had her own notions of how to run a successful operation. But Galen's fifty-one percent beat Tyler's forty-nine percent hands down. The lady might be holding queens over jacks, but he was holding aces over kings.

And this time, he intended to parlay his winnings into something bigger, something better. Something more to his liking than a damned gambling boat.

Shifting position in the folding oak deck chair to ease the perennial ache of his left leg, Galen heard the crinkle of paper in his coat pocket, reminding him of the letter that had come earlier that morning. Up to his ears in bookkeeping, trying to make sense of one of Aster's scrawled entries, he'd shoved it into his pocket and forgotten all about it.

The letter was from Brandon, his older brother. Probably three lines from Brand, who'd never been much of a correspondent, a few newspaper clippings, and a note from his sister-in-law, all about the new baby.

Galen had yet to see his new niece. Wasn't quite sure

how he felt about being an uncle. For one thing, it made
him feel old. As if life were an outgoing tide that had left
him stranded alone on a barren reef. Brand had the shipyard they'd started together. He had a wife now, and a new
daughter.

All Galen had to show for his thirty-three years on earth
was a leg that seized up on him in damp weather, a streak
of white hair that hadn't been there a couple of years ago,
half-interest in a leaky old tub that looked more like a
high-class whorehouse than a respectable gambling boat,
and a handful of plans that were taking longer than he'd
expected to realize.

Hell of a thing. A minute ago he'd been sitting on top of
the world, now here he was, wallowing in the bilge. Impatiently, he slit open the envelope and pulled out a single
sheet of McKnight Shipping stationery with a few scrawled
lines in his brother's illegible hand. No clippings, nothing
about the baby, nothing at all from Ana.

"Gale," he read. He could make out that much. He
managed to make out the next few words. "You'll be sus—
suspended? No, surprised to learn that you've inherited
two—two—" Galen squinted, trying to decipher the next
line. Ladders? Letters? *Ladies?*

"The hell I have," he muttered. Scowling, he continued
to read. Ladies couldn't be right. Probably lackeys. Last
February Brand had sent him a cabin boy who'd lost an
eye. The kid was smart as a whip, a favorite with all the
dealers. Galen had got him fixed up with a glass eye and
now he was helping tend bar in the small salon.

But what the devil was an Os—obs—osculation? Whatever it was, it was going to be arriving by rail on the fourteenth. "The fourteenth? Hell, that's only three days from
now!"

Galen raked his fingers through his hair. Here he'd managed to get rid of Aster for a few days and now his brother
was sending him—

What? A pair of old ladies to take under his wing? What the devil was he supposed to do with them, dress them up in red silk and bangles and let them hobble around serving drinks and cigars?

Damned if he wasn't tempted to do it, just to see what Aster would say when she got back from visiting her old man.

And what the devil did Brand mean, he'd *inherited* them? You didn't inherit people.

"We'll just see about that, brother. I'll feed your old ladies and put them up overnight, but then your little surprise package is going right back where it came from, with my fondest regards."

Brand had Ana to help him deal with life's unexpected twists and turns. Ana was both beautiful and sensible. Let her take on Brand's latest derelicts.

All Galen had was Aster Tyler, a sharp-tongued harridan who wasn't above fighting dirty to get what she wanted. Right now, what she wanted was to compete with the town's other gambling boat, the *Albemarle Belle*, by laying on dinner cruises, dancing, stage players, and three-day jaunts on the weekends. It was all Galen could do to stay one step ahead of her shenanigans, without having a couple of old ladies dumped into the mixture.

Judas priest, and he'd thought life was good?

It was full of surprises, that much he'd admit, but that was all he'd admit until he saw what showed up on the four-oh-five southbound.

Kathleen stood alone in the midst of a seething crowd of travelers, waiting for Mr. McKnight to return with their tickets. Tara had skipped off with him, still spouting questions quicker than a body could answer. Not that she waited for answers. Bright as a brass button, she was. It was a good thing they were leaving, else she'd wear the poor man down.

Standing stiffly on the siding, Katy diligently guarded

their single piece of luggage, trying hard not to be intimidated by the blur of sound, form, and color all around her. It helped if she focused her gaze on a distant steeple that stood out sharply against the deep blue sky.

She wasn't frightened, truly she wasn't. She had brought them this far, hadn't she? The worst was surely over.

"The worst is over, the worst is behind you." She whispered the words, as if hearing them spoken would fend off the uneasy feeling that leaving Ireland had been a grave mistake.

To Tara, it was all part of a grand adventure. Life itself was a grand adventure, which was both a trial and a blessing, for to be sure, they'd seen more than their share of sadness.

Nine years ago when their mother had died, Tara had been barely four years old. Katy wasn't quite sure how much she remembered, and how much was only her fanciful imagination.

Katy herself had been thirteen. She remembered her mother as clear as if it had been only yesterday, but with a small child and a grieving father to look after, there'd been no time to mourn. Not outwardly, at least.

Fortunately, she was both frugal and sensible. There'd been much to learn, but she'd learned it quickly.

But then they'd lost Da, too.

Fishing had been dreadful all season, the men forced to go farther and farther up the coast to fill their nets. They'd been staying in a rough camp along a barren stretch of coast some distance away when the storm had blown up. For five days it had blown as if all the banshees in the world had been loosed. They'd waited it out, knowing that fishing was often better after a hard blow. On the sixth day they had set out again, filled their nets, and were on their way in when Declan O'Sullivan had spied a man tangled in a bit of flotsam. Before anyone could stop him, he'd gone overboard, and drowned himself saving the life of an American sailor.

They'd brought his body home, leaving two men behind to care for the American, who'd lost his wits and might still lose his life. Katy remembered having bitter thoughts at the time, about how unfair it was for her father to lose his life for a stranger who would probably die in the end.

No one even knew the man's name, for he'd been nearly dead when they'd fished him out of Blacksod Bay, but the entire village had been devastated by the loss of one of their own. Neighbors who could ill afford another mouth to feed had offered to take them in, but Katy had declined. To keep from starving, she had cut and cured peat, trading it for food, hoed the barren scrap of land that was her garden, and fished.

And all the while, her dream had grown. Somewhere there was work to be done. Work that would pay enough so that Tara could go to school and learn to be a lady. So that she would never have to cut and cure peat to make ends meet.

The American had healed and her father's mates had carted him to Galway and put him aboard a ship. It was six months later when the letter arrived. Addressed to the family of Declan O'Sullivan, it had offered condolences, and made some reference to being forever in their debt. All that, plus a monstrous sum of money for the dependents of the man who had saved his life.

Katy had been sorely tempted to return the money with a letter of her own, telling the man that no amount of money could make up for the loss of a life. It had been Tara who'd stayed her hand. Tara, who was growing out of her clothes faster than Katy could cut down her mother's old gowns to make more. Tara, who wore out shoes even faster than she outgrew them.

"Oh, Katy, don't send it back. I want to go to Amerikey, I do." The child had scrunched her eyes shut and commenced swaying, the way she did when the sight was on her. "I see a ship. Oh, she's a lovely thing, she is, with pretty tables all covered in green, and money like golden rain! Oh, let's do it, Katy, let's go to Amerikey like Mr. McKnight says!"

"Well, to be sure, he doesn't come right out and say—"

"He says if ever he can be of service, we have only to ask. That's the same thing, isn't it?"

"That it's not."

"But it's what he meant to say." Tara had grabbed the letter, held it tightly to her flat chest and shut her eyes again. "He wants us to go to him. Why else would he have sent us the fare? Sure and I can hear his voice clear as a bell, that I can."

Pride had urged her to return the money, but Katy, ever the sensible O'Sullivan, knew pride alone would never put flesh on Tara's frail bones, nor shoes on her growing feet. Declan O'Sullivan had jumped overboard to save the life of a stranger and lost his own. There were those in the village who thought that stranger owed Declan's daughters something in return.

He'd been such a charmer, their da. A good man, a comely man, if never a good provider. They'd been left with no more than a moldy thatch over their heads, and that leaking and fit to fall down. But to be fair, it wasn't the first time Declan O'Sullivan had leaped without first looking. Feckless, some said, and that she couldn't deny, and himself with a heart that had never been strong.

She'd prayed over it. Tara had never said another word. With her gift, even as unreliable as it was, she must have known all along that given the choice of emigrating to America or being dependent on the charity of a poor village, they would go.

And so Katy had made her decision. Timmy O'Neill, one of her father's mates, had toted them all the way to Galway in his pony cart, and arranged passage that very day. The ship had been old and ugly, not beautiful. There'd been no tables at all, much less pretty green cloths. They'd eaten ship's fare from tin plates balanced on their knees.

At least Tara had. The very thought of food had made her own belly start to heave.

And gold? The only gold she'd seen or was ever like to see was the sun glinting off Tara's head, and that more copper than gold.

And now here she was, in a town called Mystic in America, still reeling from one endless journey, and about to set forth on yet another. And for all her sister's assurances, she was wishing they'd never left home.

Casting a suspicious glance over her shoulder at the puffing, snorting monstrous machine behind her, she thought longingly of all the friends she'd left behind, people who'd known her all her life. Their village was small, no more than a dozen or so cottages scattered in the crooks and crannies of the rugged coast.

America was big. Big and noisy and full of people who spoke with a funny accent and looked down their noses at the likes of the O'Sullivan sisters.

Not Mr. McKnight nor his lovely wife, never a bit of it. They were kindness itself. Unfortunately, Mr. McKnight was the wrong Mr. McKnight. When they'd finally located the offices of McKnight Shipping, only to be told that Mr. Galen McKnight, the man their da had rescued—the man who'd sent money for their fare—was no longer there, she'd felt as if the world had suddenly tilted under her feet.

But then, ever since they'd left Galway Bay she'd been struggling to come a-right, more often on her knees than her feet, with a bucket clasped in her arms.

It was not Mr. Galen, but his brother, Mr. Brandon McKnight, who took them in charge, gave them tea and biscuits in his office and explained that Galen now lived in a town four days' journey to the south.

Katy could have wept. Only pride had kept her despair from showing through. The gentleman had taken them to his home, where his wife had made them welcome. Tara had fallen in love with their new baby daughter, and Katy had fallen in bed and slept the clock around and then some.

She heard them before she saw them. Tara was still spouting questions. "Here we are," said the wrong Mr. McKnight, handing her two strips of cardboard.

Katy held them at arm's length, pretended to study them, then tucked them into her purse. "I thank you kindly, sir. I'll be repaying you as soon as—"

"Hush now, don't give it another thought. Are you sure you won't change your mind and stay on here for a few more days? My wife would be glad to have you."

Brandon McKnight felt compelled to make the offer. The poor child looked so forlorn. Not the young one. Frisky as a colt, she could talk the hind legs off a donkey. But the other one looked as if she still hadn't got her land legs under her.

Ana had opened her arms, her heart, and her home, as he'd known she would when he'd showed up with two strange young females in tow.

And strange they were. He'd never seen a more bedraggled pair in his life, nor a prouder pair. At least the older one. The little redhead was sharp as a tack and lively as a cricket. After they'd been fed and settled for the night, Ana had joined him in his study. "Brand, did you know that shabby trunk of theirs was filled with books? Between them they don't have enough to dress a decent scarecrow. First thing tomorrow I'm taking them both shopping."

"You do that, my dear. But first find a way to keep from hurting their pride."

"Oh, Lord, you would have to mention pride. Well, I'll work on it. What in the world is Galen going to do with them?"

"I'd give a pretty penny to be a fly on the wall when they step off that train. I dashed off a note to warn him, but they might get there before it does. Probably should have telephoned, but then he'd have talked me out of it. I figured it was best not to give him too much warning, else he might skip town."

"I have a feeling that with a few more pounds and the right clothes, and something done with her hair, Katy would be lovely. Did you notice her eyes?"

"Somehow, I don't think Gale's in the market for any more females, no matter how lovely. He's got his hands full dealing with Tyler's daughter."

"I can imagine. Brand, do you think there's something a bit strange about that child?"

"Tara? Hmmm. Our old friend Maureen would call her pisky-mazed. Fey. Probably a prank, but a harmless one. Although, come to think of it, she hadn't been inside my office more than five minutes when she broke in to tell me where that manifest was that I'd been looking for all week. The blasted thing was right where she said it was, slipped down behind the filing case, so maybe it's not a hoax after all."

"Yes, well, she told me my sister was coming for a visit, and we both know I don't even have a sister, so maybe it is."

Now, as he waited for the train to begin boarding, Brand thought about all that had transpired over the past few days since he'd been summoned to meet an immigration official and take charge of a pair of incredibly green girls.

He thought about his young brother, his only remaining brother, whom he'd come so close to losing. Galen deserved all the good fortune that came his way. Lately, fortune had smiled on him, in spite of his ongoing battle with that harridan, Aster Tyler, but Brand had a feeling Galen wasn't quite as satisfied with life as he let on. He'd sensed a certain restlessness the last time they'd been together, almost as if he were searching for something.

The O'Sullivans were probably not the answer to whatever ailed him, but Brand had a feeling things were going to get interesting, mighty interesting, once they were added to the mix.

The conductor stepped out onto the platform. Brand collected the shabby valise, which was all the luggage they possessed in spite of his wife's best efforts except for the trunk full of books he'd shipped on ahead after promising Katy they'd be waiting for her when she arrived.

Katy took out a handkerchief and dabbed at a smudge on her sister's face. "There, now," she scolded gently. "Stay clean, for we want to make a good impression on Mr. Galen."

Oh, you'll make an impression, all right, Brand thought a few minutes later as he watched them take their seats. Tara grinned through the sooty glass and waggled her grimy fingers.

Katy managed a smile, but she looked scared half to death. Probably wishing she had a bucket handy, in case train travel served her the same as travel by shipboard.

Oh, yes, brother Galen, you're in for a rare treat.

It might even be worth a trip south once Ana and the baby were up to traveling, just to see how it all turned out.

The trip was endless, for all they rollicked along at a breathtaking speed. For the first few hours, Katy's fingers gripped the edge of the seat, as if she was afraid of being thrown off onto the floor.

By the third day she'd given up hanging on for dear life. She was simply too exhausted. She'd seen cities, towns, and villages until she'd lost count, passed pastures and fields, forests, and rivers, until she was dazed by the very vastness of it all. For the first few hours she'd been fascinated, but now all in the world she wanted was a bed that didn't rock, and a cup of strong tea that didn't jiggle off the table and spill all over her lap.

"Sit down, Tara, before you fall."

"I'm hungry."

"It'll soon be suppertime."

The girl bounced a few more times, looking more like the child she was than the young lady she was on the verge of becoming. After being cooped up aboard ship for so long, it was no wonder she needed to work off her high spirits. The brief stay in Mystic hadn't been enough. Katy's heart went out to her, that it did, but there wasn't a blessed thing she could do about it. They would simply have to endure a few more hours of captivity.

"Do you think he'll be glad to see us?" Tara asked for the hundredth time.

"You're the one who said he was longing for us to join him. You're the one who said we'd be sailing on a ship of gold, up to our elbows in emeralds and rubies."

"Well, and I never said that, to be sure. I said I saw a fine ship, and gold, and lovely tables all covered in green. And I did see it, Katy, that I did, plain as day."

"The way you saw Thomas O'Neill's cow lying dead in the bog, and her all along hiding in a thicket with her new calf?"

"Well, and I can't always—"

"And the way you saw Mrs. Gillikin fall off the milking stool and break her leg?"

"It could still happen." The child's blue eyes widened under a fringe of wispy hair. For all she was still thin as a rail, she was growing up. Katy only hoped she'd done the right thing by bringing her to a place where neither of them knew a single soul. Perhaps she should have stayed with the wrong Mr. McKnight.

The child sighed and scratched a bony knee under her thin skirt and single petticoat, cut down from one of Katy's own. Not knowing how long it would take her to find work, even in this land of opportunity, Katy had hoarded every penny. Now she wished she'd spared enough for one new outfit for each of them. With the most generous heart in the world, the right Mr. McKnight was hardly going to be impressed by their appearance.

Mrs. McKnight had offered to take them shopping. Katy, painfully conscious of how shabby she must look to a woman who wore fashionable silk and cashmere, had declined, partly from a lack of funds, but mostly out of a fierce sense of loyalty to the women of Skerrie Head, each of whom had donated something of their own to see Declan's daughters properly outfitted for their new life in America.

She was wearing Mrs. Gillikin's best shirtwaist, that had been stitched by machine and had come all the way from Belfast, along with the lace collar Maura Clancy had worn on her wedding day. Tara's dress had been worn and outgrown by only two of the O'Donnough girls before their mother passed it on. It was practically new.

Wish us luck, Da. We'll not shame you, that we'll not.

Shortly before the train pulled into the depot, a sense of tired excitement began to stir among the handful of passengers getting off there. Faces were wiped, hair was smoothed, collars were straightened and wrinkles were brushed out. Katy requested a damp napkin from the porter, handed over a penny, feeling like a queen dispensing largesse, and proceeded to do her best to erase the stains of travel from her own and her sister's face.

According to Mr. Brandon, the town of Elizabeth City did a thriving shipping business, with more industry moving in every year. There was bound to be work for her here. She had only to find it. She could cut peat in her sleep, but according to Mrs. McKnight, wood and coal were used for fires. Her mother had taught her to sew and make lace. Of course, she needed a strong light to see, but the days were longer here in America, which was another good reason for emigrating.

On the long journey south, Katy's dream had come clearly into focus. She would do whatever she had to do until she earned enough money, but then, as soon as she could pay back what she owed and save enough more for a start, she was going to have her own shop. A ladies' gown shop, full of lovely things that smelled of lavender and linen, not fish and burning peat.

Katy knew better than to talk about her dream now. Who would believe her? She looked a frump in her secondhand dresses, with her peat-stained fingers and her hair all wild from weeks on the ocean. But she could still remember the way her mother had looked before her pretty gowns had become worn and stained, before work and too many babies had turned her hair gray and put lines in her face.

As much as she hated to ask one more favor, she would need Mr. Galen's help in finding a cheap room. He might even put her in the way of a job. According to Mr. Brandon, there was a fine school Tara could attend during the day, so that Katy wouldn't have to worry about her getting up to mischief.

It would all work out. She would *make* it work out.

"Do you think he'll be waiting for us, Katy?"

"Who, Mr. Galen? If not, then we'll walk. Unless you've forgotten how?"

Tara grinned, her pale blue eyes gleaming with excitement. In spite of Mr. Brandon's assurances, Katy wasn't at all certain they'd be met. For Tara's sake, she hoped so. The child still insisted that the right Mr. McKnight had sent for them to come here, and against her better judgment Katy had let herself be convinced, for there'd been no future for them back home.

She was too sensible to put all her faith in dreams, but she was no stranger to hard work. With Tara's dreams and her own strong back, there was nothing they couldn't do, given time and a bit of luck.

Galen McKnight. She closed her eyes and tried to picture the man who might be waiting for them. Mr. Brandon had mentioned his white hair and a bit of a limp, which meant he was older, perhaps even as old as her father. If he looked anything at all like his brother, he would be a handsome gentleman, even so.

She hoped he had children. It would be nice if he had a daughter near Tara's age, someone who could show her where the school was and be a friend to her so that she wouldn't feel quite so alone.

Not that she ever did. Tara had never met a stranger. The world was her best friend, which was never a problem back home, but America was different. It would pay to go carefully until they learned their way about.

"May I please go find the porter and ask him for an apple?"

"Not now, the conductor just announced our arrival."

"Oh, is that what he was after saying? If everyone in Amerikey talks so funny, how're we ever going to get along?"

"Well, we'll see, won't we? If they can't speak properly, then we'll just have to teach them how."

The remark prompted a giggle, which was just what she intended. For all her sweet nature and boundless curiosity, the child was exhausted. They'd both do well not to fall on their face once this infernal machine stopped moving.

Lagging behind a straggling line of passengers, they finally managed to disembark. Katy looked around for someone who looked as if he might be looking for them. Family groups met, embraced, and dispersed. By the time the train pulled out of the station, there were only a handful of people left, not a one of them with white hair and the look of a McKnight about him.

"Do you think he got lost on the way to meet us? What if his pony ran away and he tried to catch him and fell and even now, he's lying there, all broken and bleeding and—"

"Tara Eleanor O'Sullivan, hush your blather!"

Hiding her own misgivings, Katy continued to look around her. Beyond the station, there were handsome houses behind iron fences and blooming hedgerows. Saints preserve us, did everyone in America live like kings?

"I don't see him, Katy."

Katy didn't, either. Other than the two men she recognized as railroad workers, there was only a sweeping boy, two elderly women with market baskets, and a strikingly handsome young gentleman who kept glaring at his watch and tapping his black-booted foot.

Gathering her courage, she set out to ask if he knew the whereabouts of a Mr. Galen McKnight. She'd almost sooner have boarded the train and gone back to where she'd come from, but that was not an option.

Dangerous. That was the first word that came to mind. Wickedly handsome, but as dangerous as any hidden undertow. Heart pounding, she approached the man, with Tara dawdling along behind. She opened her mouth to speak when the two elderly women came around the corner, market baskets over their arms.

The gentleman tipped his hat, revealing hair the color of tarnished brass with a narrow streak of white above his left brow. Katy waited, fighting the urge to flee, and an equally powerful urge to go closer.

"Morning, Miss Maude, Miss Abbie," Galen said politely. One of the old women giggled. The other simpered.

Galen was fit to be tied. He'd placed more calls to Brand's office in the past few days than he had in all the time he'd been here, and not a one of them had gotten him any answers.

"I'm sorry, sir, but Mr. Brand just stepped out. I could give him a message."

Eight calls, and Brand had just stepped out before every damned one. Galen was beginning to believe his brother was deliberately avoiding him.

"Yes, ma'am, it surely is a fine day," he said, and forced a smile as the two spinster sisters hurried home to their supper.

The minute they were gone, his smile turned into a scowl. What the devil had happened to his own old biddies? The ones Brand had palmed off on him? Either they'd missed the train, or got off at an earlier stop, or Brand had been pulling his leg all along.

He had read and reread the letter. It made no more sense the last time than it had the first. For all his various skills, his brother was sadly lacking in some areas. No wonder he had an office full of clerks to keep his ledgers for him. Why the devil hadn't he simply telegraphed?

Galen checked his watch again, as if the time meant anything. The damned train had come and gone, and Brand's old ladies weren't on it. As far as Galen was concerned, he had done his duty. He shrugged and was about to head back to Water Street when a pair of ragged children approached him. Without thinking, he reached in his pocket for a coin.

And then something made him give them a second look.

Chapter Two

〜

With all the savoir faire of a professional gambler—
which he was, in a manner of speaking—Galen curled
his fingers into his palms, took a deep breath, and counted
to thirteen. Not a glimmer of emotion showed on his face.

He was going to wring Brand's neck.

No, first he was going to deal with this pair, hole up in
his private quarters, and get quietly drunk, and *then* he was
going to wring his brother's neck, if he had to go all the
way back to Connecticut to accomplish the deed.

Old ladies? They were children! A pair of ragged, faded,
exhausted waifs who looked as if they'd been thrown into
a lion's den and were waiting to be served up for dinner.
What the devil did he know about children? What was he
supposed to do, adopt them? First Oscar and now this pair.
You'd think he was running a bloody orphanage instead of
a gambling establishment.

It didn't take long to discover who they were. The minute the little redhead opened her mouth, he recognized that
brogue.

"O'Sullivan," he muttered, half under his breath. His
composure badly shaken, he tried unsuccessfully to keep
the irritation from his voice. "You must be Declan O'Sullivan's children."

The smile on the freckled face of the younger girl wavered. What did she expect him to do, throw open the gates of paradise and wave them through? "Aye, she's Kathleen Margaret Sheehan O'Sullivan, after Ma's old granny, and I'm Tara, after me da's own ma."

Which was confusing as hell and several times more than he cared to know about either of them.

Tilting her head to one side, the kid narrowed her eyes. "Are you sure you're the right one this time?"

Galen barely contained his frustration. "The right what?" He glanced at the older one, slammed head-on into a pair of pale green eyes squinting through a thicket of the longest, blackest eyelashes he'd ever seen, and momentarily lost his train of thought.

The little redhead stood on first one foot, then the other, the way kids did when they had to pee. Galen felt a wave of panic sweep over him. She was still chattering. "The right Mr. McKnight. We went to that other place first, because you said that's where we should go, but you weren't there. The wrong Mr. McKnight fed us and took us home with him, and he put us on the train. Sure and he even paid our fare, that he did, for we've all but used up the money you sent for our passage. Travel is fearful costly, it is."

The older O'Sullivan hissed her sister to silence. "We've a trunk to be collected, sir, if you would be so kind."

Galen wanted to say kindness was the very last thing he was feeling, but he didn't have it in him. She looked as if a whisper, let alone a sharp word, would drop her in her tracks. "Freight office," he growled, and tried to pull away from the spell of a pair of eyes the exact color of green grapes.

The little one hitched up her limp, faded skirts. "Do you have any children? The wrong Mr. McKnight has a little baby girl. I held her. I could look after your baby for you. I'm practically thirteen, and—" She broke off, looked him dead in the eye, and played her hole card. "But then, you're not wanting us at all, are you?"

He folded. What the devil was he to say? Pasting a sick smile on his face, he blustered something about being surprised, that was all, which was more of an understatement than an outright lie. "I expected you in on a later train."

"Then why did you meet this one?"

Lifting his hat, Galen raked a hand through his hair, buying time. Then he offered the best excuse he could come up with at short notice. "An intelligent man always hedges his bets."

"Me da said a smart man never bets on the turn of a card, but Tommy Clancy said betting on cards was no worse than betting on the horses. Me da was a dab hand when it came to the horses, he was."

A bead of sweat formed under his hat band and trickled down his forehead. He dug out a crisp linen handkerchief and mopped it away. Turning his attention to the girl in the ugly brown shirtwaist with the crooked lace collar, who was older than he'd first thought, he came up against those eyes again. This time it was the expression that got to him, not the color. She might be down, but something told him she was far from out. At the moment she was as pale as buttermilk. Not a speck of color except for those remarkable eyes of hers and half a dozen freckles.

Oh, hell. If she was going to pass out on him, he'd better get her off the street. "Miss, are you all right?"

He gave her full marks for gumption. She ratcheted herself up to her full height, which put the top of her head somewhere in the region of his collar button. "That I am, sir."

That he doubted, but had the good sense not to say so. He figured his best bet would be to get her somewhere where she could collapse in private. The sooner she got over whatever ailed her, the sooner she could start answering questions.

Such as what they were doing here.

Such as what the devil they wanted from him. He'd done

his best to make up for their loss. If it wasn't enough, then that was just too bad. He had damned well wiped out his savings, which meant he'd had to postpone his plans.

Not that any amount of money could make up for the loss of a loved one. More than most men, Galen knew that. It was beyond his power to bring back Declan O'Sullivan. The man was dead, and fair or not, he himself was alive. O'Sullivan's mates had let him know straight out they thought it was a rotten trade, but there wasn't one damned thing he could do about it other than live with the burden of guilt.

And then he'd come home to yet another tragedy. Brand had never uttered a single word of blame, but Galen knew that the blame for his youngest brother Liam's death rested at least in part on his own shoulders.

But dammit, guilt or no guilt, the last thing he needed was a readymade family!

For a man who considered himself suave, polished, cool under pressure—all of which he was, if only because he'd deliberately cultivated those qualities—Galen couldn't come up with a single thing to say that was even faintly adequate, much less appropriate to the occasion.

He gazed across the Norfolk and Southern tracks at the stately houses that lined Pennsylvania Avenue, as if the answer could be found there.

Dammit, his feet hurt. He'd thought when he'd taken over the *Pasquotank Queen* that looking the part of a dangerous gambling man would not only be good for business, it might keep some of the young bucks in line. Adopting the black frock coat, the tall western boots, ruffled shirt, and flowing tie of some of the most notorious professional gamblers he'd met out West had all been a part of the dangerous image he'd deliberately cultivated.

By the time he'd discovered that the constant wearing of high-heeled boots threw him off balance just enough to worsen the ache of his leg, it was too late to change. He'd

seen the wary looks a few of the reckless younger set sent
him, heard their whispers. Obviously, he impressed the
devil out of them, quite literally. Which had been his intention, after all.

But his legs were cramping, and his head was aching,
and now he had this little green-eyed ragbag to deal with.
"Would you, uh—care for a glass of ice tea?" It was the
best he could come up with at short notice. "And maybe a
bite to eat?" he added with grudging generosity.

"No, thank you. If you'd be so kind as to direct us to the
nearest boardinghouse, we'll not bother you further, sir."

Galen sighed. Against all reason, he found himself wishing Aster was back so that he could turn the pair of them
over to her. God knows what she'd do with them—put
them on the next train north, probably. At least his own
conscience would be clear.

He looked from one face to the other, one plain and ex-
pectant, the other wary, far too pale, yet oddly arresting.
He'd seen better-dressed scarecrows.

And that hair . . . thick, black as pitch, with the ugliest
hat he'd ever seen on any woman riveted squarely on top.

Ah, what the hell. He gave in with as much grace as he
could muster. "Come along then, I'll see you aboard the
boat and send someone for your trunk."

Not another boat. Katy opened her mouth to protest and
then shut it again as she blinked away the spots that swam
before her eyes. Warily, she watched the tall, dark-clad man
stride across the siding to speak to a gentleman wearing a
red cap. He flipped him a coin—silver, not copper. She had
a sinking feeling she might have insulted the porter by offering him a penny for the use of a wet towel.

If this was the right Mr. McKnight, they were in trouble.
She'd expected an older man, someone more like her own
da. Instead, here was this dapper gentleman wearing Sunday clothes on a Thursday morning, and him with the face
of a fallen angel.

Oh, she didn't trust him, not a bit of it. Not with those cold blue eyes and that streak of white hair. Besides all that, he had the most beautiful hands she'd ever seen on a man. Smooth, clean, with the long fingers all dusted with golden hair.

Her own hands were still callused and hard, the peat stains still evident around her fingernails. Self-consciously, she buried them under a fold in her skirt, wishing she had thought to wear her gloves instead of packing them away in her valise.

"It's not more than a block away, if you don't mind walking."

Tara was bouncing on her feet. The child had been cooped up so long, she couldn't stand still. Katy would have liked nothing better than to lie down right here on the planks in the sunshine and sleep for a week.

But there were arrangements to be made. And to be truthful, she would sell her soul for a good, strong cup of tea and a bite to eat.

The gentleman took up her valise in one hand, and crooked an elbow. Cautiously she placed her hand on his arm. The jolt that raced through her she set down to being tired to the bone.

Just to be sure, though, she peered at him under the cover of her hat brim, only to find that even from this angle, even frowning fit to scare the devil, he was so handsome he took her breath away.

With her free hand, she smoothed her limp skirt, as if smoothing away the wrinkles would make up for days of travel. They set out along the wharf, and Mr. McKnight pointed out the sights along the way. A lumber mill and a railroad wharf, the homes of a judge and a prominent merchant.

She could tell he'd sooner be left to his own thoughts, not that they were all that pleasant from the looks of him. She was searching for a polite way to tell him he needn't

put himself out to be entertaining when he nodded to two
of the fanciest boats she had ever seen in all her born days.

"The big one with the blue awnings is the *Albemarle
Belle*. Mine's the one on the far side. The *Pasquotank Queen*,
at your service."

Katy made what she sincerely hoped was an appropriate
response, but all she could think of was tea and her empty,
aching belly. There'd be time enough to look for a place to
stay once she'd had herself a bite to eat.

Tara skipped and chattered away, gawking at all the cupo-
las and fancy windows on the houses across the train yard,
at the river with its boats of every size and description, the
wharves with their warehouses and fish houses, drunks and
stevedores, and even a few painted women. She asked doz-
ens of questions without waiting for a single answer.

Katy glanced nervously at the man beside her. She had
gone over it in her mind again and again on the long journey south, wondering if she'd done the right thing by accepting the money.

She had managed to convince herself, with Tara's help,
that returning it would have hurt the man's feelings. Seeing him now, face-to-face with those cool blue eyes, with
his fine and fancy suit, she wondered if he even had any
feelings.

Surely not the kind of feelings she could ever understand.

She could hear the soft even sound of his breathing. She
could smell his scent, faint and crisp and clean, like fine
woolens and tobacco. The intimacy of it took her by surprise, for she'd never felt such a thing before, didn't know
what to make of it.

Better to make nothing at all. If the scent of a man and
the sound of his breathing could overset her, then she was
in worse condition than she'd thought.

"Here we are," Mr. Galen announced in a voice Katy
suspected was meant to sound cheerful. It didn't fool her,
not for a minute.

When he turned in alongside the fanciest floating palace ever a body could imagine, a dozen questions rose to the tip of her tongue, but before she could ask a single one, her stomach gave a noisy rumble. She flushed. Tara grinned. Mr. Galen tossed a coin to a sweeping boy and told him to see to the trunk that would be coming along directly. Then, reclaiming Katy's arm, he led them up the red carpeted gangplank.

Tara skipped on ahead. Katy tried to hang back. Sunlight danced blindingly off the water. She was acutely aware that a wharf full of strangers had stopped to stare. Men with an unsavory look about them followed their progress. Ragged little boys stopped skipping stones to whisper among themselves. A frumpy-looking woman dressed in dirty green satin called out, "You could do better than her, love."

Wanting only to disappear, Katy let herself be led aboard the gaudy stern-wheeler. As the smell of fried onions drifted out to meet her, mingling with the familiar smell of fish, her belly gave another noisy protest.

"Miss O'Sullivan? Are you coming?"

He sounded so impatient. Katy glanced around for Tara, and saw her back on the wharf again, busy chatting up the sweeping boy, who was staring at her as if he couldn't make out a word she was saying. Hardly surprising. The child could talk a chaffinch out of her nest.

Katy opened her mouth to call her back and sighed, instead. If only she weren't so terribly tired. If only her monthlies hadn't come on her three days ago. If only she'd dared eat the sumptuous meals served in the dining car.

If only she'd never let herself be talked into following a dream all the way to this big, noisy land where they were at the mercy of strangers. She'd been miserably ill on the crossing, but not so far gone she hadn't heard the whispered tales about fancy gentlemen who pretended to help innocent young girls fresh off the boat, only to spirit them away for evil purposes. She'd heard it said of London and Liverpool, but who was to say it couldn't happen here in America, as well?

And this *Queen* of his, or whatever it was he'd called her, looked to Katy like a floating den of iniquity. Never in all her born days had she seen such a monstrous fancy boat. As if to prove her right, a painted lady in a red silk gown appeared on one of the railed balconies, shamelessly flaunting herself in broad daylight.

Tara meandered along the gangplank as if they had all the time in world, gawking at everything in sight. Katy turned to go after her when a sudden wave of dizziness forced her to stop and cling to the railing.

"Miss O'Sullivan? Are you all right?"

Cold sweat broke out on her body. She felt chilled in spite of the overwhelming heat of the sun. Clinging to the wooden rail, she waited for the spots in front of her eyes to clear away.

"Take my arm, I won't let you fall."

"I'll not be falling," she whispered, accepting the extended arm and swallowing as a fresh wave of dizziness assailed her.

"Lord love us, I hope she ain't carrying a disease," someone whispered.

"Looks puny to me, don't she look puny to you, hon?"

Tara hurried up, a worried look on her face. "Katy, are you ailing?"

Before Katy could open her mouth to reassure her that she was perfectly all right, the child was explaining to everyone within earshot that poor Katy hadn't been able to keep a morsel down for weeks, nor had she dared eat more than dry bread aboard the train for fear it would return on her.

"Tara, hush," Katy whispered fiercely. For all she hadn't a wicked bone in her body, the child had no more discretion than a bleating sheep.

She managed a sickly smile for all the people who had crowded around, most looking concerned, a few merely curious. And then she was swept up in a pair of strong arms.

Clinging with both hands, she opened her mouth to protest, gulped in the familiar scent of bay rum, wool, and tobacco, and gave up the struggle.

A gruff voice somewhere above her head said, "Tara, go aboard and ask for Ila, there's a good girl."

Father in Heaven, look after her if I die here in this heathen land with not so much as a decent wake to mark my passing. Just don't let her end up in a workhouse. Or worse.

Forcing her eyes to open, Katy called on the last vestige of strength she possessed. "Tara must have schooling," she said hoarsely, addressing the square, clean-shaven jaw inches away from her face. "And our mother's books—she's to have those. Promise me!"

"Shh, you've nothing to worry about. Tea, am I right? Strong tea and dry crackers to settle your stomach? Traveling affects some that way, but we'll have you back in fighting trim in no time, that I promise you."

Dreading the return of the awful seasickness that had plagued her all the way across the ocean, Katy clung to the shoulders of the handsome devil who carried her across the deck of his fancy boat, praying he wouldn't drop her. "Strong," she managed to whisper, unsure if she meant the man or the tea. As the spots coalesced into a darkening veil, she added, "And no milk . . ."

Ila Billings, the woman who served as housekeeper and manager of his female staff, stood by the bed, hands on her broad, bony hips, a dour look on her face. Galen had just come back from paying the freight on the trunk that had been sent over from the freight office.

He peeled off his coat, flung it aside, and loosened his tie. "What's the verdict? Is she really sick?"

"Mostly needing food. As for what else ails her, it's not catching, so you can take that look off your face."

Galen flung out his hands in a gesture meant to convey innocence. He couldn't take his eyes off the small form lying so still and pale in his bed, with acres of glossy black hair spread out across his pillow.

He should've taken her to the spare cabin. "Thanks, Ila. You can go now, I'll take over here."

"I'm not going nowhere. She's a respectable girl, for all she's ragged out so poor and all."

"Give me credit for half an ounce of common decency, will you? Now go tell Willy to make us a pot of tea. Tell him to boil the stuff if he has to, just be sure it's strong enough to float nails. And no milk."

"You want I should bring up some of that pork stew we had for supper last night?"

The slight figure on the bed stirred, moaned something under her breath, and subsided. Galen lifted his shoulders and let them fall in a gesture of defeat. "I seriously doubt if Miss O'Sullivan would appreciate it. How about toasted bread, no butter, and a bit of ginger conserve?"'

"It ain't ginger she needs to settle her belly. There's times when a woman has more to bear than's fair, I'll tell you that."

"Don't bother, I don't want to hear it."

"Men!" she snorted in exasperation, but left to fetch tea and toast. At the door, she turned back for a parting shot. "I'm going to add a dollop of whiskey to the teapot. It'll help ease her miseries." She strode away in a swish of taffeta, her parting words echoing down the passageway, as they were meant to do. "Cowards, every last one of 'em. If a man had to put up with half of what a woman has to put up with in this vale of tears, you'd never hear the last of it."

Galen swore and slammed the cabin door. He grabbed the back of his neck, digging his fingers into the knotted muscles there, and then flung himself onto his sturdy oak desk chair and began kneading his thigh.

Damned old bones. Damned old boots. Where the hell had he been the day the Lord had handed out brains?

After a few minutes he swiveled around so that he could keep watch on the bed. Or rather, on its occupant.

Ila had removed her collar and loosened the top buttons of her shirtwaist. Even with the balcony door propped back and all six portholes wide open, the room was hot as blazes.

He thought about uncovering her, reached out and touched her brow, and then her hand, and decided she needed the light spread, after all. She was cold. Clammy.

He didn't want her here. Didn't need her here. God knows what he'd been thinking of, but when she'd fainted, the only thing he could think of was getting her away from all the curious eyes.

He could have put her in Ila's room, but it would've been even hotter than his. There was plenty of space here on the top deck if he'd taken the time to think things through. Originally there'd been four staterooms, but when he'd become part owner, he'd had a bulkhead removed, combining office space and sleeping quarters into one spacious cabin. The Tylers claimed the remaining two, Aster in one, her father in the other. Although he was hardly ever in town now that he'd been liberated.

Idly massaging his aching limb, Galen gazed morosely at the woman on his bed. She looked as fragile as eggshells. How the devil had she managed to come all the way from Ireland, with a child, no less, without someone to look after her?

He'd wanted to send for a doctor, but Ila had voted him down.

"The last thing that poor child needs is to wake up to some old man pawing at her. You leave her to me, I'll see to her. Lordy, if she ain't skinny as a weed. Looks like she ain't eat a bite in a year. Not like that young'un. Now that one's trouble, you mind my words."

Galen figured he would mind her words when he had time. Right now, he had to think of a way out of this mess before Aster got back. He'd changed his mind about wanting to turn them over to her. God only knew what she'd do with them. Turn 'em over to the law as indigents, probably. Dump the pair of them out onto the wharf to take up whatever nefarious trade they were best suited to.

He was in business with the woman, through no fault of his own. That didn't mean he trusted her out of sight. Aster Tyler ran her end of the business with an iron fist. He'd given in to her in the matter of the girls, the new red carpet, and matching draperies, but he drew the line at fancy dinner cruises and hired entertainment. As long as he ran honest tables, offered good whiskey and fine cigars, his customers could get by on pickled eggs and hot sausages.

But she wasn't going to tolerate this pair. Not without making demands he wasn't about to meet. Like it or not, the O'Sullivans were his own personal problem.

The kitchen boy rapped on the door and edged inside with a heavily laden tray. Galen took it from him and set it down, and the kid nearly tripped over his own feet, staring at the woman on the bed.

Galen handed him a coin and backed him out the door, closing it firmly behind him. "Katy," he said quietly. "Tea's served."

He'd never seen skin so white. It was almost translucent. Hair that black usually lacked luster, but hers reflected every color of the rainbow. He studied the eyelashes that were fanned out on her cheekbones, wondering if they were real.

Of course they were real. He'd known enough women in the past to recognize artifice when he saw it. He'd thought she was a child the first time he'd seen her.

She wasn't a child. If she'd been a child, his body

wouldn't have reacted the way it was reacting to the sight of her in his bed, lying between his satin sheets, with her hair spread over his pillow.

You're a rotten, black-hearted scoundrel, McKnight. The woman's under your protection. At least, she is until you can find someone to take her off your hands.

"Kathleen? Katy? Miss O'Sullivan?"

Katy awoke to the smell of tea. Real, honest-to-goodness tea. Smoky, rich, and strong enough to tan leather, with a hint of something that reminded her of her father. The watery brew she'd been served aboard the train hadn't been strong enough to stain linen.

She opened one eye cautiously and waited to see if the sky would come crashing down on her head. Nothing happened except that her belly rumbled.

At least it no longer ached quite so much. There were no more dots dancing before her eyes. So she opened the other, and it was then she saw the man across the room, sprawled in a chair in a way that was hardly respectable, much less respectful.

Feeling at a disadvantage, she struggled to sit up. Saints preserve us, her hair was all about. And she was unbuttoned halfway down her chest! She was all set to jump out of bed and run for the door when he held up a fat brown teapot. "I believe you requested tea and toast?"

Narrowing her eyes on the teapot, she said in a voice husky with sleep and exhaustion, "I never said anything about toast."

"No? Maybe my housekeeper did, then. She's gone below to see to some supper for your sister. I thought you might want to start out with toast and ginger conserve instead of Willy's pork stew."

The temptation, not to mention the sight of a familiar-looking brown Betty teapot, almost like the one they used to have, was too much to resist. She swung her legs off the edge of the bed, embarrassed to see that someone had removed her shoes and left on her stockings with the gingham patches where the toes had been darned too many times to hold.

"Stay there, I'll serve you. You'll feel more like getting up once you've had a bite to eat."

Not at all sure she wouldn't have fallen flat on her face if she'd tried to get out of bed, she leaned back against the pillows.

"Thank you," she said in that same husky voice she'd heard before coming from her own throat. She could yell and screech with the best of them when she wasn't so awfully, terribly tired.

She accepted a cup of tea, sniffed and wrinkled her nose.

"It's whiskey. Ila said it would help whatever ails you. If you'd rather have it plain, I'll send down to the galley for more."

She sipped and said, "No, this is fine," and then sipped again. It was more than fine, it was wonderfully restoring. When half the cup was empty, she took a deep breath and said in a far firmer voice, "Now, sir, I believe there's talking to be done."

He regarded her steadily as she helped herself to a second cup of tea. She took a scalding gulp and shuddered. Finally, he said, "Ladies first. Would you care to tell me just what—that is, just why—oh, devil take it, what I mean is—" He tipped back in his chair and gazed at the ceiling, and Katy, watching him, decided that whereas Tara's eyes were the color of a summer sky, his were more the blue of the winter sea. Perhaps not as cold as she'd first thought, but hinting at storms and mysterious depths.

"What you mean to say is that you never expected us," she said with a quiet dignity. "You never meant us to come here, after all, did you?"

The two front legs of his chair hit the deck with a loud

thud, and Galen glared at her. "Dammit, no such thing! Although I will admit I was somewhat surprised," he conceded.

"That you were. I can set your mind at ease, then. I have plans of my own, so I'll not be a burden to anyone."

How, he wondered, could any woman look so damned proud and so forlorn at the same time? "Oh? Might I inquire as to these plans of yours?"

"Well . . . I suppose telling won't hurt anything. First I mean to find a place to stay, and then I'll find a job and earn enough so that I can pay my debts, and after that I mean to save up enough to go into business for myself."

"Go into business for yourself, hmm? And what type of business did you have in mind, Miss O'Sullivan?"

He hadn't meant to sound so skeptical, but dammit, didn't the woman have a grain of sense? Nobody came to a brand-new country and set up in business, just like that. Certainly not a woman. Respectable women didn't work. At least, not outside the home. Not unless they were widows. Or orphans. Which she was.

Oh, hell. He sighed and raked a hand through his hair.

She poured herself another cup of tea and sipped it.

They continued to glare at one another, neither of them willing to give an inch. They were still glaring when someone rapped on the cabin door.

Chapter Three

With an impatient exclamation, Galen strode to the door and jerked it open. "Not now!" he snapped.

"But, Cap'n, Pierre says—"

"Tell him I'll be down shortly. Oh, and go by the galley and ask Willy to send up a plate of whatever's left over from supper, will you?"

"Aye, sir."

From across the room, Katy couldn't help but overhear. The boy called him Captain. He didn't look like any boat captain she'd ever met. Not that she'd ever met that many men. But then the captains back in Skerrie Head wore rough baggy woolens, not fancy frock coats, ruffled shirts, and black boots polished bright as a mirror.

Under the silky sheets, she stretched her legs, wriggled her toes, and studied her surroundings. There were books, all neatly lined up on a shelf, with a picture of a horse, and another picture of a woman.

She stared at the smaller one, wondering who the woman was. If she could truly be as lovely as she appeared. There was a look of serenity about her that was vastly appealing.

Katy yawned. Whatever had ailed her before no longer did. She was no longer rolling about or being rattled to death on a noisy, smelly train. Her belly no longer felt achy and heavy. To be sure, she was disappointed that Mr. Galen neither needed nor wanted them, but that had been Tara's dream, never her own.

They didn't need him, either. She had brought them this far. She would provide for them well enough. Still, a friend would have been nice.

Lifting her chin, she said quietly, "If you'll have my trunk set out on deck, then we'll be on our way, sir."

He turned back into the room. He wasn't smiling. "And which way is that?"

She looked at his nose, which was a fine, brave nose, but not as beguiling as his eyes, which were dangerous. Spellbinding. Hinting at all manner of deep, dark, brooding secrets that were none of her business.

It must be the tea, she thought, for she'd never been a fanciful woman.

"Katy?"

"Oh. Sir? Which way is what?"

Sounding exasperated, he said, "You might as well take time for a bit of supper before you go. You can start with the toast. I've sent down for something more."

All of a sudden, she was starving. All her life she'd made do on short commons and thought little of it. Tea and a bowl of porridge of a morning, scad and a potato of an evening. More for the menfolk, to be sure, and that washed down with a good strong ale, but for the women and children, a fish, a potato, and a bit of hard, yellow bread made of Indian meal, served well enough.

"Oh, well, if you insist, I'd not say no to a bit of mutton stew."

"I'm afraid I can't oblige you there. Here in North Carolina, we run more to swine than to sheep."

Bacon she liked well enough, but she drew the line at pig stew. "Then I don't believe I'm hungry, after all, sir."

He looked fit to be tied. Katy knew it was mostly her fault. If she could have thought of a comforting word, she'd have offered it, but the best she could do was bid him farewell and take herself off his lovely boat with the wide, soft bed and the fine silk sheets, and the loveliest tea in all the world.

"Dammit—I beg your pardon, but it's been a long day, and for me, it's only just beginning. What I mean to say is, you'd do well to eat something before you try to get out of bed."

"Would you care for some tea? Oops. The pot's empty, but never mind, we'll just ring for more. I read that in a book once. Ring a bell, and tea comes on a fine silver tray."

He leaned closer, peering at her suspiciously.

As always whenever something came too close to see clearly, she reared back. She mistrusted the look on his face. Clearly, he thought she meant to latch on to him, like a winkle onto a rock.

"Did I say how skilled I am at reading, writing, and sewing?" In a strong light, she was. At arm's length. "My mother taught me."

There, that should set his mind at ease. She would never be a burden to him. There was bound to be work for someone who could do so many things, and do them well. Although she'd as soon not have to sort and salt fish, for she hated the smell that got on her hands and stayed there.

Feeling warm, relaxed, and not at all frightened of the future, she went on to say, "Did I tell you about our mother? She was the loveliest lady in all Dublin, Da said, he was that proud of her. Gifted, she was. Not the sight—that comes hit or miss, and I'm that glad it passed me by."

"Gifted?"

The way he was looking at her, you'd have thought she'd claimed to be able to spin gold from straw. She tried to think over what she'd just said, but her head felt as if it were floating somewhere in the clouds. "Aye, that she was, gifted with a voice that could bring a strong man to his knees. I'm a right fair lilter, myself, come to that, but never

a match for Ma. Besides," she said artlessly, "there's no
money in it, only joy."

"Only joy," he repeated slowly.

"Aye, only joy." She beamed at him, wishing he would
send for another pot of the lovely, fortifying tea. The last
time she'd felt so uplifted had been at her father's wake.
It had taken two whole barrels of porter to see Declan
O'Sullivan on his way, for the village had lost a fine and
hardworking man.

From the look of him, Mr. Galen had never done a day's
work in all his blessed life, for all he was the most beautiful man she had ever laid eyes on.

Taking a deep breath, she resumed her recital. "Now then,
I can cut and cure peat—turf, as some call it—but I'm told
you've not much use for it hereabouts."

Galen, his eyes half closed, tipped back in his chair and
steepled his hands before him. How well he remembered
the pungent smell of burning peat. A whiff of the stuff burning in the Dismal Swamp never failed to remind him of the
weeks he'd spent lying on a crude pallet in a fishing camp,
hurting like hell, burning with fever, trying to remember
his own name and what he was doing with a gang of cut-
throats who didn't even speak the King's English.

"Is that it?" he inquired.

"It?" She stretched both arms over her head, teacup dan-
gling from her fingers. The skin on her arms was the color
of buttermilk, the color of moonlight on snow.

He had to get rid of her, the sooner, the better.

"Katy, maybe you'd better . . ."

She went to set her empty cup back in her saucer and
missed. Shaking his head, Galen removed cup and saucer
from her hand and set them aside. "Is that the extent of your
accomplishments?" Just how much whiskey, he wondered,
had Ila dumped into that teapot? There was a flush on her
cheeks, and she'd sloshed tea on his bed.

Unless he was very much mistaken, she was soused to

the gills. He had a drunken woman in his bed, hardly more than a girl, one he didn't want, only he was having the devil's own time convincing his body of that.

Now what? She leaned forward and propped her chin in her hand, her elbow on her bent knee. He cleared his throat and reminded himself that it was late. If he intended to get rid of them, he'd better see about it pretty damned fast. He could hardly send them away after dark, not knowing a soul in town.

"Toast," he said gruffly. "You'll feel better once you've had something to eat." Slathering a thick layer of ginger conserve on a slice of toasted bread, he held it out to her.

Instead of taking it, she glanced around, looking uncomfortable. Looking embarrassed, as a matter of fact.

Belatedly, it occurred to him what her problem was. "It's behind the screen. Shall I send for Ila? She can give you a hand if you need it."

With a gasp that struck him as theatrical—comically so—she flung a protective hand over her bosom, looking as shocked as if he'd offered to hold the pot for her.

"Thank you—that is, no thank you," she said, and began easing her legs out from under the spread.

The weight of the heavy spread tugged her skirts up high enough to reveal a flash of white petticoat, a sliver of pale, silky thigh and a homemade garter anchoring a coarse cotton stocking.

She nearly tumbled out of bed in an effort to cover herself, and Galen told himself he felt sorry for her. It wasn't temptation he was feeling, it was pity.

Keep talking, Cap'n, maybe you'll convince someone.

"I'll leave you to your privacy," he said. "If you need any help, pull the cord. Someone will be here in two shakes."

Stepping outside onto the balcony, he stared out across the tranquil harbor, hearing the soft beat of a ragtime band from Bellfort's boat a few lengths upriver.

What the devil had he gotten himself involved in now?

For two cents, he'd walk out on the whole mess, find another way to make his stake, and start all over again somewhere else. He might even head out to gold country.

Then again, maybe he'd stay put. He'd rambled enough for one man, sailed more seas and visited more countries than he could count on one hand. After a while a man needed to pick a place and settle down.

He'd picked the town of Elizabeth City, in the state of North Carolina. He'd followed Brand south a few years ago, liked the area, and thought, why not? It was as good a place as any to set about making a dream come true.

He'd been attracted at first to Aster Tyler, but that hadn't lasted much beyond the time it took to get to know her. If he left now, she'd be the first to wave him off. Once he was out of the way, she'd waste no time in turning the *Queen* into a floating fairground, with banquets and dancing, play actors and weekend cruises.

Oh, yes, she'd give Bellfort a run for his money, all right. And the leaky old *Queen* would sink with all hands before she even cleared Knobbs Creek, and he'd have one more black mark against him.

At the moment, however, Aster, the *Pasquotank Queen*, and his own personal plans weren't his most pressing problem. What the devil was he going to do with the O'Sullivans? A greener pair, he'd yet to meet. He was still searching for answers when the sound of footsteps pounding up the main stairway alerted him to the fact that he was about to have company. Moving down the balcony, he stepped into the covered passsageway that separated his quarters from those of the Tylers.

Oscar, the boy Brand had sent him last year, raced up to the head of the stairway, gasping for breath. "Cap'n, sir, you better—you better—"

"Slow down, catch your wind first, boy. I take it we're not on fire? We're not sinking?"

"No sir, but, Cap'n, sir, you'd better come a-running, there's trouble in the main salon."

Glass eye slightly askew, the boy waited only for Galen's nod before racing back down the stairs, eager not to miss out on anything as exciting as "trouble."

Trouble. Well, hell. If that wasn't just what he needed. He rapped on his cabin door and called out, "I'll be back shortly, Miss O'Sullivan. I'm sending up a plate of dinner, and I want you to clean up every last bite, is that understood?"

No answer. Either she'd gone back to bed to sleep off all her tea or she was primping in front of his shaving mirror.

"Cap'n? I think you'd better hurry," Oscar called up from the bottom of the stairwell.

"Coming," he called down.

Captain. It was a mockery now. There'd been a time when it had meant something. He'd sailed aboard every one of the McKnight ships. The *Mystic Winds,* the *Mystic Lady,* and last of all, the big one. At 746 tons, the three-masted *Mystic Wings* was the pride of the McKnight Brothers' small fleet.

Of the three, the *Lady* was his favorite, but he'd sailed aboard the *Wings* to find out who was taking on unauthorized cargo, diddling the manifests, delivering it on the sly and pocketing the proceeds. There'd been complaints from several brokers whose promised deliveries had never arrived. While Brand had gone over books, bills, and manifests looking for proof, Galen had shipped aboard the *Wings* to catch the culprit in the act.

He'd found proof, all right, but before he could do anything with it, the ship had gone down with all hands.

Halfway down the stairs, Galen set aside the past and focused on the problems at hand. Evidently they were multiplying faster than he could deal with them. Before he even reached the main deck, he heard the sound of loud angry voices from the main salon. Taking a deep breath, he dusted off his hands, ready to do whatever it took to bring order. Brawls, he could deal with.

Women were another thing altogether.

Pierre was waiting for him. Buck, the lookout, was right behind him, looking worried. Trouble was rare, but now and again some young blade with a skinful, out to prove his manhood, would start something and Galen would be called in to sort things out.

"Buck, what the devil . . . He broke off, staring at the slight figure standing before his dealer, Pierre's soft, white hands clamped onto her bony little shoulders. "Want to tell me what's going on here?"

"Damn it all to hell and back, Gale—!" Pierre never called him anything but Captain unless the two men were alone. He never cursed, seldom even lost his temper.

"Mr. Galen, this man won't let me play with his cards. He won't even let me watch a game."

"Tara, this is no place for a child."

"I'm *practically* thirteen years old. Why can't I stay? Those ladies are here."

Sweat popping out on his forehead, Galen shot a distracted glance at Sally and Ermaline, two of Aster's girls. "Those ladies work here. You're not old enough to be—"

"Listen here, McKnight, if you let her stay, I'm taking my business to Bellfort," exclaimed one of the town's most prominent citizens, a wholesale merchant.

"That goes for me, too, McKnight," said a retired judge.

"You don't need no fortune-teller. Pierre can sandbag us without no help from a kid."

Some twenty minutes later, Galen left Tara at Ila's cabin with instructions to stay out of trouble until he came back for her. He strode along the corridors, aching thigh bone, miserable boots and all, barely aware that he was even limping. He was too damned angry to feel much pain.

Through absolutely no fault of his own, he had one O'Sullivan sprawled out on his bed, stewed to the gills, while another one was doing her damnedest to drive his best customers away. What kind of scam had the kid been running, anyway? He still hadn't figured out how she did it—wasn't even sure he believed it, with a dozen witnesses ready to swear she was a witch.

What was he supposed to do now with a kid who claimed she hadn't meant to cause trouble, who couldn't seem to understand why anyone would get upset just because she could read a man's cards with her eyes closed?

Damn. He still couldn't believe it, and he'd seen it with his own eyes. Tara swore she'd never played poker before, didn't know faro from frogs, and had never even seen a roulette wheel. But when he'd put her to the test, she'd called nearly every shot before the bets were even placed.

How the devil could she cheat when she didn't know how the game was played? Even if she was hedging the truth, he still couldn't figure out how she'd done it.

But he'd seen what he had seen. He'd heard what the others had said. There was only one conclusion he could draw, and that was that she was telling the truth. Or at least the truth as she saw it.

Galen was moderately skilled at all games of chance. He'd always been lucky. Lucky, at least, when it came to cards. Stranded on the West Coast between ships, he'd once done a stint at dealing in a third-rate gambling parlor. It turned out to be a hell of a lot easier than working aboard a ship. But a gambler needed soft hands and nimble fingers, and his years at sea as both an ablebodied seaman and an officer had hardened his fingertips, just as too many waterfront brawls had turned his knuckles to steel.

He knew men. He had an uncanny ability to spot a cheater. Any man caught cheating aboard the *Queen* was tossed into the river. If he couldn't swim, he was fished out with a boat hook, dumped onto the wharf, and told not to come back.

As for crooked dealers, any who were discovered working aboard the *Queen* were swiftly consigned as deckhands aboard departing ships. The old tub might not be the fanciest gambling boat on the Pasquotank, but she had a reputation for fair dealing that was better than money in the bank.

So what the hell was he supposed to do with a kid who cheated without even playing the game? He still found it hard to believe that a freckle-faced runt with a brogue so thick you could cut it with a butter knife had come close to bringing down his entire operation before she'd been on board half a day.

After ordering a round of drinks on the house, he'd put Charlie in charge of Pierre's table, delivered the kid to Ila, and joined Pierre, his head dealer, in the small salon, which wouldn't open until later on that evening when the high rollers started wandering in.

"All right, suppose you start from the first and tell me what you make of it."

"If she's using mirrors, damned if I could catch her at it. I thought I knew every system on the books, but that kid beats all."

Pierre, scion of a wealthy New Orleans family who paid him twelve thousand a year to stay away, leaned against the baize-topped table, a scowl on his darkly handsome face. A soft-spoken man with pale, watchful eyes, he looked every inch the professional gambler.

Galen might dress the part, but his heart wasn't in it. Gambling was a means to an end, which, in his case, was a small shipyard specializing in shallow-draft boats suited for the sounds and rivers of the mid-Atlantic and waterway traffic.

He counted among his friends some of the town's most affluent and influential citizens—men he would need if his venture was going to succeed—but if word got out that he'd hired a little girl to do whatever the hell it was she'd been doing, his reputation as a reputable businessman was sunk.

"She's a witch disguised as a kid." Pierre, who had an unerring instinct when it came to explaining things that defied rational explanation, summed it up. "Gale, I've never seen the like of it. She stood right there and called out every card in old Judge Henry's hand. He damn near swallowed a two-dollar cigar. And what beats all is, she didn't have anything to gain. No money riding on it. It was like a game to her, like she was showing off, you know what I mean?"

"I wish to hell I did."

Galen paced. He opened the door, called for Ermaline to bring her tray over, selected a cigar, clipped it, licked it, lit it, and scowled at the thing as if the answers might be encoded on the gold and ruby red band.

"I'll have to find someplace to stash the pair of them until I can figure out what to do with them. Legally, they're not my problem, but I can't in all good conscience just dump 'em out on the street."

"Why not?" Pierre, ever popular with the ladies, wasn't known for his tender heart.

"'For one thing, I owe them."

"They're Irish. Anything to do with the gent who fished you out of the drink?"

Galen had sketched in the story, leaving out the details. "His daughters. Orphans now. O'Sullivan's mates never let me forget it, either. Believe me, they weren't any too tender when it came to sewing up my head and setting my broken leg. They laid a load of guilt on my back about him being a family man and all that. The minute they figured I could stand the trip, they hauled my ass to Galway and dumped me aboard the first outbound freighter. Once I made it home, I cleaned out my bank account and sent it to that hard-hearted devil who stitched up my scalp with fishing twine and told him to forward it to O'Sullivan's family. Hell, I didn't even know their names."

"Conscience money?"

Galen shrugged. "Next thing I knew, these two females turn up, and now I'm stuck with them."

"Until Aster comes back."

"Don't remind me."

"Isn't there some kind of mission in town?"

"Oh, hell, man, I can't hand 'em over to any mission. The older one has some highfalutin plan to go into business once she earns herself a stake. She's looking for work, not a handout."

"The kid could set up a tent and tell fortunes. The other one didn't look like much—I didn't get a good look at her, but there's always Miz Dilly's Sporting Palace."

Galen shot him a hard look. "She's respectable."

"If you say so."

"I say so, dammit. I'll have Ila ask around. She might know someone who needs a housekeeper."

Pierre shrugged. "Who's going to keep the young'un out of trouble if the older one finds work?"

"She'll be in school."

"Got it all figured out, have you?"

"I wish to God I had." Galen stared out through the port-hole at the still, black waters of the Pasquotank River. "All I know is I've got to find some way to keep 'em off my back. First thing tomorrow, I'll see what arrangements I can make in town."

"That there lace is torn. See if you can sew it back so it won't show. When you're done with that, there's that pile of stockings to mend."

Sitting cross-legged on the floor, Katy frowned at the lace. It was cheap, hardly worth the trouble to mend. Finer than anything she'd ever owned, but then, every Irishwoman, rich or poor, knew good lace when she saw it, even if she couldn't afford to wear it.

"You can use my chair, if you've a mind to," said the stern-faced woman who managed the cigarette girls and the housekeeping staff.

"The light's better over here," Katy told her, perfectly comfortable to be warm, well fed, and safe in a place that wasn't moving. Other than a slight headache she'd woken up with and the mild soreness in her belly that usually accompanied her monthly flow, she felt better than she had in months.

"I've set the girl to peeling potatoes." The words were spoken as a challenge.

"To be sure, she's glad of a chance to be useful."

"Yes, well . . . Cap'n Galen, he didn't say what to do with her, he just said to keep her out of the gaming rooms."

Katy bit off the end of a thread and squinted at the torn lace on a ruffled petticoat. "I was wondering, would you happen to know of anyone looking for help? I can turn a hand to most anything, and I'm willing to work hard."

"Work, you say? Let me tell you something, missy, work's not easy to find if you're a decent woman. Even if you find it, it don't pay near as well as the other kind, if you know what I mean. I'll be needing a maid, but that don't pay much. Not enough for two, leastwise. Now, that Jack Bellfort that owns the boat just down the river, he might be looking for help. You could ask there."

Jack Bellfort. It was somewhere to start, at least, Katy told herself as she squinted over the pile of mending in her lap. They had spent the night in the captain's bed, sleeping as snug as two cats on a hearth. Her conscience bothered her a bit, but then, surely the captain of such a fine boat had more beds than one. With any luck at all they'd have a place of their own before the day ended, and a decent, respectable job.

* * *

Humming under her breath, Tara dropped another potato into the salted water. It was almost like being back home, with the heat of the stove and the smell of bread baking, only at home there'd never been so many potatoes in the pot all at once.

Now that she'd had more time to look about—now that those old men were no longer yelling at her, she meant to learn everything there was to know about the boat and the people and the town so that she could advise Katy. Squinting at the tall window just behind the big iron range, she allowed the impressions to drift in, making no attempt to sort them out. Little bits and pieces would drift away. Important things would come clear. Sometimes she saw silly things, like the mice nesting in the pantry and a dog sleeping on the wharf in the sun. There was a glimpse of a man with a knife and a rope in his hand, but that was probably only because she had a knife in her own hand.

She dropped another potato into the pot. She could peel a tatie closer than even Katy could. It was nice to be good at something real. Something besides seeing things.

Sometimes she tried too hard and mistook what she saw, and then Katy would scold. She hated being scolded but she understood. She understood far more than anyone thought she did. She was, after all, practically thirteen years old. She already had bumps on her chest.

The captain wasn't married. There'd been a picture of a lady on his shelf for a while, but it wasn't there now. When she thought about the captain and the sad-eyed lady, she didn't feel anything at all.

Sometimes the captain hurt. Sometimes he was sad, too. Sometimes he was angry. She thought it might be something she'd done. The angry, not the sad. She wondered if she should tell him that if he took off his boots, he wouldn't hurt quite so much.

"When ye've done with them 'taters, get to work on the onions."

"Sure, and I'll be happy to." She beamed at the cook, whose name was Willy. Willy scowled back at her, but he wasn't really angry, he only pretended to be because it made the kitchen boys move faster.

Katy was fretting again. She'd been fretting over one thing and another ever since they'd left home, but then, Katy had never been a one for bold adventuring. One day Tara was going to see every corner of the world, all the places in her mother's books, from Constantinople to Timbucktoo, only first she had to stay here with the sad, angry captain and Katy, because they needed her. Perhaps when they had each other, she'd be free to set out on her travels.

Half closing her eyes, she tried to see beyond the veil. Sometimes she tried too hard, and what she saw wasn't quite right. On board the ship coming to Amerikey, she'd seen ever so much, only it was hard to concentrate on what it all meant with so many people around, most of them moaning and groaning over their buckets, with snatches of thoughts coming at her too fast from all sides.

Still and all, being near water always helped. Sometimes it helped too much. Sometimes she saw things she'd as lief not see, and then she would sing real loud to block it out, only then Katy would *think* things about her singing. She never said it right out, but Tara knew. When the gifts of the O'Sullivans had been handed out, Katy had got the voice and Tara had got the sight. Sometimes she wished it had been the other way around, but then, a gift was a gift, and had to be guarded carefully or it would turn on you.

Those men had been angry with her, and all for nothing. She'd just wanted to play their games, only they said she was too young, and besides, she didn't know how, and besides that, she had no money.

So then she'd told them that she was practically thirteen

years old, and she'd showed them that she knew all about cards, but she truly didn't have any money. Not a copper penny to her name.

Maybe if she peeled enough potatoes . . .

Chapter Four

~

It was nearly eleven when Galen set out the next morning. He was not in a cheerful frame of mind. There'd been a brawl on the docks during the night that had required police intervention. Aside from the fact that he had a personal interest in a game that was currently being played out in the shadowy world of warehouses, cribs, and fish houses, such matters were bad for business.

He'd been up past midnight going over the books. Tedious business. More in Brand's line than his own, which was why he'd gone to sea while Brand had stayed ashore and turned McKnight's Shipping into one of the more successful small shipping companies on the East Coast.

What he needed was to find himself a good bookkeeper who wouldn't crumble to Aster's demands as the last one had.

Charlie, the second dealer, had been pestering him lately, wanting to talk to him about Sally. He'd put him off again this morning. Dammit, he was no Madame Lonelihearts! He made it a policy never to involve himself in the private lives of his employees, as long as those private lives didn't interfere with their work.

He'd been halfway down the gangplank when Ila buttonholed him about a matter of draperies. Claimed the sun was fading them. As if he or a single one of his regulars cared if the things were hanging in shreds. He told her to wait and take it up with Aster.

"Yes, well, I reckon Miss Aster'll have enough on her plate with that pair of Irishers. Sews right well, the older one does, but that young'un . . . mm-*mm*! Before she was even done with her breakfast this morning, my gals were lining up to have their fortunes told. Maybe we could—"

"And maybe we couldn't." He'd escaped, feeling beleaguered, irritable, and restless after a night plagued by dreams of a kind he hadn't had in years. Dreams in which that green-eyed witch had played a starring role, which made it all the more vital to get her off his boat and settled in town, where he wouldn't have to deal with her.

With a few notable exceptions, Galen prided himself on being reasonable, fair, and even-tempered. The exceptions usually had to do with Aster, who was stubborn, opinionated, spoiled, and not above a bit of chicanery. Even so, he'd been the one to call the shots, with only the occasional strategic compromise for the sake of peace.

Until yesterday.

Some six hours later, after a thoroughly frustrating day, Galen left his horse and buggy at the livery and walked the short distance to the boat, getting soaked in the process. He'd been a fool not to drive to the wharf and let one of the boys return the rig.

It wasn't the first time he'd done something stupid, nor would it be the last, but he'd wasted an entire day. If there was one thing he'd learned in the cold waters off the northeast coast of Ireland, it was that time was precious. Far too valuable to waste.

Now thoroughly out of sorts, he was limping before he even set foot on the gangplank. In the course of inspecting every halfway decent accommodation in town, finding something to criticize in every one, he must have climbed in and out of that damned buggy three dozen times.

Who would have thought in a town this size, with all the commerce brought in by shipping, shipbuilding, and farming, not to mention the oil mill and the new cotton mill, there'd be no place for a pair of respectable young ladies to stay?

The first one he'd dismissed immediately. Too many men living there. The next place he'd tried, a block over on Fearing Street, had a single vacancy no bigger than a paint locker. He'd trudged up three flights of steep, narrow stairs to see for himself. The room contained a single cot, a chamber pot, and a dresser with one leg missing. Two dollars a week, meals not included. It was a seller's market, he concluded. Thanks to a growing economy.

He'd been tempted by a third, a handsome two-story house on one of the town's better streets. The owner had struck him as one of those starchy types who could be counted on to look after a pair of motherless girls.

But that was before he'd taken a better look at a few of the other women staying there. There was no mistaking the invitation in all those painted eyes.

Damn . . . for a minute, he'd almost been tempted. There was definitely something lacking lately in his diet. Something Will couldn't provide.

Next he'd checked out the hotels, but quickly crossed them off his list. Too many transients. Never stopping to think that she'd shepherded her sister safely over thousands of miles, he told himself that Katy was entirely too young to be staying in a hotel unchaperoned. With her looks and innocence she wouldn't last a day before some fast-talking slickster took her under his wing and into his bed.

God knows what would happen to the kid then. She'd probably wind up in a fortune-telling tent out at the fairgrounds. Either that or tucked away in the State Hospital for the Insane.

Tucked away, hell, she'd probably end up running the place.

She was one spunky kid. One spooky kid, he corrected. Pausing to brace his hands on the railing, he checked automatically for chipping paint while he thought about the pair he'd inherited. A fine misting rain beaded on the brim of his felt hat, soaked through the shoulders of his wool broadcloth coat.

To think he'd considered Tara the harmless one of the pair. How dangerous could a twelve-"practically-thirteen"-year-old little girl be, after all?

That was before she'd practically driven him out of business.

Katy, now . . . Miss Kathleen Something-or-Other O'Sullivan. She was a different problem altogether. He hadn't sent for her, didn't want her—

Well now, that wasn't altogether true.

The devil of it was, he didn't know what he was going to do with her. She couldn't stay here. Aster aside, there was no room aboard the *Queen* for anyone who didn't earn his keep.

Even if he found her a job and a place to stay, he'd still feel responsible. Once a man had sailed as captain of a ship, he couldn't help feeling a responsibility toward his crew.

Or maybe it was about Liam, his baby brother. If he'd taken his responsibility toward Liam more seriously, the boy might be alive today.

God, he didn't know. He only knew that as much as he resented having the pair of them thrust upon him, he was responsible for their welfare. He couldn't change the past, but he could see that it didn't repeat itself, not on his watch.

Shaking the moisture off his hat, he turned and sauntered slowly up the gangplank, crossing the deck and letting himself inside.

The crew was at supper, getting the jump on the first rush of traffic. He ate more often than not at the Albemarle House in town. Tonight, he hadn't bothered.

The truth was, he'd forgotten to eat. Lost track of time.

The woman was getting under his skin, interfering with his business. Before she'd been here twenty-four hours, she had him running in circles. Galen prided himself in being able to size up most men. When it came to women, he wasn't quite as fast, not quite as accurate.

When it came to Katy O'Sullivan, he was dead in the water.

He turned toward the double doors that led into the gaming rooms, his boots squelching with every step. The land was so damned flat it took forever for puddles to drain away. He must have stepped in every one between Culpepper Street and the Norfolk Road.

Entering the main salon, he stood quietly observing the play, his senses alert for anything that might indicate possible trouble. There was the occasional burst of laughter, the usual calls for drinks, cigars, fresh cards. Business as usual. Not that he'd expected any trouble.

Only a handful of strangers tonight. He knew most of the men here, including the hotheaded young blades who occasionally got out of line. His stance that of a man with nothing more on his mind than seeing that his business ran smoothly, he searched every table, looking for some clue—a giveaway sign.

There was nothing at all. It might as well have been Bellfort's place, which was more excursion boat than gambling establishment. Wholesome Family Entertainment, that was the way he billed his cruises, even though everyone knew his gambling rooms were the chief source of revenue.

It drove Aster wild. But then, everything Bellfort did drove her wild. It was Galen's opinion that her chief goal in life was to run the man out of business.

Sally was looking tired. She couldn't have been on duty more than a couple of hours. He figured it must be the weather. It affected some people that way. On the other hand, it might be female trouble, in which case Ila would have to deal with it. It was a bit out of his line of authority, thank God.

The girls were popular, though, he was forced to admit. Having them in the background, with their flashy red silk gowns and their painted faces, gave the players a feeling of being reckless devils, even though most of them were staid, respectable businessmen. An illusion of wickedness was good for business. Aster had been right about that, if damned little else.

Galen would lay odds that not one in a dozen of his regulars had ever visited Miss Dilly's Sporting House on the outskirts of town. Too risky in a place where everyone knew practically everyone else and rumors spread faster than a new hatch of mosquitoes. Besides, the place was shut down on a weekly basis. No pillar of society could afford to be caught in a raid.

As tired as he was, Galen had to smile at the thought of Old Judge Henry, with his gout and his platitudes, being hauled off to jail for illicit fornication.

Or any other kind of fornication. The man could hardly bend his creaking joints enough to sit at a table.

Quietly, he moved through the room, nodding to acquaintances, lifting an eyebrow at each of his dealers and the lookout, receiving barely perceptible nods in response. All was well. Paul Hyde, prominent attorney, appeared to be on a losing streak, but he could handle it. Sam White, on the other hand, was grinning like a hyena over his hand. Probably a pair of deuces. Maybe fours over treys. Sam couldn't bluff his way out of a paper sack, but now and again he had the devil's own luck.

Galen moved silently across the room and stood for a few minutes watching a new man deal faro. The fellow showed promise. Good hands and steady nerves. He could attack the tiger in another man's lair without so much as the flicker of an eyelash.

Could he be the one? He'd bear watching, but Galen wasn't ready to accuse any man without irrefutable proof.

Damp and uncomfortable, he went on to glance into the small salon, where the high-stakes games would be getting under way in a few hours. It was Aster's latest showplace, with new carved paneling, a couple of gold-framed oil paintings, and a brass chandelier roughly the size of a bathtub.

He'd argued against the expense, but he had to admit it seemed to be paying off. All the same, he'd rather have spent the money on another set of pumps. When Elsworth Tyler had contracted to have the *Pasquotank Queen* constructed at a small shipyard up the coast that had since gone out of business, he'd been far more concerned with what showed above her waterline than with what was hidden below.

Galen had examined her with a far more critical eye and found her sadly lacking. But what the devil—a man could hardly complain about the shortcomings of a boat he'd won in a poker game.

Satisfied that all was running smoothly on the main deck, he went below where he poked his head through the galley door and left orders with one of the kitchen boys to have a cold plate and a pot of coffee sent up to his cabin.

One more stop, and then he could get out of these damp clothes and enjoy a bit of supper. And because he was wet and despised being wet—and because the hand he was stuck with held too many jokers—he just might indulge himself in a couple of shots of Kentucky's finest.

He rapped on Ila's door and waited, knowing that if she had her nose buried in one of those books she borrowed from the lending library, the boiler could explode and she wouldn't notice. One of these days he was going to find out just what was in those things that was so engrossing.

The door opened a crack. Two pairs of wary eyes peered out at him, and then the door swung wide. Both O'Sullivans beamed up at him. Katy was the first to speak. "Sure, and she said you'd be back for us."

"Back for you?"

"Miss Ila. She gave us her cabin for tonight, but she said you were out finding us a place to stay in town. Do you want us to go now? We've our bag all packed."

Galen cleared his throat. He backed up a step. Over their heads he could see the rumpled spread on Ila's bed. There was a pile of clothing neatly folded at one end and a sewing basket in the room's only chair.

"I've been working, that I have," Katy told him earnestly. Damn, he *did* wish she wouldn't look at him that way. "I've earned our supper, so we're free to go."

"You don't have to earn your keep, I told you, you're my guests." Had he told them that? Probably not. "Look here, there's no point in rushing into anything, Miss O'Sullivan. Katy. I haven't finished checking things out in town yet, but I promise I'll find something suitable tomorrow."

"I peeled the taties," Tara put in. "Onions, too. And Katy sewed on lace until her eyes got to bothering her. She can't see all that well, you know."

"Whisht, child, hush your mouth!" the older sister hissed.

Galen looked from one of them to the other. If there was something wrong with her eyes, it didn't show from the outside. They were far and away the loveliest eyes he'd ever seen.

Which was neither here nor there. The important thing was that he was no closer to a solution than he'd been when he'd met them at the train. In fact, he was beginning to wonder if there even was a solution. Maybe he was fated to carry the pair of them around his neck, like Mr. Coleridge's albatross.

"Captain Galen, do you think there's any more of that ginger cake in the kitchen? I went back for a second piece, but Mr. Willy wasn't there, so I came right back, but I'm still hungry."

"Gingerbread?" He plucked his damp collar away from his neck and stared down at the girl. Evidently, she took it as permission to go find out. With a grin that rearranged a few hundred freckles, she darted under his arm and out the door, calling over her shoulder that she'd bring him a piece, too, while she was at it.

"I'm sorry," Katy murmured. She wasn't sure why she was apologizing, nor did she have any idea whether to invite the gentleman inside, step out into the hall with him, or shut the door in his face. Back home, she'd never had cause to worry about propriety.

He took the decision out of her hands. Looking tired and harried, he nodded and stepped past her, glanced around for a place to sit and ended up leaning against a high carved dresser.

Hands clasped in front of her waist, she stood waiting to hear what he had to say. The poor man was soaked to the skin. He needed dry clothes and a pot of the kind of tea that had restored her strength and courage last evening.

Yes, and given her the headache this morning.

According to the housekeeper, he'd spent the day searching for a place for them to go. The woman had told her he had to get rid of them before Aster came back.

Aster, it seemed, was a woman who owned nearly as much of the boat as the captain did, only she acted as if she owned it all, and Tara said everyone was afraid of her. Not that Tara's information was always dependable, but this time, Katy had a feeling she might be right.

Galen cleared his throat. She glanced up expectantly.

"Still raining," he said.

"Aye, I can see that. It rains a lot at home."

"Do you miss it?"

He sounded so hopeful, she felt her heart constrict. He was wanting to send them back without even giving them a chance. "That I do," she said, knowing that truth was the best way, even when dreams were shattered for the telling of it.

"Would you like to go back?"

"There's nothing left to go back to."

"Home? Friends? A young man, perhaps?"

She did wish he wouldn't look at her that way. She knew well enough that she wasn't looking her best, but then, not even her best was any match for the fashionable ladies she'd seen driving past in their feathered bonnets and ruffled parasols and beautiful gowns. Tara said they must be the princesses who lived in the castles on the far side of the train station.

He was staring at her, obviously waiting for an answer. "I'm sorry to disappoint you, but we'll not be going back." Not even if they could have afforded the passage. "The O'Neills moved into Da's house, for their own was falling down. I've friends, but I'd not be beholden to them. There's work to be had in this country, and none at all to be found back home in Skerrie Head."

She waited hopefully to hear that he'd found her a wonderful job and a place to stay. He was entirely too close, as the room was quite small, and while she couldn't see the fine details of his face as clearly as she'd have liked, she was disturbingly aware of his scent. That warm, intriguing blend of bay rum, damp woolens, laundry soap, and male sweat.

Even in this condition he was a fine, handsome man, with his fancy summer weight woolen coat clinging to a pair of wide shoulders and those long, powerful limbs. Easier to picture him striding across mountains than lolling about on a fancy gambling boat.

Hands clasped before her, she lowered her gaze. Even his boots were handsome. Painfully conscious of her own flat, worn boots, she peered up to see if he'd noticed them, and then glanced away.

She did wish he would leave.

No, she didn't. He looked tired. Clearing the unfinished mending from the room's only chair, she said, "Would you care to sit, sir?"

He stood his ground, but sighed. "Miss O'Sullivan—Katy—I'm going to be honest with you. There's—"

"I should hope so, sir, for—"

"Stop calling me sir, my name is Galen. Katy, we're going to have to come to an understanding, and I can't do it with you sirring me every other breath. You're neither staff nor crew, you're my guest."

Aye, she thought, *and you can't wait to be shed of us.* For all he was wet and tired, and something was hurting him, he was a spleeny devil. She admired a man who spoke his mind, even when she didn't care to hear what he had to say. "I'll call you the McKnight, then if you please."

"*The* nothing! My name might be Irish, but I'm an American. Have been for three generations." He was pressing his fingers into his thigh as if to keep from throttling her. "You'll call me by my name, dammit. I beg pardon for swearing, but it's been a long day. Now, where were we?"

"We were having us a fair brave tantrum, si—Galen. I'll take part of the blame on my own shoulders, for I know you were never expecting us, but you, sir, are a *collach,* and the sooner you're rid of us, the better off we'll all be."

He sank into the arm-sprung slipper chair, closed his eyes, and then he began to chuckle. Kathleen watched him warily. She didn't smell the drink on him, but it paid to be wary of a man who laughed when he was angry.

"Dare I ask what it is you just called me?" he drawled.

"*Collach?* 'Tis a hard-shelled crab. The gentleman crab."

"Gentleman crab, hmm? Here we call 'em jimmies." He tipped the chair at a dangerous angle, regarding her with jaded amusement.

Come along now, just a bit more lift at the corners—that's it. It's called a smile, sir, and you've a lovely one when you care to use it. She bit her lip, trying not to smile back, but she couldn't help herself. For all he was crusty as any crab she'd ever caught, shucked, and used to bait a hook, it was impossible not to respond to such a man.

"We'll soon be off your hands," she promised, using the soothing tone she used on Tara when the child needed comforting. "We'll not be bothering you a minute more than it takes to find us a place in town. We never meant to disaccommodate you, that we never did."

His smile disappeared. "No need to be in such a rush. You're more than welcome to stay until you find something that suits you, only—"

"Only Tara makes you uncomfortable, for she's different in some ways. It's the sight, isn't it? I'm used to it, but it strikes some as strange."

"Yes, well . . ." He looked so worried she found herself wanting to reach out to him, to touch him—to smooth away the lines that furrowed his brow.

"Don't say another word, for I understand. It might please you to know that I've not been entirely idle. I've spent the day darning stockings and sewing torn seams and ruffles. There's still a muckle of work to be done, but I promise I'll see to it first thing in the morning, as soon as there's light enough, and then we'll take our leave, for I never expected—"

"Katy."

"Never expected—well, that's not quite true, I might have expected, but it wasn't right, that it wasn't, and I—"

"Kathleen." He was kneading the muscles of his thigh again. It came to her then that he was hurting, and not just trying to keep from striking her. Or strangling her. Not that he ever would, for he was a gentle man, even in his anger. Tara had said so, and Tara was an excellent judge of character.

But then, Katy would have known it anyway. Her eyes might be cloudy, but there was nothing at all wrong with her other senses.

He was hurting, and too proud to admit it. She wanted to help him, but men were so full of themselves, not a one of them would own up to a weakness.

He stood abruptly, and his arm struck the basket of mending she'd set on the chest. They both reached out at the same instant to keep it from spilling. Hands touched, jerked back, then touched again. His eyes blazed, going from blue to black in the time it took her to step away.

"Kathleen—Katy—"

Suddenly, the door burst open. "Katy, you'll never guess! There's fish cakes and lemon sauce, too, and Mr. Willy said we could have it all, for I told him . . ." Her face fell. Looking from one flushed face to the other, she whispered, "Katy? Is something wrong? Is it my fault again?"

Chapter Five

❧

In the heat of a new day, the waterfront teemed with activity. Sometime during the night the rain had ended. The sun, brilliant in the clear morning air, glistened on wet masts and wet rigging, danced on the surface of the river. Katy breathed deeply, welcoming the familiar scent of fish, wet hemp, and musty canvas, missing the sour smell of sheep and salt air.

You'll not be thinking of home, for you can't go back. Your life is here now.

She'd barely slept a wink for all the noise. Trains blowing like lost, lonely souls, chugging and clacking as they picked up speed. Bursts of laughter from the gaming rooms below and occasionally the sound of a fracas outside as revelers left one of the drink houses along the waterfront. She'd been in this country for more than a week now. You'd think she'd have grown used to all the noise.

Ila had given them her bed for the night, saying she'd as soon sleep up on the top deck in Mr. Tyler's room as he wasn't here.

So many names to remember. Miss Aster and now a Mr. Tyler. She had sorted them out as father and daughter, not husband and wife. According to Ila, Aster was a rare tartar. Katy thought tartars here were the same as tartars back in

Ireland. Quick-tempered women with sharp tongues. She'd just as soon be gone before the Tylers came back.

Ila, however, was a lovely woman, for all she frowned and fussed. It was only her way. There were several old men and a few boys, and those fancy gentlemen and ladies who worked in the gaming rooms. Tara knew all their names by now, but Katy still had trouble sorting them out.

She was going to have to set out today and find a place so that they wouldn't have to stay here. She hated being beholden, especially to someone like Galen McKnight. He was far too kind to say so, but it had been plain from the first that he didn't want to be bothered with them.

It was too easy to blame Tara, but Katy knew she was as much at fault as anyone. She could have said no, but she'd wanted a better future for the child than Skerrie Head could offer.

And so here they were, and here they could stay. It was up to Katy now to make a place for them.

She yawned, stretched, pushed the ruffled curtains aside and stared out at the busy waterfront. Men were everywhere, swearing, laughing, spitting, and scratching. Men of all descriptions, dark and light, busy loading and unloading, some onto mule carts, some onto handcarts, some onto shoulders wide as a barn door. Lumber, bales of cotton, crates of fruit, barrels of what might be molasses, or rum, or even salt fish.

It was a dangerous place for children to play, yet there were a number of ragged, skinny little boys, darting in and out between carts and cargo, earning kicks and curses. Not so different from home, after all. Two moth-eaten dogs trotted down the wharf as if they owned it. An old man taking the morning air on a bench in the sun called out to one of the boys, who made a rude gesture back at him. The old man cackled and the boys laughed and skipped along until they were out of sight.

Even here, she thought, amused, the old looked after the young, who considered themselves far too old to need looking after. Some things were the same the world over.

And then she heard a familiar voice. Galen was up and about. She felt a strange fluttering feeling in her chest and put it down to anxiety. If she was going to spare him the trouble of wasting another day looking for a place to send them, she'd better hurry.

"Tara, wake up, we're going exploring."

"It's too hot," Tara mumbled sleepily.

"That it is, and bound to get hotter," Katy said cheerfully. "Come along now, Miss Ila will be wanting her room back."

"I wonder what Mr. Tyler's cabin looks like. Do you suppose we could peek inside?"

"That I do not. Up you go now, for I've a feeling we'll be moving into town today."

"Did you see us there?"

She swatted her younger sister playfully with the towel she held in one hand. "No, I didn't *see* it, missy, I've something more reliable than that to go on."

Tara sat up in bed, bony knees drawn up under her chin. With her red hair standing on end and her face flushed with sleep, she looked so young, so very vulnerable, caught between two worlds, in more ways than one. There were times when responsibility sat like a stone on Katy's heart.

"Then how do you know we'll be moving?"

"Because we must, for we can't stay here. And because Miss Ila said the man on the boat next door is needing workers." Katy picked up the ivory-backed brush that had belonged to her mother and began brushing the tangles from her hair. "I've a notion to present myself there and see what kind of work's to be had before we go looking for a room in town."

"His name is Mr. Bellfort. Johnny the knife boy says he has fiddlers and everything. You could go for a lilter."

"That I'll not. Who'd pay good money to hear a hen cackle? Out of bed now, before I empty the washbowl over your head."

By the time the housekeeper rapped on the door and stepped inside, both sisters were dressed, washed, and brushed. Katy might wish her best shirtwaist were a better match for her best skirt—one was the color of peat stains, the other of overbaked bread—but no one would know it by her smile. She had brushed her hair until it gleamed, then drawn it back so tightly that her eyes were drawn halfway up to her temples.

"Katy's going for work," Tara announced as soon as the older woman stepped inside and hung her nightgown on a hook behind a locker door. "Is it time for breakfast? We had cold fish cakes and ginger cake with lemon sauce last night after supper, but I'm still hungry."

"Hungry again," Katy corrected, but she smiled when she said it, for the child was always hungry, still *and* again.

"Captain Galen said I could—" Tara began, but Katy interrupted to tell her to gather up her nightgown and pack it away.

She didn't want to hear about the captain now. She had better things to think about. Once she'd secured employment and a place to stay in town, it might be safe to think about him, to wonder why it was that a man she'd known for such a short time could scatter her wits and make her breath catch, and put all sorts of strange notions in her head.

Smoothing the last wrinkle from the newly spread bed, she sighed, thinking of what she steadfastly refused to think about. Of the way they had both reached out at the same time to right the basket of mending, and their hands had touched. For a single moment it was as if someone had spilled fat into the fire, and it had blazed up, all sparkly and dangerous.

* * *

Now that she'd set her course for the day, Katy didn't want to take time to eat, but she knew she'd feel better for a cup of tea and a bit of toasted bread. She had a lot to accomplish today, and she couldn't afford to have her belly embarrass her by rumbling at the wrong time.

Several people were seated at the bare wooden table. Every sound stopped the minute she stepped through the door. She offered a timid smile all around, and one by one, they began eating and talking again.

Tara made a place for her between two burly gentlemen in striped jerseys. "Katy, this is Oliver. He's a pumper, but he helps out with the painting. Katy's my sister. She's going to find a job today."

There were nods and murmurs, and someone offered her coffee.

"I don't suppose I could have a bit of tea?" she said hopefully.

There was no tea made. Rather than wait, she accepted a cup of coffee from the boy who passed along the table with the blue-speckled coffeepot, then shyly asked the man seated beside her to pass the bread basket.

Grinning broadly, Willy himself heaped a plate of fried meat, eggs, stewed tomatoes, and some mushy white thing smothered in brown gravy, plopped it down in front of Tara, and said, "That there ought to hold ye for a spell, young'un."

Between huge forksful, Tara introduced Katy to the rest of the crew and explained that there were no engineers or fireman to keep the boiler going, for the *Queen* never left port, and no roustabouts, for she carried no cargo. Most of the men were deck hands. Chief among their duties was to keep the bilges dry, or as dry as possible.

Next, she was introduced to an old man with a straggly gray pigtail and a half grown boy missing three front teeth, whose duties, she was told, were to swab down the decks, empty the slops, and keep the brass gleaming.

Katy smiled and said she was pleased to meet them. She sugared her coffee, tasted it, added milk, wondered where Galen was, and if he took breakfast with his crew, tasted her coffee again, and grimaced. The man beside her took his straight from the pot. She wondered why his insides hadn't rotted away, thought some more about Galen, and decided he wasn't coming.

She was glad.

Tara explained between bites that there were five main dealers and three relief dealers and Oscar, who had a glass eye and was learning to tend bar, but all except Pierre and Oscar lived in town, and that until a few days ago, Maggie the general maid had done most of the cleaning, but her mother had got bit by a black-widow spider in the privy and needed her at home.

Katy wondered how on earth the child could learn so much about so many people in such a short time. It wasn't the sight, it was that blessed curiosity of hers.

"Maggie's only a wee bit older than I am, so if Miss Ila will let me, could I please take her place?"

Thankfully, Katy was spared having to answer when two of the girls came in wearing only slippers and wrappers, their faces bare of paint. They looked tired. Ila called them her girls. To Katy, they looked more like women, and no longer in the first blush of youth.

"Lordy, me feet hurt," said the one with startlingly red hair.

The other one—Sally, she thought—sat down, turned green, then bobbed up and hurried out again. No one appeared to notice. Katy was about to ask if she could help when the sweeping boy came in, begging scraps for a dog, and then two more men came in and Tara asked the sweeping boy if she could help feed his dog.

Katy had had enough. Enough of talk, and enough of the awful coffee. She was tense enough as it was, knowing how much rested on her securing work. Leaning over, she whispered, "Remember now, you're to keep out of the way until I get back. Lend a hand wherever it's needed if Miss Ila asks, but whatever you do, don't go near the gaming rooms."

"I will, I will, and I won't."

"And you're not to be fresh," Katy scolded, but she smiled, for there was no wickedness in the child, only high spirits. "I'll be just down the way if you need me, aboard that other big fancy boat. Wish me luck."

Eyes half shut, Tara began to sway until Katy squeezed her shoulders. "Oh, for heaven's sake, not now! There's work to be had, and I mean to have it, so keep your seeing to yourself, if you please."

Katy would just as soon not know in advance, for if Tara saw her coming away with a long face, she might not have the courage to apply.

A few minutes later she was strolling along the wharf as if she hadn't a care in the world, dodging sweaty, muscular roustabouts, carts, little boys, and all manner of freight. One of the workmen turned to send her an admiring look, which she pretended not to notice, but she was pleased all the same, for it bolstered her courage.

An old man, one of several taking their ease in the morning sun, looked up from a checkerboard and called out a greeting. She beamed him a smile. Faith, and it was a fine day. There was work to be had, and a strong, sensible, practical woman who could turn her hand to most anything was seeking it.

To be sure, the man would be a fool not to hire her.

Jack Bellfort, owner, manager, and captain of the *Albemarle Belle,* leaned on the ornate railing of the upper balcony, watching the slight figure hurrying along the wharf between Aster's boat and his own.

Technically, the *Queen* was more McKnight's boat now, but he still thought of her as Aster's. He'd come to enjoy his ongoing battle with Tyler's daughter over whose boat would rule the river.

Not that there was any real competition. His *Belle* came out the winner on all fronts. She was some older, for she'd seen service on the Mississippi before he'd bought her off a broker in Mobile, but he'd stack her up against any excursion boat operating in the area. Tyler's *Queen,* for all her brass and fancy millwork, was as landlocked as the County Courthouse over on East Main.

It was no longer about business, this contest between him and Aster. It was personal, only he wasn't about to give her the upper hand by admitting it. She'd been jealous of the *Albemarle Belle* ever since he'd first brought her up the canal and gone into business.

And though it galled him to admit it, he'd been attracted to Aster almost as long, the same as any male between the ages of sixteen and sixty would be to any reasonably attractive female.

The woman was more than reasonably attractive. The first and last time he'd invited her to have dinner with him in his private quarters, she'd countered by inviting him to dine aboard the *Queen.*

"Can you match my French chef?" he'd asked, knowing damned well she couldn't.

She'd huffed up, her bosom swelling against her fashionable low-cut gown, and said, "My William can cook circles around your Frenchman any day. What's more, he doesn't depend on fancy sauces to disguise the taste of badly cooked meat."

"Isn't he the same fellow your old man hired out of that hotel that burned down a few years ago? Better watch him around matches, darling."

He'd pushed her as far as he dared, for the sheer plea-

sure of watching the sparks fly. She'd got in the last word—
something about all his fancy women—and flounced off.
He'd rather watch her flounce than watch any other woman
strip stark naked. Seeing her march off down the wharf,
bustle twitching, elbows pumping, he let his imagination
off the rein. One of these days, he promised himself, but he
was in no great rush.

She'd been the one to draw the battle lines. All he'd done
was follow her cue. A few weeks later, when he'd hired
that troop of players from Virginia, she'd done all but turn
herself inside out trying to come up with some way to out-
do him.

Noticing her watching from the upper balcony of the
Queen, he'd taken to entertaining a few ladies—and a few
who weren't ladies—on his own private balcony. Even if
she didn't see him, word of his activities would get back to
her. The waterfront community was a small one. Privacy
was hard to come by.

But then McKnight had showed up, and Aster had taken
to flaunting him at every opportunity as if he were a personal trophy. Jack knew better. Hell, he even knew what
cards old Tyler had been holding when he'd lost the *Queen*
to McKnight.

Aster and McKnight?

Forget it. They were too much alike. Too much fire in
both their bellies. McKnight's fire might be banked for the
moment, but Jack knew men. His livelihood depended on
it. There was one hell of a lot more to the new part-owner
of the *Pasquotank Queen* than met the eye, he'd lay odds
on it. One of these days Aster was going to push the man
too far, and when she did, all hell was going to bust loose.
Jack had made up his mind a long time ago that when it
happened. he'd be around to pick up the pieces.

Meanwhile, he'd continued his weekly scheduled cruises,
even though the overhead was brutal. He'd have made far

more money staying tied up the way McKnight did and catering strictly to gamblers, but Aster didn't have to know that. Let her steam. Let her wear herself out fighting straw dogs. At least it kept her attention focused on him.

Taking his lead from the new Opera House that had opened in town, he'd hired a muralist to come and paint a woodland scene complete with overblown nudes, and made the room off-limits to the ladies, which had pleased the gentlemen. At the same time, he'd set aside a ladies' parlor with fancy velvet couches, a pianoforte, and a bookshelf full of the kinds of books ladies liked to read. It had cost him more than it was worth, but so far she'd been unable to come up with anything to top it, thanks mostly to McKnight's keeping her on a tight rein.

He happened to know she'd be back today, and when she arrived, he intended to have a fine welcome waiting for her. It had come to him when that meddling old do-gooder had tried to hand out her salvation fliers at the foot of his gangplank. He'd bundled the things up, intending to throw them away, when it had struck him. Why not hire one of the young hoodlums who lived in the alleys between the warehouses to hand them out to the *Queen*'s customers?

"Cap'n Jack, lady to see you," said one of his boys, poking his head out onto the balcony.

"Do I know her?"

"Don't think so, sir. She come off the *Queen,* says she's looking for work."

Katy could hardly wait to tell Galen about her new job. It was only for today, but it was a start. According to Ila, he'd gone out again to see if he could find work for her in town, and a place to stay. For all his good intentions, she didn't need his help. This would prove it. She'd been hired at the very first place she'd applied.

Not that she was particularly looking forward to standing about among all the men working on the wharf, which was why Captain Bellfort had suggested she stay close to the *Queen*'s gangplank, where she would feel safer.

But two whole dollars! She wasn't about to turn down the chance to earn all that for no more than handing out sheets of paper. She'd thought about taking Tara with her, but Ila said, "There now, don't you worry none about that young'un. I'll see she don't get up to any mischief. Found yourself work already, have you? Bless my soul, two dollars for handing out fliers? I might be interested in a job like that myself."

Katy thought she was teasing. She hoped so. "It's for a worthy cause. Shall I ask Captain Bellfort if he needs someone else to hand out fliers? He might like to have someone on his own boat."

"Lordy, no, not and stand on my feet all day. Run along now, but you make sure you come inside if you get to feeling weak. Captain Bellfort don't expect a lady to be out in the heat of the day."

So Katy stationed herself beside the red-carpeted gangplank. There was no one about at the moment. Most of the roustabouts were working closer to the railroad wharf. She fastened a hopeful smile on her face, ready for her first customer.

Still waiting, she wondered if the fliers advertised a local attraction. There was a market across the harbor. She could see it from here.

Holding out one of the yellow sheets, she squinted against the blinding sunlight, trying to make out the small, smudged type. If her arms had been six inches longer, she'd have been able to read it, but as they weren't, she gave up trying. Captain Bellfort had said it was for a worthy cause. As far as Katy was concerned, any cause that paid two dollars to advertise was worthy enough.

Merciful saints, but it was hot! She used a flier to fan with, and waved a greeting to the old man with the pigtail she'd met at breakfast, who was polishing a brass railing.

A few minutes later she smiled cheerfully at two poorly dressed men who staggered past, feeling sorry for them, wishing she could share her good fortune with them, vowing that one of these days, she would do just that.

What a wonderful place, America. What a beautiful morning. And how friendly everyone was. The Irish, she had heard more than a few times since setting out from Galway, were not always welcome abroad. At first she hadn't believed it, because it made no sense at all. After that, she'd been too miserable to dwell on it.

Sure, and there'd been a few snooty women on the train who had looked down their noses when Tara had pestered them with questions, but since they'd arrived in town, everyone had been kind as could be, even Galen, once he'd gotten past his surprise.

"Here, and would you have one of my papers, sir?" She beamed at a gentleman with a moustache that stretched all the way to his sideburns.

Even after Tara and that unfortunate business in the gaming room, he'd been kind. And then, last night . . .

"One of my papers, sir? And you, ma'am—will you have one, too?" Imagine being paid two whole dollars for doing no more than giving away something to anyone who wanted it. No wonder they called this the land of opportunity. At this rate, she'd soon be able to afford a cottage to live in and a room on the best street in town for her shop.

The oil mill wasn't hiring. Not hiring ladies, at any rate. The cotton mill had more applicants than they had work to be done, for half the farmers had come from the country to find work in the mill. Mr. Flora's Wholesale place at the foot of Main Street had been his last stop, but Flora already had enough clerks. Besides, he seriously doubted if Katy knew enough about buggies, building supplies, or guns to be of much use in selling them.

At this rate, he might do better to send them out into the

country. Somebody had to bring in the crops, or they'd all starve. All this manufacturing might be good for the economy, but Galen was afraid it was not an unmixed blessing. Time would tell.

Meanwhile, while he was out he'd investigated a row of rental houses over on Fearing Street. They were sound enough, and not all that costly. All the same, he couldn't see that pair living there, jammed up against neighbors on either side. He could just imagine the havoc Tara could create.

As for Katy . . .

No, it wouldn't do. What she needed was a place in the country, where she could take her time getting used to her new life. If she insisted on staying in town, he'd simply have to find some kindhearted, respectable landlady who would take a special interest in her, and not hold it against her that she was fresh off the boat from Ireland. Prejudice was something he had trouble dealing with. It was everywhere, of course, with immigrants swarming here to take advantage of the opportunities, while those who'd arrived on an earlier boat tried their damnedest to hang on to whatever ground they'd managed to claim.

He'd sailed with men from half the countries in the world, and found none of them superior or inferior by birth, only by character.

Katy was Irish. Some people would hold it against her. Settling the pair of them wasn't going to be quite as easy as he'd hoped. As much as he dreaded doing it, he was going to have to ask Aster's help. She was due back today. Due back in less than an hour, as a matter of fact. He might as well swing by the depot as long as he was out in a buggy. Aster never traveled light. If he knew his business partner, she'd have brought back even more than she'd set out with.

Besides, it wouldn't hurt to butter her up a bit. Prepare

her for the sisters O'Sullivan. Aster wasn't too fond of surprises, not unless it was something she could parlay into a winning hand in her ongoing battle against Bellfort.

Somehow, he couldn't see either of the O'Sullivans filling that role.

Chapter Six

~

It was bad. Far worse than he could ever have imagined. The usual noonday mob loitered along the waterfront, for even the roustabouts took time off in the heat of the day to down a pint or two. Men off the freighters swarmed to the local taverns. Farmers in from the country hawked watermelons, corn, and fresh peaches from the backs of their carts. A wagon from Crystal Ice Company dripped its way slowly through the melee, stopping to chip off a chunk of ice here and there. Whores, looking tired and bored in the harsh light of day, mingled with the crowd in hopes of picking up a bit of business.

And there in the midst of the familiar motley crew stood Miss Katy O'Sullivan, smiling as if surrounded by a Sunday morning church congregation instead of the Saturday morning regulars, cheerfully greeting anyone who ventured in range and presenting them with one of whatever it was she was handing out.

She was attracting some curious looks, but no one refused her offering, such was the power of that guileless smile. Galen wondered if any of them would bother to read it. Or even could.

Not that it mattered. "What the devil is she up to now?" he wondered aloud.

Aster leaned forward in her seat. "Who on earth is that creature?"

"Stay here, I'll take care of it."

"Who *is* that woman? What does she think she's doing here? She's interfering with my business!"

Galen knew who. What he didn't know and meant to find out was what. Not to mention why. By now Aster was standing up in the buggy, waving her arms. "Shoo! Get away from my boat! Move along, whoever you are, get out of here!"

Galen yanked on her skirt. "Sit down before you fall out, I'll handle it."

If he had a grain of sense he'd have bought himself a ticket on the train that had just pulled out and ridden the thing all the way to New Orleans. Maybe then he could start over without a flock of females whose sole mission was to complicate his life.

Aster leapt out of the buggy, endangering the concoction of ribbons, feathers, and cabbage roses anchored by a pair of six-inch, needle-sharp hatpins to her glossy pompadour. Tossing the reins to one of the deck boys, Galen signaled for two more to unload her considerable luggage and set it on board the *Queen*. Then, reluctantly, he set off after her to discover what was going on.

By the time he caught up with Aster she was standing toe to toe with Katy, demanding to know what the devil she thought she was doing, trespassing on private property to interfere with a legitimate business.

The entire Saturday morning crowd had stopped whatever they were doing to view the confrontation. It wouldn't surprise him one bit if bets were being placed on the outcome.

"Sweet Judas," Galen muttered. "Now hold on, Aster, I said I'd handle it."

Both women were talking, Aster's shrill voice easily drowning out Katy's soft brogue. "Who told you you could stand here, girl? This is *my* part of the wharf, I pay good money to rent it. Now, move along or I'll have you arrested. What on earth is this drivel you're peddling, anyway?"

"Hold on, Aster, there's no call to—" For his troubles, he was totally ignored. "Now, listen here, the both of you—" Still ignored by both women, he shouted, "Would you two kindly shut up long enough to tell me what the devil is going on here?"

He might as well have been talking to a tree stump for all the response he drew. Utterly frustrated, he snatched one of the fliers from the stack cradled in Katy's arm and began to read. A few lines was all it took.

"Dammit, Katy—" Yelling to make himself heard over Aster's ongoing tirade, he shook the thing under her nose and demanded to know what she thought she was doing.

Katy reared back as if he'd waved a snake at her. Leaning so close he could see her pupils widen, he shouted, "Dammit, Katy, where'd you get these things? What are you trying to do, drive me out of business?" Dropping the flier, he grabbed hold of Aster's waving right arm before she could take a poke at something.

Or some*one*.

Katy tried to back away. He grabbed her with his free hand and hung on, else she'd have gone right over the edge of the wharf. And dammit—dammit all to hell, she kept blinking those big green eyes of hers, as if she couldn't believe what was happening to her.

What the devil did she expect? Did she think he was going to thank her for warning customers away from the wickedness to be found aboard his den of depravity?

All the same, he lowered his voice. "Look, I'm sorry, Katy, I know you didn't mean—"

Aster whirled to confront him, eyes blazing. "Katy! *Katy?* You *know* this female person?"

"It's for a worthy cause," Katy whispered into a sudden

pool of silence. All around them, heads turned as one. Tears brimmed in Katy's eyes, making them look like wet jade. "I'd not do anything to cause trouble, that I wouldn't, but I vowed I'd not take another penny from you."

Aster swung around to glare at him, her beauty distorted by anger. "Money! She's your *whore*? I'll not have it! I don't care how many women you keep in town, but I'll not have them on my boat! Get rid of her. I don't care what you do with her—drown her, for all I care, but you're to get rid of her this minute, Galen McKnight, do you understand?"

He understood. So did every pair of ears between Blade's Mill and Shell's Shipyard. Judas priest, all he needed now was for Tara to come out, roll her eyes, and start telling fortunes. "Now, listen here to me, both of you." He gripped Aster's arm tightly and at the same time tried to send a silent message to Katy.

Nobody heard a word he said. He had to shout, and he was a man who never raised his voice. Coolness under fire was a large part of the image he'd worked so hard to create in an attempt to coldcock trouble before it reared its ugly head.

This time, it wasn't working.

"Would the pair of you just shut up for a minute?"

Aster glared at him, her magnolia-pale complexion splotched with patches of red. "I'm sending for the police."

"Now you don't want to do that. Think about it—a herd of policemen swarming all over the old *Queen* would really be bad for business." She was patting her foot. Bad sign. "Aster, it's no crime to hand out a few fliers. It's done all the time."

She glared at him as if he'd suddenly sprouted horns. "Fliers telling all about the evils of gambling? Not on *my* boat, it's not!"

"Shh, easy there. I'm sure Miss O'Sullivan didn't realize she was doing anything wrong."

"Didn't realize—!"

So much for coolness. "And dammit, it's not your boat! Now, what we're going to do is, we're going to go up to my office and settle this thing in a calm and civilized fashion. I'm embarrassed by the two of you, causing a public scene this way."

He managed a grim smile. Indicating with a nod of his head that the audience should go about their business, he turned toward the gangplank, then looked back to be sure the two women were following.

Aster had her arms crossed. Standing her ground, she was glaring daggers at his back. As for Katy, if he'd accused her of murder she couldn't have looked more stricken. His first impulse was to apologize. Fortunately, common sense intervened, and before either woman could sense his momentary weakness and snatch the advantage, he grabbed them both by an elbow and marched them up the gangplank.

Yellow leaflets scattered in the breeze behind them. Aster's crow feathers, ribbons, and cabbage roses trembled with every stiff-backed step she took. As whistles, catcalls, and a few obscene suggestions from the audience followed them aboard the *Queen*, Galen briefly considered shipping out to sea.

Hell, even the ice-hauler's lop-eared mule was staring at them.

Not a single member of staff or crew spoke a word, but Galen was acutely aware of all the eyes following their progress. Before they made it as far as the third deck, tongues would be flapping up a breeze.

Aster was still going strong. The woman hadn't shut up since she'd jumped out of the buggy. He cut a wary look at Katy, wishing he could see her face to better gauge what she was feeling.

God, what would she be feeling after all this? Defeat, probably. Utter humiliation. Her bowed head said it all. She looked . . .

Breakable was the best word he could come up with to describe it.

"Not now," he snapped when Oscar poked his head out the door of the main salon. He waved off his housekeeper and hit the stairway amidship, forcing the two women ahead of him. "Pipe down, Aster. Not another word until I say so, is that clear?"

"Don't you dare tell me—"

"Aster? Just stow it, will you?"

He yanked open the door. He seldom locked it. At the moment, the only person he might have locked it against was firmly in his grasp. Shoving the two of them inside, he slammed the door, pointed to the two straight chairs, and roared, "Sit!"

And then he expelled a heavy sigh that said it all. Why even bother? Why not simply walk away and allow them to fight it out between them?

His gaze moved to the slight figure sitting primly, her small, work-worn hands clasped so tightly in her lap that her knuckles showed white. He owed her his support.

He didn't know why, but he knew that much. None of this business was really her fault. Someone—and he had a damned good idea who to blame—had involved her in a battle that had begun long before she'd arrived on the scene, and would be going on long after she was gone.

"All right now, one at a time. Suppose you tell me your side of the story, Katy."

If she'd had an oar strapped to her backside, her posture couldn't have been any more rigid. Her collar was crooked. His hand ached to reach out and straighten it, and then to lift her small chin and tell her not to look so frightened, that no one was going to hurt her.

As if she'd read his mind, she lifted her head, visibly gearing up to say her piece, when Aster jumped up and opened her mouth.

Galen cut her off mid-squawk with a single look. It was not a look he used very often. As a rule, a few well-chosen words did the trick. In the case of a drunk and disorderly crew, a few words and a night in the hoosegow worked wonders.

However, this was Aster. She was tougher than the salt horse that was standard ship's fare. Meaner than cat-claw briars. So he gave her the full treatment.

Somewhat to his amazement, it worked. She sat down again.

"All right now, Katy, you go ahead and talk, and then I'll say what I have to say. I believe we've heard all we need to hear from Miss Tyler."

Aster sputtered, but didn't argue. Fifty-one percent versus forty-nine. They both knew who would win if it ever came down to a battle for control.

With a quiet dignity that impressed him all the more, since he knew she was shaking in her boots, Katy explained how she had come to be handing out fliers. "For a worthy cause," she added, "and I'm that sorry to cause trouble, but since Captain Bellfort has already paid me, I'm obligated to finish the job."

"Over my dead body," Aster muttered.

"Aster." His voice was soft, but underlaid with steel. "I believe we've heard all we need to hear. Miss O'Sullivan meant no harm, she was only—"

"No harm!" The older woman swept Katy from head to toe with a scornful look that spoke volumes. "Didn't you even bother to read what you were handing out, you stupid little twit? But of course you probably can't even read, can you? It's really no wonder so many of your kind wind up on their backs."

Galen opened his mouth, but Katy beat him to the punch. If there'd been a jeweled crown on her head, she couldn't have appeared any more regal. "As it happens, I can read and write well enough, miss. I never meant to harm you, not a bit of it, but if the words on those fliers are true, why then, perhaps it's your business you should be after blaming, and not the words."

"Touché," Galen said softly. As it happened, it was his business she was maligning, as well, but damned if he didn't applaud her courage.

Aster sputtered a few times, then turned and stalked out, slamming the door behind her. Galen suspected he hadn't heard the last of it, but he welcomed any reprieve, no matter how brief.

But when Katy rose to follow her, he waved her back into her chair. "Sit down, if you please. I believe we still have a few things to settle."

She could have bitten a lemon and not have pinched her mouth any tighter. He knew what she was thinking. He couldn't much blame her.

"Say what you have to say and be done with it, for I'll not sit here and be insulted another moment."

"I know you won't, Katy. I'd never expect it of you." He started to smile, caught himself in time, and cleared his throat instead. "Now, about what just happened—no, wait, hear me out." He lifted a hand when she started to interrupt. "I know you didn't mean any harm, but, Katy—"

"I never gave you leave to call me that."

"All right then, Miss O'Sullivan. Now, about—"

"But you can if you've a mind to."

Galen considered himself a reasonable man, possessed of a certain amount of intelligence. Which made it all the more unreasonable that, without even trying, this woman could shake up his world and rattle his brains until nothing made sense any longer. How in hell did she manage to affect him the way she did?

Strictly speaking, she wasn't beautiful. Her eyes were too large and her nose too small. She had far too much hair for such a small face. As for her figure, what he could see

of it under those wretched dresses she wore—according to
Ila, she had three of them, each one equally dismal—it was
no more than ordinary.

Galen had been deeply in love but once in his life. When
she'd married someone else, and not even her first choice,
he'd got over it. Eventually. But he'd never entirely forgotten what love felt like.

What he felt for Katy O'Sullivan bore no resemblance
to anything he'd ever felt for Margaret Kondrake. The two
women were as different as night and day. Black and white.
Fire and ice.

All the same, the sooner he saw Katy settled and on her
own, the sooner he could get on with his own plans. Plans
that had nothing to do with Aster, and certainly nothing at
all to do with either of the O'Sullivans.

"As you probably know, my dear, I've been looking
around for a place in town where a respectable young lady
and a child might stay until—well, at any rate, the trouble
is, there's nothing really suitable that's not already filled to
capacity."

She looked crestfallen. "Nothing at all? We'd not need
much, only a single room. We can share a bed if need be,
we're used to sharing."

At the thought of sharing a bed with her, Galen clean
lost his train of thought. Clearing his throat, he put on a
thoughtful expression. "Now then, it seems to me that the
best solution all around would be to find you a husband."

Warily, he watched for a reaction. Her mouth had lost its
pinched look, but he didn't care much for the look in her
eyes. "No, don't say anything yet. I've spent a lot of time
thinking about the situation, my dear." He'd spent all of
twenty minutes thinking about it, waiting for Aster's train
to pull in.

"But I don't—" she started to say, but he cut her off.

"Think about it before you make up your mind, Katy,
will you do that much?"

That pinched look was back. A crease formed between her dark winged brows as she considered his suggestion. He found himself wanting to smooth the twin furrows away.

Yes, well, he told himself, it still seemed like the best idea. Marriage. The only problem was that he didn't know of anyone offhand who would appreciate a woman like Katy O'Sullivan.

Katy was . . . special. It would take a man with sensitivity, one with a lot of patience. From the looks of her hands and what he knew about her father, she hadn't had an easy time of it. She would need a man who could not only support a wife but one who could manage to keep a young sister-in-law from setting the town on its collective ear.

He thought about the young men-about-town who sought to prove their manhood by drinking too much, smoking too much, getting sick all over his carpet, and gambling away their allowances. Not a one of them was good enough for someone like Katy.

Who did he know who was mature, sensitive, patient, and reasonably affluent? The only bachelor he knew who filled all those requirements was Pierre, his head dealer. Pierre was single. Women considered him handsome. The trouble was, he was too worldly by far for a woman like Katy.

There was also the matter of age. Pierre was even older than Galen.

Katy needed someone young, decent, steady. Someone who'd be patient with her. Someone who would appreciate her fine qualities. And while Galen would be hard-pressed to name a single qualified candidate at the moment, he was convinced such a man could be found.

The trouble was, now that Aster was back and on the rampage, he didn't have much time to look.

Katy sat there looking as if she were waiting for some words of wisdom. He tried to think of a few, but dammit, his left foot was going to sleep.

These wretched boots. He'd thought he was being so damned clever, dressing this way to head off trouble before it got started. Wild West shows were all the rage now. Everybody knew how dangerous professional gamblers were.

It wasn't working. He might as well wear jeans, jerseys, and house slippers, and arm himself with a boat hook. If worst came to worst, he could swing a hook or a fist without splitting every seam of his custom-tailored coat.

"So . . . Katy," he said, and couldn't think of another thing to say.

Katy found everything about the man utterly fascinating. She should be furious, or at least apprehensive. Instead, she sat here admiring everything about him, from his intensely blue eyes to his shapely hands, to his even more shapely . . .

Well. Everything about the man was well formed. Being in his presence seemed to rob a room of its air. She couldn't afford to be any more indentured to him than she was. She was in far too deep as it was. Over her head. It was a terrible burden to bear, and yet she knew in her heart that she'd sooner be indebted to the man for a lifetime than never to have known him at all.

Tara said he was troubled. The last thing she wanted to do was cause him even more trouble. With the best of intentions, she seemed to have done it, all the same. For that reason alone, she told herself, she was obliged to hear whatever he had to say. That didn't mean she had to go along with his plans, not a bit of it.

"Now, it seems to me that the best course would be to find a place for you and Tara to sleep here aboard the *Queen* for the next few days, until I can interview a few prospective bridegrooms."

"Bridegrooms?" Surely she must have misunderstood.

"What you need is a husband, Katy. A man to look after you and take Tara in hand."

She swallowed the words that first came to mind. "Thank you kindly, but no. I've made plans of my own."

"Your ladies' shop."

"I know it's hard to believe, but I mean to do it, Galen, and I'll do very well. I've made up my mind."

She waited to see if he had anything more to offer. From the look on his face, she knew he doubted her. The telling meant little. She could talk about what she intended to do until she was blue in the face, but it was the doing that would tell the tale. And that would take time.

"I'm grateful to you for all your kindness, Galen. Truly, I never meant to trouble you." She smiled and tried to put her heart into it, so he'd know she meant what she said.

"No, I know you didn't, Katy. You did the right thing, coming to me for help."

She wanted with all her heart to deny it, but they both knew she was here only because Galen McKnight had sent her money. They both knew why he had sent the money—because Declan O'Sullivan had jumped overboard and died saving his life.

All the same, she wished . . .

Well. Things were the way they were, and there was no wishing the truth away.

"You'll make out just fine, Katy, once you settle in. You'll meet some nice young man—"

He went on talking about the nice young man she would meet, but Katy wasn't listening. She'd already met a nice young man, and he clearly wasn't interested.

Which was all very well, for she hadn't come to America in the first place to find herself a husband. The land was rich enough to grow anything. There were jobs to be had by anyone willing to work. One small setback wasn't the end of the world. She would simply return the two dollars Captain Bellfort had paid her and ask if he had something else she might try her hand at. If need be she could tell him about Tara, who was small for her age, but was used to hard work, and offer him two workers for the price of one.

Now, what man in his right mind could refuse an offer like that?

Chapter Seven

⤜

Grudgingly, Aster apologized.
Graciously, Katy accepted.

It was Ila who brought the two women together again. As she explained it, they were short a girl since Sal had gone and got herself in trouble, and now Sal and Charlie were going to have to get married, and hadn't Aster herself said she refused to have a married girl working for her, husbands being the troublesome creatures they were?

Aster had. On the subject of husbands, if nothing else, Katy thought, she and this witchety woman agreed. As much as she hated being forced to accept his charity, she refused to allow Galen to hand her over to the first man he could find who wanted a strong, healthy woman to cook and sew and scrub and bear him a slew of sons to fish his nets and tend his fields.

It had been just such a life that had killed her mother. Work and grief. For all he'd adored his lovely, city-bred wife, Declan had given her a dearth of comfort and too many babes. Until the day he'd died, he had mourned her, but Katy knew to her sorrow that he had mourned even more having been left with only two scrawny daughters and half a dozen small graves on the hillside.

Oh, she'd loved him dearly, for Declan O'Sullivan had been a lovely man. A man who could charm the stoniest

heart with no more than a song, a smile, and a witty word.
But charm never put food on the table, or kept out the wind
and rain on a cold winter's night. It was a lesson she'd
learned early and well. Any woman with brains and a strong
back would be better served looking after her own needs
instead of placing herself in the hands of a man, no matter
how charming the scoundrel was.

The three women were in Ila's cluttered cabin, where
Katy and Tara had slept the night before. Katy stood by the
door, her hand on the glass knob. Aster had immediately
taken possession of the room's only chair. In her purple
silk and her fine, fancy bonnet, she glared at Katy, who
glared right back. Ila, her skirts and apron flipped back, sat
on the foot of the bed and rubbed her bothersome knees.

The room reeked of liniment, lavender, and unaired clothing. Katy longed to throw open the window and let in the
rich, musky smell of the river, but none of the others seemed
to notice the stuffiness.

"Like I said," the housekeeper reasoned, "Sal's gone,
and here's Katy, needing work, and with Tara to help out
we'll not even have to hire on another cleaning girl to take
Maggie's place."

"Tara!" Aster exclaimed. "Who in the world is Tara?"

There followed a noisy succession of explanations, ar-
guments, charges, and rebuttals. Before it ended, Katy had
made up her mind she'd sooner walk barefoot over a bed
of barnacles than work for such a creature.

She ventured a question to the housekeeper. "Didn't you
say Captain Bellfort was in need of workers? If I'm not
wanted here, I believe I'll—"

"Bellfort! You stay away from Jack Bellfort!" Aster
snapped.

Katy's head came up. A body could be pushed just so
far, and she'd been pushed beyond her limit. Nose in the
air, she crossed her arms over her bosom and enjoyed a
bracing surge of self-righteousness. "I was told that this is

a free land. If the captain has work to be done, and I'm of a mind to do it, then that's no concern of yours, madam."

"Why, you little—!"

"There now, Miss Aster, you been riding that dirty old train all day long. What you need is a drink and a nice warm bath."

"What I need is to come home just once in my life without having to sort out a week's worth of problems," the woman snarled without once unclenching her teeth. "Why is it that I can't turn my back for a single minute without everything falling apart?"

Ila made soothing noises while Aster grumbled out her spleen. For all her fine and fancy trappings, she looked tired to the bone. The housekeeper winked at Katy as if to say, there's more than one way to skin a cat.

Katy thought of the two dollars burning a hole in her shabby purse. Money she would have to return. She thought of Willy's heaping table, and the way he had taken Tara under his wing. She thought of the row of ragged, but friendly old men dozing in the sun outside the warehouse, and the ragged children who whooped and hollered up and down the wharf, and the prostitutes who worked the waterfront in hope of earning a meager living.

Oh, yes, she was not as naive as some might think.

And then she thought about Aster Tyler, the woman who, according to Tara, owned nearly half of this lovely boat and had every man, woman and child on board dancing to her tune.

Not Galen McKnight, to be sure, but then, Galen was no ordinary man. There was far more to him than fine clothes and a handsome face, Katy had sensed that right off. But for all his manly strength, he was no match for Aster Tyler. The poor man could use a bit of help.

Which was how Katy found herself reluctantly agreeing not long after that to taking Sally's place until another girl could be found. As the meager pay included room and board for two, plus whatever tips she could glean, she didn't dare refuse until she found something more to her liking. It was a wise woman who knew the value of a bird in hand, as old Maddie Gillikin back in Skerrie Head was fond of saying.

"That's that, then." Ila rolled up her black cotton stockings, corked the liniment bottle and set it aside. "Sal's dresses can be took in to fit. The girl can do it herself," she said to Aster. "She's handy with a needle."

"Gawd, that stuff reeks." Aster waved a handkerchief in front of her elegant nose.

Ignoring her, the housekeeper rubbed what was left on her hands into the knotted joints of her fingers. "She'll have to have shoes, though. Them boots of hers looks awful."

They discussed her—the girl—as if she weren't even present. Self-consciously, Katy drew her feet in their worn, round-toed, flat-heeled boots under her skirt. To be sure, they weren't as fine and fashionable as some, she thought, eyeing Aster's stylish kid shoes with their pointed toes and tiny spooled heels, but they'd served well enough all these years. There was nothing really wrong with them that new soles and a bit of blacking wouldn't cure.

"Oh, all right," Aster said grudgingly. "Shoes, then, but cheap ones. First see if Ava or Ermaline has a pair she can borrow." Pinning her sharp eyes on Katy, she issued a warning. "Just remember, I'll be advertising for another girl right away, so don't go getting too comfortable. You stay away from Captain Bellfort, and see that you don't go bothering Captain McKnight, either. You'll answer to Ila, and she answers to me, is that clear?"

It was more than clear. Any guilt Katy might have felt over accepting one job while looking for another promptly fled, as did her momentary admiration for another woman's independence. Aster stood to go, pretty as a picture in her fancy bonnet, her corseted waist, and her leg o'mutton sleeves.

One of these days when she owned her own shop, Katy

would dress every bit as fine, if not quite so fancy. It would never do to compete with her customers. She'd never set foot in a fancy shop in her life, but she knew exactly what she wanted to do, and had a very good notion of how to do it. Many an hour while her hands had been working, her mind had been free to roam. Wearing her oldest clothes, mended and stained, she would picture the way her mother had looked when she'd been young and strong, and the gowns she'd brought with her from Dublin had been bright and lovely.

Fortunes were as fickle as the wind, her mother had said more than once. Never put all your eggs in a single basket.

"Now that that's settled," Aster told the housekeeper, as if Katy weren't even present, "she might as well get on with taking up Sally's red dress, but just the one, mind you. She won't be here long enough to need any more than that."

That I won't, you saw-tongued harpy.

"Oh, and while she's at it, tell her to see about my new blue watered silk, will you? Some clumsy old fool stepped on the flounce at a dance the other night and ripped it half off. She might as well turn up the hem half a length all around, too. Skirts are going to be shorter next season."

Katy dressed carefully, pinning the lace collar onto her second-best gown, a gray muslin that wasn't terribly faded, for she'd worn it only a few years. She re-anchored her fat braid in a crown on top of her head and pinned her best bonnet—her only bonnet—on top. Inspecting her reflection in the full-length mirror Ila used for fitting the girls' gowns, she nodded approval. "You'll do just fine, Kathleen Margaret Sheehan O'Sullivan, that you will. I'll spit in the eye of anyone who says you'll not!"

She located Tara on the side deck outside the galley, dealing herself a hand of cards. "I'm only practicing, Katy, truly. Captain Galen said Johnny the Knife was to give them to the old men down the dock, and Johnny said he'd teach me to play a game with them first if I showed him how to tell how many spots a card had without looking at the front."

Katy rolled her eyes. "Give the cards back. You know better than that, Tara."

The child was gifted, but that didn't mean she wasn't crafty as a fox. "I will, Katy. I only wanted to play."

"I know, love, but please try to stay out of trouble until I get back."

Katy considered taking her along, and thought better of it. It wasn't that she didn't trust the child, but there were times when responsibility sat so heavily on her shoulders, she wasn't sure she could bear up under it. Then the guilt would come over her, and she'd remind herself that she was all that stood between Tara and the workhouse.

Besides, she loved her more than anything else in the world. All they had was each other now. Once Katy got her bearings, things wouldn't seem quite so overwhelming. It simply took a few days to get used to new people, new places, new ways.

But first she had to return Captain Bellfort's two dollars. To think she'd woken up this morning with such a fine lilting feeling in her heart. Not a note had passed her lips, for singing before breakfast tempted fate, but fate must have heard what was in her heart.

"Good morning, girlie," called out one of the old men who spent his days resting on a bench outside a tavern— one of those places Ila referred to as three-cent houses.

At least she was young and strong. She had her health. "Top of the morning to you, sir," she caroled, and felt better for seeing his bony old shoulders lift and square. There were worse things in life than having to give back money a body hadn't earned.

Things such as despising another woman, even while she admired her gumption.

Things such as being an ocean away from home and knowing she'd never see it again but in her dreams.

One of the old men called out something that sounded almost like a warning, not that she could understand a word of it. She glanced back, then turned to continue on her way and tripped over something that darted between her feet. At the same moment two little boys lunged at her knees.

Down she went, skirts flying up over her knees. Her purse slid out of reach, and before she could grab it something dug into her leg up under her petticoat. Reaching down to brush it away, she caught hold of a pathetic scrap of fur and bones.

A cat. Hardly bigger than a baby chick. "Faith, and what else can go wrong?" she gasped, still sprawled flat on her bottom, hat down over her eyes and skirts up over her knees.

The kitten yowled, twisting to free himself. Sheer instinct made her hold on to the wretched little thing.

"Gimme my cat, lady!" A lad who couldn't have been more than five years old reached for the kitten as Katy struggled to her feet.

An old man with a crutch hobbled over, retrieved her purse, and then turned to lend her a hand. She caught her breath at the stench that wafted around his tattered rags. She righted her bonnet and accepted her purse. "Thank you very much, sir," she said breathlessly.

He could have kept it. They both knew it, just as they both knew he'd considered it. "I'll not forget your kindness," she told him, and turned back to the boys, who were doing their best to snatch the kitten from her hand. Holding it out of their reach, she scolded them. "If this wee creature is yours, you should be ashamed of yourselves. He's naught but skin and bones and matted hair, the poor darling."

One of the boys snickered. The other one quickly hid a sack behind his back. Katy clutched the kitten against her throat and received a scratch on the cheek for her troubles.

The old man cackled, hawked, and spat. "It ain't their'n, girly. They was gonna drown it like they done drowned the rest o' the litter. Fer a penny, they'd drown their own ma, if they had one."

Katy's face must have reflected her shock. "Is that true? Let me see what you've got in that sack."

"We've not got nuthin', lady." Shamefaced, the boy wearing a ragged shirt that came down past his scabby knees held out the limp cloth sack. It was empty. "We done drownded the rest a'ready. Orek and me, we dropped 'em off the end o' the pier, all but this'n. She runned away."

Katy felt like crying. She felt like taking them both by the scruff of the neck and shaking them until their teeth rattled. Not that they had more than half a gumful of teeth between them, and those black as tar.

Besides, it wouldn't have done a speck of good. They weren't really wicked, they were hungry and poor. A penny could buy a heel of bread—although she suspected their earnings would have been spent on a licorice whip, instead.

The old man scratched his head, examined his fingernails, and flicked something away. "There's too many cats, missy. They keep the rats down and clean up what fish scraps don't get stole fer the soup pot, but when the livin's too easy, they breeds like lice, and has to be thinned out."

She didn't need this, not today, of all days.

Helplessly, she glanced back toward the *Queen,* and there was Galen. Arms crossed, with one of those thin, fragrant cigars he favored held between his fingers, he stood watching from the top balcony.

Her head went up. Her backbone stiffened. She saw his teeth flash in a grin, and before she could turn away, the boys had fled, leaving her with a smelly old man and a wretched animal who wanted no more of her than she did of it.

But if she let it go, it would be caught and killed, and she didn't want that on her conscience. So she clutched the tiny scrap of fighting fur to her breast with one arm while she dug into the purse that dangled from her wrist.

"Then, here, give them this. Tell them the kitten is mine now."

The hand that accepted the coin was black with grime, the fingers horribly twisted. She wondered briefly if the boys would ever see the coin, decided it didn't matter, and with a curt nod, went on her way.

You foolish fumbler, your wits have gone begging, that they have! For a penny you can ill spare, you've gone and bought yourself another mouth to feed.

Having obviously thought better of the situation, the kitten stopped squirming and set up a pitiful cry. "Ah, sure and you're frightened, you wee whelp," she crooned. "A bath and a bowl of milk will set you up, that it will, but you'll have to be quiet. Until I can find us a real home, we're all here on sufferance, you and me and Tara."

The back of her hand was bleeding. Her cheek had begun to sting. "Whisht now, you're an ungrateful wretch, but I know how you're feeling, that I do." Holding it up to her face, she gazed into a pair of cloudy blue eyes and whispered, "You'll not believe it, but half the time, I'm so scared myself I could jump at my own shadow." The cat let out a pathetic wail. It was a girl cat, not a boy cat, which made it all the more dear. "We girls have a hard row to hoe, that we do. Hush now, Katy has you safe."

She began to sing, her voice clear as a silver bell against the din of clattering wheels, hucksters' cries, and the ever-present creak and groan of rigging. " 'Ah, whiskey, ye're the divil, ye're leading me astra-a-ay.' Hush now, ye're safe in Katy's arms-o."

"And what have we here, Miss O'Sullivan? Is that a moth-eaten muff you're singing to?"

Her fingers tightened around the kitten's bony middle. The little wretch promptly reacted by scratching her again. "Faith, and you'll have me heart leaping out of me gullet, Captain Bellfort!" The words slipped out, she was that startled when the very gentleman she'd come to see loomed up in front of her. From the time she was weaned, her mother had drilled her in the proper way to speak. She had learned well, and done her best to set a good example for Tara, but now and again in a moment of stress, she backslid.

"And how did the morning's business go, Miss O'Sullivan?"

"I suspect you know very well how it went," she snapped, far too embarrassed to guard her tongue. "I'm sorry, sir. I was doing well enough before I ran into a wee spot of trouble."

"A wee spot of trouble, hmm? Now that's what I'd call a perfect description of Aster Tyler. Raked you over the coals, did she?"

She nodded. They were still standing on the wharf, drawing more than a few curious looks. For all she knew, Galen was still watching from the deck of the *Queen*, moored not a stone's throw away. Sighing, she looked up into Jack Bellfort's twinkling eyes. "I tried to explain that it was for a worthy cause, but Miss Tyler took exception."

Tucking her free arm under his own, the captain steered her toward his boat. "If I know Aster, she was too busy tearing a strip off your—ah—dressing you down to listen. From the looks of you, I'd say she wasn't the only one you've run afoul of today. Come aboard and I'll have someone look at those scratches of yours. Cat scratches can be the very devil for going septic. Risky place, a waterfront."

"Aye, that it is." She thought of the two boys. She thought of the old man—of all the old men soaking up sunshine. Her heart went out to them, for every one of them looked ragged and lonely and hungry.

Katy had seen hungry men before. She'd known hunger herself when March came and the mackerel never showed up, when day after day, the seines came up empty, the sheep fell ill, and even the potatoes rotted before they could be dug.

At least those young scamps had been trying to earn a penny instead of stealing it.

The captain led her to a spacious cabin as fine as any she'd seen aboard the *Queen*. Indicating a velvet padded chair fit for a palace, he yanked on a tapestry ribbon, and not a minute later there came a knock on the gleaming paneled door. A cheeky lad wearing a dark green uniform poked his head inside. "Yessir?"

"Sherry for the lady, whiskey for me, and a bowl of cream—oh, and tell Jeannie to bring soap, a basin, and bandages."

Katy held the squirming kitten on her lap and stroked its scruffy head until it settled down. "I've come to give you your money back, sir," she said, hoping she didn't sound as reluctant as she felt to part with her earnings. She'd been hoping to send a few pounds to her friends back home once she got settled. She had that to do, and Galen to repay, all before she could begin to set aside money for her business.

"Let's not talk about that now. First, we'll see to your injuries, and then—Ah, Jeannie, here you are. The young lady here has gone and got herself clawed by a tiger. See to it, will you?"

Jeannie, a pretty girl wearing dark green silk with a lacy apron, knelt and made over the kitten. "Here, let's set him to his supper while I do something about those scratches."

The cabin boy brought in a tray holding two glasses, two bottles, and a bowl of cream. Heather, for Katy had decided to call the kitten that for the color of its eyes, sniffed suspiciously at the bowl, then went to lapping it up.

Captain Bellfort filled the two glasses and handed the smaller one to Katy. Like the kitten, she sniffed it first. Then she sipped it, made a face, and said, "Tastes like medicine."

"You might call it that. Don't tell me you've never had wine before?"

Not wanting to appear as green as grass, Katy shrugged her shoulders. "Oh, I've had me a bit of this and a bit of that."

"Sit still, ma'am," cautioned the woman who was sticking a plaster to the scratch on her cheek. "There now, don't let that wicked little imp get at you again. Cat's claws carry all kinds of filth. If it don't heal right away, you'll likely have a scar. I knew a man that died of a chicken scratch." Rising, she collected the basin, soap, and roll of bandages.

Jack Bellfort grimaced, but held the door for her. "Jeannie, Jeannie, always the alarmist." He kissed her on the cheek as she passed by with the basin, and left the door open behind her. "Thanks, love, I knew I could count on you."

"Is Jeannie your wife?" Katy inquired when he turned back to her.

The gentleman laughed. He had a fine, bold laugh.

He was a fine, bold-looking man. Not quite so handsome as Galen, but handsome enough in his own way. Dark hair, dark eyes, with a crooked grin that was as wicked as it was winsome.

"Jeannie's a good friend. She works for me."

"Sure, and that's what I came to talk to you about—work. That and to give back your money, for I never earned it, but first, sir, would you mind closing the door?"

He lifted his eyebrows. "Are you sure?"

The kitten had finished the milk and was exploring the cabin. If she got out, she'd be the very devil to catch, for she was wild as could be.

He closed the door, tugged at the knot of his tie, and Katy cleared her throat. She dug out the two paper dollars and thrust them at him, and then launched into the brief speech she'd rehearsed on the way to his boat, before she'd tripped over Heather and been knocked off her feet by that ragged pair of young rascals.

She was just getting to the part about how she was a

hard worker, and could read, write, cipher, and sew, and had plans to own her own business one day, when someone knocked on the door.

Jack Bellfort, a look of amusement on his face, said, "Excuse me, darling, let me get rid of whoever this is, and we'll talk about what you can do for me."

Chapter Eight

❧

It was a sight to gladden a maiden's heart, two such fine, handsome gentlemen, one dark, the other golden, with eyes as blue as Moy River on a fair summer's day. Katy's mouth hung open until she remembered to shut it.

"McKnight, welcome aboard," Jack Bellfort said expansively, right hand outstretched. "Come to scout out the competition?"

"Come to retrieve my property," Galen said evenly. Not once did he look directly at Katy, yet she knew as well as she knew her own name that he was aware of her presence.

"This scruffy creature belongs to you?"

Her eyes widened. She'd seen lightning blast a stone wide open in less time than it took Galen to react. Ignoring the outthrust hand, he grabbed hold of the other man's cravat, practically lifting him onto his toes. In a voice made all the more dangerous for being little more than a whisper he said, "If you've laid a finger on her, Bellfort, you'll answer to me."

Katy waited for the captain of the *Albemarle Belle* to explode.

Instead, he began to chuckle. Slowly, Galen loosened his grip. When his hand fell to his side, Jack straightened his necktie and nodded toward a chair. "Simmer down, man, all I did was offer her a drink. Under all that grime and matted hair, how was I supposed to know she was your lady?"

Without a bit of warning, Galen's fist shot out, catching Bellfort on the jaw. The captain of the *Albemarle Belle* staggered, but managed to catch himself on a nearby bookcase.

Galen grimaced and rubbed his knuckles.

Katy covered her mouth with both hands.

Bellfort righted himself, moved his jaw experimentally, and said in a voice smooth as silk, "If I were you, man, I'd take better care of my property. The world's a dangerous place for someone as innocent as our kitty here." He scooped the filthy yellow kitten from halfway up the velvet draperies, where it had been clinging by its claws. "Finished your cream, have you, love?"

Galen looked from Katy to the tiny animal twisting and hissing at the end of Bellfort's outstretched hand, and back again. His eyes narrowed. "Tell me the truth, Katy, did Bellfort touch you? If he so much as laid a finger on you, he'll curse the day he was born, I promise you that."

"I believe you've said quite enough, McKnight." Carefully, Bellfort handed the kitten to Katy.

"Aye, he touched me, but— Galen, stop that! Don't you dare strike that poor man again, he was only trying to help." She uttered a Gaelic curse.

Both men stared at her, making her wish she'd held her tongue. Bellfort recovered first. "Poor man?" he murmured ruefully. "Gad, I feel insulted myself."

The kitten, who'd had quite enough of it all, jumped from Katy's lap and scrambled under a small table covered in a fringed tapestry cloth. The cloth began to slide, and the three of them watched, immobile, as two glasses and a crystal decanter crashed to the floor.

"Well, hell." The plaintive remark came from Jack Bellfort.

"Would somebody mind telling me what the devil is going

on?" Galen's plea was directed to Bellfort, but it was Katy
who replied.

"Behave yourselves, the pair of you. For all I might be
small and scruffy, I don't belong to either of you."

When both men tried to speak at once, Katy cut them off
with another Gaelic oath. She wasn't sure of the precise
meaning, but she'd heard it from her father often enough
when he came stumbling home after a night of drinking
and brawling with his mates.

Turning to Jack, she said, "As for you, sir, I gave back
your money. Now that we're even, I've another favor to
ask of you."

Bellfort shot Galen a smug look, his crow black eyes
gleaming with amusement. "Anything, love, you've but to
name it."

"But first"—she turned to Galen—"I want you to understand that I'm grateful for all you've done for me and
mine, and I'll not let you down, I promise. I agreed to take
Sally's place until Miss Tyler can find someone better, but
I've only myself to depend on, so I'd best be about finding
something more permanent. Ila said there's work to be had
aboard Captain Bellfort's boat, and I mean to have me a go
at it."

She turned back to Bellfort, awaiting his response. Had
she left out anything that needed saying? She tried to be
fair and aboveboard in all her dealings. It saved trouble in
the end, and trouble was one thing she could do without.

She waited. The sharp scent of whiskey tickled her nostrils, reminding her that she'd not taken time to eat more
than a bite of breakfast. Here in this fancy room, surrounded
by all these fancy furnishings, with two fancy gentlemen
staring at her as if she had oats growing from her ears, she
wondered if she might've bitten off more than she could
swallow.

It wouldn't be the first time. She could hear her father

saying plain as day, *Katy, me girl, ye'd best try the river before ye go leapin' into the current.*

Too late, Da, I fear I'm in over my head.

"The lady is working for me, Bellfort," Galen said flatly. "Katy, what happened to your face?"

"She got scratched. I've already taken care of it, and the lady doesn't have to work for you, McKnight. I've already hired her to work for me."

"Doing what?" Galen jeered. "Handing out more leaflets?"

Bellfort's mouth twitched. He was far enough away so that Katy could see him quite clearly. "That was a dirty trick, I'll admit. If I'd thought it through, I'd never have set her up, but knowing Aster was due in today, I couldn't resist." Looking at Katy, he added, "Sorry, love. I'll explain if—"

"Cut it out, Bellfort, I don't need you to explain anything. Come on, Katy, let's go."

"The lady is staying. As I said before, she's working for me. I've hired her to take Addie's place."

"Addie?" Katy repeated.

"My chanteuse."

"But I don't know anything about—about chantoosing."

Bellfort's smile held both warmth and amusement. "Addie is a songster. That is, she sings here on Friday and Saturday evenings. Unfortunately, she recently came down with a dose of—that is, a case of—well, never mind that. I've been looking for a replacement."

"Oh, but—" Katy tried to interrupt, and was ignored for her troubles.

"Miss O'Sullivan is not a singer. She'll be working under my supervision, selling cigars at night and helping Ila during the day."

"Now, that would be a sheer waste of beauty and talent. Don't tell me you've never heard the lady sing?" Bellfort breathed on his manicured nails and then buffed them on the lapel of his white linen coat. "Tell me this, Katy, my love, do you play the piano as well as you sing?"

Katy stared at first one man and then the other. She couldn't believe they were arguing over her. Not that either man truly wanted her, it was simply the way men were. Let a one of them plant his boot on a hummock, and along would come another one to knock him off and take his place.

Galen looked as if he'd bitten into a lemon and his teeth had locked together. Katy took the opportunity to speak for herself. "My mother played the harp, but Da sold—that is, I didn't bring it with me."

"Never mind, love, Casey can play for you. Come along, I'll introduce the two of you and you can start working on your repertoire."

"I'll not go for a singer, I'm that sorry, but there's other things I can do, and do well. I'm not afraid of hard work, sir, that I'm not."

Galen eased in behind her. His voice came from over her head, as a hand came to rest possessively on her shoulder. "As I said before, Bellfort, the lady's spoken for. Now, my dear, if you've finished what you came to do, we'd better get back before that sister of yours gets into any more trouble."

Katy turned a worried look on him, but he shook his head imperceptibly. "She's fine," he murmured. "Just fine."

They left as soon as Katy could recapture the kitten. It was not a particularly dignified exercise. All the way back to the *Queen,* she could feel Galen's eyes on her. She had a feeling he was scowling, but lacked the courage to look and see. Before they even left the main deck of the *Albemarle Belle,* with Captain Bellfort watching their progress from his canopied balcony, he had tucked her free hand under his elbow and kept it there, clamped tightly against his body.

She'd have freed herself if she dared. Never had she been so aware of her lack of inches. Or of the heat and strength of another body. Of the scent of him, and even the sound of his breathing.

Sweat trickled under the brim of her hat, beaded her neck, and trickled down to pool between her breasts. If he was bothered at all by the miserable heat, he hid it well. One more sin to lay at his feet.

"Do you ever jump into the river for a swim?"

"Good Lord, no. Whatever gave you that notion?"

She marched along beside him, taking two steps for his every one. Her two little boys ducked between buildings, and she wondered if they ever swam in the river. Wondered if anyone watched over them. Wondered if one of the old men would go in after them if they were to get into trouble.

"So you suppose—" she blurted, then broke off.

"Do I suppose what?"

Slipping her hand from the crook of his arm, she fanned her damp face. Galen handed her a crisp, folded handkerchief, and she fanned with that, then blotted her forehead.

"I was only wondering if the children ever fall overboard."

"From the looks of them, neither one has been in close contact with water lately. Why?"

"Don't they have anyone to watch over them?"

He sighed. They were nearly at the *Queen,* by then. "Katy, Katy, you can't take on the whole world."

"They're too little to run wild."

Galen could have told her that wild they may be, but that didn't mean they were entirely without supervision. His own crew kept an eye out. He had an idea Bellfort's did, too. There were official ways of dealing with the hungry and homeless, but for the most part, the waterfront looked after its own.

Five days later, Galen wondered if he wouldn't have been wiser to let Bellfort have the pair of them, with his blessings.

They had both been on their best behavior, Katy assured him of that at least once a day.

And every day he watched her scurrying around, trying to make herself indispensable, trying to keep an eye on Tara. He found himself actually seeking her out, listening for the sound of her voice. Was she aware that she hummed when she worked? That she poked the tip of her tongue out the corner of her mouth when she was trying to thread a needle? It took her at least half a dozen tries, and by that time, he was usually so damned aroused he had to go back to his own quarters and wrestle with the books to get himself under control.

Katy, of all women. It didn't even make sense.

Aster hadn't said anything lately, but he could tell she was just waiting for a good excuse to boot them out. The more dead set she was on getting rid of them, the more determined he was to keep them. Which was one more thing that didn't make sense.

All week he'd been trying to locate a suitable place in town where they'd be safe until he could find Katy a husband. Nothing was working out. The timing couldn't have been worse. His land deal was coming to a head. The little problem on the wharf wasn't anywhere near solved. As for Katy and company, if he didn't dispose of them in the very near future, Aster was going to land on him with both feet.

And if he did, his own conscience would do the job. Either way, he couldn't win.

It didn't help matters that nearly his entire crew was enchanted, except for one or two dealers who threatened to quit if the kid came anywhere near their tables again. Among the enchanted was Willy. The grizzled old son of a sea cook was going to bankrupt him, cooking twice as much as it took to feed the crew and allowing the kid to pass out what was left over to anyone on the wharf who looked hungry.

Naturally, they all looked as if they were hovering on

the edge of starvation. He knew damned well there were soup kitchens in town, but this was easier. Why walk a block for food when it could be delivered to your doorstep?

Aster would have a fit if she ever got wind of what was going on. The lady never let go of a dollar without expecting a five-dollar return. Galen, on the other hand, wasn't against charity. While it had been years since he'd set foot inside a church, he tithed unofficially. A matter of conscience. Just in case gambling was the mortal sin some claimed it was.

Also a matter of conscience, he made sure Tara didn't wander outside alone with her charity baskets. Either Johnny the Knife or Oscar went along with her. Neither complained about the chore. The little minx had them both wrapped around her thumb.

Also among the enchanted was Ermaline, who had ended up with a new pair of shoes in a larger size so that she no longer hobbled around with that long-suffering look on her face. Meanwhile, Katy, wearing Ermaline's old shoes with cotton stuffed in the toes, swished around the gaming rooms in Sal's cut-down red silk dress, selling cigars, cigarettes, and handing out free smiles.

She'd quickly become a favorite with his regulars, which both irritated and amused Galen. He set it down to the way she smiled when one of the men paid her an extravagant compliment.

"Some of the high rollers are claiming she brings them luck," Pierre said in a quiet moment one Thursday evening, before the crowd settled in. "They call her over to stand by whenever they're in a tight spot. From the tips she collects, even when they lose a pot, it won't be long before she can set herself up in whatever business she wants. I only hope it's not gambling."

Galen hoped so, too.

"Maybe she'd like a partner. When you move on, maybe

Katy and I can take over the old *Queen*. I've got a few ideas about expanding I wouldn't mind trying out."

"Stay away from her," Galen grumbled.

"Dog in the manger?"

"You're pushing your luck, old man." Galen shot him a hooded look, and the New Orleans gambler chuckled.

"Still, you have to wonder why the other girls aren't raising hell. She's easily raking in twice the tips they are, after no more than a week on the job."

"Maybe they like her," Galen said with a shrug.

"I like her myself. She doesn't play favorites. She might be a tad clumsy at times, but you can't help but like her, even when she trips over her own feet and spills her tray all over the floor. What do you think about this notion she has of going into business for herself?"

"I try not to think about it," Galen snapped. It was bad enough that he couldn't sleep for dreaming about her, without wasting time swapping gossip when he should be looking after business.

"Might not be a bad idea to look into it."

It would be a lousy idea. He admired ambition in anyone, man or woman, but hers had about as much chance of being realized as a snowball in hell.

Galen told himself he was overdue a visit to Miss Dilly's Sporting House. Obviously he'd neglected certain matters of a purely physical nature for too long. Sex was like any other appetite. When a man was hungry, he ate. When he was thirsty, he drank. When he was—

Yes, well . . .

The first time he'd seen Katy in Sally's red silk dress, with her face powdered and rouged to disguise the cat scratches and her hair all curled and caught up in a silver ribbon, he'd damned near swallowed his cigar.

She was stunning. All the more amazing, she didn't even seem to realize it. Ila had brought her up to his cabin for a

final inspection that first night. She'd held out her skirts
and whirled around, then kicked out first one foot and then
the other in her new secondhand shoes that were at least an
inch too long, admiring the flash of white ruffles.

"I never saw so many storebought underclothes in my
whole life, and not a single layer of wool," she'd exclaimed,
grinning from ear to ear. "I'm all cambric and lawn, with
ruffles and ribbons down past my knees and clean up to
my gullet. Who'd have thought a body needed so many
layers just to be decent? Faith, and here I've been indecent
all my life, and never even had the pleasure of knowing it."

At the innocent disclosure, all in the lilting Irish brogue,
Ila's usual pinched expression had given way to a reluctant
smile. A childless widow, his housekeeper was totally under the spell of the Misses O'Sullivan, not that she would
ever admit it.

As for Galen, he hadn't known whether to laugh, sweep
her up and take her to bed, or reprimand her for talking
about her underclothes in front of a man.

If she even thought of him as a man.

Did she think of him at all? Other than as an employer,
that was? Did he want her to?

Oh, hell yes, he wanted her to. And that, unless he got
himself back on course pretty damn quick, was going to be
a problem. "Ah, Katy, Katy," he murmured now, studying
the glowing tip of his cigar. "What am I going to do with
you?"

At least there'd been no more hocus-pocus trouble with
Tara. He'd have heard about it if there'd been any further
incidents like the one that first day.

How the devil had she done it?

He wasn't sure he wanted to know. Better to put the incident behind him. The old *Queen* might be a tub, but she
had an impeccable reputation for honesty, and he intended
to keep it that way for as long as he was here.

With his tie and collar loosened and his bare feet propped

on the railing, Galen gazed out across the gleaming reflections that snaked across the river's surface. He could hear strains of music coming from Bellfort's orchestra.

Katy? A singer?

Not if he had anything to say about it. Katy had her own dreams, and as impractical as they were, they were a damned sight better than anything Bellfort could offer her.

Everyone had dreams. Hell, even Aster had her dreams. He'd heard more than he ever wanted to hear since the day he'd taken over Tyler's ownership. And while he couldn't in all good conscience allow her to take the old tub out of the harbor, once he was out of the picture she could hire herself a fancy chef, a dance band—hell, she could hire on a damned circus if she felt like it.

Stretching, he tossed away his cigar. It was going to be one of those nights. There was something in the atmosphere tonight. He had a sixth sense for trouble, which was why he'd taken his break early.

Reluctantly, he buttoned his collar, adjusted his cravat, put on his boots, and went below. Outside the double doors to the main salon, he paused and adjusted his expression to one meant to tell the world he was one armed and dangerous dude. Quietly, he moved from table to table, alert for signals from his dealers. Ava and Katy were working the main salon, which meant Ermaline was handling the high rollers tonight. They took turn and turn about. The crowd was a bit more unpredictable in the larger room, the tips usually higher in the small salon.

It was noisy. All the tables were busy tonight, both rooms filled to capacity. He'd come to hate the constant din, the smoke so thick a man needed a foghorn to navigate. The rosebud in his lapel was already wilted. Another part of his don't-mess-with-me, I'm-a-dangerous-man image was the nightly rosebud he affected, the only spot of color he allowed himself in an age when most men sported striped shirts and flowered waistcoats, not to mention neckties that rivaled the ladies for flamboyance.

Image. Was that what it had come down to, after all these years? he wondered tiredly. His father had been a success-ful horse breeder, his grandfather had owned a shipping business. And here he was, at an age when most men were already established in their chosen career, operating a leaky old gambling tub in a town he'd never even heard of a few years ago.

It had to be the weather. He could remember thinking not too long ago that he had about as sweet a setup here as any man could wish for. That life was good, and getting better every day.

Among his many vices, he added the vice of self-delusion.

He was still distracted by a vague sense of disquiet when suddenly, the room erupted. A chair flew past his head. Men cursed. One woman gasped and another one squealed, and then he heard the ugly sound of flesh striking flesh. By the time he managed to work his way to the center of the crowd gathered around the faro table, he had a sinking feeling the trouble was just beginning.

"What seems to be the problem here?" He might have known Katy would be right smack in the middle of it. "Katy, do you have something to say for yourself?"

Her face almost as red as her dress. She was standing on a chair, holding her empty tray as if it were a weapon. The table and floor were both littered with chips, cigars, ciga-rettes, and overturned glasses.

Pierre was helping a young man up off the floor. Waving off the two relief dealers moving in from the left, Galen said blandly, "All right, gentlemen, go back to your games, everything's under control now."

Naturally, not a soul moved an inch. Hell, nothing was under control. "Katy, get down off that chair. Pierre, would you mind telling me just what the devil is going on?"

"She was trying to cheat me, that's what she was doing!"

the young man on the floor shouted. Galen had never seen him before, but judging by his appearance and his slurred voice, he was well under the hatches.

"Katy, is what the gentleman said true?"

She didn't move a muscle, didn't utter a word. Nor did she climb down off the chair.

Galen grasped her by the waist and swung her down, not releasing her immediately. Her eyes had a glassy look, as if she'd backed into a situation she didn't understand, and it scared the hell out of him. Instinct urged him to get her out of here, to take her upstairs, lock her in his cabin, and throw away the key.

Fortunately, reason prevailed. "Katy?" Her face was no longer red. She was white as a bedsheet except for a pair of snapping green eyes, two blotches of rouge, and a handful of freckles. "Did you try to cheat the gentleman?"

She was trembling. "Sure, and I would never do such a thing," she retorted in a voice so soft it was barely audible.

"No? I'd like ta know whacha call it." The young man was on his feet by now, just barely. Still looking dazed, he rubbed the top of his head. At closer range, he didn't appear quite so inebriated.

"Pierre? You want to tell me what happened?" Katy tried to pull away, and he tightened his grip. "Stay right where you are, young lady."

Pierre nodded to one of the boys, who hurried over and began cleaning up the litter. "Near as I can make out, this gentleman here wanted to buy a cigar. Katy came over with her tray. He took his choice, paid his money, and the next thing I knew they were going at it, tooth and nail. Then Katy—"

"I gave her a double eagle! She gave me back a nickel! I figured she wanted to do a bit of business on the side, so I told her to go on to her room and get in bed, that I'd follow her as soon as I'd finished the game, and damned if she didn't kick me. Knocked the cards right out of my hand. Best cards I'd seen all night."

"He grabbed my—my—he put his hand on my—"

"Katy, pipe down. Pierre, did you see what happened?"

"They're both telling the truth. He gave her a twenty-dollar gold piece. I didn't see what kind of change she gave him, but . . . ah, there's been some trouble before tonight about the way she makes change. A tip is one thing, but . . ."

"Katy? Did you try to cheat this man?" Galen deliberately kept his voice devoid of the impatience and frustration he was feeling.

It didn't help. She was going to cry. He should have waited to deal with her once he got her alone, which was what he'd intended to do all along, but dammit—!

"That I did not."

"She sure as hell did!"

"It felt like a quarter," she exclaimed. Her lower lip was quivering. Galen stared at it until she began to speak again. "I didn't look at the color, for my eyes were burning from all the smoke, but I was sure he'd taken a twenty-cent cigar."

"I don't smoke crap!" the young man shouted.

"Well, how was I to know what you smoke? Any man who would touch a lady on her—on her—"

"Lady? Ha! If you were a lady, you wouldn't be strutting your stuff in a place like this! You been giving me the come-on all night, admit it! I don't mind a little sport, but dammit, not when I'm holding a winning hand. I was fixing to rake in the biggest pot I've seen all week—I was all set to celebrate with a good cigar and a quick tumble when you turned into a damned wildcat."

"I did no such!"

"The hell you didn't! We had us a deal. You gave me the eye, you took my money and then, first thing I knew, you were beating me over the head with that damned tray. Man, this place stinks! I'm getting out of here, but not before I get my money back."

"I'm sorry for the misunderstanding, young man. Pierre will settle up with you." The room was still as a morgue. Every eye in the room was fixed on the small tableau gathered around the faro table. Galen, his face set in a chilly smile, nodded to the spectators. "Enjoy your evening, gentlemen. Sorry for the disruption—merely a misunderstanding."

It was Pierre who announced that the next round was on the house. Galen nodded to the bartender, and then he got out before something else could go wrong. Ushering Katy out before him, he waited only until the doors swung shut behind them, and then he grabbed her by the wrist and headed for the stairway, his long stride eating up the distance.

Halfway up to the top deck, Katy dug in her heels, nearly jerking him off balance.

She freed her hand and shot him an accusing look. He saw her rub her wrist, which was turning red, and it was the last straw. On top of everything else, he was a bully.

It was *her* fault. He'd never had this kind of trouble before. His girls sold cigars and cigarettes and that was all they sold. He'd have been out of business before he'd ever opened his doors if he ran that kind of operation. A place like his had to be doubly careful not to step over any lines.

"You think it's all my fault, don't you?" Standing three steps below him she looked incredibly small, incredibly vulnerable.

"I didn't say that."

She was still rubbing her wrist. Trying to make him feel guilty. Dammit, he hadn't held her that hard. "If you're waiting to hear an apology, don't hold your breath. I'm not about to apologize until we get to the bottom of this."

Eyes so clear and direct ought to be against the law. Whatever had happened down there, she'd been right in the thick of it, whether she'd deliberately sent out any signals or not.

He thought not. He'd stake everything he owned on her honesty.

But that didn't mean she was off the hook. Trouble was second nature to the O'Sullivans. Before they'd been on board more than an hour that first day, Tara had nearly shut down his entire operation, single-handed.

And now this. "Katy?"

"I didn't do it. Not what he said I did."

"I know you didn't. That is, I'm sure you didn't do it deliberately." He didn't want to have this conversation at all, much less out here in the open, where anyone could come along at any moment. "Katy, I'm not blaming you. Now come along, there's a good girl. You don't want Tara to hear us and get all upset, do you?"

Her chin quivered once before she got it under control. She clamped her lower lip between her teeth, sent him a look that defied interpretation, and then trudged up the last few steps.

What the devil was he going to do with her?

He was tempted to let it drop until tomorrow, to send her below and hide out in his own quarters until he felt more like sorting it all out.

But dammit, he was the captain here. He was in charge.

Wordlessly, he led her to the door of his cabin, opened it, and stood aside, waiting for her to go in. Her head was on a level with his wilted rosebud. She refused to look at him. With a sigh dredged up from the depths of his weary soul, Galen rested his hands on her shoulders.

And then he made the mistake of tilting her face up to his.

At least she wasn't about to cry. If she'd started crying, he didn't know what he'd have done. Dry-eyed, she met his gaze with that soul-searing guilelessness of hers, and he groaned. "What am I going to do with you, Katy?"

Her lips parted, but she didn't utter a sound. Her eyes

widened, then narrowed, then blinked several times in succession.

And then it came to him. "Oh . . . my . . . God. You're blind as a bat, aren't you?"

Chapter Nine

❧

It's not going to work. You're going to have to get rid of her." Leading the parade, Aster barged into Galen's quarters two days later, catching him with his shirt unbuttoned, razor in hand, his face still half lathered.

Tara, wearing an apron left behind by the recently departed maid that wrapped twice around her middle and dragged the tops of her thick-soled boots, was right behind her, with Katy bringing up the rear.

"They'll never notice, Captain Galen. Sure, and I didn't even notice myself," Tara pleaded earnestly.

Ila shoved in front of the trio. "I done my best, Cap'n, but all the paint in the world's not going to hide them specs."

Standing in the doorway, feeling like nothing so much as a leg of lamb on a butcher's table, Katy knew it was true. No matter what Tara said, she'd be a laughingstock dressed in the red silk gown and high-heeled shoes, with her hair all done up fancy and a pair of spectacles on her face.

Galen had taken her to the eyeglass doctor the very next morning after the misunderstanding in the main salon. He'd waited for her, trying to hide his impatience, while she had tried on one pair of spectacles after another. She'd been concerned about the cost, concerned because Galen was angry with her, concerned because so far nothing had turned out the way she'd expected. No matter how hard she tried, one thing after another seemed to go wrong.

Now, on top of everything else, she had to get used to seeing everything in reverse. Instead of sharp at a distance and fuzzy up close, things were clear as a bell up close, but blurred at a distance unless she remembered to take off her spectacles.

"You'll be able to make change," he'd told her on the way back to the *Queen*.

"But I'll never be able to find my way about."

"Katy, you're not supposed to wear them constantly," he'd said, sounding as if his patience was sorely tried. "They're magnifying glasses. You wear them for close work and take them off when you're finished."

"Sure, and I knew that." Knowing it and getting used to doing it were two different things. Magnifying glasses were what old people depended on when their eyes wore out, but she was only twenty-two years old. Which was hardly young, but not really old, either.

They'd strolled down Main Street, and Katy had counted all the people they passed who wore eyeglasses. A few, not many. She'd felt as if everyone was staring at her. She'd been wearing her new glasses to get used to the feel, but she'd removed them again when they'd passed a small shop with a window opening onto Main Street. "Ohh," she breathed reverently, standing back to admire the gold lettering on the storefront.

Then she'd put them on and moved closer to stare at the display window. It was still blurred.

What was it Da used to say? Damned if I do, damned if I don't.

While Galen had waited, arms crossed over his chest, she'd taken in every single detail of the lavender taffeta gown, the purple straw bonnet with a single lavender plum, and the tiny pair of gray kid slippers beside the dress form, a bouquet of silk violets in the left one.

Someday, she'd vowed silently, she would have a window that would make women stop and say, "Ahhh . . ."

"Seen enough?"

She'd nodded. He'd been more than patient with her. More than generous. Her debt was quickly adding up to a staggering sum, which was depressing enough under any circumstances, but even more depressing when the last thing she wanted from him was money.

For one long moment as they'd continued on their way back to the wharf, Katy had allowed herself to think of what it was she *did* want from him.

And then she'd been even more depressed.

"Remind me to introduce you to Mrs. Baggot over on Poindexter Street. She's dressmaker to most of the ladies in town. She might be able to use you in some capacity or another now that you can—"

"Now that I can see to make proper change and sew a seam with the raw edges inside instead of outside?"

"Well, you have to admit, my dear, it does make a difference."

They'd both laughed a bit, and Katy had thanked him again, promising to repay him as soon as she earned enough. He'd brushed off her offer, but she was determined. And she did feel somewhat more optimistic about the future.

That is, she had until she'd dressed for work this evening and caught a glimpse of herself in all her finery, with a pair of owlish spectacles perched on her nose.

She'd added another dusting of rouge, and with her little finger, dipped into the red salve Ila had given her and smeared it on her lips, hoping to distract attention from her eyes.

It only made things worse. Even Tara had laughed, and Tara's tastes were—to put it charitably—rather exotic.

She had scrubbed off every smidge of color from her face. She'd pulled back the curls Ila had made with her hot iron, and flattened her hair as much as thick hair could be flattened, but it only made her spectacles stand out more.

"You're going to be late," Tara had reminded her.

Desperately, she'd tried to ram the wire frames in her bodice, where she could take them out to make change, but by then her skin was damp with perspiration because it was hot and she had on so many layers, and they jammed halfway in.

She'd uttered a bad word, to Tara's delight. And then Aster had barged in, and now here she was, causing trouble again.

Awash with guilt, she waited for Galen to explode. Men had no patience, none at all. Some things were the same on both sides of the Atlantic.

She hadn't long to wait. Galen slammed his razor down on the washstand, spattering flecks of shaving soap onto the ruffled bib of his starched white shirt. "For God's sake, can't a man have any privacy around here?"

Arms crossed over her bosom, Aster swapped him glare for glare. "I told you to get rid of them. Didn't I warn you? But oh, no, you and your bleeding heart, you have to take in every stray that turns up with some far-fetched story."

Katy opened her mouth to say she was not a stray, but before she could get a word out, Aster was off again. "Well, I hope you're satisfied. The tables are already filling up downstairs, and it's not even dark, and now we're short a girl. She can't go in there looking like that, they'd laugh her out of the place. God knows, she's already caused enough trouble!"

Holding her breath, she waited for Galen to explode.

Ila's eyes were round as marbles. Tara wasn't even breathing. Quietly, Galen said, "Is that it? Are you finished?"

"No, I'm not! Let me tell you something, Galen McKnight, the *Pasquotank Queen* and I will still be here long after you've given up and gone back to where you came from. We've more than enough carpetbaggers without you, so don't think we can't do without you anytime you feel like selling out and going back up north where you belong."

If a pin had hit the floor, they'd all have jumped out of their skins. Galen laid aside his razor. He toweled the lather from his face. Turning to Ila, he said, "Katy looks just fine to me. More to the point, she sees just fine. Now, if there's nothing more I can do for you, I'd like to finish getting dressed."

Aster flung out her arms, endangering seams that Katy had only recently repaired. "Well, I never—!"

Katy felt like crawling into the nearest mousehole. Tara rolled her eyes and started to sway. Fortunately, Ila herded them all outside before the child could utter a word.

The next few days were unexpectedly peaceful. Katy gave up on trying to paint her face. Ila tied a black ribbon to her spectacles, and she wore them around her neck, using them as she needed them, letting them hang in between times. Not a single gentleman remarked on it.

Not a single gentleman leered, grabbed her by the behind, and made an improper suggestion, either. Katy didn't know whom she had to thank for that, but she thanked them all. Buck, the lookout, Pierre, the head dealer, Charlie, who looked embarrassed, and the other dealers, whose names she still hadn't sorted out.

Tara in her wraparound apron gathered up laundry to be sent out, dusted furniture, made beds, and ran errands. She carried her baskets of food to her newfound friends along the waterfront, always with Oscar or Johnny the Knife in attendance.

What with Oscar's glass eye and her own spectacles, Katy thought Galen must owe a fortune to the eye doctor. At the rate her own debt was adding up, she might just be able to pay it off in the next hundred years. Her dream of a shop of her own grew more and more distant, but she refused to be discouraged.

Ila insisted on giving her a pair of earbobs that had been given to her by her late husband. "Won't do an old crow like me a speck o' good, gussyin' up in pearl earbobs. I come across 'em the other day and I said to myself, Ila, I said— it's time to start getting shed of all the things you don't use no more. First thing you know, you'll up and die and then that meddling sister-in-law of yours'll have herself a field day, going through your private, personal things."

Katy's face had crumbled, she'd been that touched. She'd tried to refuse, but the housekeeper had started crying, too, and then they'd both had a good blow and a wipe and Ila had told her all about the scamp of a traveling salesman she'd been married to for seventeen years, who'd kept more ladies happy than a frog had freckles, not that Ila had suspected a thing until after he'd got drunk, stepped off a ferry-boat, and drowned in the Chowan River. There'd been so many grieving females wearing full mourning at his funeral that even the undertaker had been confused.

So along with her red silk gown and her spectacles and Ermaline's pointy-toed, high-heeled patent leather shoes with a wad of paper stuffed into each toe, Katy wore Ila's pearl earbobs. It was far too much, she knew that, for she'd inherited her mother's taste for understated fashions, but there wasn't much she could do about it.

Aster stayed busy with some mysterious new project that kept her in town most of the day. Ava and Ermaline slept late, came to breakfast in their wrappers, and everyone laughed a lot more.

And Tara was on her best behavior. No swaying, no far-away, unfocused look in her sky blue eyes. If she experienced any sightings, she kept them to herself, although she did confide in Katy that Captain Jack showed off his fancy women only because he knew Miss Tyler was watching, and he liked to rile her.

"How do you know that?" In Katy's opinion, any man

who enjoyed making Aster Tyler angry was daft, but it was no concern of hers.

Tara looked smug. "I just know, that's all. What if Miss Tyler's trying to get Captain Galen to marry her?"

"Tara," Katy said warningly. "You promised."

"I didn't *see* anything, I was only thinking about it. Did you know she's taken her dinner out on his balcony three times this past week? I know, because I've heard them up there talking."

"Well, and why shouldn't they be talking? They're business partners."

"Huh! He has an office for talking. Why does he have to invite her out onto his balcony and feed her egg custard in a glass with whiskey sauce? Willy makes me eat my custard out of a bowl, with only molasses on top."

Getting dressed for her evening shift, Katy squinted through her spectacles as she tried to attach one of the pearl earbobs. She murmured an absentminded response. "It's better than no custard at all."

Tara snorted. "Aren't you even listening? Katy, we have to do something. What if he marries her?"

She didn't want to think about it. It made her stomach tighten into knots to think of him holding a woman, lying down with her, kissing her. . . .

"Oh, drat," she muttered, wishing she saw more to admire in the looking glass. "My shoes—hand me my shoes." She couldn't afford to be late. Ila lined up all her girls for inspection promptly at half past four. Already she could hear the sound of early arrivals trooping up the gangplank.

"Katy? Did you hear what I said?" Tara flopped down a set of freshly laundered pillow slips, sighing dramatically. "I do wish you'd pay attention. I said, I think Miss Tyler's trying to get the captain to marry her, and whether or not you help me, I mean to save him. She's not near good enough for him. She's mean."

Knotting her shoelace, Katy looked up. "Well now, that's not a kind thing to say."

"But it's the truth. Katy, he can't marry Miss Aster, he's far too good for her. I know who'd make him the best wife of all, do you want me to tell you?"

"That I don't, and don't you go trying to see, either. The captain is old enough to find his own wife."

Tara had that smug, I-know-something-you-don't-know look on her face. It never failed to make Katy uneasy, as trouble was seldom long in coming.

"Quit your blatherin' now, girl. When you're done putting away the linens, go see if you can help Willy."

Tara left, carrying a stack of folded linens to be parceled out to the cabins. There was a knowing look on her face that made Katy want to lock her away before she landed them both in hot water.

Fluffing out her skirts, she hurried to present herself, breathless and barely in time, at Ila's cabin door. Ava arrived next, complaining about a garter that refused to stay fastened. Ila looked them over, yanked Ava's bodice higher, flipped up the back of Ermaline's skirt and adjusted a sagging petticoat, paused before Katy, and finally nodded approval.

Katy let out the breath she hadn't even known she was holding and followed the other two women to the game salons. Each day she expected to be told she was no longer needed. Told that Aster had hired someone else. Each day she promised herself she could look for work in town. She didn't fit in here. The smallest and plainest of the lot, to her way of thinking, she couldn't hold a candle to either of the others.

At least she had no more trouble making the proper change, nor did any of the gentlemen cause her a speck of trouble. By midnight all tables were filled, the noise-level deafening. Her head was beginning to ache, but she had already collected seven dollars in tips tonight.

She thought of the money tucked away in her valise, thought about how she would parcel it out. One dollar a week toward a school outfit for Tara. Fifty cents for books? She had no idea how much books cost here in America. There would be rent to pay, and food to buy, but every penny she could spare would go toward what she owed Galen. Once she had Tara outfitted and enrolled in the public school over on Pool Street, she could set aside even more against her debt.

Katy hadn't forgotten Galen's promise to introduce her to Mrs. Baggot, the dressmaker. She liked that plan far better than his other one. Finding her a husband. She knew precisely what she wanted in life, and it wasn't a husband chosen for her by someone else.

As it turned out, it was Aster who set into motion the wheels of the future by announcing that she'd hired a new girl. Annie Matlock would be moving aboard to take Sal's place and Sal's old bed, which meant that Katy was no longer needed.

"I told you right from the first the job was yours only until I found someone else," the older woman reminded her.

Katy nodded. "Aye, that you did, ma'am, and I'm that grateful to you."

Aster harrumphed. She did a lot of that sort of thing when she couldn't think of a proper set-down. Katy was coming to know her quite well.

"Then I'll be packing our bags, and as soon as I've found a place in town, we'll be off."

She refused to give in to fear. Instead, she would go to Mrs. Baggot herself and offer to work ten hours a day—twelve hours a day, if needed, doing whatever needed doing, and all for a modest wage to cover the cost of a single room and two meals a day for both Tara and herself. And a fish and a bit of cream for Heather.

She would simply make herself indispensable, and then,

one day when business was slow, she would ask to be allowed to design and stitch a gown from the cheapest mate-
rials. Katy knew good clothing, even if she couldn't afford
to wear it. She could still remember the way her mother
had looked before she'd grown pale and thin, and her gowns
had hung on her.

It was Katy who had remade every one of those gowns
after her mother died. She knew every seam, every dart and
gusset, and just what each accomplished. She had her mother's old fashion journals, long out of date by now, but good
taste was good on either side of the Atlantic.

She might have known it wasn't to be so simple. Nothing
ever was. They weren't even finished packing before Galen
rapped on the door. "Would you mind telling me just where
the devil you think you're going?"

Hiding her panic with a smile, Katy glanced up from
tucking her spare pair of stockings into her valise. Never
had she wished so hard to be tall, poised, and elegant, instead of small, plain, and shabby. She managed a smile,
but her wits completely failed her.

"Katy? What do you have to say for yourself?"

"I've only this to say. You recommended Mrs. Baggot, if
you'll recall. I've a mind to see if she'll have me."

"What I said was that I'd introduce you."

"I can introduce myself, for I've a tongue in my head."

"That, at least, I can vouch for," he retorted, a hint of
amusement softening the sharpness of his voice.

She could tell he wanted to argue. She couldn't miss the
way his gaze took in the sorry condition of her old brown
dress, but he had sense enough not to say anything. At
least, not about the way she looked.

"I see. Have you thought about where you'll stay? Not
every landlady welcomes pets. And what about Tara? What
do you intend to do with her while you're at work?"

She fastened the flap of her valise, her fingers tightening convulsively on the stained and threadbare tapestry. Hadn't she worried herself sick about those very same questions?

"Katy, you don't have to go. At least wait until I can—"

"It's time, Galen."

For a long time, he stared at her, as if searching for answers to questions neither of them dared voice. Katy told herself she was being fanciful, but she wasn't. At least, not entirely.

"Promise me something," he said finally.

She nodded. Couldn't have uttered a word if her life depended on it. She was half convinced it did.

"If you need help—if you can't find a decent place to stay—if anything at all happens, and you need me—"

The smile cost her more than he would ever know. She hung on to it as long as she could, and then turned to smooth the spread she had already smoothed. "Yes, of course. And thank you."

He held out his hand. She stared at it, and then at him, and he said, "Oh, hell—Katy, don't go."

Somehow—it didn't make a bit of sense, but somehow, she was in his arms, and he was holding her, rocking her from side to side, saying her name over and over in a despairing tone of voice.

She didn't belong in his arms, but oh, how she wished she did. Just for a moment, because she wasn't quite as strong as she needed to be, she let herself surrender to all the dizzying needs that swirled inside her. Caught up in the rip, torn away from the shore by a current more powerful than anything she had ever known.

Never leap into the current, Katy, before you test the river.

Too late, Da, too late.

He didn't kiss her. Later, after he'd gone without a word, Katy fought back the disappointment, willing her common sense to rise to the occasion, but oh, how she missed the strength of those hard arms wrapped around her, holding her close, so close she could feel the throb of two hearts beating as one.

It was almost a relief when Tara burst into the cabin, her small face avid. "Katy, d'you know what I think?"

"I'm afraid to ask."

"I think we're lucky Miss Aster found somebody else, and you lost your job, and do you know why?"

Katy didn't. Again, she was afraid to ask, but Tara needed no prompting. "Because a ladies' shop will be the perfect place to look for a wife for Captain Galen."

Her smile was far too ingenuous to be trusted. "You'll do no such thing. Tara, I'm warning you—no trouble. No seeing, and no speaking out of turn. It was one thing back home, where everyone knew you and remembered Granny, but people in America don't believe in such things."

"That they do, else why would they blow on dice and close their eyes and whisper before they roll them across the table?"

"Have you been in those gaming rooms again? No, don't tell me, I don't even want to know. Just go find Heather and see if you can borrow a basket. We'll leave the trunk here until we decide on a place to stay."

"Maybe Mrs. Baggot won't hire you. Maybe we won't find a place to stay. Then can we come back here?"

"She *will* hire us, and we *will* find another place to stay," Katy said firmly. She would beg if she had to. She would promise to work twice as hard for half the wages. What businesswoman could turn down such a bargain?

"Did you see her saying yes? Did you see us moving into a—"

"That I did not! Go along with you, and don't cause any more trouble than you must." She swatted her little sister on her negligible behind, but she was smiling. It was either that or weep, and she'd long since done with weeping.

* * *

Leaving Katy, Galen sent for his rig and drove directly into town. He knew Inez Baggot slightly, the way he knew most of the town's small business community. He left after twenty minutes of hard bargaining. It was the slack season, when most of the town's best families were still at the beach. Mrs. Baggot used the time to make up a supply of ready-made garments, some with a particular customer in mind that could be finished in a day's time.

She argued that she had all the help she needed until fall.

Galen argued that this was the perfect time to train a new worker, when there was no great demand on the staff.

They didn't discuss salary—that was a matter between employer and employee. All the same, when he asked suggestions as to a respectable, affordable boardinghouse for a woman and a young girl, she thought a moment and gave him a name and an address.

He drove around and looked the place over. It was roomier than the shared cabins on the *Queen,* but that was about all it had to recommend it. Given more time, he might have found them something more suitable, but time was the one thing he couldn't control. A certain tract of land he'd been trying to buy for nearly a year was coming on the market. He would have to move fast to work out the details. Thanks to Judge Henry's advance warning, he had a good shot at it, but there were three other interested parties. He had to move fast.

Katy. Damn. His head was still swimming, and it wasn't on account of being so close to taking the first step in realizing his dream.

The woman was half waif, half witch, and entirely too distracting, at a time when he couldn't afford to be distracted.

If he was smart, he'd get on with his idea of finding her a husband. The last thing he needed was a wife. Besides, he was too old. She was hardly more than a child.

She hadn't felt like a child in his arms. That had been no

child looking back at him, her lips so near it was all he could do not to take what she was offering.

Galen told himself she hadn't been offering anything. That was only his overheated imagination.

He told himself that while widows were given more latitude, respectable, unmarried young ladies didn't live alone in public accommodations, unchaperoned. They didn't own their own businesses. Even working in a shop was borderline.

For both their sakes, he was going to have to find her a husband. Quickly, before he did something incredibly foolish.

Chapter Ten

～

He missed her. Found himself thinking about her at the damnedest times, when his mind should've been too busy going over plans, options, offers, and the like to have room for anything else.

Found himself looking up, hoping to catch a glance of her, listening for a snatch of one of those funny, plaintive little songs she sang.

Gaelic. He thought it must be Gaelic. Whatever it was, he missed it, missed the sound of her footsteps, crisp on the hardwood between carpeted areas.

You're daft, man, he told himself, and then grimaced, catching himself using a word Katy used when he'd have said crazy, or nutty.

Feet propped on the railing of his balcony, he studied the glowing tip of his cigar as his thoughts drifted back over the past twenty-four hours.

Things had gone surprisingly well, thanks to Judge Henry's advance warning. He'd managed to ace out the competition by being first in line, with a sizeable amount of cash in hand and three prominent names as security on a note for the balance. He didn't know if the reputation he'd so carefully cultivated—that of a man whose past was shrouded in mystery, a man who dealt with trouble quietly, and with deadly efficiency—had had anything to do with the speed at which the sale went through, but it probably hadn't hurt matters.

Barring unforeseen complications, the property was his, signed, sealed, and delivered. There was easily enough waterfront for his purposes, with plenty of additional acreage for outbuildings. There were even a couple of houses at the far end, one that might even be brought up to standard with a bit of work.

There was an overgrown flower bed in front, and before he could stop himself he was picturing Katy kneeling, trowel in hand, setting out slips of this and that. She'd be good with flowers.

He hadn't bothered to look inside the place. Later, when he wasn't quite so distracted, he'd look the place over and decide whether to raze it or repair it.

Now that he had the papers securely locked in his safe he could afford to admit that he'd been nervous as a cat on ice, afraid something would go wrong at the last minute. His first choice had been a tract some half a mile east of Knobbs Creek. New in town, he'd been unable to arrange the financing in time to beat out another buyer and unable to swing the deal on his own, thanks to having sent most of his savings to O'Sullivan's bereaved family.

The last thing he'd intended was for Declan's daughters to use the money to emigrate, much less to show up at his door.

He had a dream. Now, when it was so close to being realized, he couldn't afford to let anything interfere.

Every man, if he had the guts to admit to it, had a dream. Brand had dreamed of taking what was left of their grandfather's shipbuilding business and bringing it back to life. Galen had gone into the business with him, but it was largely due to Brand's leadership that the place was now a growing and prosperous concern.

As for Liam, their youngest brother, whatever brief dreams he had dreamed had ended in a nightmare. He'd had the misfortune to marry the wrong woman, a woman Galen could have—should have—warned him about. A woman who had married a lad who was too young to know better, and proceeded to lead him down a short, straight road to destruction.

Against all reason, Galen found himself wanting to tell Katy about his dream of starting his own yard, where he could build ships of his own design.

And how that dream was suddenly within his grasp. And about Liam, dead now for nearly three years. And about the guilt he still felt—would probably always feel—for not having taught him to be wary of treacherous women who would marry a man for his money, strip him of all he possessed, including his pride, and then leave him to die by his own hand.

Galen belched discreetly and set his empty glass on the rail. He allowed himself one drink a night. Tonight he'd had three, in celebration. He stared at the dead ash on the tip of his cigar. As swiftly as it had arisen, the intoxication of success fled, leaving him feeling tired. Feeling old. Feeling . . .

Unfinished. Empty. Wanting to talk and having no one interested enough to listen. He blamed it on the whiskey. It always affected him this way, which was why he seldom drank. The quick jolt of euphoria, followed by headache and depression. Their father had been the same way. And Liam. Liam, who was buried in the hills of Connecticut.

God, what a fake he was. The mysterious Captain McKnight, who was rumored to have killed a man for holding one too many aces. A man who was rumored to have played poker with Bill Hickock and won, to have turned down an offer from Bill Cody to star in his Wild West Circus.

He could ride as well as the next man—better than most. But hell, one of the reasons he'd left home in the first place instead of following in his father's footsteps as a horse breeder was because he was no more fond of horses than he was of taking orders.

Katy would have understood. She'd had the courage to strike out on her own. In her case, it had been a dangerously foolhardy thing to do, especially being solely responsible for a child like Tara. But she'd done it. On her own, he thought lugubriously, with no man to protect her or guide her or tell her how to manage, she'd come all the way from Ireland with some half-baked notion of opening a dress shop.

A dress shop. It had been all he could do not to laugh when she'd confided in him. Dressed in the most godawful getup imaginable—two shades of muddy brown, topped off by the ugliest hat he'd ever seen—and she was going to open a dress shop?

Even the red silk Aster had chosen for her girls as flashy, but not too flashy, was an improvement. For Katy, green would've been better. With a higher neckline and a longer hemline. Something a lot more modest. Something that wouldn't encourage men to take liberties. He was going to have to take her in hand, but first he'd have to come up with a way to do it without hurting her feelings.

And then he remembered that she was no longer his to take in hand. No longer here. And he started missing her all over again, imagining the way her big, nearsighted eyes would look up admiringly while he told her all about lumber sheds and shallow draft hulls and steam engines versus sail, versus the new gasoline-powered engines.

Without understanding half of what he was saying, Katy would have understood his dreams.

God, he couldn't believe how much he missed her.

It was dark by the time Katy and Tara left the shop to return to their room. They had gone in at seven that morning and worked steadily, with only a brief break at midday.

Katy had taken one look at the row of sewing machines and nearly cast up her accounts on the spot.

"You do sew, don't you?" Mrs. Baggot had asked.

"Sure and I've been sewing practically all my life," Katy had assured her, praying the woman wouldn't set her before one of those contraptions until she'd had time to watch a bit and see how it worked first.

"I'll start you on hand basting. It's easier to pick out when you make a mistake."

Katy had whipped out her spectacles and set them on her nose, vowing silently not to make a single mistake. She hadn't missed the way the woman had looked her over. It was up to her to prove her worth, and she set out to do it.

She'd spent the morning on buttonholes after first doing two samples, one bound, the other one stitched. Tara had been set to ironing flatwork—dress parts cut out and ready to be basted, fitted to one of a dozen dress forms, each with a discreet name attached, and then stitched by the three seamstresses bent over the noisy machines.

After hours of doing buttonholes, Katy had started on hems that had been measured and marked with chalk by Mrs. Baggot. She'd pinned them, pressed them, and stitched them with tiny, invisible stitches, a feat that would have been all but impossible without her spectacles.

Even with them, her eyes were tired at the end of the day. Before they could leave there were spools and trimmings to sort out and put away, bolts of cloth to roll up and stack on the shelf, the sweeping to do, and the trash to take out.

"I'm worried about Heather," Tara confided on the walk home. "What if Mrs. Riggins finds out about her?" As eager as they were to get home in time for supper, their steps dragged wearily.

"I'm more worried about Mrs. Baggot's finding that section of skirt you scorched. Count yourself lucky there was enough fabric left on the bolt for me to cut out another to take its place."

"I don't like her."

"Sure, and she doesn't much care for you, either. See that you keep your nose clean."

Tara promptly crossed her eyes in an effort to see her short, freckled nose, not that there was enough light to see much at this time of day. "Oscar says that, too. He says I'm more trouble than a peck of weasels, but he doesn't mean it, he only says it because Captain Galen makes him go with me to carry food, and he'd rather watch Charlie and Pierre. He wants to be a dealer, not a bartender."

"I hope we haven't missed supper tonight," Katy murmured as they turned the corner onto Martin Street. The house was an old one, not far from Mr. Allen's Cotton Gin. It was noisy and none too clean, and what's more, they'd been warned by the old man in the room next door that when it rained, the roof leaked like a sieve.

They had missed supper, but Mr. McGinty had saved them two chunks of cornbread and a bowl of clabber to spread on it. He'd kept Heather in his own room all day, feeding her bits of fish left over from breakfast. Katy hadn't been able to eat more than a bite or two of breakfast, she'd been that nervous about her first day at work.

"I miss Willy. I miss Ila and Oscar and the captain," Tara said while Katy brushed and laid out their second-best outfits for the next day.

Katy wasn't even going to think about who it was she missed. "Don't fret, love, you'll be starting school in a few weeks. Then you'll have lots of new friends."

Tara, her skinny legs doubled up before her on the bed, trailed a bit of string for the kitten to chase. "It won't be the same. They'll laugh at me because of the way I talk."

"Sure, and they'll do no such thing. They're used to strangers from all over, with all the boats from every port in the world."

"That's only on the waterfront. Ava says the people in town are snooty. She says the people who live in those big houses on the other side of the train station are the snootiest of all, and that—"

"Whisht now, child, haven't I warned you not to listen to gossip? You'll never hear a bit of good in it. Now, stop teasing the cat and try to get a bit of sleep. Tomorrow will be here before you know it."

Tara crawled under the thin spread, her bony shoulders heaving in a vast sigh. "I'm hungry."

"That you're not, for didn't you just put away a nice bit of bread and a bowl of clotted cream?"

"It's not clotted cream, it's soured milk. It's not the same thing at all."

"Don't whine. A lady never whines."

"I'm not a lady yet, I'm only a child."

Katy refrained from reminding her that she was, in her own words, practically thirteen.

"Besides, a lady never gets to have any fun."

Katy yawned, too tired to argue. Perhaps they didn't. Her mother had had little enough fun. Sometimes when she tried hard enough, Katy could almost remember hearing her mother laugh, but mostly she remembered her looking tired and worn and old before her time.

The rain came on gradually. At first it was only a whisper against the one small window. By the time it grew to a noisy drumming on the slate roof, drops were splatting on the floor with monotonous regularity.

Katy shoved the chamber pot under the drip. She glanced up at the stained ceiling, counted the blotches, and tried to think of what else she could use to catch the leaks. Heather thought it was all a game. She twitched her ears and pounced as the next drop fell on the mattress.

"Tara, you'll have to get up and help me move the bed out of the way."

Tara whined, but slid out from under the spread and

flopped her weight against the painted iron frame. They managed to shift the bed to a place where the ceiling seemed less stained. Katy was used to leaking roofs, for she'd spent the better part of her life dodging drips and listening to Da explain that he'd see to replacing the thatch once the fishing season was over.

The trouble was, the season never ended, it only changed from May mackerel, which were caught in March, to scad, to pollock, to lobsters, and never enough of any.

A wet floor was nothing new, but she drew the line at sleeping in a wet bed.

"I forgot to change Heather's dirt box," Tara said once she'd crawled back under the sheet.

"Then you'll just have to do it before we go to work tomorrow."

"Could we go visit the captain tomorrow? He misses us."

Her glasses sliding down her nose, Katy gave her a sharp look. "We'll not be after bothering the captain again."

"But, Katy, he really, really misses us."

"Tara O'Sullivan," Katy said warningly.

"But he does, Katy. He was thinking just tonight that he wished we were back on the *Queen*. He'd be that glad to see us, I know he would. You could wear your lace collar and we could—"

"Go to sleep, Tara."

Gusting a sigh, the child rolled over, the kitten tucked up under her chin. Rain plunked steadily into the chamber pot. It splatted in the washbasin and plopped on the painted floorboards. Lying awake, Katy thought about how each drop of rain struck a different note. The night noises in town were different from those aboard the *Queen,* and those had been far different from home.

It came over her then, that deep sense of loneliness. By all rights she should be dancing with joy. Today she'd taken the first step toward realizing her dream. Every day would be a day closer to the time when she would be independent.

Had Galen truly been thinking of them?

Perhaps Tara had been mistaken. He'd probably been thinking of how good it was to have them settled and off his hands. Between the things the child saw in her mind—and as often as not misread—and the things Katy desperately wanted to believe, there was no way of sifting out the truth.

Katy believed what her eyes and her common sense told her.

Tara believed what she thought she saw and wanted to be true.

They were a fine pair, they were, but at least they were here. They'd come this far. There was no reason why, with a bit of hard work, they couldn't go farther still.

Mr. McGinty rapped on the door just as the sky was beginning to grow light. The old man, a retired ship's carpenter whose joints were so knotted with age he could scarcely get about, had offered to wake them, claiming he never slept but in brief snatches.

"Thank you, and a fine good morning to you, sir," Katy called softly through the door. Aside from the storage rooms, there were only two other rooms on the third floor, both cheap because of the stifling heat in the summer, the cold drafts in the winter, and the leaks whenever it rained.

Breakfast was a rushed affair. Tara hated to wake up mornings almost as much as she hated going to sleep at night. She wasted so much time in getting dressed that there was scarcely time to change the dirt in Heather's box before leaving for work.

Katy tucked two biscuits in her pocket for a noonday break. Mrs. Baggot allowed them twenty minutes off in the middle of the day, and kept a kettle on for tea, which they were welcome to share. Even so, by the time the day's work was done, Katy felt as if she could fall into bed, shoes, bonnet, and all, and sleep for a week.

"Could we just walk down to the waterfront on the way home today?" Tara had hit her stride. Full of energy in spite of having cleaned floors, waxed display cases, and polished glass all day, she was ready to play.

"It's not on the way, and well you know it."

"Yes, but it's not all that far. I promised Oscar I'd visit."

"What about your supper?"

"Willy would give us something. He promised he'll go on saving me whatever he can for my friends."

"What do you suppose your friends did before you came along with your baskets?"

"Stole. Drowned kittens. Picked pockets. Whored."

"Tara Eleanor O'Sullivan!"

"Well, they did. What else could they do, for they've no homes to go to. Nobody to look after them. Sam and Mickey—those were the boys who were chasing Heather—their ma's a whore. She got sick and died last winter, and Sam said—"

"Tara, I've told you before, I'll not listen to gossip. Now, come along, it's getting dark, and if we've missed supper again, you'll just have to go to bed hungry."

"What about you?"

"I'm too tired to eat."

"We could see if Willy—"

Tara sighed. Katy wondered how long dreams could survive aching feet, an aching back, and a hollow belly.

Last night's rain had left puddles on the road, and where there weren't standing puddles, there was mud. Even from here, she thought she could smell the river, the rich scent mingling with the smell of raw cotton, garbage, and the heady fragrance of a flowering vine that grew on a nearby ditch bank.

"Good evening, ladies."

They were halfway up the front steps of Mrs. Riggins's boardinghouse when the dark figure rose from the front porch swing.

Tara flung herself at him, her skinny arms wrapping around his lean waist. "Captain Galen! I knew you were wanting to see us, didn't I say so, Katy?"

Katy remembered to close her mouth . . . just barely. Torn between embarrassment at Tara's uninhibited greeting and a surge of unfamiliar vanity, she wished she'd taken the time to tidy her hair and brush the lint off her dress before she'd left the shop.

She started to put on her glasses, the better to see him, but thought better of it and shoved them back into her shabby purse.

"I wasn't—that is, it's nice to see you again. I trust you've been keeping well."

"I trust I have," Galen replied, sounding angry and amused all at once, which was impossible, as anyone with a grain of sense would know.

"What are you doing here?" She was no better than Tara when it came to schooling her wretched tongue.

"As to that, you left in such a hurry, I hardly had time to say good-bye."

He had said good-bye. They both had, if not in so many words. Katy remembered now as if it were happening all over again. What's more, she thought he was remembering, too.

"As a matter of fact, I just checked by to be sure you were well situated. Why the devil didn't you tell me the woman had moved you into the attic, Katy?"

"We weren't moved anywhere. That is, we're still in the room we were shown."

"The devil you are. I was told you'd be in one of the rooms on the second floor, and I come back to find you stuck up there in the attic with a lecherous old sot—"

He was angry with her. Katy didn't know what he was going on about, but somehow, it was all her fault. She lifted her head and went to pass by him. "Come along, Tara, our supper is waiting."

For someone who'd claimed to be starving only minutes before, Tara showed no interest at all in food. "In a minute, but first I want to tell Captain Galen about the sewing machines. You wouldn't believe how much noise they make. And the women have to raise their voices to talk over them, and they look down their noses—" she broke off and stuck her own nose in the air. "Like this. And they make fun of the way I talk, but I don't care, because I don't like them anyway."

"Tara, I'm going in now. If you're wanting supper, you'd better hurry."

"In a minute, but first I need to tell Captain Galen about how it rained last night, and we had to move the bed and put the chamber pot in the middle of the floor, and I nearly fell over it this morning when I got out of bed."

Katy rolled her eyes, wishing the child had never learned how to talk. Or at least, learned when not to. "The captain isn't interested, Tara. Now, will you please come inside? Heather needs taking out for a walk."

Galen looked from one to the other. "I've paid off the week's rent. The maid packed your things—those damned books are a nuisance, you know that? Anyway, your cat's in the basket and I've cleared a storage room where you can stay until I make other arrangements."

It was the last straw in the haystack. Grimly, Katy said, "You shouldn't have bothered. We're perfectly well satisfied here."

"Are you, now? Even though your neighbor next door is a nasty old man with a habit of peeping through keyholes. I hope you didn't afford him any entertainment while you were here."

"Mr. *McGinty*? Why would you say such a wicked thing?"

"Because it's true."

By then Tara had found Heather's basket, stacked along with the rest of their things on the front porch behind the railing. "Did you know about the woman who lives next door? She knows he watches her with his spyglass when she takes her bath, but she doesn't care."

It was too much. It was all simply too much. Katy could only stand there with her mouth gaping open until Galen stepped forward and tipped it shut.

His voice was gruffer than usual when he said, "Come along now, I've sent for the buggy to haul your trunk back to the *Queen*. Tara, you take the cat and I'll take the valise. That'll do for tonight."

And such was her state of mind that Katy followed him down the front walk and allowed him to take her arm and lead her back home to the waterfront.

Chapter Eleven

Tara was still snoring softly beside her, the kitten curled on her chest, when Katy opened her eyes. It took only a moment to establish her surroundings, to remember how she happened to be there. They were back in the storage locker.

Why on earth had she allowed herself to be swept up like a ball of house moss? She'd had herself a job and a place to stay, and if the roof leaked a bit, it wouldn't be the first time they'd shared a leaky roof. Now she would have to start all over again and find another room.

As for her job—

"Merciful saints preserve us, I'm doomed." With a stricken look at the sunlight dancing on the far wall she rolled out of bed and started dragging on her clothes.

By the time she dashed into the galley, Willy and the two kitchen boys were having their own breakfast. Tara had gone back to sleep, and in despair, Katy had left her there. Galen wanted them?

He could have them. At least he could have Tara until she could make other arrangements.

"If there are any biscuits left, could I please take two with me? I'm terribly late."

"Set ye down, missy, I'll pour ye a cup o' coffee for dippin'."

Breathless, Katy explained that she didn't have time for coffee, that it was a good twenty-minute walk to the shop, and that it was terribly, terribly important that she not be late, and merciful saints, she already was.

"Miss Katy, can Tara stay here?" The request came from one of the kitchen boys, who was attacking a plateful of buttered grist, or grits, or whatever the tasteless stuff was called. "Please, ma'am, can she? She promised to teach me how to read tea leaves."

Katy prayed for patience. "Don't you believe a word of it, it's pure frummery. Willy, please tell her she mustn't fritter away the day with such nonsense. She knows very well we must work for our keep."

"Don't you fret none, missy, I'll keep an eye on the young'un. Go along now, else you'll be late." The grizzled cook handed her a walking bundle done up in a napkin. More than biscuits, from the feel of it.

She sniffed it and smiled. "Bacon? Bless you, sir, I'm that grateful." Holding her bundle in one hand, purse in the other, she dashed out to the stairs, wondering what time it was, not daring to take the time to find out.

Not until she reached the top step did she look up, and then she nearly fell back in surprise. Galen grabbed her by the shoulders. "Slow down, where's the fire?"

"G'morning to you, I've no time to talk now." She gasped, trying to dodge past him. She stepped to the right just as he moved left. She slammed into him again, boot to boot, nose to chest.

Impatiently, she shifted again. So did he. "If it's a game you're playing," she exclaimed, "then I'd as soon you found yourself another playmate, for I've no time to spare." She went to grab his arm to hold him in place until she could pass, but he only laughed and patted her hand.

She nearly swung her bundle at him. "Do you *mind*? I've better things to do than dance a jig all day."

Already there were sounds outside of a new day getting

under way. Cheerful curses from a freighter being unloaded down at the railroad wharf. Sound carried on the water. The crisp clip-clop of the delivery wagon from Crystal Ice Company, momentarily drowned out by the melancholy wail of a departing train. The creak and groan of hoists and rigging. The whine of a lumber mill saw starting up.

One by one, the regular residents of the waterfront began emerging to take their place in the sun. To warm aching old bones, to cadge a penny for a cup of coffee and a biscuit.

"Did you sleep well?" Galen said softly, his eyes twinkling like sunlight on stormy waters.

"Yes, and I'll have a word with you about that if you please, but not now. If I'm late, Mrs. Baggot will turn me off. She's not at all pleased with me, as it is."

She managed to get past him and dashed outside, skidding on the dew-wet deck before she reached the carpeted gangplank. He was right behind her. Without even looking around, she could feel his presence. She waved a quick greeting to the old man who had come to her rescue the other day. He called out something she didn't quite catch, but she smiled and pretended she had.

"You're never thinking to walk with me all the way uptown."

"I'm not?"

She snorted, lengthened her stride. They crossed the wharf, and then stepped across the tracks. Galen took her arm and forgot to release it when they turned off onto Pennsylvania Avenue. They didn't talk. She was too anxious, too irritated. Even more irritated because she wanted him there, and knew she shouldn't.

Walking quickly, they passed Broad Street and then Walnut. Picking up her pace, she counted off Cypress and Pleasant and then Pearl. The houses, set back from the street, gleamed like jewels in the fresh morning light, but she didn't dare take the time to admire them.

I'm going to be late, I'm going to be late.

Her small feet in the too-large shoes flashed in rhythm to the mantra. She kept waiting for Galen to turn back. She wished he would, for he was far too distracting, all freshly shaved and smelling of coffee and bay rum, dressed up like a racetrack dandy at this hour of the morning.

Bay rum, indeed. The man had never done a lick of hard work in his life.

"Katy, about last night. I might have been a bit high-handed, but—"

"That you were," she snapped back. "If I'd had my wits about me, I'd never have let you talk me into leaving, that I wouldn't."

"That you wouldn't," he agreed solemnly. It was the hint of laughter that was her undoing. How could a body stay angry with such a man? For all he was a complete rascal, he was a lovely man.

"Why was Mrs. Baggot angry with you?"

"Did I say she was angry?"

"You implied as much. Did it have anything to do with Tara?"

"Not a bit of it. I made her promise before we ever set foot over the threshold that there'd be no swaying, no seeing, no dire predictions."

"Swaying, seeing, and . . . dire predictions?"

"Tara, not Mrs. Baggot. And they're not always dire," Katy admitted. "It was the gold and the green tablecloths that brought us here, after all. It might have been misleading, but to be sure, there was nothing dire about it."

"The gold and green what?" In the middle of Matthews Street, he stepped in front of her. It was either halt or plow into him. Katy halted. A motor car chugged past on the left, another ice wagon on the right. Caught up momentarily in the spell of blue eyes and bay rum and a mouth that was ever so slightly tilted to the left, she hardly even noticed the traffic.

"Green and gold—?" she repeated dazedly. "Oh. You mean the tablecloths. Well, there's your green—your gambling tables. As for the gold, I suppose it's the money that changes hands, though it's more silver and paper than gold, which is still better than copper."

Slowly, he shook his head. "Katy, Katy. I'm beginning to wonder which one of us is halfway round the bend."

Katy didn't know which bend he was talking about, but she did know she was late and getting later by the moment. "There, now, you've done your duty, you can go back now."

Duty was the last thing on Galen's mind. With all he had to do today, he had no time to waste playing games, but she was irresistible, damned if she wasn't. He'd always liked puzzles. Crossword. Jigsaw. Chinese.

Katy was a puzzle, all right. All pluck and backbone, dressed like a refugee from the missionary barrel, thinking she was going to set herself up in the fashion business.

She just might do it, too. Might surprise them all. He was coming to believe there was more to Miss Katy O'Sullivan than met the eye, and what met the eye was impressive enough.

"Go back, Galen. Truly, I appreciate what you're doing, trying to make me feel safe and all, but I don't need you."

Safety hadn't even entered his mind. This was downtown Elizabeth City on a weekday morning, not Saturday night on the waterfront with its sundry assortment of drunks, thieves, and gamblers. "Are you sure?"

He wanted her to need him. Which meant he'd lost his wits. Brain fever. It had to be that, there was no other explanation. "As it happens, I'm going this way."

It was no lie. He'd been on his way to a breakfast meeting with a couple of businessmen, but then he'd seen Katy barreling up the stairs as if her skirttail were on fire, and the meeting had gone clean out of his mind.

"You are? Well, that's just lovely, then." She tucked her

hand inside his arm and they set out again, with her purse swatting him in the thigh with every step, the scent of bacon wafting up from the bundle in her other hand.

And then the courthouse clock struck the half hour, and she gasped. "Oh, saints preserve us, I'm late!" Before he could stop her, she grabbed her hat and was off and running down the street.

Galen stared after her, slowly shaking his head. What a mess she was. Of all the women in the world, why did it have to to be this one? Why, he mused, watching her flying down the sidewalk in her shabby dress and Ermaline's too-big shoes, did he find everything about her so completely fascinating?

Before letting herself out the back door that evening—the staff was not allowed to use the front door—Katy sought out Mrs. Baggot to be sure there was nothing more that needed doing before she left.

"Come in half an hour early tomorrow to make up for today. I'll not dock your pay this time, but see that it doesn't happen again."

Thus the day ended as it had begun when she'd walked in thirty-two minutes late that morning. Mrs. Baggot, arms crossed over her black silk bosom, had looked her over from head to foot, making her miserably conscious of every single flaw in her appearance, right down to the patches on her stockings.

"Where's the girl? I don't tolerate tardiness."

"Tara? As you're not paying her, I thought you'd be pleased not to have her underfoot."

"I said I wouldn't pay her in coin, but out of the kindness of my heart, I'd allow her to stay, seeing as you're both new to town and you've nowhere else to leave her. No law says she can't make herself useful, is there? And don't think I didn't see that skirt she ruined yesterday, either, missy. I go through every speck of trash before it's carted off to be sure nothing gets thrown out that shouldn't be thrown out. You'd be surprised what some folks will try to sneak past me."

Katy fought her temper to a standstill, something she'd been forced to do all her life. "Yes, ma'am. I'm sorry about that. Tara's never used an electric iron before."

After that, it had been one small thing after another. Most of it she'd been able to ignore. Despite the fact that there was little traffic, as most of her best customers were still at the seashore, Mrs. Baggot found more than enough to keep her entire workforce busy all day. The seamstresses stitched "ready-mades," their gleaming black machines clattering noisily, but not noisily enough to drown out the clatter of their tongues.

Katy had been forced to listen to speculations as to who she was, where she'd come from, what she had to do with Captain McKnight, and whether the little girl she'd brought with her yesterday was actually her sister, as she'd claimed, or her illegitimate daughter, in which case, who could the father be?

Has to be that gambling cap'n off'n the boat. Show me a man who wears high-heeled boots and a rosebud in his lapel who ain't a devil with women.

A man who wears only boots and a rosebud? Saints preserve us.

Lips pinched from a lifetime of holding pins and dipping snuff, the speaker cast a glance at Katy to be sure she'd overheard. She'd heard, all right, just as she was meant to hear. Not that she understood half of what she heard, but only a fool could fail to recognize the malice behind the words.

What had she ever done to these women to make them want to hurt her feelings?

Off and on throughout the day, as she basted seams and pinned and pressed hems, Katy allowed her imagination full play. For years that imagination was all that had kept her from losing heart. Cutting turf for peat, sorting fish, her hands chapped and raw from stickers, she would go off somewhere in her mind, and there they'd all be, strolling the streets of some fine city, window shopping, stopping for tea, going to concerts all dressed up in fine clothes, with everyone wondering who the handsome couple with the two lovely daughters might be.

Over the years that image had slowly faded. Now, in its place, came the image of a Galen McKnight dressed only in boots and a rosebud. It was wicked of her, she knew, but then, where was the harm?

And imagining Galen in the altogether was a temptation she didn't even try to resist. Parts of his body were a bit unclear, for her imagination would stretch only so far. Even so, it was enough to bring a flush to her cheeks, which she tried to pretend was due to the heat of the iron she was using.

Across the room, one of the machines grew still as a bobbin was changed. "Skinny as a rail," Katy heard one of the woman mutter. "And them clothes of hers, did you ever see the like? Wouldn't think a man'd like to bed a bundle o' bones."

"Them glasses don't help none, either. Reckon she wears 'em to bed?"

"Law, don't reck'n she'd need to, not if she's sleepin' with that gambling man. He'll show her where everything's at and where to put it, if I know men."

"How many men've you ever known, Sudie Ann?" All three women cackled.

"More'n you have," the one called Sudie Ann said over the sound of treadles picking up speed.

"But not as many as *she* has, from the looks of her."

From the ironing board on the other side of the work-room, Katy heard every word, as she was plainly intended to do. In spite of telling herself she didn't care, that these women meant nothing to her, it hurt.

She told herself they were only jealous, but didn't believe it. What reason would anyone have to be jealous of her? She was practically penniless, over her head in debt, with a child depending on her, her only security what she could earn with her own two hands.

Closing the back door behind her that evening, Katy made a silent vow. She would do what she was told, hold her tongue, collect her pay and work harder than ever. To fix her dream more firmly in her mind, because there were times when it was in danger of slipping away, she walked around to the front and stared at the display in Mrs. Baggot's show window.

Navy blue. She would do her first window in navy blue, with white gloves and a tiny chip straw in matching blue. Quiet good taste, that would be her hallmark. The wrong Mr. McKnight's wife had worn a navy silk gown. Even now, as tired and frightened and confused as she'd been at the time, Katy could remember every detail—the way the skirt had fit around the hips, then flared off behind into soft folds. The sleeves full at the shoulder, fitted on the arms, with covered buttons and . . .

"Katy? Are you ready to go home?"

Spinning around, she let out a yelp and clapped a hand to her bosom.

"Sorry. I didn't mean to startle you."

"You never do, do you?"

"It's hardly my fault you're so spooky."

"I'm not spooky, as you call it, what I am is . . ." She was going to say startled, but instead, her shoulders sagged. It was all she could do not to admit to being tired and discouraged and worried about the future.

"Come along, my dear, ride home with me."

"Never say your meeting is just now finished."

He never said, and so she let him lead her to the buggy he kept in a livery stable, let him help her up onto the high seat, all without speaking a word. He twitched the reins, and the neat little mare set off at a walk, her hooves punctuating the still evening air.

The remnants of a gold-and-purple sunset cast its splendor over the town, lending a momentary dignity to the drabbest warehouse. The plaintive wail of a locomotive broke the stillness. Already she was getting so used to the sound she hardly even heard it.

"Thank you," she said belatedly.

"You're welcome."

Feeling his gaze, she tried to sit up straighter. She'd been given more to do today than yesterday, and yesterday had been bad enough. If tomorrow was worse, she might not be able to keep up.

"Have you had anything to eat?"

"Biscuits and bacon. Willy gave me a bundle this morning."

Without another word he turned the buggy around and headed back toward Main Street. Katy wondered if he had suddenly remembered an errand. She did wish he hadn't mentioned food. Now she was starved. All in the world she wanted to do was fall into bed and sleep for a solid week, but first she had to make sure Tara was all right, and then she had to eat, and then she really should see about finding another room. She hated staying where she wasn't welcome.

A few minutes later Galen pulled up before an impressive brick building, tossed the reins to a curb boy, and handed her down to the sidewalk. "When's the last time you enjoyed a thick steak?"

He waited expectantly. If all she'd had was a couple of biscuits, it was no wonder she was looking so limp. He had a feeling Inez Baggot milked every penny's worth from her employees. Ila had worked for her briefly, before she'd left and gone to work for Aster.

"Katy? They serve the finest beef this side of Chicago here. I make it a habit to dine here at least once a week."

His smile slowly faded. He'd expected a bit of gratitude,

at the very least. Was that too much to ask? Simple gratitude? It wasn't as if he had nothing better to do. Even
before he'd left, the crowd promised to be a good one.
There'd been trouble last night but no one had gotten hurt.

Dammit, he didn't have time for this.

"Dinner, that's all I'm suggesting, Katy. Nothing more
than a steak and maybe a bit of dessert. You'd like that,
wouldn't you?"

It was a hotel, but it wasn't *that* kind of a hotel. Surely
she didn't think—

He watched her square her shoulders, stiffen her back,
and lift her chin. He was coming to recognize the signs.
"You want me to hold your high horse while you climb
aboard?"

He was reduced to sarcasm, a weapon he usually reserved
for a more worthy opponent. "Katy, I'm sorry. You're tired.
I'll take you home, all right?"

Katy could have whacked him. She could have wept if
she'd had the strength, not that it would've done a speck of
good. "It's kind of you, to be sure, and you go right ahead
and enjoy your bit of beefsteak. I can walk, I meant to all
along."

"That was before I drove you several blocks out of your
way."

Katy knew she should insist—it was never wise to depend on anyone else—but she was simply too tired. She let
herself be helped back up onto the black leather seat, re-
sisted the temptation to close her eyes, and wished everything weren't so complicated. Back home in Skerrie Head,
life was simple.

Galen reached over and covered her hands with one of
his own. She wanted to turn her hand and curl her fingers
with his, but she didn't dare allow herself even that small
comfort. Comfort was too beguiling. A body could come to
depend on it all and then, when it was snatched away, what
was left?

She had only herself to depend on. Da had said, depend on him, tomorrow's catch would be better and then he'd repair the roof and buy her a new frock. Only it never was, and he never did, and then he'd died.

"Katy? Why so glum? If you don't like your job, we'll find you something else. No law says you have to work there if you'd rather do something else."

"Don't be too kind to me, Galen, for I've trouble enough sorting things out, as it is. It's a different kind of work. It takes some getting used to, that's all, but I'll manage."

"I'm sure you will, my dear."

And don't call me your dear, she wanted to say, but had better sense. Calling her that might mean that he cared for her, and she couldn't allow herself to believe such a thing.

Because you want to believe it so very much.

"Katy, Katy, you'll never guess what!" Tara came racing down the gangplank to meet her. "There was a fight, and a man got hurt really bad, but he wasn't one of our friends, and—"

"I'd like a word with you, Miss O'Sullivan, if you please," said Aster.

Katy watched the woman march down the gangplank, and her heart sank. "Of course. If it's about our being here," she said calmly, unconsciously mimicking the way her mother used to speak when she'd had about all a body could take, "then let me assure you that Tara and I won't be burdening you with our company much longer."

"Now, Katy," began Galen.

Aster whirled on him, lips clamped together in a way that made her look years older. "You keep out of this! If it weren't for you, none of it would have happened!" Turning back, she jabbed a finger toward Katy's modest bosom. "I want the pair of you off my boat this minute!"

"That will be quite enough, Aster." Galen didn't raise his voice. He didn't have to. He held out his arm. Katy placed her hand in the crook of his elbow, compelled by an authority she didn't even try to understand.

Tara fell in behind them, leaving Aster standing at the foot of the gangplank, gaping like a stranded cod, much to the amusement of the ragtag collection of waterfront regulars.

A few hundred yards away, on the balcony of the *Albemarle Belle,* Jack Bellfort looked on with great interest.

Chapter Twelve

Katy didn't want to hear about it. All she wanted to do was take Tara and walk away. And keep on walking until she found a place with no people and no squabbles and no one scolding her and telling her things she didn't want to hear.

Not surprisingly, she wasn't about to get her wish. Aster was going on and on, Galen was over by the stairway talking in an undertone to Pierre, and Tara was hanging on to her arm, jabbering at her, her eyes round with excitement. "There was a policeman and he said a lot of bad things, and threatened to shut us down, and—"

"Shut who down?"

"Us. The *Queen*. He said we were a—Katy, what's a nikkedy?"

"A . . . what?"

"He said we were a den of nikkedy, and if there was any more skulduggery, he was going to padlock the whole damned shooting match. I didn't hear any shooting, but—"

"Would someone please get that child out of my sight?" Aster screeched. "She probably started the whole thing!"

"Katy, I didn't."

Katy saw her face turn red, her eyes grow damp, and her chin begin to wobble. She stepped between Tara and

Aster, as if her presence alone could block out the hateful words.

"Never mind, love, things are different in America," she said softly, wondering where she could go to get away before anything else happened.

"But, Katy, I didn't do anything wrong," Tara wailed. "Won't you tell her that?"

"I know, I know, sweetheart, it's all right." What she knew was that Aster wouldn't listen to her any more than she listened to anyone else. Except perhaps Galen. She was still railing, something about abusing her good nature and what she refused to put up with.

Galen took her arms and tried to steer her inside. "Lower your voice, Aster, you've an audience."

"I don't care if the whole damned town hears me, I want them off—my—property!"

"Whose property?"

"Don't give me that forty-nine, fifty-one percent argument, I want them *gone*! There, is that plain enough for you?"

It was more than enough for Katy. She had no idea what had started the trouble, nor what had actually happened. She did know that with Tara involved, nothing was ever quite as simple as it appeared. With the best intentions in the world, the child attracted trouble, even back home where everyone knew her and made allowances.

The crowd refused to disperse. Galen swore briefly and caught Katy's eye. Upstairs, he mouthed, and she nodded. She didn't want to go with him, but she could hardly stay there on the deck.

Aster shoved past them and stormed up the stairs, elbows pumping. From a few steps below, Katy glared at the elaborate pompadour that bounced with every step.

"I don't think she's pretty at all," muttered Tara. Katy turned to shush her and surprised a smug expression on her face.

Where were the tears that had been threatening to fall only moments before? "What are you up to?" she demanded in a fierce undertone.

"Why would you be thinking I'm up to something?"

"Because I know you, Tara O'Sullivan. And I'm warning you, I'm at my wit's end. Unless Mrs. Riggins will have us back, we'll be sharing a bench with the likes of all your fine friends." She tried to sound stern, but her heart wasn't in it.

"I don't care. And Mr. McGinty is nice, even if he does like to watch his lady friend through the window. Katy, why do you suppose he lets her lead him around that way?"

"Mr. McGinty and his lady?"

"No, silly—Aster and the captain. If he had a wife, she wouldn't dare take on so. I was thinking, you could—"

"No more thinking. You've thought us into enough hot water, as it is."

By then they'd reached the top deck. Galen ushered them inside. "You two wait in here," he said to Katy. Turning to Aster, he said, "Out on the balcony, if you please."

With a last malevolent glare, Aster stepped outside. Galen followed, shutting the glass-topped door firmly behind them.

If it was privacy they were after, Katy thought, they'd be better off down in the boiler room. Even from here she could catch snatches of music from the *Albemarle Belle*.

Outside on the balcony, Aster immediately began to pace. Katy watched through the door as she passed back and forth, her jaw never ceasing to move.

"—can tell that wretched cook of yours to pack his things and get off my boat, and don't think I won't have his bags searched before he goes, either! Wicked old—"

Katy, with Tara's hot hand clutching her fingers so hard they were numb, waited to hear Galen's defense.

Unfortunately, his voice was nowhere near as carrying as Aster's. He murmured something, and she came back with, "Believe me, the next time I hire a chef, it won't be a toothless old fool who lets himself be talked into robbing me blind. And those two *females* you took in won't be around to cause trouble, either!"

"Aye, madam, that we won't," Katy vowed softly.

Tara shot her a worried look, but then, Galen was speaking, and they both strained to hear.

To no avail. Aster had launched again. The woman could drown out a tree full of crows. "I warned you, they're nothing but trouble! That little tramp is making a complete fool of you, and all you can do is follow her around with your tongue hanging out! Honestly—men. Between you and Papa, you've not got the brains of a walnut."

"I've never seen the captain sticking his tongue out, have you, Katy?"

"Shhh."

"Well, have you?"

"Tara, please . . ."

"It wasn't about the food, Katy, honestly. There was a fight—I think it was a bad one, and one of the dealers came running out, and then everybody started yelling, and the policeman came and . . ."

She sighed and rested her head on Katy's shoulder. All was quiet out on the balcony. Katy thought Galen must be speaking. After a few moments, Tara whispered, "I didn't start it this time, Katy, truly I didn't."

Heartsick, Katy only patted her hand. Long before Aster marched off down the balcony to her own quarters, Katy had made up her mind. She had left home rather than accept charity from her neighbors. She would rather starve than beg from a stranger.

Galen came through the door, looking tired and defeated. She rose to meet him, determined to have her say before he could undermine her decision. "I'm truly sorry for all the trouble we've caused, Galen. We've been a burden to you. You've been nothing but kind, and for that we're grateful, but if you don't mind, we'll be on our way now."

His face was pale with strain. Nevertheless, he cocked an eyebrow. "Oh? And which way is that?"

Which way, indeed. She hadn't thought beyond the moment. "I'm certain Mrs. Baggot will allow us to sleep in the workroom until I can make other arrangements," she improvised. She was certain of no such thing, but she'd go to her grave before she'd admit it.

"Sit down, Kate."

"I don't believe—"

"Tara, sit down. Please."

Tara sat, and after a moment, Katy did, too. The odds were two to one against her.

Galen looked from one to the other, his gaze coming to rest on Tara. "All right, Tara, I've heard several views of what happened. Would you care to tell me your version?"

"Aster said it was the food, but I don't think that was it at all. The man who got hurt wasn't anyone I know. But if it was the food, I'm sorry."

Galen sighed. He looked as if he were searching for just the right words to explain something. "There was more to it than that," he said at last. "But, Tara, about your baskets— I'm sure you have only the kindest intentions, but it will have to stop. I run a business, not a charity mission."

"But Willy said—"

"Willy's a soft touch. I assure you, I'm not."

"But we only gave away what was left over after everyone had finished. Willy said he wouldn't trust a stew past the third day, not even in the icebox."

"Then he can cook less of it from now on. He's been cooking enough to feed an army."

"But he said you've never turned away anyone in need. Sure, and didn't you send Katy and me the money to come to Amerikey when we were cold and hungry and desperate?"

"*Ta*-ra!" Katy hissed. She glared at Galen. "That we were not, sir. We never once wanted for anything, I assure you."

"But, Katy, you said—"

Katy shot her a warning look, for all the good it would do. It wasn't that the child lacked pride, she simply lacked judgment. "You misunderstood," she said with all the dignity she could summon, while she silently added up the cost of a week's worth of meals for a dozen indigents and tacked it onto the huge sum she already owed the man.

At this rate she would go to her grave in debt.

"All the same, child," Galen reasoned, "you can't simply invite all your friends and all their friends to come for dinner whenever they take a notion. Willy was hired to cook for crew and staff. It's not that I begrudge the food, but having strangers wander on and off the boat complicates things for all of us."

"But they're not strangers, they're our neighbors."

"That's as may be, but, honey, there are places in town that look after the poor."

"B—but my friends don't like those places. They like Willy's cooking better. Besides, what harm can it do to give away food that would only go to waste?"

Galen turned to Katy for help. Katy turned to Tara. Something told her the child wasn't quite as guileless as she appeared. There was more to this matter than the food, and Tara knew more than she was telling, but getting to the bottom of it would take time and energy, and Katy had run out of both.

She did her best. "Tara, Miss Tyler doesn't like having a policeman aboard the boat. She says it's bad for business."

"But he didn't stay long, and besides, the *Queen* belongs to Captain Galen. If he says it's all right, then why can't they eat here?"

Katy sighed. Galen raked his fingers through his hair. Tara looked anxiously from one to the other and said, "They didn't mean to cause any trouble. When I never showed up yesterday with my basket, they came to see if I was ailing, and Willy told them I had me a job, and the table was all set for dinner, and—"

"And so naturally, they took it as an invitation," Galen put in dryly.

"But Willy was their mate. He wanted them to stay."

"I beg your pardon?"

"Sure, and he must have told you. Before he came to work here, Willy sailed on a coaster with Mr. Bynum. He knew Mr. Smith from jail, and—" Breaking off, she clapped a hand over her mouth. "Oh, I never meant to say that."

Katy closed her eyes and prayed for patience. "Tara, we had an agreement."

The child looked desolate. Suspiciously desolate. "But, Katy, I never saw it, I only heard it. You didn't say I couldn't talk about what I heard."

"I give up," Katy said with a sigh. To her horror, her belly chose that particular moment to give a great rumble that could be heard clearly, even above the music from the *Albemarle Belle* and the noise from the gaming rooms below.

"Have you eaten anything today?" Galen asked quietly.

"I haven't had supper yet," Tara said quickly.

Katy wasn't about to admit to having skipped breakfast and then gobbled down her biscuits and bacon before noon. Saints alive, it was hard enough to hang on to her pride without that.

Galen yanked the cord beside his desk. In less than a minute someone answered his summons. "Send up two plates of whatever's left in the kitchen, will you? Oh, and a pot of tea and a glass of—?" He looked from Katy to Tara and back again, lifting a questioning brow.

"Milk," said Katy, at the same time Tara stated her preference for coffee.

"But Willy always lets me have—"

Katy glared her into silence. She couldn't refuse outright if the child hadn't had her supper yet, but when the food came, she found she couldn't eat a bite. While Galen sat with his fingers steepled, staring morosely at a calendar on the wall, its curling surface covered with scribbled notes and numbers, she shoved greasy bits of meat and cabbage about on her plate and tried to sort it all out in her mind.

Aster was fit to be tied. Katy couldn't really blame her. She didn't know who to blame, but the moment Tara laid down her fork, Katy stood and said, "We've packing to do. Come along now."

"There's no rush, you're not going anywhere tonight."

Katy met his eyes bravely, but looked away almost immediately, afraid of what she would see there. Afraid of what she wouldn't see.

"That I am."

"Katy, be sensible. If you won't think of yourself, then think of Tara. You can't drag her through that mob without even knowing where you're going. For once in your life, think of someone besides yourself."

That hurt. She couldn't believe how much it hurt, but he was right. Lifting her chin, she said quietly, "If you don't mind then, we'll spend one more night here and leave first thing tomorrow. I thank you very kindly."

Galen nodded. He looked as if he wanted to hit something. Oddly enough, she wasn't frightened. She might not understand what was going on, but she did know he'd never intentionally do either of them any harm.

On their way to the door, Tara paused before Galen, her lower lip trembling. "Don't you dare cry," Katy muttered in a fierce undertone.

"I don't care what that policeman said, Mickey and Sam aren't crooks." Her eyes were brimming, but not quite overflowing. Katy had a sinking feeling the little imp was doing it deliberately.

"I know that, Tara," Galen said. Looking beyond her,

his gaze met Katy's. For one long moment, both of them forgot the child.

"The policeman pulled on their ears, that's why Mickey called him a lick-spittle bastard."

"Yes, well—" Galen cleared his throat. Katy looked away. "I'm sorry to have to burst your bubble, love, but people aren't always what they appear to be."

Katy closed her eyes and prayed for patience. Tara knew very well what she was saying. Even back in Skerrie Head, men were sometimes careless with their language. Trust a child to pick out exactly what words she shouldn't.

Stepping aside, Galen held the door open. "Go to bed now. We'll sort it all out tomorrow."

Katy made the mistake of looking up again as she passed. There it was again. The heat of his body. That crisp, clean scent of bay rum and tobacco, laced with a hint of something more personal, something more masculine.

It was a good thing they'd be leaving tomorrow. She was beginning to believe she wasn't quite as sensible as she'd thought.

Feeling an uncomfortable mixture of guilt, frustration, and tenderness, Galen watched them go. It wasn't that he was a selfish bastard—though he'd be the last to deny it. It wasn't even that he lacked judgment. He knew damned well he had no business feeling the way he was feeling, but at least he was man enough to admit it. It might not stop him from feeling the way he felt, but forewarned was forearmed.

The timing couldn't have been worse. If only they'd waited until he could get his old business handled and his new business up and running, he could've handled it.

At least, he wanted to believe it was only a matter of timing.

Sure it was. Because he had too much on his mind, he wasted time brooding about a woman—hardly more than a girl—lining up all the reasons why she needed a husband and then shooting them down again.

Because his timing was all off, it took two drinks instead of the one he normally allowed himself to help him sleep. And then he dreamed. Dreamed about a dark-haired, green-eyed beauty with a waist he could span with his hands, hips that filled his palms, and a pair of. . . .

He woke up, swearing. Another bad habit he'd fallen into lately. Even during his seagoing years, he'd been moderate in his habits. A modest amount of drinking, a modest amount of fighting, a modest amount of wenching. A moderate man, all in all.

One thing he'd never done—he'd never imagined himself in love with a woman nearly young enough to be his daughter.

Katy was eleven years younger. Margaret, the only other woman he'd ever considered himself in love with, had been several years older. One of these days, maybe he'd get it sorted out.

Reluctantly, he buttoned his coat, straightened his tie, and headed back downstairs to see what else had busted loose.

The night was still young. Unfortunately.

Things appeared to be quiet. Buck, the ex-convict he'd hired to collect bets, watch for skulduggery and generally keep the peace, gave him the thumbs-up sign.

Buck had been the first one Galen had thought of when the trouble had started. Random occurrences, at first—a big win, a few too many drinks. The area was well lighted around the boats, but there were dark places where trouble waited. The first few times it had happened, a man knocked over the head and robbed, he'd issued a warning and considered it sufficient.

But then it had happened again and again, always to men who had won big pots, never the penny ante winners.

A pattern had begun to appear.

In a matter of weeks, he'd be ready to put his share of the business up for sale. The last thing he needed was this kind of trouble.

Behind the gleaming mahogany bar, Oscar poured two drinks at once without spilling a drop. Glass eye and all, the boy was turning out to be quite an asset. The girls all liked him. So did the dealers. Brand had done him a favor by sending him south.

Charlie was back. Galen had given him a raise after he'd married Sal. With a baby on the way, the poor guy would be needing it.

Pierre was his usual debonair self. It took more than a waterfront brawl to ruffle his feathers. The new girl, Sal's replacement, was giving him the eye. Galen could have told her she was wasting her time. Pierre had a wife somewhere in Louisiana. When his family had banished him, she had chosen to stay behind, where the real money was.

He was better off without her, in Galen's opinion. Not that he'd ever offered that opinion. Like most men, Pierre preferred to keep his private life to himself.

Galen would have preferred to do the same thing. Unfortunately, his own private life was becoming increasingly and embarrassingly public.

Moving easily from one table to the next, from the large salon where Ava and the new girl were working to the smaller room where Ermaline was earning herself a few laughs and a tidy sum in tips, Galen told himself he would be glad to walk away from it all. Gambling had never been his chosen profession. The opportunity had come his way at a time when he was at loose ends, a time when he'd had a half-formed notion in his mind, and at a time when his bank account was at its lowest ebb.

He'd spent a little more than two years here, and didn't regret it. All told, there were very few experiences in his thirty-three years that he did regret.

Of those few, losing a brother topped the list. After that

came losing a ship and an entire crew. Declan O'Sullivan was somewhere in there, but Margaret, the one true love of his life, was little more than a dim memory, although there'd been a time when he could have sworn his life was ruined forever.

Evidently a man stopped feeling pain when a certain threshold had been reached.

Leaning against the bar nursing a shot glass of cold tea, he studied the new girl who had replaced Katy, who had replaced Sal.

She showed promise. She'd need to quit switching her hips and batting those painted eyelashes. According to Ila, the trick was to smile a lot, tease a bit if the occasion demanded, but to stand well back from the tables. Few men would risk tipping their hands for a sample of something that wasn't for sale.

Without seeming to, he studied the girl, whose name was Dolly—Polly—something like that. He'd forgotten already. She was pretty. Aster insisted on pretty girls, but not too pretty. He'd noticed that about her. For a competitive woman, she was careful to keep the odds in her balance when it came to other women.

Funny, he'd never thought about it before. Usually the first thing he did was size up the competition, search out his opponents' weaknesses, and figure the best way to use them.

Probably because she was a woman, he'd never applied the same rules to Aster.

Just as well. Things were complicated enough, as it was.

"Good house tonight," murmured one of the relief dealers, just coming on duty. "Looks like that little ruckus earlier settled things down some."

Galen nodded. "Keep an eye on the table by the door. Young Blakely's got a snootful."

"Sure will," the young man replied, and Galen watched him snake his way between tables and wondered if he was single.

Back to Katy again. He knew damned well what he was doing. It wasn't going to work. If he'd lined her up with a husband right off the bat, it might have worked out. Now it was too late. He might try to convince himself it was still an option, but Galen knew he would never let her go.

He didn't know what he was going to do with her—hell, the last thing he needed was a wife—but he knew she was his.

Long after Ila had slipped in with two mugs of hot cocoa and an offer to look after Tara and keep her out of Aster's sight until Katy could find them another place to stay, Katy lay awake, going over the past few hours in her mind.

She'd made a few colossal blunders in her life, but never one as big as this. Back home they'd had a roof of their own, a tiny plot of dirt where they could grow a few turnips, potatoes, and cabbages. She could have gone on the same way for years until Tara was grown and married. She might even have found someone for herself, eventually.

But oh, no, they'd had to come to America, land of opportunity. Land of lovely green tablecloths, where gold rained down from the sky. The trouble with dreams was that sooner or later, a body woke up.

Tara was up to something, Katy knew the signs.

She closed her eyes and tried to block out the sound of laughter down in the pump room below, the muffled rumble from the gaming rooms overhead, and the smell of mildew and paint in the stuffy little locker room.

After a while, she drifted into a dream. Familiar faces, familiar voices . . . but not familiar, after all. Deep blue eyes, smiling eyes, a cap of curly hair the color of tarnished brass, with a streak of white running through it . . . and a pair of short, curved horns.

Someone was laughing. She was shouting, but no one would listen, they just kept laughing and laughing. Lips moving in her sleep, she tossed and muttered until Tara roused and punched her in the back.

"Go to sleep, Katy, it's nearly morning."

So she slept again, and this time she dreamed of a monstrous deep tunnel. She'd fallen and was sliding down a rough rocky surface, going faster and faster while someone who looked like Galen McKnight stood by, laughing, until darkness swallowed her up.

Tara was sluggish as always the next morning. Katy was at her wit's end when Ila tapped softly on the door with a tray of coffee and a basket of mending.

"Oh, heavens, I've overslept again. Tara, wake up, we'll have to hurry."

"You go along, honey, and leave your sister to me. Miss Aster's gone shopping for new curtains. She'll not be home for hours."

With a harried smile and a sense of guilt, Katy rushed through her dressing, sipping Willy's strong, scalding brew between buttoning herself into her gray muslin and lacing up her shoes. A few minutes later, she dashed down the gangplank just as the courthouse clock struck the hour.

"Merciful saints, she'll murder me."

"Just in time, I see," someone called out.

With one hand on her purse, the other holding on to her hat, she glanced up to see Captain Bellfort in a shiny black motor car. "If you're daring enough, I'll drive you into town," he offered.

Daring was the last thing she felt, but she desperately needed whatever it took to keep her from being late again.

Katy had never set foot in a motor car before, hadn't even seen more than a few of the noisy contraptions, but such was her distracted state of mind that she climbed in without a thought to her bodily safety.

"Captain Bellfort—"

"Jack."

She took a deep breath and started again. "Jack, then, and thank you for the privilege. Jack, would you happen to know of a cheap, respectable boardinghouse where I might find a room for Tara and me?"

"Leaving the *Queen*'s hospitality so soon? Now, why am I not surprised? Could it be that McKnight's famous charm is finally begining to wear thin?"

Oh, for heaven's sake, Galen McKnight's charm had nothing to do with the matter. She barely managed to keep from saying so. She hadn't so many friends she could afford to squander a single one.

Before she could frame a reply, however, the captain came back with a proposition that knocked the wind clean out of her sails.

Chapter Thirteen

"Sure you won't change your mind and come and work for me, Katy?" She stared at him wordlessly. Laughter lurked in those dark eyes of his, as if he didn't seriously expect her to take him up on the offer. "And how much would you be offering me if I said I would?" she probed cautiously.

"How much are you worth?"

Katy hadn't the slightest idea of how much a real singer was worth, not that she would even consider doing such a thing. She sang the way everyone in Skerrie Head sang. For the joy of it. Because there were songs to be sung.

He watched her expectantly. "Two dollars a night," she replied. There. That should put an end to his teasing.

"Shall we say eight?"

Her jaw dropped. "Eight . . . what?"

Eight songs, she thought. Two dollars for the mere singing of eight songs. "The Cobbler" and "Barbara Allen." "Maggie Pickens" and "The Month of January," and—

It would be thievery, pure and simple. She knew hundreds of songs, and sang them every one for the pleasure of it.

"Eight dollars a performance. I provide the costumes, accompaniment, plus room and board. In exchange you'll do two sessions a night, possibly more on cruise nights."

Even if she could have made her tongue work properly, Katy couldn't have found the wind to reply. "Eight dollars a *night*? And room and board for us both?" she managed finally.

The captain touched his collar. His eyes went all lazy, and Katy told herself it wasn't disappointment she was feeling. She'd known all along he was only teasing her.

But then he began to chuckle. "Ah, you mean your sister. Yes, of course. A room and meals for the both of you, plus a starting salary of eight dollars a night."

"But it's far too much."

"We'll see, Katy, my love. We'll see. I have a feeling we're going to get along just fine, but first, here we are. I suppose you'd better go in and tell Inez you won't be her slave any longer."

She thought about it. Eight dollars a night, plus room and board for two. All morning she ironed and swept up scraps around the cutting table, put away spools and bolts and cards of trim. And she hummed under her breath.

You're a fool, Katy O'Sullivan. A fair lilter you may be back home where you're among folks who've known you since you were cradle-bound, but it's a fool you are in America.

Nevertheless, she hummed while she worked. While the three seamstresses clattered away on their machines, raising their voices to pass back and forth snippets of gossip, Katy sang snatches of "Amhram Dochais" and "Sean Dun Na Ngall." She hummed "Lark in the Morning" and "Rocking the Cradle," songs she'd known all her life.

Eight dollars a night.

Why that was almost as much as she'd been promised for a week of working from seven in the morning until six in the evening for Mrs. Baggot.

Steam drifted up from the heavy electric iron, causing

her hair to curl around her face, bring a flush to her cheeks and a film of sweat everywhere else.

Twelve dollars a week added to eight dollars a night—

Mercy. At that rate she'd be out of debt in no time. She'd be able to pay off her debts and set aside enough to rent her a shop. Nothing fancy. Two rooms was all she would need. With a window. She could see it now, her name in modest gold letters on the door. Miss Katy's, with curlicues on the M and the K. Or perhaps, Miss O'Sullivan's.

Miss O'Sullivan's what? Dress Shop? Clothing Emporium? She wasn't entirely sure what an emporium was, but it sounded big and proud and important.

With a look of dawning delight, she whispered, "Miss O'Sullivan's House of Fine Fashions. *Yes!*"

It was perfect. Of course, it would take a door as big as a barn to hold it all, but she could sort out the details later.

Finally, finally, she was on her way! Impulsively, she plopped the iron onto the board, hoisted her skirts above her ankles, and jigged a few impromptu steps around a dress form, grinning from ear to ear. Grinning like a possum, as Willy would say. Whatever a possum was, it couldn't be any happier than she was.

"Miss O'Sullivan!"

Oops. "Yes, ma'am?" The stench of scorched linen drifted up to her nostrils. With a stricken look, she hurriedly reached for the iron, knocked it over, but caught it before it could fall to the floor.

Inez Baggot stood in the workroom doorway, black eyes snapping fire. All three seamstresses turned to watch. The only sound in the room was a tiny whimper from Katy. She gripped her right wrist to keep the pain from shooting all the way up to her shoulder. It didn't help.

"This will cost you dearly." The veiled threat was all the more terrifying for being softly spoken.

Between stark terror and the agony of a blistered palm,

it was all Katy could do to defend herself. "But it's only a single panel, ma'am. I can soak it in lemon juice and set it out in the sun, and—"

"I don't sell damaged goods. If there's not enough linen left on the bolt to cut a new section, you'll pay for the entire thing. Otherwise, I'll only dock you for what it takes to recut the panel. Now, see to it. And when you're done with that, you can go next door and wash down the walls and scrub the floor. There's men coming tomorrow to paint and put down carpet."

"Next door?"

"Are you hard of hearing? I announced in the paper last week that I was expanding my showroom. Now, go see if there's enough material left on the bolt. If there is, set it out on the table with Miss Eppie's pattern, and then go fetch a bucket and pail and get to cleaning."

Katy refused to cry. It wasn't the first time she'd had to ignore a burn. Back when her mother died, when she was twelve, and she'd had the cooking and washing to do for Tara and Da, she'd blistered herself more than once before learning to use her apron to drag a pot off the fire.

Following her own long shadow, Katy made her way slowly back to the waterfront that evening, blind to the splendor of a setting sun reflected on the mirrorlike surface of the river.

A motor car rattled noisily past, causing two horses to whinny and cavort. She didn't bother to look around. If it happened to be Captain Bellfort, and if he happened to smile and say something nice to her, she just might break down and cry her eyes out, she was that miserable.

Thank goodness she wouldn't have to sing for her supper tonight. She could hardly remember a time when she'd felt less like singing. Captain Bellfort had promised to give her until the weekend to get settled and go over a few bits of music with his pianist.

At least there was no crowd gathered on deck when she stepped aboard the *Queen*. Two well-dressed gentlemen followed her up the gangplank. When one of them tipped his hat and held the door, she managed a weary smile, but it took nearly all the strength she possessed.

"Thank you, sir," she murmured.

"My pleasure, miss."

The small kindness brought ready tears stinging to the surface. Katy fought them back, bracing herself for what lay ahead. There was no sign of Tara, which was good.

Or perhaps not.

Telling herself it was folly to borrow trouble, she hurried down the stairs and turned toward the hastily furnished locker room. She didn't see a single soul along the way, but heard the sound of laughter coming from the galley at the other end of the corridor.

Tara would be having her supper, or lingering to help wash up afterward. Willy had promised to keep her busy and out of trouble.

Carefully, Katy unpinned her hat, smoothed the modest ribbon band, and placed it on top of her trunk. Absently, she brushed at a speck of lint on her skirt, and gasped as pain streaked up from her blistered palm.

She allowed herself three deep breaths, and then stiffened her shoulders. There was Tara to find, and packing to do, but before she could use her hand, she'd better beg a bit of butter or tallow from Willy. She had tied her handkerchief around her hand when she'd finished scrubbing, hoping it might ease the pain.

It hadn't. She didn't know which hurt more, the streak of raw blisters across her palm, or her aching feet. Except for the time she'd spent on her knees, scrubbing years of filth from a splintery floor, she'd been on her feet all day long.

Without thinking, she sank down onto the stool in the

corner. She leaned back against the wall and allowed her eyelids to close. Just for a minute. A single minute . . .

"Katy, wake up, wake up! Can you hear me? I know I promised, but this time, it's important!" Tara was shaking her shoulder, going on and on about . . . sickness? Something about a roomful of desperately ill people?

"They were all moaning and groaning and throwing up in buckets, just like on the boat coming over, only it was right here. It was Charlie and Ava and Johnny the Knife and Oscar. It's the cholera, Katy, I'm sure of it. Please, please wake up—we have to warn the captain."

"Shhh, go 'way," Katy murmured, certain she must be dreaming.

"But, Katy, I *saw* it!"

Without opening her eyes, Katy said, "There's no cholera here. They have rules about such things in America."

"I know, it's mostly Asia and places like that, but, Katy, I *saw* it, and it wasn't one of those foreign places, it was right here. Katy, please open your eyes. What are we going to do?" The child grabbed her hand to pull her up off the stool. Unfortunately, it was her right hand. Katy screamed, Tara jumped back, and then the door burst open and Aster stood, hands on her hips, demanding to know what was going on *now*.

"I told you you had to leave. Didn't you think I meant it?"

"Oh, but—" Tara began when Katy waved her to silence. By then she was awake. Wide awake and wishing she were still sleeping.

"We've only our packing to do, and that won't take long. I'm sorry we couldn't leave sooner, but I just now got back from—"

"I'm warning you, I fully intend to go through your bags before you set one foot off my property. Aren't those Ila's pearl earbobs you're wearing? We'll just see what she has to say about that."

Katy could only stare at her. She'd awakened from one nightmare, only to find herself mired in another one.

"Miss Aster, are you feeling all right?"

Aster glared at Tara briefly before turning back to Katy. "There's nothing wrong with me that getting rid of the pair of you won't cure. You won't be coming back again this time, so take that ugly cat of yours with you."

"Heather's not ugly, she's only—Miss Tyler, are you sure you're not feeling ill? You're shaking all over and your face is all splotchy."

Throwing her hands in the air, Aster spun on her heel and marched out, skirttails flying. The door struck the jamb and bounced open again.

"I think she's coming down with it, Katy," Tara whispered.

"Stop it. Just stop it right now. I don't want to hear one more word about cholera, do you understand?"

Tara looked hurt, but then Katy was hurting, too. What's more, she was mad as a hornet. The woman had all but accused her of being a thief.

Saints preserve us, how could everything go so right and so wrong, all on the same day? "Gather up everything and pack it away in the valise, we're leaving. Where's your clean underwear? Hurry, because I don't want to walk down the wharf after dark. And don't forget Heather's basket."

"Where are we going?"

Patience, Katy admonished herself. Tara was hardly to blame for Aster's nastiness, or Katy's weariness, or her carelessness with the iron. "You'll never guess. Captain Bellfort has invited us to move aboard his boat and work for him."

Cholera was forgotten for the moment. Tara brightened, but Katy reminded herself that she wasn't the only one who was tired. The child was drooping. She'd probably spent the day scrubbing pots for Willy and running errands for Ila.

"There now, doesn't that sound exciting?" Forcing a cheerful smile, Katy pinned on her hat again, glad there was no mirror in the room to remind her of what she must look like.

Cholera, of all things. It came of reading all those books her mother had brought to her marriage, along with a trunk full of fancy gowns and a service for six in heavy sterling flatware. By the time she died, all that was left were a few gowns that Katy had since cut down and turned until there was little left, and a complete set of encyclopedias. No one in Skerrie Head had wanted the books enough to pay her father's asking price.

They worked with silent efficiency. Packing everything they possessed hardly took more than a few minutes, and then there was only the trunk to be dealt with. Shoulders sagging as her excitement began to fade, Tara took the cat basket on her arm and went to find someone to haul their trunk up on deck, while Katy took one last look around the room to make sure they hadn't left anything behind. Not that they had much to leave. Even the kitten's bowl belonged to Galen.

She would miss Ila. She'd miss Willy, too, and the old man who polished brass and windows, and Oscar, who always had a smile and a cheerful word.

And Galen. She knew very well he expected her to fail, he'd as good as told her so. They both knew she would've had to work until the spirit had all gone out of her, sweeping and ironing, scrubbing and polishing for Mrs. Baggot, to pay off all she owed and save enough for her business.

She would miss him. She didn't dare think of the other dream that had been growing inside her ever since she'd first seen him outside the depot, looking like a fallen angel in his black suit, his shiny black boots, with that odd streak of white across his tarnished brass hair.

She refused to put a name to it. That second dream. At

least she would have the satisfaction of seeing the admiration in his eyes the day he saw her name in gold on her very own storefront. Until then, she'd do better to try and forget him.

Eight dollars a night. Even to think of standing up and singing for a roomful of men terrified her. She would do it, though, because she had to. If she didn't believe in herself, no one else would, and then where would they be?

"Not another word, young lady."

"But Captain Galen, I saw it as plain as day. People were moaning and carrying on, and there was Charlie and Oscar, and Ermaline was crying holding her belly, and—"

"Tara, not now, please. I'm busy."

"Yes, but—"

"I told you, there's no cholera. We have laws against it. They're called quarantine laws."

"Yes, but—"

"I realize that with ships coming and going from every port in the world, there's always the possibility of spreading disease, but in a town this small, it's hardly likely. Believe me, if I thought there was the slightest danger, I'd close down so fast your head would swim. Now run along like a good girl, will you? I'm due back on the floor, and I'm already running late."

"Well, but . . . I saw it, I really did, clearer than I've seen anything since the tablecloths and gold coins."

With an exaggerated sigh, Galen turned away from his safe. The IOUs would have to wait. How the devil was he supposed to concentrate on business with a hysterical kid carrying on about something she thought she'd seen.

Dreamed, more than likely. After the supper she'd put away, it was no wonder she had nightmares. Willy said she ate more in a single sitting than most full grown men did in a day.

Years of going hungry, he suspected, feeling almost guilty because he'd never personally experienced real hunger.

Hunger was the last thing he felt after spending the past two days wining and dining bankers, lawyers, and building contractors at the Albemarle House.

"Tara, Tara. What am I going to do with you?"

She looked so damned miserable with her homely little face and her big sad eyes, he felt like holding out his arms and letting her pour out her foolishness on his shoulders.

She sniffed. Her face was pale, the freckles standing out like specks of rust. Her lips were quivering. If she was doing it deliberately, he had to admit she had it down to a fine art. He'd seen professional gold diggers who couldn't play on a man's guilt half as well.

A piteous yowl came from the basket on her arm. She shifted on her feet and said, "I guess I won't be seeing you again, then."

"Of course you will," he exclaimed with patently false cheerfulness. "Has Katy found you another place to stay?"

She nodded, still on the verge of tears.

"Well, then, I'll be seeing you around town. Elizabeth City's a small place. We're bound to run into one another sooner or later. Besides, you know you're always welcome to visit."

"Miss Aster doesn't want us. She hates cats."

"You leave Miss Aster to me."

The look she gave him then defied description, and Galen decided he was imagining things. She was a funny child. Maybe all children were that way, imagining pirates and robbers behind every tree. It had been too many years, he couldn't recall.

"Want me to tell Katy good-bye for you? She'll probably be too busy being famous and entertaining rich men to come visit."

"Being famous, huh? I see Mrs. Baggot had better look to her laurels."

She opened her mouth to reply, but then shut it again, looking so miserable he wondered if she could possibly be jealous of her older sister. Having grown up the middle son of three, he did remember something about sibling rivalry.

He told himself he'd do well to secure Katy a husband before Little Miss Trouble dreamed up another escapade, but knew he wouldn't do it. Didn't know what he would do, but knew he wasn't about to hand her over to another man.

The door opened a crack, and Katy peered in and said, "There you are. I've been searching everywhere. Come along now, we'd best be leaving."

Galen stood and shoved his chair under the desk. "Katy, if you've a moment—?"

"I'm sorry, but we're in a grand hurry. Galen, thank you for—"

At a moan from Tara, she broke off. They both turned in time to see Tara crumple onto the nearest chair, clasping her belly. Her face held a greenish cast, and for once there was no doubt at all that she wasn't acting.

Tara was the first victim. Johnny the Knife was next. After that, the pumpers fell ill, and before the doctor could arrive, it seemed that everyone aboard the *Queen* was wretching and moaning.

All thought of leaving was forgotten as Katy and Galen, with Ila's help, settled the victims in whatever quarters could be made quickly available. By the time Ila threw up, gasped out an apology, and then fled from the room, the doctor had arrived.

"It all came on so fast, doctor. Is it—cholera?"

"Cholera? Lord love you, no, madam. There's scarlet

fever in town, and one or two cases of the summer in-
fluenza, but this looks to me like plain old food poisoning.
Happens every summer. You take a spell of hot weather,
with the ice man running behind in his deliveries—What
with picnics and all, folks get sick. Happens every summer.
Wait'll the Fourth of July, I'll be run clean off my feet trying to keep up."

There was no question of Katy's leaving. For all she knew,
she might be the next one to fall ill. Tara was returned to
the locker room, to the bed they'd shared for the past two
nights. Katy would have set the cat free to look after herself, but she knew Tara would be heartbroken, so she made
her a place with a box and a bowl of milk, and prayed the
milk wasn't tainted.

Aster had been moved into Ila's room, too sick to offer
more than a feeble protest, and Ila was in with Ava and Ermaline. One by one in rapid succession, the entire staff had
succumbed. The male crew was scattered among the few remaining quarters, mostly on pallets on the floor. It made
nursing far easier, having them all on one floor.

Or deck, as Katy reminded herself. To be sure, after the
past few hectic hours, she couldn't have said where she
was, nor which end was up.

Most of the customers had long since fled. The few who
came late were turned away. Galen placed a sign at the
foot of the gangplank, letting everyone know that the gambling rooms would be closed until further notice. While he
was at it, he called over one of the waterfront regulars. The
two men conferred briefly, and then Galen handed over
a sheaf of bills. The bilge pumps could go unmanned for
a day or so without serious consequences. He could use a
nurse, but didn't hold out much hope of securing one at this
hour of night.

Sandwiches, though . . . neither he nor Katy had had
time even to think about supper. Under the circumstances,

neither of them had much of an appetite, but they had to
eat to maintain their strength.

"Poor Willy," Katy said with a sigh. "He tried to apologize. I told him it wasn't his fault, but I don't think it
helped."

"He's not as bad as some of the others. A few of the
boys are turning themselves inside out."

"Tara's asleep now. I wish she hadn't eaten so much
supper."

"Did you?"

"Did I what?"

"Have any supper."

They'd met in the corridor, shoulders drooping, and lingered a moment to compare notes. Galen told her about the
sandwiches waiting in his office, and she groaned. The handkerchief she'd tied around her hand earlier was filthy. The
pain was a constant dull ache, but she'd ignored it.

She managed a glimmer of a smile. Galen stared at her.
Neither of them could manage to look away. "You're for-
ever trying to feed me. It's a good thing I was too busy.
There's far worse things than going hungry."

"Honey, you've got to eat something. Half a sandwich.
Two bites."

She wrinkled her nose. He reached out and touched the
very tip of it, and she closed her eyes against the temptation to lean against him and let the world and its troubles
disappear.

"It might have been better if you'd sent out for help instead of food," she told him.

"I did that, too. Your friend, Mr. Bynum, offered us the
services of Red Satin. For a fee."

"Red—what on earth would we want with satin?"

"It's a woman, or rather, she is. Red hair, satin . . . well,
whatever."

Katy's mouth rounded into a startled O.

"Take a break, honey, before you drop in your tracks. If I have to look after the lot by myself, I might jump ship."

"You never would, not you. You've far too great a conscience." She raked back her hair. She'd misplaced her hat, and her hair was tumbling from its once tidy knot. Earlier when they'd passed in the corridor Galen had paused, stripped off his tie, turned her back to him, and secured the unruly mop as best he could.

She'd told herself she only imagined his hands lingering there. As weary as she was, it was no wonder her mind was playing tricks on her.

"Katy?" His voice was a husky whisper, soft so as not to disturb anyone who might be sleeping in the rooms on either side. "Come upstairs. Two bites, five minutes, that's all."

"Oh, all right. Five minutes, then, but no more. Are you sure you left a bell in every room?"

"Bells, buckets, and plenty of towels."

As they were close to the galley, and as always, there was a kettle on the stove, Katy made tea. She had an idea Galen would have preferred coffee; she didn't ask and he didn't complain.

Galen carried the brown betty teapot and two stout mugs. It was all Katy could do to carry herself up the stairs and out onto the balcony. She'd left Tara in bed with the kitten curled at her feet. The child had emptied out her belly again and then fallen into an exhausted sleep.

"I think Johnny and Ermaline might be over the worst," she said after collapsing into one of the chairs Galen had dragged outside.

He unwrapped a thick sandwich and handed it over. "Here, eat as much as you can and I'll give you some tea."

"I want tea while it's hot. Now. Right this minute . . . please?"

"Demanding little tyrant, aren't you?" He poured her a

mug, stirred in three spoonsful of sugar and handed it over. "You look awful, by the way." The words were offered with a crooked grin, and Katy couldn't find it in her heart to resent it. In his sock feet, with his shirt unbuttoned halfway down his chest, the tails hanging out and the sleeves rolled up over tanned, muscular forearms, he looked more than ever like a tarnished, jaded angel.

She emptied her cup, closed her eyes, and sighed. "That was lovely."

"Eat."

"I'd rather sleep."

"Katy, I know you would, but just this once, trust me to know what's best."

"I trust you," she said without opening her eyes. And she did. She would trust him with her life. Hadn't she come nearly five thousand miles on blind trust alone?

She felt his hands on her arms, and then he was shaking her. "Dammit, wake up! Don't go to sleep on me yet. Take one bite, just one little bite, and I'll put you down for a nap."

She shook her head. Galen stared down at her, his expression one of hunger, frustration, and exhaustion. "Stubborn woman," he muttered.

He could almost swear she smiled without opening her eyes. "Come along then, I'll let you sleep awhile, but then you're going to have to eat a whole sandwich. Do we have a deal? Katy?" He wasn't entirely sure he could carry her without dropping her, he was so damned tired after playing nursemaid half the night. It wasn't his line of work. Not that he wasn't willing, but a man felt so damned helpless, watching a kid retch his guts out over and over without being able to do a damned thing to ease the pain.

He bent over her chair to scoop her into his arms, and it was then he noticed her right hand. It came to him that she'd had that rag tied around it all night, only he'd had other things on his mind. She hadn't explained, and he hadn't asked.

Now he carried her inside and lowered her onto his bed. Her lips moved, but other than that, she didn't stir.

He opened her collar, unbuttoned it all the way down to the edge of her chemise, to where the soft swell of her breasts began, and felt like a dog for looking.

He unlaced her shoes and slipped them off, cursing softly when he saw the wad of paper crammed into the toe. Damn Aster and her penny-pinching ways!

And damn him for not paying closer attention to what was going on.

Next he reached for her hand. The handkerchief was knotted, the knot pulled tight. It was damp, which made it all but impossible to pick loose, but he managed. She didn't stir. Not even when he lifted her hand, examined the palm and began to swear.

"Katy, Katy, what am I going to do with you?"

He used shaving soap because it was mild, and daubed on whiskey, knowing it would sting like the very devil, hoping she would sleep through it. Ila had something in her room she used on everything from cuts to earache, but he wasn't sure where she kept it, and didn't want to leave Katy long enough to go search.

So he folded her hand over the raging raw place on her palm, lifted it to his lips and kissed her knuckles. And then he leaned over and kissed her lips, which were slightly parted, and wanted to do more. As tired and distracted as he was, it took almost more willpower than he possessed to sit there beside the bed and watch her sleep when he would have sold his very soul for the right to lie down beside her.

To take off her gown and whatever she was wearing under it, and then take off his own clothes and lie down beside her. Not to make love, because he was too tired and she was too tired, but to hold her. Flesh to flesh, skin to skin, to hold her while she slept, to sleep with her, and after a while . . .

Chapter Fourteen

〜

Galen told himself it was one of life's small ironies. The last time he'd lost his head over a woman, that woman had been seven years older than he was. A neighbor's daughter, he'd always known her, but hadn't thought much about her one way or another until after she'd come home from a two-year stay in France.

Instead of the quiet, shy girl he'd known all his life, who used to beat him at checkers and dominoes, she'd come home a poised, elegant woman, speaking with just the hint of a foreign accent. He'd been about eighteen at the time. Maybe even younger. He'd considered himself suave, handsome, everything any woman could want in a man, a favorite with all the ladies, from grandmothers to granddaughters, servants to socialites.

In other words, he'd been a complete ass.

For all her newfound sophistication, Margaret had been unfailingly kind. Looking back, he had a feeling she might have had something going with Brand, but if so, nothing had ever come of it. Years later, when they'd met again, they had both smiled over it. By then she'd been married to a banker-turned-diplomat, and appeared to be serenely approaching middle age.

Now it was happening to him again, only in reverse. Katy was little more than a child. She might be almost twenty-two years old, but in experience, she was hardly older than Tara. Innocence stood out all over her. Innocence and pride and a stubborn conviction that all she had to do was want something enough and work hard enough, and it would fall into her hands like a ripe plum.

Katy, Katy, what am I going to do with you?

He had a feeling if she heard him asking, she'd have a ready response. One he didn't particularly care to hear.

Leaving her there, he made the rounds again. Tara was sound asleep. Still too pale, too frail. There were shadows under her eyes that didn't belong on a child. But then, as she reminded anyone within hearing whenever her status was questioned, she was *practically* thirteen years old.

He smoothed the light cover up over her shoulders, touched her matted hair, and then her forehead. It was cool, thank God. He told himself it could have been a lot worse. She'd said cholera. The last bad cholera epidemic had been—hell, he hadn't even been born then, but it still cropped up now and then.

"Sleep well, honey," he whispered. At the sound of his voice, the kitten stretched, curled her paws, and then closed her cloudy blue eyes again.

Ila was sitting up in a chair, but she looked awful. He'd estimated her age at about forty. He revised it upward a couple of decades.

"Over the hump?" he asked softly.

"Reckon I'll live. Not sure it's worth it." She nodded to the bed where Ava and Ermaline still slept. "Ava woke up a while back. Didn't ask for the bucket this time. Must be over the worst."

"I'd better look in on Aster."

"I don't envy you none. She'll be ridin' high on her broomstick after this, just you wait."

Galen chuckled. Ila managed a weak smile. Ava snored, and Ermaline muttered something in her sleep about a full house.

Aster was on her knees holding the chamber pot in her arms, but at least she'd recovered enough to send him a malevolent look and tell him where he could go. Closing the door quietly, he decided she was on the mend. An hour ago she hadn't been able to hiss at him, much less swear at him.

Willy was on his feet again. Tough old bird. He'd just come in from emptying a pail over the side. "Sorry 'bout this, son. Won't happen again. What don't get et up first time around, I'll give it away or chuck it over the side."

"How're the boys?"

"They'll make it. Johnny come around wantin' grits and coffee."

"Godamighty." Galen couldn't remember the last time he'd been sick in his belly, but he did know Willy's boiled coffee was no remedy. The stuff would dissolve paint. "You need a hand here?"

"Naw, we're doin' real good. You take care of the little missy. Way that young'un eats, she'll be bad off."

They talked for a minute more, and then Galen left. Katy hadn't moved. Her right hand was curled half open on the pillow beside her head. He angled it toward the light and studied it.

Still raw. It was going to be a problem for the next few days, but at least there were no red streaks running up her arm.

She didn't stir, so he held onto her hand a few minutes longer. Poor baby, she was exhausted. He was fairly certain she'd had no more than a couple of biscuits and a few cups of tea in the past twenty-four hours. It wasn't enough to sustain any woman who worked as hard as she did, but in this case, it had spared her a lot of misery.

He glanced at the clock, then checked the weather outside. Another day on the horizon. Maybe rain, he couldn't be certain. For once, his bones didn't ache—either that or he was so damned tired another ache or two went unnoticed.

There were papers on his deck that needed his attention. There were clothes draped over bedposts and chair backs—a few more on the floor. He was inclined to be tidy, possibly a relic of his years at sea. A place for everything and everything in its place, that was the seaman's credo.

Or was it one of Ila's sayings? Or his mother's?

At a time like this, who gave a damn? Not him. He was too tired. Too tired to do anything except shed the rest of his clothes, right down to his drawers, and crawl into bed.

It was a wide bed. He remembered thinking just before his head hit the pillow that there was plenty of room for two people to sleep peacefully without disturbing one another.

Fever. Either that or hellfire was licking at his flesh. Heat and the constant drone of rain on the water, rain beating down on the canopy, rain pounding down on the overhead deck. . . .

Galen opened his eyes one at a time. And discovered the source of the heat. It was curled around him like a serpent twined around the branch of an apple tree. With the same effect.

Temptation. Full, throbbing arousal.

Mere inches away, her lips were an open invitation. "Katy?" he murmured.

"Mmmm."

She could hear him. That meant she was awake. That meant he wasn't taking advantage of a sleeping woman. He moved his head only enough so that his lips brushed against hers. It wasn't really a kiss. It was no more than the light tug of damp flesh against damp flesh.

Her lips were parted. He thought she sighed. Angling his head for better contact, he went back for more, pressed his mouth against her slack lips, felt them stir and grow firm, and his hand moved to cup her cheek.

Ah, Katy . . . what have you done to me?

She tasted salty and sweet—a hint of tea. Something smoky and musky, laced with an intoxicating essence that was purely irresistible. Galen rolled over so that his upper body covered hers. When her arms came around his neck, he told himself she was fully aware of what was happening. The muffling sound of a driving rain shut out any guilt he might have felt. The unsought intimacy of waking up together on rumpled silk sheets in a room lit by a single lamp robbed him of any common sense he might once have possessed.

There was no past, no future, only now. Only this.

Her breasts were small but surprisingly firm. They fit perfectly in the hollow of his palms. Through whatever thin layers she still wore, he could feel her nipples harden and lift to meet him.

With clumsy fingers, he finished unbuttoning her blouse and laid open the two sides. Still too many layers. He tugged at a shoulder strap, a narrow band of worn white cotton, but it refused to give way.

"I want to see you, Katy," he rasped. "All of you."

To see if she was as beautiful as the woman he'd dreamed of too many times. The woman in his dreams was small, her skin paler than ivory, paler than moonstones. Nipples like carnelian, and lower, past a waist so small he could span it easily—below the imperceptible swell of her belly— a nest as dark as midnight, hinting of unimaginable treasures, pleasures. . . .

In his dreams, the woman never opened her eyes, but if she had, he knew what color he would see.

His hand moved over her breast to her waist. His mouth left her lips to taste her throat, lingering on the pulse that throbbed in the hollow there. He explored the faint indentation of her navel, and felt his own taut flesh jerk in response.

"Katy, are you sure? We won't go any further unless you—"

"Cap'n, suh, is you in there?"

Galen came back down to earth with a solid, bone-jarring thud. Eyes closed, he took a deep, shuddering breath and began to swear silently, lethally, the words directed toward himself. Toward his own stupidity. His own damned, unbelievable selfishness.

Katy opened those incredible green eyes. In the gray half light of dawn she looked dazed, disoriented.

"It's all right, darling, everything's all right. Stay here, go back to sleep, I'll handle it."

Some forty-five minutes later, Katy stuffed the clothes she'd worn for the past two days into the valise at the foot of the bed. The dress she changed into was creased where it had been packed since yesterday.

Yesterday? It seemed more like last week.

At least she was clean from the skin out.

"Katy, I'm hungry. Heather wants her breakfast."

"I'm sorry I woke you, I tried to be quiet." She had bathed and changed her clothes in the darkness, with only the light of a single candle set on the floor where it wouldn't shine in Tara's eyes.

"Could I have something to eat?"

"A bit of broth, then. The hunger's a good sign you're mending, but you're not ready for food yet."

"I hate broth. Couldn't I have some gingerbread? Willy always has gingerbread, he knows I like it."

"Willy's been sick, love. Everyone has."

Tara's face crumpled. Katy could tell she was working herself up, and no good would come of it. She'd be sick all over again, and there would go their chance to slip away quietly, before Galen—before anyone could stop them.

"Can I just have some bread and jam, then?"

Reluctantly, Katy gave in. "I'll go and see if I can find a bit of bread and milk, but if you're well enough to eat solid food, then you're well enough to get up and put on your clothes." Thank goodness they hadn't far to go.

"I'm not that well," Tara whined.

Katy was having none of it. They'd be here forever if Tara had her way, and then Aster would rant and rail, and Galen would be forced to defend them. Or not . . .

"The rain's let up. If we hurry we can make it as far as Captain Jack's boat before it starts again."

The note had come just in time. Katy didn't know how he'd found out, but Jack Bellfort knew all about the sickness, who had it and who didn't, and what had caused it. He could have seen the doctor coming and going. She didn't know and didn't care, as long as he never learned of Katy's own private shame. Of what she'd done, or nearly done. What she'd wanted so desperately to do.

Aye, and there was the shame of it all. Perhaps fifty years from now, when she was an old, old woman, she might be able to look at Galen and not remember the way it had felt to lie in his arms and feel his hands on her body, his mouth on hers. To want—

"I want some coffee, too," Tara said petulantly.

"Shhh, you'll wake the others. They've all been sick, even Aster. If she hears you, she'll—"

"I know, she'll make us leave, but Captain Galen won't let us go. He wants us to stay, Katy, I know he does. I saw—"

"Tara Eleanor O'Sullivan!" Katy whispered sharply.

"I'm sorry. I know I promised. I forgot. But, Katy, can I please at least have something to eat?"

"The hell you say. When did they leave?"

Oscar shrugged. "Less'n an hour ago. She said to say good-bye and thanks for everything."

"The hell she did!"

"Cap'n, sir, is something wrong?"

Galen paced, kicking aside a chair that got in his way.

The note had been for Katy, delivered by one of the water-front urchins. He'd tipped the boy, handed it over, and waited for her to tell him what it said.

Instead of reading it right away, she'd looked at him so pointedly he'd mumbled something about checking on Tara and the others and started looking around for his shirt and trousers.

He'd almost sooner have gone down to the crew's quarters in his drawers as to have to scramble into his clothes while she sat there watching. Nakedness had never embarrassed him before, but there was something demeaning about getting dressed in front of a woman he'd nearly made love to, and hadn't. Regardless of the reason, it felt too much like failure.

"No, nothing's wrong, son," he said in belated response.

Nothing except the fact that Katy had walked out and left without even giving him her directions. Nothing except that his leg hurt, and his head ached, and black wool was too damned hot when the mercury barely dipped into the eighties, even in the middle of the night, in the middle of a damned rain squall.

It was drizzling again, the wharf nearly deserted, by the time Katy, with Tara lagging after her, marched up the gangplank of the *Albemarle Queen* and plopped her valise on the trunk Oscar had carried aboard. He'd offered to take it inside, but he still looked a bit green and unsteady. Besides, she hadn't known where to direct him.

"Go on back and go to bed," she told him. "I'm sure Captain Bellfort will send someone to help with the trunk."

She had more on her mind than finding a new home for her books. She couldn't afford to be late for work again, and there was still Tara to be settled. If things hadn't been so awkward, she could have left her with Ila instead of dumping her in the lap of strangers.

"Do I have to go to work with you?"

"I don't know. We'll see." It was the best she could do for now.

"Captain Galen wouldn't want me to get sick again."

"Don't you dare think about getting sick again," Katy said quickly, and then felt like gathering the child in her arms and keening her heart out. "We'll find you a nice bed, and you can rest all day and play with Heather. There now, you'll like that, won't you?"

"I'm hungry."

Katy was hungry, too, but there was nothing she could do about it. First she had to get Tara settled, and then she had to get herself to work. The good thing was, she would be far too busy to waste time thinking about what had happened last night.

Had she really woken up in Galen's bed? Woken up in his arms, with his mouth on hers, and his hands touching her body in ways no one had ever touched her before—ways she'd never even imagined?

Or had she only dreamed it out of sheer longing?

Hearing a low murmur of voices, she opened a door, poked her head inside, and looked about. Jeannie—Janie—what had been the name of the woman who had taken care of her cat scratches?

Several boys wearing white aprons were arranging trays. One of them glanced up and said, "Ma'am? Did you want something?"

"Captain Bellfort is expecting me. I'm Miss O'Sullivan, and this is Tara, my sister. If you'd kindly have someone collect our trunk and show us to our room, I'd be much obliged to you."

Everything had gone like clockwork. Everyone had been lovely. Still, Katy worried. She couldn't help it. Worry was second nature to her, after years of doing all the worrying for the entire O'Sullivan family. "Are you sure?"

"Of course, I'm sure. Would I lie to you?"

Her eyes sought his, needing reassurance. Jack Bellfort had told her she wasn't expected at work today, that he had arranged the day before with Inez Baggot for her to work three days a week, on the days she wouldn't be singing. In exchange, Mrs. Baggot would get to make costumes for Katy and a school wardrobe for Tara.

"But why are you doing all this? I don't understand."

She hated her own suspicions, but she couldn't help it. She'd heard too many tales on the way to America. Men didn't do favors for women without expecting something in return.

Not even Galen.

"Would you believe my heart overflows with the milk of human kindness?"

She studied the wicked twinkle in his fathomless eyes for a moment, then shook her head. "That I wouldn't. You're offering far too much in exchange for a lilter to entertain your guests four nights a week. I'm not worth it."

"That's for me to say, isn't it?"

"Captain—"

"Jack. Katy, don't ever underestimate yourself. I know you're not a trained singer, but your voice is true and clear and delightful. Besides, you're a novelty. You can offer something we don't often hear in this neck of the woods."

"The Gaelic, you mean."

He nodded. "That, too. But no matter what you're singing, it's the way you do it that makes it special."

"I'll be terrified."

"You'll do just fine. You're going to have to teach Casey your tunes, but as he plays by ear, that shouldn't pose much of a problem. A voice like yours doesn't need a heavy backup."

They'd settled on a practice schedule that first day, one that wouldn't interfere with the pianist's regular duties. Then Jack had told her she'd be going into town for her first fitting after lunch.

The next three days were a whirlwind of activity. A maid, hardly older than Tara herself, was assigned to look after the two of them, and to her amazement, Katy found herself living in the lap of luxury, with daily fittings and lovely sandwiches and tea for the asking, and a roomful of books she was welcome to borrow.

There wasn't a word from Galen. Not that she'd expected any. He could have asked after Tara's health, though. He could have at least done that much. It wasn't as though he was that far away. If she listened hard enough, she could catch a familiar voice now and then from someone aboard the *Queen*. A snatch of laughter. Jimmy the Sweep whistling as he went about his duties.

She tried not to think about it, but twice in the darkest hours before dawn she awoke from a dream, feeling as if something incredibly valuable had slipped away before she could reach out and catch it.

Her costumes were cotton, not silk. Summery colors, with flounced overskirts and too many ruffles, but underneath all the trim, Mrs. Baggot had an excellent eye for line and color. It took only a few hours to make over the gowns once she got them back to her room. She was afraid Jack would object, but he didn't.

"You're the one who'll have to wear them. I want you comfortable. My sole aim is to create an image to go along with your repertoire."

Katy wasn't entirely comfortable with being an image, much less one created by a man. For eight dollars a night, however, she would have buried herself in frills and furbelows. And the new kid slippers that went along with her new gowns were certainly far more comfortable than Ermaline's high-heeled shoes with the paper in the toes.

Although she hadn't asked Katy to scrub any more floors, Mrs. Baggot couldn't exactly be said to treat her with respect. When she timidly inquired about trying her hand at cutting from a pattern, she was told that it would hardly be worthwhile.

"I don't know what game Jack Bellfort's playing this time, but it's not like him to let his ladybirds out of the cage."

"Ladybirds? Is that something like a songbird?"

"Humph," was all the older woman said, but her eyes spoke volumes.

So Katy continued to sort and put away, fetch and carry when customers came in to see the new fall fabrics and patterns, while Tara stayed on board the *Belle* and played checkers with Patsy the maid, and pestered the chef for scraps of cookie dough and bowls of cream for Heather.

Katy rehearsed every afternoon at four, going over songs she'd sung all her life, and telling Casey how they used to gather in first one home and then another, and sing the night away, while the men drank poteen and the women piled all the bairns into one bed, and how they danced and how her father was always the life of the party until he fell asleep.

It was a tremendous relief to find out that her first performance was to be on a Sunday afternoon in the Ladies' Parlor. She'd dreaded singing before an audience composed mostly of men. They would be cruising as far as Nags Head, putting in for an overnight, with guests from the hotel there coming aboard for an evening of music, dinner, and gambling.

It was a relief, but still she was terrified.

"I'll forget every song I ever knew, that I will. There I'll stand, with my mouth open, and not a note will come out."

"You'll do just fine," Jack assured her. He'd stopped by to hear her final rehearsal before they sailed. Several of the staff had wandered in. A few maids. Two waiters, and even a dealer or two.

Casey smiled encouragingly. He struck a few chords, and she closed her eyes and launched into a familiar ballad about the tragedy of a broken heart and a jilted lover. By the time the session was over, the knots in her belly had miraculously dissolved. She had carefully avoided looking out at her small audience. Which was why she was totally unprepared, when she gathered her shawl and the books she'd selected to take back to her room after rehearsal, to glance up and find Galen studying her as if he'd never seen her before.

Chapter Fifteen

"A re you certain you want to do this, Katy? It's not too late to change your mind."

Of course it was too late. His gaze moved over her face, as if searching out all her secrets. Couldn't he tell how much she'd missed him? How many hours she'd wasted thinking about him, dreaming about him?

"I'm being paid eight dollars a night for singing. On the days when I work for Mrs. Baggot—"

"Is this about money?" Anger tightened the planes of his face. "Because if that's all it is, you don't have to do it. Katy, I can—"

"You can do what? Pay me to stay away? The way Pierre's family pays him not to go home? No, thank you, I already owe you far too much, I'd not—"

"Dammit, Katy, you don't owe me anything!" His eyes suddenly narrowed. "What do you know about Pierre? I wasn't aware that the two of you were particularly close."

"Tara said—"

"Ahhh. Tara said." Arms crossed over his chest, he rocked back on his boot heels. "And what else did Tara say? Has she told you yet about the explosion that's going to rock the waterfront in a couple of days?"

"An explosion? Merciful saints, did she say that?"

"That and a lot of other bilge."

"It's not bilge. Not always. She was right about the sickness."

"She called it cholera."

"To be sure, she might have mistook what she saw and said it wrong, but she saw it right. The moaning and misery and sickness and all."

"To be sure," he acknowledged.

Katy examined his words for mockery and found none. "But there's no mistaking an explosion," she stated flatly. "Was it aboard one of the boats? Have you told the authorities?"

He shook his head slowly. "Katy, Katy. Do you know what day this is?"

She looked perplexed. "Thursday?"

"Right. Thursday the second of July. And every Fourth of July, we have a big fireworks exhibit. Rockets flying, exploding powder, shooting sparks. In other words, an explosion. A regular explosion of explosions."

"Yes, but—"

"I'm sure she meant well, but she didn't realize how we celebrate our independence every year, with fireworks. It's only natural—"

"That she did! We know all about your Independence Day. It's all there in the encyclopedia, even the exploding fireworks. She forgot, that's all, but you can't say she was wrong."

His features relaxed. As the fine lines around his eyes eased, the creases in either cheek deepened. "No, I suppose I can't, but, Katy, back to the point—are you sure you want to work for Bellfort? You don't have to put yourself before the public and—and—"

"Make a fool of myself?" Hurt the size of a fist clogged her throat. She told herself it was anger.

"That's not what I said. Katy, I don't want you to feel as if you have to do something you're not comfortable doing just because you feel responsible for your sister."

"I am responsible for Tara. I never asked you to—"

"That's right, you never asked me for anything, did you?" Without giving her a chance to argue, he went on to say, "You show up out of the blue and I'm supposed to dump you out at the nearest boardinghouse and forget about you, is that it? Katy, give me credit for—"

"If it's credit you're wanting, sir, then it's yours, but I'm the one with the duty." She was mortified, but determined not to show it. Head held high, she faced him bravely, challenge in every inch of her body.

Arms crossed over his chest, he glowered down at her. Sparks flew. A dangerously short fuse sparkled between them. Galen ground his teeth, while Katy fought back tears. Tears of anger, not of disappointment. Why did he have to go and remind her of all she owed him now? Now, when she desperately needed his support? The least he could have done, she told herself, was to wish her luck.

But it wasn't wishes she wanted from this maddening, meddling man. Her heart knew the truth, even if her mind refused to accept it.

He looked her over, from the tip of her black kid slippers, to the crown of her newly styled hair, taking in everything in between, from the simple stylishness of her new yellow sprigged gown to the ragged patches of color that suddenly bloomed in her cheeks.

Slowly, he shook his head. "I can't talk to you anymore. You used to be fairly reasonable, but in a matter of days you've turned into a stranger. I don't even know you." And then he turned and left her.

She was tempted to hurl something at him, to grab that streak of white hair with both fists and yank it out by the roots. To shake him until his teeth rattled, and bury herself in his arms.

Reasonable? She had never felt so unreasonable in her entire life!

But the anger faded almost as swiftly as it had arisen,

leaving only a hollow sort of bitterness in its place. A sense of loss. She told herself it was only seeing him here so unexpectedly. Why couldn't he have wished her luck? Why couldn't he have said, *Katy, I like your songs. Katy, you're looking pretty in your new dress. Katy, I'm sorry you left, but I'm that glad you're doing well.*

"Aye, and, Katy, your wits have gone wandering," she muttered. Taking a deep breath, she squared her shoulders and marched off in search of Tara. Evidently the child had gone visiting again. She spent entirely too much time aboard the *Queen*. It would have to stop, only Katy didn't know how to forbid it without explaining, or how to explain what she didn't understand herself.

The Katy who had come to America so full of hopes and dreams and fears had been a different woman. Or perhaps only the hopes and dreams had changed.

They sailed the next morning with a full load of passengers. Scores of children of all ages crowded the railing to watch the town slip away as they left the protected harbor. Little girls waved or cried, depending on their ages and temperaments. Little boys poked each other in the shoulders. Nursemaids threatened naps, promised treats, and warned against flying sparks and falling overboard, with Tara in the thick of it all, making friends with the older children.

Most of the women were inside, either getting settled in one of the passenger compartments or lolling about the ladies' lounge, looking over the latest selection of books or exchanging gossip with friends. As for the men, they were already getting down to the serious business of gambling.

Katy stood apart, waiting for the first sign of seasickness. Through the thin soles of her shoes she could feel the vibrations, sense the urgency as the boiler worked up a full head of steam. To think that not too long ago, the only form of travel she'd ever known was a pony cart and the occasional day trip in one of the village fishing boats to one of the tiny islands that dotted the bay. Since then she'd journeyed on ships and trains, and even an automobile. She wished her mother could see her now.

Nervous about her first public performance, she clung to the thought that Captain Bellfort must have known what he was doing when he'd hired her, even if she didn't. And it wasn't as if she'd be entertaining the entire group. Her audience would consist of women and a few of the older children.

She told herself it was all wildly exciting. That she was the luckiest woman in the world, to be paid good wages for doing no more than singing a few songs. She told herself that from now on she'd be far too busy to think about Galen. That he was a part of her past, not her future.

And she wondered why she didn't feel more elated.

At least her belly felt just fine. As the *Belle* moved out onto the river proper, there was no sign of queasiness. As for stage fright, her father used to say, "Katy, me girl, the higher ye roost, the easier ye are to knock off yer perch."

She wasn't about to set her heart on a singing career. All the same, eight dollars a night for as long as it lasted would move her a good bit closer to her dream.

Tara was happy as a grig. "It's nothing at all like home," she exclaimed over and over. Warm, sandy beaches sloping gently down to the water. Children romping about in swimming suits while their nursemaids tried to keep up with them.

During the morning, Katy ran over her music with Casey one last time. The closer she came to her debut—that was what Captain Jack called it—the more her belly tightened up. By the time she walked through the room that evening, a brittle smile fixed on her face, and took her place beside the piano, she had to remind herself to breathe.

The lights had been lowered so that only the first row of chairs could be easily seen. It helped. Tara had a front row seat, not because she was eager to sit through songs she'd heard all her life, but because Katy had insisted. "Just this one time, and I'll not ask it of you again. I'm nervous, Tara. Shaking in me slippers, truth be told."

"Ha, I can always tell when you're scared. You talk like Da."

"You'll do it, then?"

"Can I eat cookies in bed?"

They had a running argument about eating in bed. "Just for tonight—"

"And tomorrow night."

"All right, but you'll have to sweep away every last crumb."

"Heather'll eat all the crumbs. She likes cookies."

Katy rolled her eyes. Jack Bellfort couldn't possibly have known what he was taking on when he'd hired Katy and her dependents. She only hoped he never learned that Tara had already made friends with his kitchen staff, and bribed one of the waiters to supply her with milk and scraps for Heather and whatever was left over in the way of sweets at the end of the day.

Just then, Casey struck the opening chords of "The Lark in the Morning." Katy closed her eyes, lifted her head, and pictured herself back home at her own hearth, with Tara just outside the door and Da whistling his way up the path for supper.

Galen stayed until the very last notes faded away. The handful of men who'd been coerced into accompanying their wives had slipped out along about the third or fourth song. Even at that, he had an idea they'd stayed longer than they'd planned on staying.

Easy to see why. She was spellbinding. Not that he hadn't heard better voices—trained voices, with a far more sophisticated style—but never had he heard sheer magic woven around a few simple themes.

The accompanist knew better than to even try to follow her, much less to lead. He wondered if Katy had even noticed when he'd left off playing altogether.

" 'Tis a sad song, but then, the best ones are always sad," she'd told her audience after a lament for a lost sailor. He wondered if she was thinking about her father.

Galen found himself wondering quite a lot of things as Katy shyly thanked her audience for their patience and stepped down off the low platform. One of the things he wondered most of all was what the devil he was doing here, with a dozen different things back in town clamoring for his attention.

He knew the instant she saw him. Her jaw fell and her eyes widened. Every vestige of color drained from her face, reminding him of the way she'd looked the first time he'd seen her. He could have kicked himself for so thoughtlessly spoiling her triumph.

Someone had turned up the lights once the performance was ended, and now women were stirring about, moving over to the bookshelves, or to the table where coffee, tea, and assorted cakes were being served.

"What are you doing here?" she whispered.

He could have told her he was here because he couldn't stay away. He could have told her he just happened to be in the neighborhood. He could have said any of a dozen things, but he said nothing at all.

The truth was, he didn't know why he was here. He only knew that when he'd watched Bellfort's boat churn its way past the point, he'd felt something akin to panic. Earlier that morning he'd seen the sloop that distributed freight, mail, and a few passengers along the Outer Banks. Galen had met the ferryman when he'd first come south looking for Brand. At least once or twice a year since then he hitched a ride on the rugged skipjack to visit his old friends, the Merriweathers, at a place called Merriweather's

Landing on Pea Island. Nags Head was one of the stops along the way.

He'd watched Katy sail away, seen Pam's skipjack tied up at the Globe Fish Market dock, and acted on impulse.

"You're good," he said quietly.

"Thank you."

He'd seen more give in a piece of tungsten steel. When had things changed between them? He'd thought they were friends. "By that I mean, you're well worth whatever Bellfort's paying you. If I said anything yesterday to make you think—"

"It doesn't matter. Is Aster here with you?"

A bark of laughter erupted from his throat. "God, no! What makes you think I'd bring her along?"

She shrugged, and he noticed the way light from the gimballed brass lamp shone down on her shoulders, making her skin gleam like pearl.

"Katy, could we go somewhere and talk?" The women in the room were beginning to send them curious looks.

"I'd better see where Tara went, she rushed out before I'd even finished."

"Probably just getting ahead of the stampede." Horrified at what he'd implied, he stammered a retraction. "I didn't mean—that is, I only meant—"

"There now, I understand what you meant. Sure, and I lost half my audience before I even got to the song about crowing women and cackling men, and it was the best one of the lot." She smiled the kind of smile that should have made him feel better, but didn't. She was being tolerant. Dammit, he didn't want her tolerance, he wanted her—

He wanted her.

"Come along, we'll go out on deck. I could do with a bit of air."

Galen tugged at his collar. He could do with a bit of air himself, only he had a feeling it wouldn't help what ailed him. Somewhere along the way, without realizing when it had started, he'd got so all he had to do was see her, to catch a drift of her subtle wildflower fragrance, to become instantly aroused.

Compared to the more fashionable cutaway morning jacket, a frock coat had its uses.

He led her outside, up a set of stairs that led to the third deck balcony. At this hour of the evening, it was all but deserted.

"Are you staying aboard the *Belle*? Why haven't I seen you?"

"I'm staying over tonight at the hotel. Tomorrow I'll catch a ride back with the ferryman who dropped me off here."

"Mmm."

He noticed she'd forgotten about Tara. He'd like to believe it was because she had her mind focused on him, but with a woman like Katy, a man couldn't afford to take anything for granted. The more he came to know her, the more he realized that her mind didn't work the way most women's minds worked, and he fancied himself something of an expert on the workings of a woman's mind.

"So . . . have you given up on the notion of having your own shop?"

"Not a bit of it. Once I earn enough to repay you for our passage, I'll be setting aside every penny I can spare. I've thought of a name, but I'm not sure it's quite right."

Galen hunched his shoulders, gazing out at the glow of torches along the shore. "Katy, I told you, you don't owe me anything. I wanted to pay your passage. It made me feel—but you know all that. We've been over it before."

"That we have. I'll not take charity when I can earn my own way. You did what you thought best. Are you begrudging me the same right?"

Exasperated, he started to explain, thought better of it, and set off on a new tack. "I don't know how it is in Ireland, I wasn't there long enough to learn much about your ways, but, Katy, women here don't set themselves up in business. It's just not done."

"Mrs. Baggot did it."

"That's different. Inez is a widow." Besides, while it wasn't common knowledge, she had a backer with whom she shared more than a business relationship.

"Aster did it. She's not a widow."

"You're not Aster."

"No, I'm not. Aster doesn't have a younger sister depending on her. What would you have us do, line up on the wharf and wait along with the others for one of Willy's baskets?"

He opened his mouth, discovered he didn't have a ready retort, at least not one he cared to offer, and then muttered something under his breath when a couple strolled past, holding hands and murmuring softly.

Katy waited until they were out of earshot, and then she said, "There now, you've said your say, and I've listened. Galen, it's not that I want to be troublesome, but I'll not let you marry me off to a stranger just to ease your conscience. You might as well go back, for I'll not change my mind on it, I'm that stubborn."

He felt like shaking her. Never in his entire life had any woman been able to rattle him so easily. Didn't the little fool even realize how unreasonable she was being? "Fine, then if you won't marry a stranger, you can marry me!"

He didn't know which one of them was more stunned. If he could've bitten back the words, he would have swallowed them whole, but it was too late.

Her head came up another few notches. There was a dangerous glitter in her eyes. "I thank you for asking me. To be sure, it's a great honor you're offering, but you're no more wanting a wife than I'm wanting a husband."

And if that didn't put him in his place, Galen didn't know what it would take. Feeling lower than a snake, he waited for relief to overtake him. When it didn't, he resorted to anger.

"Then go ahead and ruin your life. Make yourself the talk of the town. Take away Tara's chance of growing up in a respectable home with a decent family, just don't expect me to keep on coming to your rescue."

"I never expected that of you," she said quietly.

"Fine!" He'd never felt so impotent in all his life. To think he'd actually asked a woman to marry him. Katy O'Sullivan, of all people.

To think she'd refused him!

Wheeling away, he stalked off toward the main stairway. Halfway there, he turned and strode back to where Katy stood rooted to the deck, eyes glittering like wet jade. Words churned in his head and his heart, fighting for expression.

"Fine! Tell Tara I said good-bye." Dammit, that wasn't what he wanted to say.

"I will."

He opened his mouth and then snapped it shut again. How the devil could she look so calm and composed with tears streaking down her cheeks? What the hell did she have to cry about, anyway? He was the one who'd just been rejected.

"And—and tell her to stay off the *Queen*. She's been over there every day this week."

"I'll tell her she's no longer welcome there."

"Oh, hell, you know I don't mean it. Katy—"

She swallowed hard. As he watched her throat convulse, his last shred of reason fled. He hauled her into his arms, pressing her against him as if she were a part of him. If she'd shown the slightest resistance, he'd have released her, gone back to the hotel, and put her out of his mind once and for all.

Instead, she curved herself against him as if she'd been designed to fit every inch of his body, her head in the hollow under his shoulder, her breasts pressing up against his heart.

Cradling her face in his hands, he kissed her, pouring out all the frustration of all the sleepless nights, all the anger at his own weakness. One hand strayed over her shoulders, down her back, and he held her tightly against the growing hardness of his groin, angling his head to take full advantage of her mouth.

There was nothing gentle about the kiss. It was the kiss of a man driven by temptation, a man tired of fighting a losing battle with his own reason.

He knew the instant she recognized what was happening to him. It would take more than a few layers of clothing to disguise his fierce arousal, even for someone as inexperienced as he knew her to be.

Bending over her, he buried his face in her throat and fought the urge to sweep her up in his arms and carry her off to his hotel room. She wouldn't stop him. Whether she knew it or not, she wanted him every bit as much as he wanted her, it was there in her innocent response.

Another couple strolled past. Galen groaned. There was no privacy here. Lamplight glittered on the water, on polished brass railings, on Katy's hair. Through the open doors below came the sound of laughter and music, the clatter of the roulette wheel. The humid night air was filled with the smell of salt, of wild grasses, of arousal.

Dammit, there had to be a secluded corner somewhere aboard this floating crap game where they could be alone. If they went to her room, Tara would be there.

But what if she wasn't? What if they made love? Then, she would have to marry him. Honor would demand it.

"Honor," he muttered, his hands curling into fists on her back. Reason returned, driving into him like cold, drenching rain. He deserved to be hanged, to be keelhauled, to be tarred and feathered for what he'd been thinking. This was Katy, not one of Miss Dilly's girls! Had he completely lost what was left of his mind?

It was the hardest thing he'd ever had to do, but he set

her away from him. Once he could trust his tongue to listen to his brain, he said, "For what it's worth, Katy, I'm sorry. I don't have any excuse to offer."

Half a century passed while she stared at him, not saying a word. Did she know anything at all about lust? About the way it could spring up without notice, making fools of otherwise sensible men and women?

Did she understand what had just happened to them? Did she have any idea how many marriages had foundered on that particular reef?

He could have told her. God knows, he was old enough to have seen something of the way things worked. The only marriages that had a snowball's chance of succeeding were ones in which both parties were reasonably close in age and experience, had similar backgrounds, and shared similar goals.

Katy and he failed on all counts. He was eleven years older than she was, a hundred years older in experience. Their backgrounds couldn't have been more different, and as for their goals, they were worlds apart.

As the eldest, it was up to him to be wise for both of them. The trouble was, he didn't feel wise. What he felt was needy and angry and frustrated.

Clearing his throat, he tugged at the knot of his tie, buttoned his coat, and told himself he'd just had a narrow escape. The trouble was, when he touched her on the shoulder, kissed her briefly on the forehead, and turned to go, it didn't feel like a narrow escape.

It didn't feel like an escape at all.

Chapter Sixteen

The Fourth of July celebration had been all she'd expected and more. Katy had stood beside Tara at the railing while flags fluttered overhead, horns tooted everywhere, fireworks exploded on shore. She'd told herself she was the luckiest woman in the world. Here she was living in America, with a wonderful job that paid a fortune and another that paid less, but that taught her things she would need to know before she could set up her own business.

She was the happiest woman in the world. It might not feel like happiness, but to be sure, that's what it was. If now and then she got confused and wanted something more, something she had no business wanting, why then, that was only to be expected. She had left behind a row of graves on a hillside, her home, and all her friends. She was beginning to settle in, but it would take time to replace all she'd lost, if she ever could.

Tara was happy. School would be starting in a few weeks, and she had already made friends with several children from town, thanks to the Wednesday dinner cruises and the weekend excursions. Katy and Jack had compromised on her school dresses. In exchange for a bit of mending, Katy allowed Jack to pay for the material, but she insisted on making them herself.

It was something to do in her spare time. Peggy had told

her about the hurricane deck and she'd dragged a chair up there. The light was perfect, and there was often a welcome breeze. The heat didn't bother Tara at all, but Katy had trouble getting used to sweltering, even in her underwear.

So on fine days she took advantage of the breeze and the good light. Glasses perched on the tip of her nose, she stitched away, singing softly, trying to remember all the words to songs she hadn't thought of in years.

If now and then she glanced over her shoulder toward the *Queen,* that was only to be expected. Sometimes she rested her eyes by studying the sawmill. Sometimes she watched trains go and come and wondered at their destination. Wondered what else there was to see in this vast land. Now and then she gazed at the tops of all those fine houses on Pennsylvania Avenue and wondered what it would be like to live there, and whether or not the people who did live there resented the noisy, smoky trains or wondered, as she did, where they were bound and what exciting places they would pass along the way.

Sometimes she looked at the *Queen* and wondered what Galen was doing, and if he ever thought about her. She hadn't seen him since he'd gone to Nags Head for her debut on the Fourth of July. Not that it mattered. With all she had to do and all she had to think about, she hardly had time to waste on daydreams.

Tara had said, "But why can't I go over there?"

"Because I need to know where you are at all times."

"But if I tell you I'm going over to visit my friends, then you'll know, so why can't I go?"

"I might need to fit something on you." It was a poor excuse and they both knew it. "Tara, please do this for me."

"It's because of Captain Galen, isn't it?"

"No, it's not," she lied.

Tara had given her that knowing smirk that always made Katy feel as if she were the child and Tara the adult. "It is, too. You miss him, don't you? He misses you, too. Just yesterday he—"

"Tara," Katy warned.

They'd reached an understanding about that sort of thing after the Fourth of July explosion. No more seeing. Or at least, no more telling what she thought she'd seen, because people here didn't understand. It was hard enough for Katy to understand, and she'd lived with it all her life.

So Katy sang and sewed and walked into town three days a week to work for Mrs. Baggot, who treated her with a tad more respect after Katy had taken the first of Tara's dresses she'd finished to show her.

Together, they went over every stitch, testing seams and gussets. "Kind of plain, isn't it?" Inez Baggot suggested.

"I'm making a pinafore to wear over it. Do you like the bias cut of the skirt?"

"It'll sag."

"Feel the material, there's no give there."

After that, Katy had been allowed to help with the cutting. She'd even been called in once or twice to help fit a gown on a customer.

Everything was perfect, she told herself. She was earning a fortune doing things she loved doing. Tara was happy. What more could a body ask?

Two weekend excursions later, after several midweek dinner cruises around the harbor and out into the surrounding waters, Jack Bellfort suggested that she might start thinking about a somewhat more sophisticated repertoire.

"I'm not sure I know what you mean."

"Nothing vastly different. Pick out a few of your songs that deal with more—shall we say adult subject matter? I'm thinking of trying you in the blue salon." That was the smaller of the gaming rooms, where Adeline and a three-piece band entertained the gentlemen for an hour or so each night.

"Oh, but—"

"Naturally, your pay will reflect the additional time."

"Oh, but . . ."

She fell silent. To be sure, she knew bawdier songs. Hadn't she heard Da and his mates sing them time and again, when they were in their cups? The women knew songs that would even shame the men. They sang them and laughed together sometimes in their kitchens, but to sing them before a roomful of men—

She would die of mortification. "I thank you kindly, but I don't believe I will."

Jack Bellfort lifted his glossy black brows, and Katy found herself trying to explain. The more she stumbled and blushed, the more he grinned, until finally she stood, shoved her sewing back into the basket, and left with some excuse about needing to fit a shirtwaist across Tara's shoulders.

Saints preserve us, she thought, fanning her face. She wasn't about to turn into *that* kind of songster, not for any amount of pay. She would scrub floors for Mrs. Baggot before she would wear a gown cut halfway down her chest and sing for a roomful of men about Diddling Tom and his Walking Stick.

Nothing more was said, and Katy continued to sing about lost seamen and sheepherders and lamenting ladies. She sang what she could recall of "Druimin Donn Dilis," and if her Gaelic was a bit rusty, no one complained. Now and then someone requested a particular song, making her feel as if she were among friends.

It was several days later when she left work—through the back door, for Mrs. Baggot hadn't thawed enough to allow her the use of the front entrance—that she emerged to find Galen waiting for her. There'd been more than enough time to put him out of her mind, but she took one look and forgot how to draw breath.

"Good evening, Katy. Are you in a particular hurry today?" His soft deep voice purred over her skin like a velvet glove, leaving gooseflesh in its wake.

By the time she found her tongue, he was explaining that he'd had to come into town on business, and while he was here, he thought he might drive her out and show her a tract of land he was in the process of acquiring. "That's if you're interested," he added.

As if she could say with any truth that she wasn't. She was interested in anything that interested him, but she would carve out her heart before she'd admit it.

"I've a few minutes to spare," she allowed. "I don't sing on the nights when I work late in town."

Ignoring the quick surge of emotions, Galen handed her up into his gig and climbed in beside her. Not by so much as a whisker did he allow his feelings to show, but in one quick glance he took in every detail of her appearance. She looked even more beautiful, if that was possible. There was a new confidence about her. He happened to know Inez Baggot was treating her with a good deal more respect, and resented the fact that Bellfort was responsible for it, not himself.

What else was Bellfort doing for her?

"Are you happy working two jobs, Katy? Are they treating you well?"

"Yes." Hands folded in her lap, she sounded breathless, almost as if she'd been running. He cut her another quick glance. When she didn't return it, he took a moment to admire her profile, with the smooth, high brow, the short, straight nose, and that surprisingly firm little chin.

And then they were crossing the Charles Creek Bridge, and he tooled along the riverside road, past the cotton mill and Shell's Shipyard. She admired the view and the fine houses set back from the river's edge, and he swelled with pride, as though it were all his doing.

"The property I'm buying is just around the next bend.

Only about three hundred feet of riverfront, but it goes back a thousand feet."

She murmured something vaguely appreciative, and he told himself he was a fool to think she'd be interested in another stretch of eroding shoreline and a few acres of scrub forest with a couple of rundown old houses, just because the deed had his name on it. Or soon would.

"I guess there's not much to see at this point," he said almost apologetically. "By the end of the year, I hope to have several buildings under construction and start setting pilings for a railway."

She glanced around at that, and he was caught up again in those remarkably clear green eyes. "Railway?" she repeated.

"For launching boats, not trains." Was she interested at all? Was he clean out of his mind to think she might be? "I plan to build my own shipyard. The one my brother and I took over in Connecticut was started by our grandfather. Brand operates it now. Not that he does much building these days, he's mostly involved in shipping now. I turned over my interest to him when I came south, since I'm more interested in designing and building than I am in the shipping end of the business. Over the next five years I plan to—"

God, would you listen to him. No wonder she had a glazed look in her eyes. "Sorry, Katy. Once I get off on the subject of boat building, I never know when to shut up."

"You were never interested in gambling, were you?"

He'd climbed out of the gig, and now he handed her out. They stood there while the mare cropped wild grass, and gazed out past the row of cypress trees to the calm dark waters of the Pasquotank River.

"How'd you guess?"

"Tara told me. And don't ask me how she knew, she just did." He shook his head, and she said, "Then why do you do it?"

So he explained about how he'd won fifty-one percent interest in the *Queen,* and how it seemed logical to parlay that particular windfall into something more to his liking. He didn't bother to mention the image he had deliberately fostered, one designed to disguise his lack of interest and keep potential troublemakers in line.

"Then you're using gambling as a means to an end, the way I'm using my singing."

He nodded. Distracted by the lilt of her voice, the way the late-afternoon sunlight spun rainbows around each strand of her glossy black hair, he lapsed into silence.

If he could have handed her her dream on a silver platter, he would have done it, no matter how impractical, how unworkable that dream was. Instead, he had cleaned out his savings and sent it off as a token payment on a debt that could never be repaid. And now he'd wiped out all he'd managed to acquire since and put it toward the purchase of his own dream.

He felt like a selfish clod.

"Katy, I—"

"This is lovely. It's a fine bit of property."

Galen tried to see it through her eyes, which was when the first doubts crept in. It was boggy—probably flooded after a rain. He might have waited and found a better place, but the way the town was building up, good acreage was in demand. This piece had come on the market, and the price had been within his range.

Had he made a mistake? If he'd been a little more patient, a little less distracted, could he have done better?

He wanted to blame Katy. Ever since he'd kissed her, held her, he'd felt this crazy mixture of lust and tenderness that got in the way of his concentration. But it wasn't Katy's fault. He'd always been prone to impulsiveness. He liked to think of it as decisiveness, following his instincts, but lately, he wasn't sure what to think.

"Well, it's mine now, for better or worse. I've staked everything I own on it. I've put the *Queen* on the market and borrowed the rest." He didn't know why he was telling her all this. He never tipped his hand. Not even Brand knew the details of his finances.

He managed a sickly grin. "So . . . if you've got any spare shamrocks stashed away, I could use a run of good luck."

She was deep. Deeper than any river, he decided. It had to be the way she listened without interrupting, without passing judgment, that made him want to bare his soul to her, to share his deepest dreams.

They stood there for several minutes longer, watching the river traffic. Watching a muskrat emerge from the water, climb up on a cypress knee, take his bearings, and slide soundlessly back into the river.

Katy thought about all he'd told her. She was almost sure he hadn't intended revealing quite so much. He wasn't a man to share his dreams, much less to share his doubts. She could have told him she was earning a fortune and would soon be able to start repaying him, but she knew how he would react. A man had his pride, after all. Taking money from a woman, even in payment for a debt, would not come easy to a man like Galen McBride.

"It's getting late," she murmured.

"I'd better get you back, but first, if you can spare a few more minutes, I'll show you my two houses."

"Two of them. Fancy that." She deliberately sounded a teasing note to hide what was in her heart.

The houses weren't much by Elizabeth City standards. By Skerrie Head standards, they were fine, indeed. One of them had once been painted yellow. There was an enormous magnolia tree and a tangle of roses falling over a broken fence. Before her imagination could take hold and start building one more dream, she turned away and said something about getting back for the second sitting for dinner.

"I've kept you too long. Sorry—they're not worth seeing, I just thought as long as you were out here . . ."

The houses were worth seeing. It was just that she

couldn't afford to let herself be distracted, and looking at houses with Galen McKnight was a major distraction.

"They're lovely, it's only that I don't like leaving Tara alone too long."

"I understand." He handed her back up into the gig, and Katy told herself it was only her imagination that made her think his hand lingered on her arm a moment longer than necessary. Or that his eyes lingered on her face just a beat of the heart too long.

If he'd never kissed her, she wouldn't be feeling such things, but he had. And she wanted him to do it again, and it probably showed on her face, in her eyes.

Looking everywhere but at the man beside her, she tugged at a button on her sleeve, slipped it through the loop and then back again.

Ignoring her as if she weren't even there, he clucked up the mare, and they wheeled around on the weed-choked riverbank and headed back toward town.

"Nice sunset," he observed after several minutes had passed in silence.

"Indeed it is."

After a while he said, "I hear you're thinking of singing for the men."

"No such thing. That is, I was asked, but I declined." She stole a sidelong look at him and caught his grin.

"You declined, hmm? Now, why doesn't that surprise me?"

"Well, as to that, I can't say."

"No, I don't suppose you can, but, Katy, half your audience is male anyway. At least the whole back row. What difference would it make to move to a larger room with a larger stage?"

She had noticed a few gentlemen accompanying their wives for the early evening entertainment. To keep from being nervous, she'd put it from her mind. "How did you know? You weren't there."

"There aren't too many secrets on the waterfront, Katy. Your friend Mr. Bynum was saying just the other day that if it hadn't been for your cat, Bellfort would never have heard you sing, and if it hadn't been for those two boys, you'd never have found the cat. So I guess you owe your fame and success to Heather."

"Malarkey."

"Malarkey? I thought her name was Heather."

"No, I meant malarkey to my fame and success. Well . . . not my success, because I'm earning prodigious sums of money, but never fame."

"Prodigious sums, hmm," he said, and she cut him a quick glance to see if he was making fun of her.

When they came to Poindexter Creek Bridge, she began gathering up her purse and her sewing basket. Why couldn't he have stayed away until she'd taught her heart to behave in his presence? Given a few more weeks she might have forgotten the way his hands looked on the reins, so strong and square and capable. The way that tiny little scar deepened at one end of his mouth when he smiled. The way sometimes he would touch her and his eyes would change color, going dark as night for no reason at all.

He drove her right to the edge of the wharf and helped her down from the high seat. She tugged at the flat brim of her hat and then brushed a wrinkle from her skirt, all the while trying to think of something clever to say to keep him there for a little longer.

Just until she could think of some way to keep him forever.

"Give my regards to Tara. Tell her she might want to show off her card tricks to Bellfort's customers, I'm sure they'd be fascinated."

His voice was so droll, she had to look a second time to be sure he was teasing. "There's the devil in you, sir, and I'll do no such."

He took her hand and lifted it to his lips. If the world

had come to a blazing end at that moment, Katy was certain she wouldn't have noticed.

"Katy, Katy, wake up," someone hissed in her dream.

Katy swatted the dream away.

"You have to wake up! Katy, someone is getting murdered."

"Oh, Tara, not now . . . can it wait until morning?"

"Please, oh, please—it's awful! You have to do something!"

Knowing there would be no more sleep until the child unburdened herself, Katy sat up and shoved her braid over her shoulder. "All right, what do you think you saw this time? Another explosion? A gunshot? Lovey, automobiles make all sorts of horrid sounds. What you heard was probably—"

"No, Katy—listen to me, I didn't hear anything, I saw it, and it was real. His eyes were popping out, and his mouth was open, and then his back bent out and he was falling—it was awful!"

"To be sure, it must have been, but even the worst dreams don't last once the sun comes up. It must be almost—"

Tara grabbed her by the shoulders and shook her. She looked ready to burst into tears. "Don't go back to sleep, Katy, please. Would you please go get Captain Galen? He'll know what to do."

"Be sensible. We're not on the *Queen* now. Go back to sleep, and I promise I'll go see Galen tomorrow and tell him—"

Tara was crying noisily, clutching handsful of Katy's nightgown. "You have to do something," she wailed. "He can't breathe. He's right outside now, near the foot of the gangplank. Please!"

"All right, lovey, stop crying, Katy will take care of it."

Reluctantly, Katy got out of bed and reached for her wrapper. *Something* was happening—or had happened. Or

soon would happen. Certainly not a murder, but she knew
well enough that neither of them would sleep until she'd
gone and looked and come back and told Tara that all was
peaceful.

She left the child huddled fearfully in the middle of the
bed, her red-rimmed eyes still fearful. "Promise you'll call
someone?"

Katy promised. "If I see anything at all troublesome, I'll
send the watchman to wake up Captain Jack."

"What if the watchman's asleep?"

"Then I'll wake him up. Now, hush and let me go."

So that I can get back and claim a few more hours of
sleep before I have to get up and go to work, Katy added
silently. Not that she'd be able to sleep. Neither of them
would sleep, even if there was nothing at all to see. Tara's
bad dreams—or seeings, or whatever they were—even when
they were entirely without foundation, were disturbing.

There was no sign of the *Belle*'s night watchman, which
was hardly surprising. Nothing ever happened once the gamblers went home to gloat over their winnings or explain
their losses. There was nothing to guard against.

The town clock struck four. The last echo faded away,
and then all was quiet. Nevertheless, Katy tiptoed across
the dew-wet deck and leaned against the rail. The only light
came from a few lanterns left burning outside one of the
warehouses, and the lights from the freight depot. It took
several moments for her eyes to adjust. And then, in the time
it took to draw in a strangled breath, she saw him.

He was standing near the edge of the wharf, about fifty
feet away, holding something in his hands. She couldn't
see what it was. A bit of string, perhaps. Light from the
warehouse lantern shone on the side of his face. She stared
hard, hard enough to know she had never seen him before.

For endless moments, they gazed at one another. He
looked as surprised as she was. She started to call out, to
ask if anything was wrong, but thought better of it. At least

he was alive. He wasn't being murdered. He didn't look as if he'd been injured.

And then he was gone. Just like that, he disappeared. She thought she caught a glimmer of movement between the warehouses, but it could have been a dog. Or a shadow.

For the first time since she'd left Ireland in a cool, foggy drizzle, Katy felt cold clean through to her bones.

Chapter Seventeen

༄

Tara was sound asleep. It wasn't the first time she'd roused the household with a nightmare she mistook as a seeing, and then, once she had everyone all upset and rushing around to prove it was all a dream, fell asleep again. It was as if, in the telling, she had discharged her responsibility.

Perhaps she had. After living with Tara's gift all these years, Katy was no closer to understanding it.

Lying in her own bed, she thought about what had happened. She probably should tell someone, but what to tell? That Tara had dreamed she saw someone being murdered, and there was a man standing outside on the wharf?

But he was alive, not murdered. There'd been no sign of a body.

Katy thought of the cholera that had turned out to be food poisoning. She thought about the explosion that had turned out to be a celebration. Likely, there had been another fight on the docks. Such things happened. Men drank; men fought. Tomorrow they would nurse their battle wounds together, and tomorrow night they'd likely drink together and fight together again.

It was a bleary-eyed Katy who set off for work the next morning. Tara, with never a word about what had happened, was helping Peggy spread the beds, having already devoured an enormous breakfast of fried fish, fried potatoes, and preserved figs.

Some of Katy's tiredness lifted, however, when Mrs. Baggot allowed her to help select pattern pieces for a morning dress for one of her best clients. They decided on a straight skirt with all the fullness in the back, a plain band collar, and leg o'mutton sleeves, with gold buttons and three rows of gold piping. The rich brown brocade needed no further embellishment.

Jack Bellfort met her that evening after work, having had business in town. He was driving the Duryea. There were several steam-powered automobiles in town, but Jack's was the only gasoline machine. Katy thought he rather enjoyed the distinction, from the grin on his face when people scurried out of the way and then stared until he was out of sight.

She was coming to know him fairly well.

Talk was impossible over the noise. While he stopped in at Mr. Robinson's General Store, she thought about whether or not to confide in him. In the end, she decided she would sleep better if she told someone. She was as bad as Tara, passing on the responsibility, but he was in a far better position to know how to deal with it.

So she told him about the nightmare Tara had had the night before, that was so real she'd had to get out of bed and go up on deck to assure the child that no one had been murdered. She even managed to laugh in the telling of it.

"Murdered?" he repeated, standing there with a crank in one hand, a pair of driving goggles in the other.

Katy shrugged. "It might have been all the salty ham and sweet potato biscuits she ate for supper. And pickles. A body can't sleep easily on a supper that heavy."

"Hmmm," he said. He fitted the crank in place, and Katy got herself in again, flinching at the roar of the engine when the thing caught up on the fifth try.

Well. She'd done her duty. There was some satisfaction in that. They drove the rest of the way with no further comment. When he shut off his popping and snorting contraption, she climbed down and thanked him for the ride.

"You're most welcome. And Katy—about this business with Tara—don't mention it to anyone else, all right? Not that there's anything to it. If there'd been a murder last night, believe me, the news would be all over town this morning. All the same, gamblers are a superstitious lot, and I'd as soon not give them anything to fret over. God knows there's been trouble enough without that."

Katy wanted to ask, what trouble? She decided she was better off not knowing. None of it concerned her, anyway.

Two evenings later, Galen came to hear her sing.

Jack Bellfort met him coming on board. "What's the matter, McKnight, not enough going on aboard the *Queen* to keep you busy? I heard you'd put the old lady up for sale."

"News travels."

"Then it's true? I'd be interested in hearing Aster's reaction."

"I'm surprised you didn't hear it all the way over here."

Jack pursed his lips. "Like that, huh? Is she going to take it off your hands?"

Ignoring the question, Galen switched topics. "I understand Miss O'Sullivan will be performing for a larger audience tonight."

Jack looked amused. "You know damned well where she'll be singing. If you'd like to stay for the concert, you're more than welcome. And, McKnight—rest assured Katy will come to no harm while she's under my protection."

"I believe I'd rephrase that, if I were you, Bellfort."

"No need. I look after my people, McKnight. Katy no longer works for you."

Galen was well aware of that fact. If he didn't feel quite

the relief he'd expected to achieve in having the two of them off his hands, that was no one's business but his own.

When he would have paid his way, Bellfort waved him on through the doors. "Professional courtesy. I might drop over one night to take in your entertainment."

Galen shot him a sour look and took a seat as far away from the small stage as he could find. Already, men were leaving the tables to find a chair. Aboard the *Albermarle Belle,* one end of the grand salon had been set aside for entertainment, the rest of the area set up with tables that could be moved out for dancing. The hard-core gamblers were in another salon on the second deck.

Moments after he took his place, the lights were lowered. Three musicians stepped up onto the low platform, and then Katy came out. He could tell by the way she carried herself that she was tense. Even from here he could see the whiteness of her knuckles as she held her hands knotted before her.

He wanted to touch her, to draw the tension from her slight frame onto his own shoulders, as if such a thing were even possible. Swearing silently under his breath, he reminded himself that he was present only as a well-wisher. After all, he was her sponsor in a way. He was responsible for her being here.

Good luck, sweet Katy. You deserve it.

He'd walked off in the middle of another fight with Aster. Ever since he'd done her the courtesy of telling her he was selling his share of the *Queen,* she'd been hounding him to sign over his shares and allow her to pay it off with a portion of the profits over a period of years. She'd put up her usual full-volume argument. The louder she'd got, the quieter he'd grown. A man just naturally didn't like to argue with a woman, especially a termagant like Aster. Especially when she flat-out refused to listen to reason.

"You owe me that much, Galen McKnight! You can't expect me to go into business with a stranger!"

"Your father did."

"Leave my father out of this! And how could you do it to him? You love this boat! How can you turn it over to someone who'll run it into the ground?"

He'd refrained from mentioning that the one most likely to run her aground was Aster. To call her headstrong was like calling the river moist. "Aster, listen—in the first place, I care enough about the old tub not to want to see her sink. In the second place, I can't afford to take on any more paper. I'm mortgaged up to the hilt, as it is. In the third place, I'm not a gambler. Never have been; never wanted to be."

She'd scoured him from head to toe with a mocking look. "Of course not," she'd jeered. "That's why you take such pains to dress like a stodgy old businessman."

Painfully aware that his somewhat theatrical attire, fashioned after an infamous gambler from Nevada, stuck out like a sore thumb in the small, southeastern town, he'd said, "But then, that's what I really am at heart. A stodgy businessman. It's all I ever wanted to be."

And while it hadn't always been true, it was true enough now. He'd lost his taste for adventure the hard way. "Like any sensible man, I took advantage of a windfall and made the most of it while it suited my purposes."

She'd screeched some more, largely repetitive. Galen had walked out mid-screech and strolled down to the *Belle*. Earlier, when Ila had mentioned that Katy would be performing in the main salon tonight, he'd had no intention of coming to hear her. Even now he wasn't sure if he'd have come if Aster hadn't been after him for hours.

What he needed was Katy, singing one of her funny Irish ballads in that clear, lilting voice.

What he needed was a nightingale, not a fish crow.

Flexing his shoulders, he forced Aster and her demands from his mind and concentrated on the tableau before him.

Katy was wearing silk again. There were shadows under her eyes. Unless he was mistaken, she was wearing cosmetics, and that irked him, because this particular lily didn't need gilding. Certainly not in a room full of reckless young blades who might mistake a painted face for enticement.

What's more, that gown she was wearing was cut far too low. He could almost see the shadow of the valley between her breasts. And dammit, she had no business showing that much ankle! She was a singer, not some high-kicking showgirl.

But then the music struck up. Katy lifted her head and began to sing, and he allowed the spell of her voice to wash over him.

She was good, he had to admit it. No trills, frills, or flourishes. No flirtatious moves. She sang—he'd heard her say it once—for the joy of it. It showed. After a lengthy ballad about a sailor who went down off Holland, leaving a brokenhearted lass behind, one of the cigar girls leaning against the far wall wiped a tear from her eye. One or two gentlemen cleared their throats, and one even flourished a handkerchief.

She sang a number he'd never heard before, partly in Gaelic, partly in English. The words meant nothing, it was the quality of her voice that got to him. Clear, sweet, and true. Like Katy herself.

Galen never moved a muscle. Aster and her demands were forgotten as the music wove its spell around him, transporting him to another time, another place. God knows he'd never been so miserable in all his life as he'd been during those interminable weeks he'd spent in a cold, damp fishing camp on Ireland's rugged northwest coast.

And yet, it had brought him Katy. And Tara. And in his weaker moments, which seemed to come more and more often lately, he was forced to admit that his life would have been far poorer without them.

* * *

Katy didn't know quite when the muscles in her throat began to ease. Somewhere between "An Bhruinnlin Bheashach" and "Rocking the Cradle."

Somewhere between looking out into a sea of strange masculine faces and focusing on one familiar face.

He'd come to hear her sing, to wish her well. She almost wished he hadn't. The sooner she got over her foolishness, the sooner she could get on with her future. With all the luck in the world, it wasn't going to be easy. She didn't know why she hadn't realized it before, but then, a dream never seemed so real as when it was viewed from a great distance. It was only as it grew near that the flaws and cracks and hidden hazards began to show.

After forty-five minutes, she bowed to indicate the end of the program. There were a few calls for more, but she smiled, touched her throat, and shook her head. The applause was long and enthusiastic, despite the fact that a few men had slipped away to return to the tables. Galen was still here. She told herself good manners made him stay till the end, but when the musicians tucked their instruments under their arms and she turned to follow them, he suddenly appeared at the edge of the stage.

"Katy, do you have a moment?"

Her knees threatened to buckle, not entirely from exhaustion. If he'd left without speaking to her, she'd have been crushed. Now that he'd spoken, she felt . . . breathless. "Aye, a moment. I doubt I'm much good for talking, though, for my throat's parched."

"We'll find something to drink and a quiet place, then. I only wanted to tell you—well, two things, actually, but they can wait for tea." He hailed a passing waiter and asked for a pot of tea and two cups. Bellfort was watching from across the room, the gleam in his eyes visible even from here. Galen glared at him. Jack nodded, crossed his arms, and watched until the waiter brought the tea, and then turned away.

Katy said, "I know a place. It'll be quiet there. I could use a bit of quiet." There was tension in her voice now, and a huskiness that hadn't been there when she was singing.

Galen, carrying the tray, followed her up to the hurricane deck. He'd seen her up there a number of times, watched her at her sewing, with her glasses perched on her nose. Sometimes she brought a book and read. Once she'd obviously washed her hair, for it was hanging down her back, drying tendrils blowing in the light, warm breeze.

He'd seen her glance occasionally toward the *Queen*. Had she seen him looking back? Did she realize he was aware of almost every move she made? If he didn't see her, there was always someone to keep him informed.

"Saw Miss Katy today. Her'n the girl set out toward town."

"My, Miss Katy's looking fine and fit. That cat of theirs got loose today and they was a-chasing it all over the docks."

He couldn't bring himself to tell them that he wasn't interested. They obviously knew he was, else why the constant litany of Katy did this, and Katy said that?

He wondered if she felt as foolish as he did, sneaking looks at a woman who was sneaking looks back at him, as if they were two kids, afraid to speak what was on their minds.

"No milk. Sorry. I forgot." He grumbled the apology.

"Never mine, it's wet and strong, and that's what I'm needing."

There was only the one chair. Katy took that and poured. Galen accepted his cup, stepping back to lean against the railing. Silently, they sipped tea and looked anywhere but at each other. Katy studied the tips of her shoes in the gleam of lantern light. Galen gazed out across the river at the wavering lights reflected there. River traffic, he'd been told, had fallen off considerably after the railroad had come through, but there was still more than enough to keep a small town going.

More than enough to keep him building for years to come.

He cleared his throat. "I enjoyed your concert, Katy. I was afraid you'd be nervous, but I might have known better. You're a seasoned trooper by now."

She eyed him over her cup as if she didn't know if that was a compliment or not. Come to think of it, he wasn't entirely certain himself.

And then it was her turn to break the awkward silence. "Have you found a buyer for the *Queen* yet?"

Galen told himself it was no more than a polite inquiry. He'd like to think it was more than that, but then, she had her own dreams to follow. "Matter of fact, Aster mentioned being interested." Which had to be the understatement of the year.

"Will you sell it to her?"

It wasn't what he'd come here to talk about. "It depends," he said enigmatically.

She nodded. "I understand she wants to do cruises."

"Now where did you hear that?" he asked, half amused, half irritated. There were few secrets in a small town.

She shrugged, but didn't reply. So he changed the subject. "How's Tara? She doesn't come to visit as much as she used to."

"You asked her not to."

He had. He regretted it.

"She never means to cause trouble, to be sure, but somehow, trouble has a way of following her. I thought it would be better if I kept her close."

"Ila was asking after her this morning. Willy's got his boys passing out all the leftover food every day. Ice is no problem now that I've installed a couple more ice boxes, but he claims the waterfront community expects it."

"Oh, my." She lifted a pair of stricken eyes, all set to apologize again when he told her it was all right, not to worry, because he'd just as soon not take any more chances.

It was her duty to worry. She started to worry about what

would happen to her waterfront friends once Aster took over. They'd go hungry, most likely. Unless Katy could persuade Jack to take over.

"Katy? Why the frown? Nobody's going to starve. One way or another, they'll all be taken care of, I promise you."

It was that rough note of tenderness that did her in. She could no more help turning to him than a sunflower could help turning toward the sun. "I promised I'd not mention it, but . . . have you heard of any unusual trouble on the dock lately?"

He frowned. "Unusual? In what way?"

"Oh, well . . . as to that, I couldn't say. Fights, perhaps. Robbings. That sort of thing."

"Robbings? None recently. There was a spot of trouble last month, but it seems to have cleared itself up. One of my dealers—you remember Charlie? It seems he and Buck were tipping off a friend outside whenever there was a big winner."

She didn't know Buck well, but Charlie? Sweet, pudgy Charlie with his slicked-down hair standing up like a rooster tail in the back? "Saints preserve us, they never," Katy exclaimed.

"Afraid so. Buck's idea. Charlie said he only wanted a stake so he could take Sal back to Ohio and buy into her uncle's hardware business."

"Oh, poor Charlie. I hope no one was hurt." Katy knew good and well it wasn't Charlie's round face she'd seen on the wharf that night, nor Buck's, either.

"Being coshed in the head and robbed is no picnic. We haven't rounded up the others yet, but Buck and Charlie will serve time, which means Charlie won't be taking Sal to Ohio to have her baby. Ila's already making arrangements for her."

Katy murmured something vaguely sympathetic, but her mind was busy elsewhere. "It wasn't Charlie I saw. Are you sure there's been nothing else?" And without waiting for a reply, she shook her head. "No, of course not. It was only a dream, I know that."

Galen waited. When she went on staring past him that way, her eyes unfocused, he said, "What was only a dream, Katy?"

"Nothing. You know how Tara is. Let her dream of rain and she'll be building an ark."

"Tell me about Tara's dream."

"Now, why should I do that? I told you it was nothing. A nightmare. Didn't I go up on deck myself and look to see? There was only a man standing there, not a sign of any trouble. We looked at one another, and I do believe he even nodded. And that was that. When I went back down, Tara was already asleep again, so it can't have been all that dreadful."

Galen didn't know whether to swear, to shake the truth from her, or to bundle her up and get her out of town. Chances were she was right, and there'd been nothing at all out of line, but what if there was? What if she'd seen something . . . or someone . . . she had no business seeing? Just because Buck and Charlie were in jail, that didn't mean the waterfront had been swept clean of all crime. There were at least two more men involved, and until they'd been captured, he didn't want Katy anywhere around.

She slapped her cup back into its saucer and stood. "If you're fixing to read me a lecture, I'll thank you to keep it to yourself. I knew I shouldn't have said anything. I promised Captain Bellfort I'd not mention it."

"You promised *what*? What does Bellfort have to do with this?"

"There now, you're going all red in the face."

"I'm no such thing. Katy, what did you tell Bellfort? Why did he tell you not to say anything?"

"Because—well, how would I know that?"

He took a tight turn around the small enclosure, coming

to a halt before her. "Listen, Katy—I want you to promise me something, will you do that?"

It was an indication of his intensity—or her need—that she nodded.

"All right now, I want you to promise me you won't go wandering out alone. No more chasing that cat up and down the wharf, all right?"

"Oh, but you can't think—"

"Promise me. I'll check around and find out if there's been any more trouble lately. I haven't heard of any since Buck and Charlie were picked up for questioning, but that doesn't mean it's entirely safe."

"You made fun of Tara's seeing."

"No, I didn't—well, perhaps I did. Oh, hell, Katy, I don't know what to think. Maybe she's a bit more perceptive than most, but as to her dreams? No, I don't buy it."

"Then why must I be on guard?"

"Because—" He raked a hand through his hair. "Because the waterfront's no place for a decent woman after dark. You need a place in town. You need a—"

"A husband? No thank you. I've managed quite well for twenty-two years without one. Tara and I will be just fine, and I thank you for your concern."

She watched his brows come together, saw the lines on either side of his mouth deepen. "Then tell me this. Why did you bother to say anything at all?"

When she didn't reply, he began to shake his head slowly from side to side. "Katy, Katy. Don't let that foolish streak of independence lead you into trouble."

She wanted to say, then don't look at me the way you're doing. Don't speak to me with caring in your voice, for I'm not near as strong as I want to be. As I need to be.

If he'd opened his arms then, she would have fallen into them. She suspected he knew it, too. But he only cupped her face in his hands and stared down at her for the longest moment.

And then he left her there. She waited until he came out below and watched him set out down the wharf. When he swung onto the *Queen*'s gangplank, she was still standing there, too tired to resist the truth any longer.

Chapter Eighteen

By the first day of school, Tara was almost sick with excitement. She had spent hours before the mirror, trying on first one new dress and then another. Tying her hair back with ribbons, braiding it, and finally tugging on the wild corkscrew curls with both hands. "Why do I have to be so curly?" she wailed. "And red! It's such an ugly color!"

"That it's not, it's a queen's color. It's the color of rubies, of—of—"

"It's the color of winter turnips. Why couldn't it be yellow? And, Katy, I'm getting bosoms."

"That you're not! Tara O'Sullivan, don't you dare go and sprout bosoms after I've made you four new dresses."

After a few tearful giggles and a last-minute search for her new pencil box, they set off to school together. It was a few blocks out of the way, which meant setting out a bit early, but it was a fine morning, and Katy didn't mind at all.

She was keeping her fingers crossed that all would go well. Thanks to years of reading the Encyclopaedia Britannica, Tara's education was far advanced in many areas, but when it came to mathematical skills, she lagged behind.

"I already have three friends in the fifth grade."

Katy hoped it was true. She remembered from her own youth that girls on the edge of young womanhood could be somewhat unpredictable in their loyalties. Not that she'd had time at that age to worry about such things, for her mother had died the year she'd turned twelve, and after that, there were Da and Tara to look after. She'd had no time for girlish things.

Now that the summer season was nearing an end, most of Mrs. Baggot's customers had returned from the seashore, ready to begin selecting their new fall wardrobes. Katy was called on to help out on the floor. She was excited, but determined not to show it.

"Yes, Miss Stevens, the blue is a perfect match," she agreed serenely. "Mrs. Baggot has a wonderful eye for color."

"No, Mrs. Baggot, I don't mind at all staying to finish the cuffs."

A week passed, and while she was still snubbed by the three seamstresses, who accused her of setting herself above her station—whatever that was—Katy found herself working alongside Mrs. Baggot more and more often, fitting pattern pieces to the dress forms, adjusting dress forms when one of their clients added or lost a few pounds. Even sorting the mail when it came in.

She was learning how to run a business. She couldn't have been happier, and told herself so at least once a day.

It was Tara who noticed the man watching her in the middle of the second week of school. They walked together every morning, admiring late-blooming flowers, kicking leaves from the sidewalk. Tara had found a four-leaf clover the day before, which wasn't at all the same as a shamrock, although here it apparently meant the same thing.

"I miss home, Katy," she confided. "I miss all the green. Grass isn't as pretty here. And I miss Tammy Clancy and Old Mollie's dog, and—and everything."

They walked and talked about home, and Katy was trying to tease her into looking forward to Halloween when

Tara glanced over her shoulder and then ducked her head. "He's there again," she whispered.

"Who's where again?"

"That man. Remember, I told you a few days ago I saw him looking at you? I don't think he's very nice, Katy. In fact, I'm sure he's got bad things inside him." Her eyes started to take on that glazed, faraway look, and Katy huffed a sharp breath.

"Stop it. Just stop it this minute, Tara O'Sullivan. I thought we'd decided that the sight doesn't work on this side of the ocean. Or perhaps you're growing out of it."

"But, Katy, I saw—"

"No. You saw a man, that's all. The town's full of men."

"But he looked at you."

"Sure, and is that surprising? I've been told I'm not quite the homeliest creature of all, in spite of being old as the hills." Katy made a comical face, and Tara giggled, and the moment was forgotten as they crossed the bridge and turned off onto the footpath leading to the schoolhouse.

All the same, at odd moments during the day Katy caught herself wondering who the man could be. He could be someone who had come to hear her sing, or perhaps even a friend of Mr. Bynum or the other old men on the wharf, who was looking for a handout.

Or the man she'd seen that night on the dock, standing there with something—a bit of string, perhaps—held in both hands.

In spite of the late-summer warmth, gooseflesh puckered the skin on her arms, and she shivered.

Two days later she was waiting on the corner of Main and Poindexter for the way to clear after a wagon loaded with sweet potatoes had broken a wheel and overturned just as morning traffic was at its busiest. Carts, buggies, and a few steam-powered automobiles were backed up several deep in all directions as the farmer's sons gathered up bushels of sweet potatoes and several men struggled to shove the cart off to one side.

Katy was running late. She stepped off the curb, and then stepped back again as traffic began to move. Tucking her purse under her arm, she waited impatiently, looking in both directions for an opening.

Suddenly, something jostled her from behind. The breath knocked from her lungs, she went sprawling into the street, purse flying in one direction, hat in another.

There were screams and curses as a huge iron-clad cart-wheel passed within inches of her left hand. The driver had swerved to avoid her, narrowly missing her fingers. Her poor purse had been crushed flat.

A dozen pairs of hands were there to lift her. Someone collected her ruined belongings. Everyone expressed shock and sympathy and outrage, and Katy tried to placate them all. "I'm all right," she managed to gasp. "Please—thank you, but I'm—oh, ouch. Oh, no . . . my poor hat."

She accepted her poor crushed straw, slapped it on top of her lopsided knot, and felt for her hatpin to anchor it. The pin was gone, the hat slid off again, but she was too busy trying to take in what had happened to notice. She murmured something about being clumsy—about tripping over her own feet, and tried to recall what had happened the instant before she fell.

Had something struck her between the shoulder blades, or had she only imagined it? Already her knees and elbows were beginning to sting. She couldn't seem to stop shaking. Someone mentioned shock, and someone else placed a man's coat around her shoulders.

"Dagnabbed motor cars," a red-faced gentleman muttered. "Ought to be a law against 'em."

"It was the mule that done it, not no steam automobile. Ma'am, are you sure nothing ain't broke?"

"Give the lady some air, if you please. Stand back, stand back." It was one of the regulars from the *Queen,* the one called Old Judge Henry. She fought the urge to lean on a familiar figure.

Someone held a parasol over her, although the sun had barely cleared the horizon. A plump matron in lavender taffeta shoved a bottle of smelling salts under her nose, making her eyes water.

"Please—thank you all, but I'm late for work." She clutched her ruined hat in one hand, her ruined purse in the other, her eyes a bit wild as she looked for an opening in the crowd.

"—lie down a spell—"

"—take you home, ma'am—"

"—ought to be a law, dagnabbit!"

Katy wanted to break through and run, to run until she could breathe freely again. She felt as if she were being smothered by kindness. She would give her soul to feel the cool damp wind off Skerrie Head blowing in her face.

But she smiled and thanked everyone again, assuring them that nothing was broken, that she was only a wee bit shaken. The crowd began to disperse. Traffic was once more trundling past. Mules pulling farm carts and freight wagons. Traps and buggies drawn by sleek horses.

"Are you sure?" asked the judge. "You look pale to me."

I am pale. I've always been pale. Is there a law against being pale?

She wanted to shove everyone out of the way so she could breathe. Instead, she smiled and said firmly, "Thank you all so very much. I'm quite all right now, truly I am." She kept on smiling, daring them to argue.

No one argued, but two kind gentlemen and the woman in lavender insisted on seeing her to Mrs. Baggot's establishment. It was easier to go along than to protest.

They left her at the door. Mrs. Baggot took one look at her and led her into the cluttered closet she called an office. "There, look at you now, if you're not a mess."

Katy took it in the sense it had been offered. As concern.

She accepted a cup of tea, was told that until she felt steadier on her pins, she could stay in here and address envelopes, and when she finished that, she could look through the new *Delineator* and see if they would need to order new fall patterns, or if the old ones could be adapted.

It was not until she finished her tea and reached for the pattern catalog that she discovered her glasses had been crushed. It was the crowning blow. Her gloves were ruined, her stockings laddered, there were smudges on the front of her skirt, and now this. Her lovely new spectacles. How in the world was she going to be able to work when she couldn't see?

For the next few hours, she managed the same way she had managed ever since her eyes had begun going bad. By turning up the lamp and stretching her arms to their full length. Long before noon she had developed a pounding headache, not to mention aches in nearly every other portion of her body.

The woman in the lavender taffeta who had been so kind to her had warned her that the soreness and stiffness would come later. She'd been right. It was all Katy could do to hold back the tears. She wanted to cry because everyone had been so kind, and her a stranger, not yet even a citizen.

And because she was very much afraid that she'd been pushed from behind just as that freight cart had come rumbling past in front of her.

It was Tara who told Galen about the accident. Katy had wanted to. Had wanted to hurl herself into his arms and cry out her pain and fears, and let someone stronger and wiser than she deal with them, which was the very reason she hadn't mentioned it to anyone but Tara. And Peggy, of course, when she'd had to explain the sorry state of her clothing, not to mention various scrapes and bruises.

It was Peggy who had told Jack, and evidently everyone else within five city blocks. By the time Galen came storming aboard the *Belle,* demanding to see her, Katy was so stiff she could barely hobble. She'd been sent home early from work and told not to bother to come in again until she was feeling better, which was both a boon and a worry. What if Mrs. Baggot discovered she could get along quite well without her?

"Why is it I seem to take three steps back for every step I take forward?" Peggy was sponging the stains from her skirt when Galen rapped on the door and called out, asking if she was decent.

"No, I'm not," she snapped just as Peggy invited him inside.

Katy was sitting in the easy chair Jack had brought down to her room, with a stack of books from the library beside her, also provided by Jack, who knew her reading tastes by now.

He'd forgotten, though, that she could no longer see to read without straining, and as she'd already strained every muscle in her body, it was hardly worth the effort.

"You look awful," Galen announced. He stopped just inside the door, hat in hand, feet braced apart, and gawked at her.

"How sweet of you to notice."

"Sarcasm? Katy, you're beginning to sound like Aster."

"If you're done paying me compliments, you may leave now. I'm busy, as you can plainly see."

"Peggy, would you go see if you can find us a pot of hot, strong tea? Steer it by the bar on the way back and see if you can stiffen it up a bit."

The maid flashed her molars in a grin. "Yes sir, Captain McKnight." She took off with a swish of petticoats, her mahogany face alight with amusement.

Katy didn't see anything at all amusing.

Galen dragged up a stool and sat down without waiting for an invitation. He took her hand, turned it over, and winced at the abrasions near her wrist. "Ouch. This town hasn't exactly been kind to you, has it? First a face full of cat scratches, now this."

Katy had spent the whole afternoon shoring up her defenses. Telling herself she wasn't hurt, that she wasn't frightened—that no one had intentionally jostled her, causing her to fall.

Without even trying, Galen sent every stone in her pitifully inadequate fort a-tumbling. "I suppose Tara told you," she said sullenly, wishing she didn't look quite so awful. "So now you've come to gloat."

"I never gloat. Poor sportsmanship."

"Then what are you doing here?"

"I came to say good-bye."

The last stone rolled silently away, leaving her utterly defenseless. To her everlasting shame, tears seeped into her eyes. If there was one thing she hated even more than she hated being seasick, it was letting anyone see her cry. She wasn't weak, she truly was not.

"Katy? Can't you even wish me farewell?"

"Then you've sold the *Queen*? I'm happy for you, but what about your shipyard?"

Reaching out, he tucked his fist under her chin, lifting her face to stare at her red-rimmed eyes. "Don't look at me," she hissed.

At that moment, Galen wondered which of them was hurting most. It killed him to see her like this. He wanted nothing so much as to sweep her up in his arms and take her with him, but it would only complicate an already complicated affair.

He was halfway in love with a woman far too young for him. A woman who had come five thousand miles following a dream. A woman, damn her, who was far too stubborn to understand why it wasn't possible.

Women—young women—respectable young women, especially those without a backer—simply didn't set themselves up in business. It wasn't done.

Yet he knew he would have helped her if he could. The trouble was, one dream was all he could afford to buy. His own dream made sense. Hers didn't, but he lacked the courage to tell her so when she was hurt and discouraged.

God, he wished he knew more about women. He'd known his share of them—more than his share. Known some intimately, some only casually, but with very few exceptions, he'd enjoyed them all.

But not a one of those women had been anything at all like Katy. He had yet to figure out how her mind worked. Right now, she was extremely fragile, juggling a prickly mixture of pride and determination, stubbornness and vulnerability. The slightest wrong move on his part could break her spirit, and he'd be damned before he could risk that.

"Katy, if there was any way I could get out of going, you know I wouldn't leave you at a time like this. I—"

Her eyes took on that glittery look he'd come to distrust. "A time like what? Saints preserve us, it's not like I lost both jobs and broke my neck besides. I tripped, is all. I've never been known for my grace and nimbleness."

Something inside him twisted painfully. *Keep your hands off her, McKnight. Just keep your bloody damned hands off her!*

"Right. You tripped and scraped your cheek raw, bruised both elbows, skinned both hands, and strained a shoulder. Other than that, there's nothing much wrong with you."

"How do you know all that?"

He could have told her that both Tara and Peggy had filled him in, but then she'd probably take their concern as some sort of betrayal. "I spoke to the doctor. Bellfort says your glasses were broken, but he's already ordered you a new pair. I would have done it, Katy, you know that."

He saw it coming. Saw the tears spill over. Watched as the tip of her nose turned bright red. At the sound of the first sob, he opened his arms, and she fell into them like a fledgling bird from a broken nest.

"I d-don't know why I'm crying," she sobbed.

"It's all right." He patted her shoulder, stroked her back, tried to think of a magic word that would make everything all right for her.

Had she considered the possibility that someone might have tried to kill her? There was no way of knowing, but ever since he'd heard about the incident the possibility had stuck in his mind. Torn between wanting to warn her and wanting to dismiss it from his own mind, he'd gone to the police with his suspicions, downplaying Tara's part in the affair. He'd talked to Bellfort. He'd even talked to Sal, who refused to say anything that might get Charlie into any more trouble than he already was.

The best he could do was wait and see what developed. And at the moment, he couldn't even be here to watch over her personally, not without breaking a promise and disappointing someone he loved very dearly.

So he'd sketched in his suspicions to Bellfort, who'd agreed that Katy would be guarded at all times, just in case it hadn't been an accident. When she was ready to perform again, he would personally vet the audience.

Knowing Katy, it wouldn't be long before she would insist on singing for her supper. She had a thing about being beholden to anyone for any reason. He had spoken to Inez Baggot. Her job there would be waiting for her whenever she felt like going back. It seemed that Katy had turned out to be far more valuable than expected.

The best he could hope for now was that she wouldn't insist on going back until she had her new spectacles, which would take at least a week. By then, Galen would be back in town.

He'd been on his way out when Bellfort had brought up the matter of the *Queen*. "I'm interested, if we can come to an agreement on the price. What are you asking?"

His mind still on Katy, Galen had mentioned a figure.

Bellfort had countered with a lower one. "We both know she's a tub. All show and no go."

"We'll talk about it when I get back if you're still interested." Galen's mind had been on more important matters. Still was.

Sniffles and a growing restlessness indicated that Katy had about used up all her tears. He managed to ease his handkerchief from his pocket and shove it into her hand, all without loosening his hold.

He could have held her this way forever. It was a good thing he was leaving town. This odd mixture of protectiveness and possessiveness, not to mention a healthy dose of lust, was beginning to get out of hand. "All right now?"

She sniffed and nodded, and stepped back from his arms. Reluctantly, he let her go. "Sorry," she whispered. "I've wet your shirt."

"It'll dry. Like I said, Katy, if I didn't have to go—"

"You don't have to explain."

"You see, she's old and not quite as clear-minded as she should be. I promised her I'd be there. She's just as apt to forget it herself as not, but I can't take that chance. If she takes it in her head to get her feelings hurt, it's hard to make her understand."

"Who is she? No, you don't have to tell me anything."

"Her name is Drucilla Merriweather. Everyone calls her Miss Drucy. She lives with her husband and staff at a place called Merriweather's Landing, about a day's sail from here."

"Sail?" Katy sniffed again, wiped again, and blinked her matted lashes at him. "But what will you sail?"

"Ferry boat. A small one. The facilities there can't handle anything much larger. Like I said, I'll be back by the end of the week. Meanwhile, if you need anything, Pierre or—"

"I won't. I'll be just fine. Tomorrow I'll be back at work. Mrs. Baggot promised to let me try my hand at adapting a

pattern, and if she likes it, then I can choose the fabric and
make one up. Did I tell you she's starting a line of ready-
mades this fall?" Her watery smile nearly broke his heart.
"So you see, I'm already on my way to success, and here
you said I couldn't do it."

"Don't say it," he warned.

I told you so, she mouthed silently, eyes sparkling with
mischief through the tears.

Taking both her hands in his, Galen tried to think of
some way to warn her not to set her hopes too high. If he
knew Inez Baggot, that lady wasn't going be too eager to
train her competition, no matter how it might look now.

"Don't rush into any agreements. And, Katy—plan on
taking a few more days off before you go back to work. If
you think you're stiff and sore now, just wait until tomorrow. I've been launched off enough horses to know that the
second day can be worse than the first, and there's pains
that wait a week to show up. Promise me?"

She refused to promise him anything. Instead, she smiled.
It occurred to him that when she looked at him the way she
was looking at him now, tear stains and all, whatever common sense he possessed went down the drain.

Maybe it was a good thing he was leaving. A little per-
spective might not be a bad thing. "I'll be leaving about
ten, so if you need anything before then—or if Tara has
any more wild dreams . . ."

He squeezed her hands, muttered an apology when she
winced, and left before he could do any more damage. If
she'd called him back—if she'd spoken another word, he
might have revised his plans. When months ago in one of
her more lucid moments, Miss Drucy had invited him to
her birthday party, he'd accepted gladly. He'd had no way
of knowing at the time that Katy was going to burst into
his life, complicating it beyond all comprehension.

He tried to tell himself that it was nothing more than a
simple accident. Katy wasn't used to city traffic. A kid had

a dream about seeing a man being murdered. Next, she imagined a man staring at Katy. What man in his right mind wouldn't? Tara was hardly the world's most reliable witness, especially as she'd been sound asleep when she claimed the murder had taken place.

All things considered, Galen told himself it wasn't a bad idea to get away for a few days. He needed a clear head, and with Katy screwing up his concentration, that was all but impossible. He wasn't getting enough sleep. He'd lost his appetite. He was snapping heads off right and left, and all he had to do was think about her to grow instantly, embarrassingly aroused.

The news was all over the waterfront even before the police arrived. By the time the wharf was swarming with vagrants, stray dogs, and uniformed men, everyone this side of Road Street knew that a body had washed up on the other side of the lumber mill with a mark that could have been made by a rope or a wire on the front of his neck. According to the coroner, he'd been dead before he'd ever hit the water.

Galen wasn't going anywhere. Not yet. And definitely not alone.

Chapter Nineteen

~

He sent word to the Merriweathers by Pam, the ferryman, that he would be a day or two late. That something had come up that demanded his personal attention. As fond as he was of the elderly couple who had taken him in when he'd come south in search of his brother, Galen was discovering that his priorities had shifted rather drastically.

Katy hadn't wanted to cooperate. The fact that Bellfort wanted something from him had made it easier for the two men to work together. Between them they persuaded Katy that it was in Tara's best interest to move back aboard the *Queen* until this business could be cleared up. Playing on her greatest weakness, he had suggested that as school hours were shorter than Katy's workday, Tara might need more supervision than Bellfort's staff could provide. "I'm sure they'd do their best," Galen said, "but it's not like having Willy and Ila and Oscar keeping an eye on her."

"But—"

"Now, we don't know that all this is even connected—Tara's dream—your accident—and now a body turning up. But if it is, and if word gets out that Tara thought she saw someone . . ."

Katy's imagination had done the rest. Galen felt almost guilty. God knows, he didn't want to take advantage of her, but he needed her right where he could watch her every minute, day and night. The rest of his business could go to hell for all he cared, but if anyone tried to hurt Katy again—or Tara—Galen would personally deck him and haul his ass off to the county jail.

Aster had reacted predictably to the news that the O'Sullivans would be moving back aboard the *Queen*. When she'd lit into him, Galen hadn't even bothered to argue, he'd simply given her The Look. Part of his armed-and-dangerous act. He was amazed she'd even fallen for it, but she had.

With Aster momentarily silenced, he'd set Ila to readying their old room and gone to escort them back, which was when Katy dug in her heels and demanded to know why they couldn't stay where they were at night, and let Tara spend her days aboard the *Queen*.

After a long day, his patience was on a short fuse. "There's no point in arguing, it's all settled. Ila's even made your bed. Besides, it's not like I was asking you to move across town."

"Exactly. That's my point. Why move at all?"

"We went over all that," he said patiently. He hadn't wanted to remind her that there was a stiff in the county morgue that had yet to be identified, and that somewhere there was a murderer walking around on the loose. The whole town was buzzing over it. It wasn't the town's first mystery, nor would it be the last, but until it was solved, no one was going to rest easy.

Tara had to chase Heather and stuff her into the basket. Then, with Galen carrying the bags Peggy had packed, the trio set out. Several members of the *Belle*'s staff and crew lined up to see them off, already whispering among themselves. There were a few openly curious looks, but no one asked any questions.

Not much doubt about what the chief topic of conversation would be over the dinner table that night. Anyone would think the two of them were suspects and he was taking them into custody.

As of course he was. Protective custody.

From the corner of his eye he saw Bellfort up on his private balcony, watching silently as they set off down the wharf. They'd never got around to agreeing on a price for the *Queen*, but it could wait. Another few days wasn't going to make or break him.

Katy was moving stiffly, as if she hurt all over. If he thought she'd allow it he would have carried her all the way in his arms, but knowing that prickly pride of hers, he didn't even offer. Besides, he didn't want her feeling any more helpless and vulnerable than necessary.

Tara didn't even try to conceal her excitement. There was a certain I-told-you-so smugness in her expression as she skipped along beside them, swinging a protesting Heather in the covered basket.

"Hold her still, you're making her seasick," Katy warned.

Galen said, "Remind me to have one of the boys fill a dirt box for you, I don't want you going off alone."

"Oh, good. I didn't bring her old one, it smells bad." Then, without even batting an eye, Tara dropped her bombshell. "When you two are married, we won't need dirt boxes, we'll have a yard. And then we won't have to keep moving around."

Katy stopped dead in her tracks and stared, aghast, her face so pale the bruise on her cheek resembled a smear of coal dust. Galen was only marginally better at hiding his own reaction.

With highly suspect innocence, Tara looked from one to the other. "But—but, Katy, I saw—"

Color flooding her face, Katy said harshly, "Tara, I've had enough of your foolishness, and so has Captain McKnight!"

Galen didn't know what to say and so he said nothing. The most important thing now was to get them below, out of sight, until he could figure out just where the greatest risk lay and how to deal with it.

Looking somewhat less assured, Tara shrugged. "All I meant was that once we're all married we can live in a house with a dog and a fence and neighbors, and then we won't have to worry about people getting strangled and thrown overboard."

Galen went cold. So far as he knew, the details of the murder hadn't yet been released. As the body had been fished from the river, it was generally assumed that he'd drowned. How could she possibly have known that the poor devil had been garroted first?

She was only guessing. She had to be, otherwise . . .

"Come along, Tara, your sister's tired. Ila has your room all ready, and Oscar's standing by to walk you to school in the morning."

"Oh, good. He tells the best stories. He said if I tell him how I can see cards without even looking, he'll tell me about the time he spent three days in jail when he was only nine years old. He said there was this great big rat that was—"

"Tara, that's enough," Katy said repressively. "I'm not entirely sure a gambling boat is the most wholesome atmosphere for an impressionable child," she said to Galen.

"You're right. Maybe a house with a yard and a fence and a dog would be better." He was teasing Tara, only it didn't quite come off that way.

"I never meant that at all," she whispered.

She was embarrassed. Oh, hell. "Katy, I was only joking, of course you didn't mean anything by it."

Another woman might have hinted at a commitment, but never Katy. If she had anything to say, she came right out and said it with no beating around the bush.

Which made it all the more surprising that he found himself dwelling on the notion long after he'd turned the pair of them over to Ila.

Ila started clucking like a broody hen reclaiming a couple of straying chicks. "Go on about your business, Galen, they'll come to no harm as long as there's breath left in this old carcass." She took the cat basket, scooped out the miserable, squalling animal, and managed to dodge sharp claws while she set her on the floor. While Galen hovered uncertainly in the doorway, she muttered words to the effect that what Katy needed was a husband, and that a dress shop was all fine and good, but no job ever took the place of a good man.

Which was quite an admission coming from a woman whose husband had been a notorious philanderer.

All the same, having heard more or less the same sentiment twice in less than an hour, the words stayed with him. That evening, while Katy slept and Tara regaled Willy and the kitchen staff with all the gory details of her dream, plus all that had happened since, Galen sat out on his balcony, a cigar in one hand, a drink in the other, and let his mind range free, visualizing a hawk on the hunt. It was a trick he'd picked up back when he'd been trying to help Brand figure out who'd been robbing McKnight Shipping, and how it was being accomplished. He had learned from experience that while the conscious mind might be hampered by inhibitions and expectations, the subconscious mind had no such limitations.

So he allowed his mind to soar, and it homed in on its prey.

A husband, he mused. If they were married he could get her out of town, take her on a world cruise if necessary, away from the scene of the crime until all danger was past.

But they weren't married. And a lady didn't go off with a gentleman not her husband, not even with a twelve-year-old sister in tow.

Of course, there were different types of marriages. All but a few of the ones he was most familiar with were what was euphemistically called marriages of convenience. Brand

and Ana were the rare exception. Even now they were disgustingly in love.

Most of his friends had married either for money or position, or to fulfill a family's fondest wish. Most of them now lived in a state of armed neutrality, at best—war, at worst.

Worst of all had been the case of Liam and Fallon. He would go to his grave bearing part of the guilt for that tragedy. He'd met Fallon a few weeks before he'd moved to Mystic. It hadn't taken long to see through her surface beauty to the shallowness, selfishness, and complete lack of scruples.

It had simply never occurred to him to issue a warning. Fallon had been staying with some cousins in another town. There was no reason to believe they'd ever meet. Liam, handsome and popular, had run with a younger crowd. He was a fine young man, a bit naive, perhaps, but sound as a dollar.

Only once Galen and Brand had signed over their shares in the family business, assuring each other that it would be the making of him, he'd been a sitting duck.

As marriages went, Liam and Fallon's had never even stood a chance. Not until much later had they learned that before the ink was even dry on the wedding papers, she'd spent every cent she could lay her hands on and started selling off everything of value.

Blindly in love, Liam hadn't even seen what was happening. Brand and Galen had been too wrapped up in rebuilding the shipyard and working out the problems to notice. By the time Fallon had tricked him into risking his neck on a foolish, drunken horse race, the marriage was already in ruins.

Liam had been drunk, the horse nearly blind. The result had been inevitable. By that time, Galen was supposedly lost at sea, and Brand had been out of touch. Neither of them had known what was happening back in Litchfield.

With Liam critically injured, Fallon had sold off everything the two of them hadn't already sold off to pay for their
wild way of life. Before anyone realized what was happening, she had disappeared, leaving her injured and embittered
husband to take his own life.

So much for living happily ever after.

Sighing, Galen sipped his whiskey and brooded. Admit-
tedly, not all marriages were doomed to failure, otherwise,
civilization would have long since come to a screeching halt.

But he'd made up his mind years ago that that particular
form of bondage was not for him. He valued his freedom
too much. The freedom to take on a leaky old tub, milk it
for all it was worth, and then trade it for a down payment
on something he really wanted, without having to justify
his decisions to anyone.

He'd been doing very well before Katy and Tara had
erupted into his well-ordered life. Since then, nothing had
gone according to plan.

Galen finished off his whiskey, tossed his cigar over the
side, and massaged his aching thigh bone. More than most
men, he knew the feeling of going under for the third time.

Because there was only space for one bed in the room Tara
and Katy were to share, Ila had insisted on taking the child
into her own cabin. "The last thing Katy needs," she told
Galen when he stopped by to inquire, "is a wigglesome
young'un hogging the bed. I made Katy take a hot tub soak
with a good handful of salts, and then, since she'd already
napped some today, I mixed her a dose of my special recipe
to help her sleep."

"Thanks, Ila. I owe you." Everyone on board knew the
reason he'd brought the O'Sullivans back here where he
could keep a close eye on them. If there'd been any doubt
left, it was gone now. Tara would have regaled them all with
her highly colorful account.

"It'll be just like it was before, we'll look after the pair of them. Now you go along and visit with your friends down to Pea Island, and don't you worry a bit."

"Who's sitting with Katy now?"

"Ethel. She's the new maid I hired."

He nodded, knowing he wasn't going anywhere until things were settled. Wasn't even going back up to the tables. Pierre could handle anything that came up.

God knows what Ila had put in that potion she'd given her. Galen had sniffed at the glass, but the ingredients remained a mystery. Whatever it was, Katy was sleeping like a baby.

Tipping back his chair, he watched her. He'd dismissed the maid, who'd been snoring away in her chair when he'd tapped on the door and entered.

"Katy, Katy, what am I going to do with you?" he murmured to the still figure on the bed. She slept on her side with one fist tucked under her chin. He counted the handful of freckles, swore silently at the darkening bruise, and wished he dared climb into bed with her and hold her, the way he had once before.

No, he didn't. With his objectivity already shot to hell and back, the last thing he needed was to sleep with her again. Even if all he did was sleep.

The trouble was, sleep wasn't all he wanted to do, and that was a problem. An increasingly uncomfortable, insoluble problem. Why now, he asked himself, just when everything was finally going his way?

For the second time, the subject of marriage had come up between them. The first time, he'd scared the hell out of himself by actually proposing.

Not that any woman with a spark of pride would have accepted a proposal framed in that manner. All the same, if they were married, he could take her away somewhere safe until all this blew over.

And then—?

If they were married, she could forget this crazy notion

of setting herself up in business. She wouldn't have to support herself or Tara, he would take care of them both.

If they were married, he could still build his shipyard. Nothing would change except that he would have someone to come home to at night, someone to talk over his plans with. Someone to bounce his ideas off. Someone to share his triumphs.

If they were married, he told himself when the hour grew late and the rattle of dice, the slap of cards, and the muffled roar of revelry gradually died away, he might stand a chance of dealing with this crazy mixture of fear, lust, and tenderness that was making mincemeat of his brain.

He must have dozed. He woke up with his mouth open, a crick in his neck, and an ache in his groin that had nothing to do with the slat-back straight chair he was about to fall off of.

She was staring up at him, her features softened by sleep. The lamp was turned down low, casting grotesque shadows on the wall behind the bed.

"Did I wake you up snoring?" he whispered. He'd sell his soul for a drink. Water, not whiskey.

"No, I dreamed . . ."

He didn't pick up the lead. Didn't want to know what she'd been dreaming. He knew what he'd been dreaming; the evidence was clearly visible. He cleared his throat and hooked the heels of his boots on the top rung of the chair, using his knees to cut off her view. It wasn't all that unusual. Most men awoke mornings with a slight erection. It wasn't morning, and his wasn't slight, and it was more than a physiological reaction. He wanted her so much it was all he could do not to take advantage of her semicomatose condition.

Thank God he hadn't sunk that low.

"Go back to sleep," he whispered, hoping she wouldn't.

Hoping she would. Hoping she'd invite him to join her in bed for the few remaining hours of the night.

"Not sleepy," she murmured, her voice slurred. "Thirsty."

"Yeah, me, too. I'll find us something. Lock the door behind me, all right?"

She nodded, but didn't make a move to get out of bed.

"All right, forget it. Look, I'll be back in two minutes. Stay right where you are, and yell your head off if anyone tries to get in."

She blinked, as if trying to focus her eyes, and then nodded.

Lurching down the corridor toward the galley, Galen told himself there was nothing to worry about. He opened one of the new ice boxes he'd bought and chipped off half a dozen chunks of ice, dumped them in a pitcher, filled it with water from a jug, and grabbed two tumblers. By the time he got back, she was on her feet, standing behind the door with an umbrella in both hands. She looked scared to death.

He barely managed to set down the tumblers and pitcher without dumping the lot. "What the devil's wrong? What happened?"

"Nothing. Nobody came, but what if they had?"

The air went out of him, leaving him limp as a wet string. And then somehow, his arms were surrounding her. Somehow, he was holding her, face buried in her hair as he waited for his heart to stop thudding and settle down.

Only instead of settling down, it began to beat faster, driving a heavy tide to his lower regions. He felt himself swelling all over again.

He needed that pitcher of ice water, and not necessarily to quench his thirst.

"I was afraid someone would come," she whispered.

"You'd have handled it just fine. Nobody's going to come looking for you, sweetheart, I promise you that. You're not going to be out of my sight again until this mess is finished."

Wordlessly, she nodded. Her arms tightened around his waist. She was a hell of a lot stronger than she looked.

"Katy, I've been thinking—you know, Tara's right. Maybe not about the house, at least not right away. The first thing we need to do is get you out of town, someplace where strangers stick out like a sore thumb. As it happens, I've got the perfect place in mind."

By now she'd recovered enough to argue, which was a good sign. However, she hadn't recovered enough to release her stranglehold around his middle. Galen didn't know if that was a good sign or not.

"Why do I have to be married to go there? Couldn't we just go?"

He'd been running on instinct, not intellect. Now he tried to come up with a logical reason, but none came to mind. All he knew was that she was his, and one way or another he was damned well going to keep her safe, if he had to marry her to do it.

He didn't expect her to buy it, not right off. Not without an argument. Not his Katy. She had more pride than was good for her, but pride alone wasn't going to protect her.

The way she was gazing up at him didn't make it any easier to think straight, but he gave it his best shot. "Look, these are personal friends of mine. They're pretty strait-laced, but if you went there as my wife, they'd look after you as if you were one of their own."

They would look after a chance-met stranger if they thought that stranger needed it. They'd taken him into their home and made him a part of their family. Even poor Miss Drucy, who didn't know Tuesday from a hat rack half the time.

"Trust me, it would be better if I could introduce you as my wife, and Tara as my sister-in-law."

"But we're not."

He edged her over toward the bed, reached for one of the tumblers, and placed it in her hand. He needed to put some space between them if he was going to pull this off.

And suddenly, it was vitally important to him that he bring her around. While he didn't necessarily want a wife, he wanted Katy. That was enough for now. At the moment, her need took precedence over his own.

Tara was wild with excitement. "You mean I can go on our honeymoon, too? Oh, that's the most grandacious thing I ever heard of!"

She was collecting a brand-new vocabulary from Oscar. Lord knows where Oscar came by it.

Katy said, "Now, you must understand, this isn't precisely a—"

Galen cut her off. He knew what she was about to say, and he didn't want it said. Maybe it wasn't going to be a regular church wedding. Maybe it wasn't going to be a regular honeymoon. It wasn't even going to be a regular marriage.

But from the outside looking in, it was damned well going to be as regular as he could make it. And for that, it had to be legal. After that, they'd simply take it one day at a time. They were both sensible adults. At least, one of them was.

Although at the moment, he couldn't have sworn which one.

They were married in South Mills, which was the fastest way to get it done around these parts. Sign on the dotted line, hand over the fee, and a couple of minutes later it was all over.

Tara looked disappointed. "We didn't even have any music," she said softly.

Ila was crying. She looked at him as if he'd just committed a crime.

Not until they were outside in the brilliant sunlight did Galen look at the small figure clinging to his arm.

"Ah, Katy . . . I'm sorry, darling. There was just no time—if I'd thought, I could have . . ."

Could have what? Laid on a church and flowers and a wedding cake with all the bows and ribbons?

Married was married. He hadn't thought beyond securing the legal right to look after her.

"It's all right. To be sure, it was a lovely wedding. With the . . . um, the flowers and all."

The flowers were a bunch of wilted rosebuds provided at the last minute by the florist where he had a standing order to supply his trademark boutonnieres.

There was cake and champagne waiting for them back aboard the *Queen*. Willy had outdone himself. Johnny the Knife had hurled rice over the wedding party and then he and Jimmy had got into a fight over who was going to have to sweep it up.

Bellfort came, bearing gifts. A Waterford bowl for Katy, which brought tears to her eyes. "Something from home," he told her, making Galen wish he'd thought of it first. And a doll for Tara, who clearly thought she was too old for such a gift, but who was too polite to say so. "I'll make a special place for her when we get our house. I think it's going to be yellow."

Galen didn't even try to interpret that one.

And then Pam arrived. He'd tied up just behind the *Queen,* impatient to be off as they had a long journey ahead of them. He did accept a bowl of champagne punch, but judging from his expression, Galen thought he would have preferred a shot of Buffalo City's finest.

They set off, the four of them, in a flurry of good wishes. Someone had scattered the rose petals on the water. He thought it might have been Ermaline. She had a soft spot in her heart for Katy.

Most of the people who'd ever met her did. His own soft spot was in his head.

At least he'd given her a ring. Guessing at the size—

correctly, as it turned out—he'd chosen a pink diamond set in platinum with a matching band, all without giving a single thought as to how far that same amount of money would have gone toward bulkheading his waterfront.

With practiced ease, Pam made the most of the light breeze until they cleared the harbor, and then with a slight shift of the tiller, he caught the wind, and they set out on a course that would eventually take them to Merriweather's Landing on Pea Island, on the Outer Banks of North Carolina.

Chapter Twenty

❧

"You're going to put in at Nags Head? We've still got an hour of daylight left." Galen scanned the slate gray streaks across a lemon-colored sky.

"Wedding gift, son. It come to me while you was off getting hitched that if I was to take the young'un on down to The Landin', you and the missus could have a nice little honeymoon all by yerselves there to the hotel."

Galen's gaze shifted forward, where Katy and Tara were hanging over the rail, watching a school of fish pass underneath the hull. The offer had caught him off guard. He only hoped Katy hadn't heard. His sole purpose in marrying her was to keep them both safe from any possible threat. He preferred his life just the way it was. Or rather, as it had been until recently. Unfettered, uncomplicated, without ties of any sort, either physical or emotional.

A single word had blown all that. Honeymoon. Now he couldn't think for all the images swimming to the surface of his mind. Visions of Katy, bruised, terrified, and trying so damn hard not to show it. Katy in red silk, her big green eyes hidden behind a pair of gold-rimmed spectacles. Katy asleep in his bed, exhausted from taking care of a boatload of miserably ill people.

Katy wearing a simple cotton gown, bringing tears to more than a few eyes with her songs about a place not a single member of her audience had ever seen, nor was ever likely to. Katy in her mud brown shirtwaist with the yellowed lace collar.

Katy in nothing at all.

A honeymoon.

Was she expecting one? He didn't think so. Choosing his words as carefully as any lawyer, he had more or less told her that he didn't expect marital intimacy. Not right away, at least.

Eventually? Well, they were man and wife, after all. Women usually wanted children. He could take them or leave them, but as he believed in fidelity, and as they were legally married, any children she had would be his. Most definitely his.

Before he could slam the door, another image slipped in, this one of Katy, nursing his son.

He felt the ground shift under his feet.

" 'Ware for'ard, comin' about!" Pam hauled in the main, eased the boom over, and the little sloop heeled over and glided in toward a long-legged pier jutting out from the pink sandy shore. "Comin' up on the hotel, son. You fixin' to get off here?"

Galen swallowed hard and loosened the knot of his tie. "Well now, that's a generous offer, my friend, but Tara—"

"She'll take to the Merriweathers like a tick to a coon dog. Her an' Maureen can talk Irish to one another."

Galen had forgotten that Merriweather's cook was Irish. She'd been in America for at least fifty years, but still lapsed into Irishness when it suited her purposes. "Yes, well—"

"I'll come back an' fetch the pair of ye tomorrow an' haul ye down there." The old man grinned around the stem of his corncob pipe. "Reckon that'll be enough time to get the job done?"

The bawdy old salt, he knew damned well this was no regular hearts-and-flowers affairs. Galen didn't know whether to be amused or irritated.

He did know enough not to pass up a golden opportunity when it came knocking on his bedroom door. "Then if you don't mind the fast turnaround, I believe we'll take you up on it."

Now, all he had to do was convince Katy.

With the shank of the season behind them, the hotel had rooms to spare. Katy had dragged out half a dozen reasons why they should all go on to The Landing as planned, but in the end, Galen had managed to convince her that this way, there'd be no question about the validity of their marriage.

"Sure, and you said it was valid, even though we weren't properly churched. Are you telling me now that—"

"All I'm telling you, Katy, is that we might as well go through the motions. That way, there'll be no question of . . . well, of anything."

"Who'd know? Who'd be likely to question us?" she asked as they stood on the dock and waved Tara off. He had a feeling she was having a few second thoughts.

"Maybe no one at all. But possibly whoever shoved you under the wheels of a freight wagon. Whoever thinks you might have seen him commit murder."

"Oh, I see. But now that I'm married, I'll not be a threat. Is it my sight I'm supposed to have lost, or my wits?"

Put that way, it didn't make much sense, he had to admit. "Katy, I don't mean to frighten you, but you need to take this business seriously."

Her eyes grew round as silver dollars. "Oh, but I do. I married you, didn't I?"

That wasn't the answer he wanted to hear, only he hadn't realized it until she'd said it. Even now, he had a feeling she might be teasing him. Or testing him. With Katy, a man could never be quite certain.

"Yes, well . . ." He searched for just the right tone. "Neither of us was looking to get married, but now that the deed is done, for whatever reason, I believe we're both mature enough to make the best of it."

Mature enough to make the best of it? Go ahead, sweep her off her feet, you romantic fool!

They dined in the public dining room. Galen had toyed with the idea of having dinner brought up to their room, but that might have seemed too intimate. Now that they were alone together, he was beginning to have a few second thoughts of his own.

Such as the fact that they were too alike in some ways, too different in others. That he was too old, and she was too young. That she didn't love him. Sometimes she barely tolerated him.

Such as the fact that he had done what he'd sworn never to do. He had entered into a marriage contract for reasons that had nothing to do with love.

He stared out through salt-hazed windows at the flickering torches lighting a walkway around the hotel. He studied a lithograph on the wall. He looked at the other diners—the room was only half filled. Looked everywhere but at the woman across the table.

"More tea?" the waiter asked, standing by with a heavy pot wrapped in a towel.

"Yes, please," Katy said eagerly.

She'd already downed enough tea to float a three-masted schooner. It occurred to him that she was every bit as nervous as he was about what happened once they left the dining room.

"And bring dessert, will you?"

"Yessir, right away."

Neither of them had done justice to the first four courses. Neither of them did more than poke at the charlotte russe with their spoons.

It was going to rain. "Would you care for a stroll outside before we go upstairs?" Damned necktie had shrunk. He cleared his throat.

"Oh, yes, a bit of fresh air would be just the thing." She latched on to the offer as if it were a lifeline.

Sand gritted underfoot on the sun-bleached boardwalks. They trudged twice around the hotel and then by mutual consent headed for the pier, where Galen pointed out the few constellations still visible above the rapidly climbing cloudbank. A narrow streak of moonlight silvered the far horizon, and they both stared at it silently for a while until Katy smothered a yawn.

Galen did his best to smother a vision of his bride in her white cotton nightgown, lying in that big double bed on the second floor of the hotel, his for the taking.

Legally his, if not morally.

Thirty-three years old, and he was acting like a green kid, discovering girls for the first time. "So . . . Mrs. McKnight," he said, forcing a teasing note as they turned back toward the hotel, "think you'll be able to get used to being Katy McKnight?"

"I think Galen O'Sullivan has a finer ring to it.'"

"Oh, so I've married myself a New Woman, have I?" And then he had to explain about the suffrage movement that was making headway across the country, state by state. By that time they were back at the hotel entrance, and neither of them could come up with a single excuse to delay the inevitable.

Katy covered another yawn and begged his pardon. Galen stifled a surge of disappointment. It wasn't going to be easy to share her bed and not touch her, no matter what he'd promised.

Promised himself. They hadn't actually discussed the matter, not in so many words. But it had been more or less understood that he wouldn't push for intimacy right away, not until they'd had time to get better acquainted.

The room was a corner one. Not the honeymoon suite, that would have been entirely too suggestive. It was a fine room, though. Large, well furnished, with four windows and a small fireplace now filled with potted ferns. There was a small table flanked by a pair of his-and-her wing chairs.

Katy sank into hers. After checking the door and opening the windows halfway to let the warm, salt breeze blow through, Galen settled into the larger one.

Silence. Katy brushed a loose thread from her sleeve.

Galen took out his watch, frowned at it, held it up to his ear, and then frowned again. It was barely nine o'clock. Back aboard the *Queen,* the evening would just be getting under way.

"Where in Ireland?" Her voice was barely audible against the sound of the nearby ocean.

"Where in what?"

"You said the Merriweathers' cook is from Ireland. What part?"

"Oh. Ah . . . Wicklow? Does that ring any bells? I believe she mentioned something about Wicklow Hills?"

"Oh." She toyed with her rings, which looked too new, too big, too ostentatious. He should have chosen something simpler, but he'd wanted her to know. . . .

To know what? That he cared for her? That he valued her friendship? That he lusted for her body? That he . . .

Might even love her?

Hell, he didn't even know what love felt like, much less how to feel it. The crazy urge that came over him whenever he looked at her, or touched her, or even so much as thought about her—it was probably no more than a passing fancy. Lust. All men felt lust. It was part of nature's plan. It was perfectly natural.

So did that mean he could use her body to slake his lust for as long as it was convenient, thank her for her generosity, and then go on about his business?

He'd done a few things in his life that he wasn't particularly proud of, but one thing he would never do. He would never intentionally hurt Katy. No matter what his reasons for marrying her—and he was beginning to think those reasons might not be as straightforward as he'd admitted—he vowed never to promise her more than he could give, and never take more than she offered freely. And if that meant a sexless honeymoon, so be it.

"I don't know much about it."

About *sex*? He nearly dropped his watch. "You, uh . . . don't?"

"My mother was widely traveled before she married my Da. She said the mountains there are the loveliest shade of blue."

Wicklow Mountains. "Yes, of course." He ran a finger inside his collar, which had suddenly grown a size too small. "Would you, hm, care for a bit of privacy before we—that is, before you go to bed?"

"Yes, please. I'll not be but a minute."

She looked relieved. Small and vulnerable, she was trying so hard to appear cool and poised that Galen felt one more crack in his armor. At this rate he wouldn't be able to fight off a paper tiger, much less a flesh-and-blood murderer. "Why don't I just step outside and see what the weather promises for tomorrow?"

It promised rain. He didn't have to step outside to know the clouds they'd seen earlier now covered the entire sky. There'd be no moon to light his wedding night. Fitting enough, he thought with an edge of bitterness.

He chatted for several minutes with the desk clerk, stood in the door of the solarium, and watched while a few couples danced to the strains of something slow and romantic, as rendered by a trio of earnest, sweating musicians. He gave her as much time as he figured it would take her to bathe, put on her nightgown, climb into bed, pull up the covers, and pretend to be asleep.

And then he went back upstairs.

Wide awake, she was sitting up in bed, pillows plumped behind her, covers tucked around her hips. From the waist up she was shrouded in that ugly brown shirtwaist she'd been wearing the first time he'd seen her, minus the lace collar.

The expression on her face was militant. The set of her jaw said it all. Do-or-die.

"Not sleepy yet?"

"Somebody forgot to pack my nightgown," she said grimly.

He blinked. "Forgot your nightgown?"

"This isn't mine." She tugged at her neckline, pulling out a wisp of white lawn and gossamer lace. "I don't know who could have made such a mistake. This must belong to Ava or Ermaline, or maybe the new girl. It's not mine."

Galen's lips twitched. He had a very good idea who had switched nightgowns. Ila was a romantic, bless her soul. She knew as well as anyone that this wasn't a real marriage, but that didn't keep her from hoping.

"Does it fit?"

"No, it doesn't, it's far too small."

"Skimpy, hmm? I hate sleeping in anything that binds. You could always take it off, I guess. I won't look."

"Bite your tongue." She glared at him, but he could tell the humor of the situation was beginning to get through to her. Katy was not without a sense of humor. It was one of the things he lo—liked most about her.

"Well then, if it will make you feel any better, I'll wear something equally miserable. Let's see . . . there's my boiled shirt and bat's wing tie. I didn't bring along a cummerbund, but you could lend me a corselet."

Katy threw a pillow at him.

He grinned, and then they both fell to laughing. He took off his coat and flexed his shoulders, and it came to her that he must be even more exhausted than she was. Hers came more from tension than actual labor. While she'd soaked away the remnants of her stiffness and slept like a log, Galen had been busy making arrangements. She had

barely seen him at all before they'd set out on the drive to
South Mills. He'd scarcely spoken a word on the way, and
Katy hadn't dared. She'd kept telling herself she would wake
up any moment and discover it was all a dream.

Perhaps she was still dreaming.

From behind the screen came the sound of splashing,
the sound of muttered cursing, and then Galen poked his
head around the corner and said, "I dropped a cuff link.
Did it roll under the screen?"

"I'll look." She leaned over and peered down at the gold-
and-blue-leaf-patterned carpet. How could anyone hope to
find something so small on such a busy design?

Reluctantly, she folded back the covers and climbed out
of bed. Wearing only the shameless nightgown and her muslin blouse for the sake of modesty, she padded silently across
the carpet.

Something glinted near one of the chairs, and she hurried to investigate. "There you are," she exclaimed, snatch-
ing up the tiny bit of jewelry. It was gold, cast in the shape
of a horse's head. "I'll put it in the dish on the dresser," she
called softly.

"Thank you. It belonged to my father, I'd hate to lose it."

He spoke from so close behind her she nearly dropped the
thing, she was that startled. "I didn't hear you," she gasped.

His warm breath stirred tendrils of hair that had escaped
her braid. The rich scent of tobacco, shaving soap, and bay
rum mingled with the smell of lavender potpourri, beeswax
furniture polish, and the pungent iodine smell of the sea.

"Barefooted." His voice was a full octave lower.

And then his hands closed over her shoulders, and he
was turning her to face him, and she was afraid he would
see everything she was feeling, plain as day. He would know
she was afraid of what was about to happen, yet at the same
time, sick with anticipation.

He would know she'd been thinking about it almost from

the moment she'd heard herself agreeing to this crazy marriage. Thinking about it and calling herself a fool, because he didn't love her. Telling herself she would be even more of a fool not to take whatever he was able to give her and make the most of it.

Her mother had done that when she'd fallen in love with a handsome fisherman. In the end it had brought her little more than heartbreak, yet Katy knew that in between the sorrows, they'd shared love and laughter and sometimes joy.

He had the look of a stranger. His eyes were almost black. "Katy," he whispered, "I want to kiss you. I know I promised, but I want to sleep with you the way a man sleeps with his wife. Do you understand what I'm saying?"

Wordlessly, she nodded.

"I know I said I'd give you time—that is, I meant to say it, even if I never got around to putting it into so many words. But, Katy, you're as aware of it as I am—this thing that's between us."

She nodded again, helpless to tear her gaze from his face.

"You know how much I like you. I respect you. I want you more than I've wanted any woman in a long, long time. Is that enough for now?"

If it was all he could offer her, then it would have to be enough, but in her deepest heart, hope still flickered like a candle in a draft. Katy was an optimist. She had come five thousand miles following a dream. Now that her dream led her in another direction, what could she do but go on following?

He led her to the side of the bed. Shyly, she allowed him to unbutton the brown shirtwaist she'd worn to hide the sheer lawn nightgown with the bosom-bearing neckline that someone had put in her valise.

Shyly, she stole a peek at the golden thicket of chest hair as he unbuttoned his own ruffled shirt. At the lean muscular loins and fascinating bulges delineated by his close-fitting black trousers.

Gently, he eased her arms from the blouse and tossed it aside. She lifted her face for his kiss, leaving her eyes open until the very last as if to convince herself that this was Galen. This was her husband. She wasn't dreaming, it was truly happening to her.

The kiss started gently, almost tentatively. Then, like a spark to tinder, it flamed into something far more volatile.

Galen led, and Katy followed. With his lips and tongue, his hands and his body, he taught, and she learned, lured on by tastes and textures, intoxicated by wild feelings in parts of her body that weren't even close to her mouth.

Shaken and breathless, they broke apart, and she watched as he quickly shed the last of his clothing. Any remaining embarrassment she might have felt gave way to awe and admiration. She'd seen boys before, naked, splashing in the shallows back at home. This was a man. Every inch a man. Every proud, lean muscle and sinew shouting, celebrating his manhood.

"Saints preserve us," she whispered, and turning, she dived for cover.

Laughing, he followed her there. "Don't count on it, precious, I've locked the door. No saints allowed. Now, come here and let me show you how beautiful you are."

He demonstrated, touching each treasure first with his eyes, then with his fingertips, then with his lips. Outside, a gust of wind rattled shutters, heralding the first bank of rain. Neither of them noticed as they explored, discovering together a whole new universe that left them stunned, shaken, desperately hungry for more.

Her sweet, awkward touches, her unschooled responses, the kisses she spread more and more daringly over his body, were making a total wreck of him. He caressed her breasts, tugged at her nipples, kissed and then suckled her.

And then she returned the favor. Had his small, flat nipples always been so sensitive, or was it Katy?

He had a sinking feeling he might never be the same man.

When his fingers brushed her nest, and then explored the moist thicket to find her trigger, she nearly came up off the bed.

He brought her to her peak of pleasure, savoring the way she panted and caught her breath in tight little gasps. Patiently, more for his sake than hers because he desperately needed time, he explained the similarities between that part of a woman that was tiny, concealed and incredibly sensitive, to the part of a man that was every bit as sensitive and blatantly exposed for all the world to see. Which could be embarrassing at times.

And then she set off exploring on her own. He had taught her well. Almost too well. But as it turned out, she taught him even more. No other woman, no matter how experienced, had ever affected him this way.

Katy had never dreamed such feelings existed. They hadn't even done all that husbands and wives were supposed to do—the part that made babies, that was, and already she'd learned how to drive him wild with a touch, a kiss. Was this the drab, sensible Katy O'Sullivan she had known all her life?

She felt bold, powerful—almost beautiful.

"Here," he rasped. Taking her hand, he moved it to the place where he ached to feel her touch. When her fingers tightened around the silken steel of his shaft, he gasped, threw back his head, and clenched his jaw.

Katy stared. For one brief moment, he was a stranger, Blue-white lightning played over his harshly etched features, sharpening angles, flattening planes. He was trembling.

She was trembling, too. "You feel it, too, don't you?" she whispered. "Do you think it could be electrical? I've heard electrical vapors can do all sorts of strange things. Could they cause a body to . . . tingle?"

"Electrical vapors? That might explain it." Galen uttered a sound that was one part laughter, nine parts desperation. She was ready. He was barely hanging on by a thread. It had nearly killed him, but he'd taken things slowly, made it as easy as possible for her. He'd never before bedded a virgin, but like most men, he knew in theory what to expect.

He only hoped she did.

There would be pain the first time. Just how much, there was no way of knowing in advance. He had explored as far as he dared, had brought her gasping and shuddering to climax, which had nearly carried him over the edge, as well.

"Love, I can't wait much longer."

He could feel her bracing herself. "I'm ready."

"If I hurt you—if the pain's too much, just tell me and I'll stop, I promise."

"Galen, I'm not a child."

No, indeed she wasn't. But neither was she an experienced lover. Lifting himself above her, he parted her thighs. The hot spicy scent of arousal drifted up around them, heightening the sexual intoxication. He lowered himself until the tip of his rod was nestled at her entrance, and then he bent over and kissed her. "Katy, Katy . . ."

She waited, but he said no more. Instead, she felt herself begin to fill. It was the strangest feeling. Not painful, exactly, but . . . strange.

Then came a sharp pain, and then more of the stretching until she thought she might come apart. But before she could ask him to wait until she got used to the fullness, the brief memory of pain was replaced by something else.

She shifted her hips. He groaned and pressed down against her, and she began to throb like a drum being beat too fast, with a heavy stick.

He whispered her name. "Katy, Katy," he said. She waited for more, but that was all he said. She wanted to hear the words, but more than that, she wanted desperately to reach out and capture this strange, throbbing sensation that was part pain, part pleasure—exquisite, unimaginable pleasure. Like a wild bird, it came close, then soared off again. Close, and then away . . .

She whimpered, wanting, needing—

He moved, riding her as he might ride a wild horse, head thrown back, eyes closed, sweat gleaming on his hard body. Instinctively she rose to meet each thrust, raced to catch the beautiful bird, to capture the light, the pulsating rainbow that hovered just out of reach.

And then it was all around her. She cried out . . . something, she never knew what. Words.

He made a sound in his throat, said her name again, and then he collapsed, rolling onto his side and carrying her with him.

During the night another storm broke over them. Lightning filled the room with a cold brilliance. The wind blew a shutter loose, and it clattered until someone fastened it back.

Katy slept through it all. Galen waked, eased himself out of bed, and filled a basin with water that had cooled until it was barely tepid.

Tenderly, he bathed away the seeds of his pleasure, the evidence of her innocence.

He came back to bed and held her until morning, unable to sleep, knowing that for better or worse, his life had taken a different course.

Chapter Twenty-one

❦

Once again they were strangers. Polite strangers. Katy stared at her new husband as he checked them out of the hotel, remembering in amazement the things he had done to her the night before. The things she had done to him.

Could she really have done all that? Surely she must have dreamed it. The Katy she knew would never dare touch a naked body the way she had touched his, not even her own, and she had known herself for twenty-two years.

"Are you ready, my dear?"

His dear. Was she truly his dear? If this tall, well-dressed stranger even *had* a dear, she was sorely afraid she wasn't it.

The image of a perfect oval of a face, with pale, perfect hair and a perfect, unfreckled nose swam to the surface of her mind. She pushed it away. Whoever the woman in the picture was, whatever they'd once meant to each other, it was Katy he had married. Katy who bore his name, and would one day bear his sons.

At this very moment she might be carrying his child. The thought made her catch her breath, and unconsciously, she brushed her hand over the front of her four-gore skirt.

The ferry was waiting at the end of the pier. Galen handed her aboard, passed down the bags, and turned to tip the bag boy. Pam the ferryman wouldn't stop grinning. Katy wondered if he knew—

Well, of course he knew. The whole world probably knew. It had been their wedding night, after all. Did he suppose they had spent it playing dominoes?

The rain had ended for now, but the sky was still overcast. That and the familiar smell of burning peat brought a painful surge of nostalgia. Galen had told her about the way lightning sometimes started fires in the nearby Dismal Swamp. Fires that could smoulder underground for years, with the ash and pungent smell carried for miles by the wind.

I want to go home, she thought, feeling as lost as if she'd been set adrift on an uncharted sea.

Pam dried off a section of white-painted bench, and she smiled and thanked him. Bracing herself for the journey to yet another new place where she would feel rootless, she took her seat.

You have a husband now. You're a citizen. You belong.

But no amount of reason made her feel as if she belonged.

Low clouds sagged overhead. A flurry of raindrops struck her face, her shoulders. It wasn't going to rain. She refused to allow it. Not on her honeymoon.

Galen cast off bow and stern, moving as surely as if he'd done it all his life. He probably had. This was his territory, not hers. Not yet.

Feeling the need to secure something—anything—she re-pinned her black straw more securely on top of her head. From across the small cockpit, Galen glanced at her face, her hat, and then back at her face again.

She knew very well he hated this hat. She hated it herself, even with the new ribbons, but of the two she now owned, she had deliberately chosen to wear her old one this morning, as if to remind herself of who she was. Her name might have changed, but she was still Katy O'Sullivan. Practical, sensible Kathleen O'Sullivan, a woman accustomed to duty and responsibility.

Her face must have reflected something of her grim

determination. Galen touched her on the shoulder. "You're not feeling squeamish, are you?"

"Not a bit of it." She manufactured a smile in spite of the fact that she was increasingly aware of being stiff and sore in places she had never before been aware of at all.

He propped a booted foot up beside her on the bench, making her acutely aware of his virility, of all the things she'd never even noticed about a man before. "We'll be coming in sight of The Landing in about half an hour. Oh, and by the way, if you notice anything unusual about Miss Drucy, try to ignore it, will you? She has a tendency to live in her own little world these days."

Katy tucked her skirts closer and nodded. He had given her a brief description of the people she'd be meeting to-day, and she'd tried to keep them straight in her mind. She looked forward to seeing Brandon and Ana again. And the baby. They would be there, along with the elderly Merri-weathers' son, Tom, and his two sons. She'd thought at the time that the boys might provide company for Tara.

She looked forward to meeting Maureen, if only to hear the lilt of a familiar accent again. In a place as vast as America, anyone from Ireland was a neighbor.

"It's her birthday. Miss Drucy's. Not that she'll remember, but it serves the purpose of a family reunion. Brand met the Merriweathers when he came south the first time. Our father had been dead only a few years, and then Liam . . . died. And Brand thought I'd been lost at sea—he'd just got back from months of searching. The Merriweathers took him in, no questions asked, when he was in desperate need of something to hang on to. It was here he met Ana."

Katy nodded again. She'd heard part of the story before. She did know what it meant to need something to hold on to.

Galen moved away to talk to the ferryman. A little while later, on the far side of a swift-running inlet, they made a final tack into a narrow channel. Returning to her side, Galen

pointed out the turreted structure known as Merriweather's
Castle on the narrow, windswept spit of land that was Pea
Island.

Unconsciously bracing herself, Katy searched among the
figures gathering on the shore for a glimpse of a familiar
coppery head. Even now she found it hard to believe she'd
been selfish enough to send Tara ahead to stay with strangers
just so she could be alone with her new husband.

She stole a look at him, standing so tall beside her. A
glimmer of pale sunlight glanced off his hatless head, high-
lighting the narrow streak of white hair that set him apart
from all other men.

As if he needed anything to set him apart. Blindfolded,
she could have picked him out among a shipload of men.
Her heart would have guided her.

"There's George Gill, the all-around man. He's the giant
on the end. And Brand—he's the one waving. The one in
the wheelchair is Mr. Merry." One by one, Galen identified them all as Pam dropped the mains'le and they glided
toward the wharf. All but the woman standing off to one
side, an infant in her arms.

The woman in the photograph.

Long before she was close enough to see her face clearly,
Katy knew. The picture had disappeared from Galen's bedroom weeks ago, but she knew that face as well as she
knew her own. A tiny flame that had been ignited inside
her only hours before flickered out, leaving only cold ash
in its place.

The woman was wearing gray, simply but beautifully
styled. The shade could have indicated half mourning, or it
could have been chosen because it matched the color of the
wearer's eyes.

A closer look was enough to tell her it had been chosen
to match the color of a pair of large, sad eyes. The same
eyes Katy had seen gazing up from the photograph.

Later she learned that it also indicated mourning. The

woman's name was Margaret Ruff, and she had lost her husband five months earlier. Ana, suffering from a sprained wrist, had invited her to travel south with them, to help look after the baby on the trip south.

And because Margaret had been traveling in the same direction on her way to Atlanta to visit her late husband's parents, she had agreed to stay with her until the Merriweathers' staff could take over.

Galen, once he recovered from his initial shock, wondered just what the devil was going on. In an aside to his brother, he asked whose idea it had been to invite Margaret along.

Grinning, Brand said, "Whose do you think? You know Ana, always trying to play matchmaker. I do believe you put a kink in her hawser, little brother."

"You mean she was thinking—?"

Brand nodded. "Now that Margaret's available again, why not? Only now, I reckon she'll have to set her sights on Tom. Or maybe George Gill."

Katy thought later it was a wonder her smile hadn't cracked and fallen right off her face. She'd smiled and greeted her host and hostess and their staff. She'd smiled and greeted the other two McKnights and made over the baby, and then she'd smiled some more and allowed herself to be introduced to the woman her husband loved.

It was all there, plain as day. She had watched him closely when he'd greeted her down at the landing. He'd taken both her hands in his and she'd heard him say quite clearly, "Margaret."

Just that. Margaret.

The way he'd said "Katy," the night before when she'd been aching to hear words of love.

Had Margaret wanted to hear those words, too? Had he ever spoken them to her? Some men had trouble putting their feelings into words.

Katy didn't know what to think anymore. She knew only

that she was confused, suffering from a lack of sleep, and aching in more than just her heart.

Dinner was a festive affair, with family, friends, and staff all sitting down together. With the help of the maid, Simmy, and Tara, Maureen served a wonderful meal, then took off her apron and joined them at the table.

Mr. Merriweather asked blessings on them all, and especially his dear wife, and they all began to talk. Katy had little to say. Not that anyone seemed to notice, as her silence was effectively covered by laughter and the clink of cutlery. Toasts were made and Katy, along with the others, including Tara, lifted their glasses time and time again.

Later they adjourned to the living room, where a fire had been lit in spite of the warm evening. The conversation continued as small groups formed, moved on, and reformed. Galen and Margaret had settled onto a window seat and remained there, talking quietly. At the moment, Margaret seemed to be doing most of the talking, with Galen nodding from time to time.

Ana explained, "They haven't seen each other in ages. I'm sure they have loads of catching up to do." Katy was holding the baby, who was plump and pink and somewhat damp. "Margaret used to live next door to the McKnights' stud farm near Litchfield, if you can call a few miles away next door. She's a bit older, but they grew up together. They've always been close."

Close. Just how close? Katy wondered. Margaret had married someone else, and now that she was free again, Galen was not. She smiled and nodded, just as if her heart weren't breaking.

Tara left the card game she'd been playing with the Merriweathers' two grandsons and wandered over to the table where Miss Drucy was cutting paper dolls from an old magazine. The two boys started arguing, and Tom spoke to them with quiet authority. The eldest one—Caleb or Billy,

Katy couldn't remember which was which—grinned and pointed at Tara.

Katy, remembering what had happened that first day aboard the *Queen,* caught Tara's eye and frowned.

Tom shook his head and turned back to George Gill.

Bits of conversation flowed like a warm current through the room. Something about the stock market—a few words about China. Someone mentioned oysters, and Maureen declared her old knees were about to give out on her.

The room was overheated to Katy's way of thinking. She had yet to get used to the warmer climate, without a fire on the hearth. Yet there was something undeniably comforting about the smell of woodsmoke mingling with the lingering scent of roasted chicken, of juniper paneling, coffee, and beeswax polish.

She did her best to take comfort, but in a room filled with people, she felt utterly alone. Already, Tara acted as if she were part of the family, helping Maureen, jumping to retrieve Mr. Merriweather's lap robe when it slithered to the floor. Teasing the two boys and playing with Miss Drucy as if the two of them were the same age.

And she really was growing a bosom. Somehow, that was the most depressing thought of all. That the day would come when Tara would no longer need her.

Katy jiggled the baby, who was beginning to fret. She searched for some resemblance to Galen in his niece's tiny face. Her name was Lianna, for Liam, the brother who had died. Ana had laughed and said it was a stretch, but it was either that or Hespeth, after Brand's mother.

Katy allowed her mind to drift away. Gale? A daughter could be named Gale. A son could be called Galen Declan, or perhaps—

"Don't you agree?"

"Don't I—?"

"I was saying I do believe a woman can have a career as well as a man if she managed it correctly. Who better than a woman can juggle half a dozen tasks without even blinking an eye? We do it all the time. Every housewife I know is a manager, even if she has a houseful of servants. Not that you'll find many men who'd agree," she added with a mischievous smile.

"What are you doing, darling, stuffing this young woman's brain full of your radical philosophy?" Brand stood over them and held out his arms for his daughter. "Come here, pumpkin, if Mama won't change your napkin, then I guess it's up to Papa."

Ana batted her eyelashes until Katy had to laugh. "But you do such a lovely job of it. How could I, a mere woman, ever manage such mathematically precise corners?"

Katy handed over the fussing baby. She envied them their strong bond of love. Perhaps one day . . .

She glanced over at the window seat, where Galen and Margaret sat talking, their heads close together. Across the room, Miss Drucy got up from the table, scattering scraps of paper, and wandered over to Galen. For several moments she stood there, her head tilted to one side. "Did I used to know you?"

With firelight flickering on his angular features, Galen stood and cupped the withered face between his hands. "Yes, you did, madam. Last year on your birthday you trounced me at checkers and cut up my best necktie for your rag rugs, but I love you just the same. Happy birthday, dearest Drucy." He kissed her gently on the brow.

She looked puzzled for a moment. "And it rained. Didn't it rain? I thought it did, but perhaps . . ."

Tom came and led her away. "Bedtime, Mother. Boys, come hug your grandmother good night."

Simmy and Tom led the old woman upstairs. And then Ana and Brand carried the baby up. Katy waited until they'd all disappeared and then she slipped away, too, not daring to glance at the window seat, where her husband sat with the beautiful woman from his past.

* * *

Galen waited almost a full hour. He had known the very moment she'd left to go upstairs. If Margaret hadn't been right in the middle of a rather lengthy and tedious description of her husband's last illness, he would have left much sooner.

"That must have been difficult for you," he murmured.

Katy, wait for me. Dammit, I can't just walk off and leave her. It would be rude.

"Well, it's not as if we didn't know what was coming. The trouble was, as the lawyer put it, the clock didn't start until poor Allen actually passed away, and by that time, things were in such a mess. I suppose you went through the same thing when Liam died, although it's different with a brother than it is with a spouse. Still, I felt so awful for you when I heard. We were in Austria at the time. Allen was attached to—"

And on, and on, and on. Galen had heard more about the life and times of the late Allen Gitman Ruff, banker, diplomat, husband *extraordinaire,* than he ever cared to know. And how much Margaret had suffered through it all, uprooting herself time after time to follow her husband from pillar to post as his financial support to the party paid off and he was given two ambassadorships in the space of seven years.

Had she always been this boring?

Probably. Only he'd been too young to notice much beyond her elegant cheekbones, her willowy body, and the mysteries hidden behind those quiet gray eyes.

The attributes that had once struck him as serene, mysterious, and romantic now struck him as boring and self-absorbed. No man should ever have to meet his first love after years of glorifying her in his mind, measuring every other woman against the impossible standards she'd set.

She hadn't even asked him about his narrow brush with

death, or about what he was doing now, or about Katy and his plans for the future.

Katy was sleeping when he finally managed to escape. On her side, with her fist curled under her chin and her thick braid trailing across his pillow, she looked small and incredibly vulnerable. He happened to know she wasn't. Any woman who could leave home with a child and a trunkful of encyclopedias, and come five thousand miles to live among strangers, was far from frail.

Quietly, he removed his clothes, hanging them in the closet beside her gown. On impulse, he lifted a sleeve and inhaled the faint scent of her body—that clean soap-and-wildflower fragrance that was as much a part of her as her green eyes, her thick black hair, and the handful of freckles that were more visible now than when she'd first arrived.

"Katy, Katy, what am I going to do with you?" he whispered, not for the first time.

He knew what he wanted to do, but because she was probably sore, and because he didn't have the nerve to wake her from a peaceful sleep and demand she do her wifely duty, he settled beside her, thinking of all the nights and all the mornings to come.

How had he managed to get so lucky?

The message came just after daylight. Galen, already awake, had been toying with the notion of easing Katy's nightgown off her sleeping body, wondering how she would react to waking up naked. His own reaction was already in evidence.

It was Evard, the young handyman, who rapped on the door, and called, "Cap'n? Message just come from the station for you. Surfman that brought it said if you wanted to send a reply, he'd wait and take it."

So much for his plans for a lazy morning spent making love to his wife. "Half a minute, I'll be down."

It could only be from the sheriff. He had left word where he could be reached. Unfortunately, the only way of getting word to him was through Pea Island Lifesaving Station, as wireless communications didn't extend to private homes here on the Outer Banks, not even for people as wealthy as Maurice Merriweather.

He hoped to hell it was good news. The thought of Katy's being in danger was enough to turn the rest of his hair white.

Half an hour later he was trying to explain why he had to go, and why Katy couldn't go with him. It was an uphill battle. "Listen to me, I don't have time to argue. Pam will be here in less than an hour and I need to go over a few things with Brand first."

Her lower lip thrust out. There was more fire in her eyes than pale green eyes were supposed to generate. But then, he supposed any bride, being told that her husband was leaving her two days into their marriage, might be upset.

"It's just that the *Queen*'s not fit to sail, and Aster damned well knows it. Bellfort tried to talk her out of it as soon as he heard she'd hired a pilot."

"A pilot?"

He sliced the air impatiently with a hand. "No ship can leave harbor without a river pilot. It's the law. Trust me, she's up to something, and if I don't get back before she goes through with it, the *Queen* and all hands are apt to end up on the bottom before they even clear the harbor. Now, I've told Brand and George Gill about the trouble back in town, and what to be on the lookout for—"

"You're not thinking he'll be coming here, to be sure."

"I'm not taking any chances. You're to stay within plain sight of the house at all times, is that clear?"

Her jaw took on a certain rigidity that usually spelled trouble. He had dealt with it before; with any luck at all, he'd be dealing with it for the next fifty years. But right now, he didn't have time. Aster had the jump on him, and if he didn't move fast to save his investment, he might lose it, and if he lost it, he just might lose his shipyard before it was even out of the planning stage.

"Promise me you'll behave, Katy?" She refused to look at him. He waited as long as he dared, feeling torn, hating the feeling. "You know I wouldn't leave you if I had any choice. I'll be back before you know it. You and Tara can have yourselves a nice beach holiday. You can compare notes with Maureen. Get her to tell you about her favorite recipe for punch. Ana swears it's Irish whiskey and prune juice."

He was trying to tease her into a better mood, as if she were no older than Tara. Katy was ashamed of herself. Taking a deep breath, she smiled. "We'll be just fine. You go along now and do whatever you have to do. Aster's probably just wanting attention. Some women are that way."

He burst out laughing. "You never cease to amaze me, you know that? Come and give me a kiss, and see if you can whistle up a breeze while you're still puckered. Otherwise, I might have to get out and walk."

"Or whistle up one of those noisy motor launches."

The good-bye kiss nearly tore her apart. She had thought they'd have a chance to talk last night, but she'd been more tired than she'd realized. By the time he'd come up to bed—if he ever had—she'd fallen asleep.

Of course he had come to bed. Just because he hadn't been there when she'd woken up, that didn't mean he hadn't been to bed at all. His pillow was rumpled. His town clothes had been hanging in the closet next to her own.

She put her heart and soul into the kiss, telling him all the things she lacked the courage to put into words. Hoping he would understand. Hoping he would come back to her quickly, before her doubts could overshadow her dreams.

"God, I hate to leave you like this," he whispered hoarsely, after kissing her until her knees nearly buckled. She touched his face, his neck above the collar of the soft blue

shirt he'd put on for the journey, a complete change from
the ones he usually wore.

He looked so different without his narrow black boots,
the narrow black pants, and the elegant black frock coat he
wore so well. She liked the way he looked now, with the
sunlight glinting down on his bare head. "Go along with
you, we'll be waiting when you get back."

"Katy, I—" She waited, but instead of saying whatever
it was he'd been going to say, he kissed her again. She
clung to him until he gently set her aside and left, and then
she hurried to the bedroom window to watch as he emerged
below on the boardwalk, and strode down to the waterfront,
where . . .

Where Margaret waited, her luggage stacked beside her.

Chapter Twenty-two

They were going at it tooth and nail when Galen loped up the gangplank. Dropping his hastily packed bag by the nearest stanchion, he was half tempted to turn around and go back to The Landing.

Face red, hair awry, and her eyes blazing, Aster looked ready to take on all comers. Bellfort was glaring right back at her, his grooming for once less than impeccable. Neither of them paid the slightest attention to their growing audience.

"Dammit, you're not taking her out, Aster. I can't allow it."

Fury jerked her chin up another notch. "*You* can't allow it! You can't *allow it*? Let me tell you something, Jack Bellfort, nobody tells me what I can or can't do!"

Arms crossed, Galen leaned against the bulkhead and watched. They were well matched, but his money was on Aster. Bellfort was too much the gentleman to fight dirty. Dirty was Aster's favorite technique.

Bellfort caught sight of Galen and shook his head. Galen interpreted the look as butt out, I can handle this. He nodded, reassessing the odds.

"I'll have you thrown off my boat! You have no right—!"

"I have every right," Bellfort said calmly. Galen could have told him that with Aster, calmness would carry him about two minutes into an argument. After that, it was no holds barred.

Those members of the crew and staff not on duty had gathered to watch the match. No doubt money would change hands, based on the outcome. Ila edged up beside him, her thin lips pursed in disapproval. "Reckon you heard the ruckus all the way down the Banks. Lord help us, if she sets off in this old bucket, I'll not be on board. I've known Elsworth Tyler since the day he come to town selling patent medicine. That man never spent a penny in his life on nothing that didn't show. Silk shirt and threadbare drawers."

"Or as they say out West where I spent a few memorable months, big hat, no cattle."

"Where's Katy? Don't tell me you two busted up already."

"She's still at The Landing. And no we haven't, so you can climb down off your high horse."

She poked him in the arm and said, "Humph!"

Bellfort cast him a look of appeal. "Would you please enlighten my new business partner, McKnight? I can't seem to get through to her."

"What new business partner?" Aster demanded, suspicion momentarily undermining her anger.

"Haven't you told her yet?" Galen asked Bellfort, feigning innocence. They had barely opened negotiations when he'd had to drop it to get Katy out of town. Now he tried to recall if Bellfort had actually agreed to his asking price. He queried with the lift of a brow.

Bellfort replied with an imperceptible nod.

Galen turned to Aster, "Sorry, I thought I'd made it clear before I left. Bellfort's bought my shares. He now owns fifty-one percent of the *Pasquotank Queen*. I believe that gives him controlling interest?"

Damned if he didn't feel sorry for her. She looked like a kid left holding a sucker stick while a dog ran away with her candy.

Evidently, Bellfort thought so, too, because he moved in

on her left flank, took her arm under his, and said, "Now
that we've settled that, how about joining me for dinner
aboard the *Belle*. I have a business proposition for you."

Galen had an idea that the proposition might involve a
little more than business. This time, though, he wasn't placing any bets. Shaking his head in amazement, he watched
them stroll off, arm in arm.

"Looks like a case of April and May to me," Ila said
smugly.

"Dream on. Bellfort would never—Jack and Aster? You
really think so?"

"Too many sparks not to be no fire."

Well, hell. He'd broken off his honeymoon for *this*?

"Why didn't he just tell her he was buying me out? Why
the devil did I have to come all this way for nothing?"

"A woman like Aster, she's got to see proof. She don't
believe nothing a man says without he can prove it."

"Comes from being her father's daughter. Anything new
about the murder?"

"Come on inside where we don't have every ear in Pasquotank County listening in, and I'll tell you all I know."

Over two mugs of Willy's hard-boiled coffee, the telling
didn't take much time. Sal was having trouble keeping food
down. There was some question of whether or not she'd be
able to carry the baby full term. The doctor had gone to
Charlie, who'd panicked and spilled his guts in exchange
for a shorter term, with the result that the police were in the
process of winding up the whole affair.

"You mean it's all finished?"

Ila nodded. "If it's not done yet, it will be once they pry
that feller out of that huntin' lodge. He went to earth over
near Johnstown. Once they rounded up Buck—"

Galen knew about Buck, but still he was disappointed.
He would have sworn the ex-convict he'd taken on as a
bouncer was a reformed man.

"Don't look so surprised, you can't save 'em all. It was

Charlie and Buck that tipped off the outside man. His name was Shy—well, I reckon it weren't his real name. All the same, Buck would go outside for a break, pass the word to Shy, and Shy and this other feller would be waiting to relieve the night's big winner of his poke."

"Just which one did Katy see, Shy or this other fellow?"

"Shy was the one that got a wire twisted round his neck and was throwed overboard. Doc told Charlie, and Charlie told Sal, and she told me, that the way he figured was, the murderer snuck up behind Shy, caught him around the neck with the wire, then shoved him overboard. Charlie was some scared, I can tell you."

Ila finished her coffee and slid the cup onto a cluttered nightstand, while Galen tried to sort it all out in his mind. He kept thinking, Charlie and Buck. Damn. Right here under his nose, all the time.

What if Tara hadn't come to him? What if he'd thought the whole thing was just another of her fanciful tales? He could have lost Katy. He could have lost them both.

Ila shook her head. "Awful business. I don't mind telling you, I had myself a glass of whiskey before I went to bed last night so I wouldn't dream about it." She lifted her feet onto the bed, dislodging Tara's kitten. The kitten promptly jumped up onto Galen's lap and began exercising her claws on his thigh.

"Falling out among thieves, that's what old Judge Henry called it. Reckon he ought to know, he's seen enough of 'em in his day."

Galen was depressed. "Buck and Charlie. Damn, I hate that. They were both good workers. I trusted them."

Ila nodded sagely. "You give 'em a chance, that's all any man can do. It's not your fault they didn't take it. Like I said, you can't save 'em all." She folded back her skirts, rolled down her black cotton stockings, and rubbed liniment into her knee, totally unself-conscious in the presence of her employer. "Now, you want to tell me how come you set out with Katy and come back with another woman on your arm?"

"Speaking of trust," he said. His smile had a bitter edge to it. "Don't you trust me to be a faithful husband?"

"About as much as I trust anything in pants. No, I take that back. You're no brighter than most men, but you're a darn sight more honest. So who is she? How come you left Katy behind and brought this other woman with you? How does Katy feel about it?"

"Katy's just fine. She knows how I feel about her."

Did she? Or had he been too busy impressing on Brand and George Gill the importance of not letting Katy or Tara out of their sight to do justice to his new role as husband?

At Ila's skeptical look, he said, "In case it escaped your notice, Margaret's not with me, she's on her way to Atlanta." Easing the kitten off his lap, he sketched in a relationship that went back to a time when they'd all been dirty-faced kids running wild in the woods.

Not that Margaret's face had ever been dirty, or any other part of her so far as he knew. She was the kind of kid who could stay clean making mud pies. "Margaret was always the princess, the one we rescued. Mostly Brand did the rescuing. Liam usually tripped over his shoelaces, and I was always delegated to tote him back to the house, squalling his head off. Standard kid stuff."

"Yes, well—that didn't look like any kid I saw escorting to the depot before you even let me know you was back in town. Looked to me like you was sneaking around, trying to hide something."

What he was hiding—not too successfully—was the fact that Katy was a full day's sail away, and it was killing him. That he couldn't just reach out and touch her, or hear her voice, or watch that funny-wise-innocent smile light her eyes when he least expected to see it.

If he'd known it was going to be this bad he'd have told Bellfort to handle the problem on his own. But when the message came, he hadn't stopped to think, he'd simply reacted.

Eyes burning from the smell of the liniment and a lack of sleep, he said, "Don't worry about Margaret, she's just an old friend. Her husband died a few months ago, and she's not handling it too well. Ana felt sorry for her." He had an idea his sister-in-law had also had something else in mind. "She was ready to leave, and we happened to share a ferry ride, that's all."

"Yes, well . . . I hope you know what you're doing. If it was me, and my new husband took off with another woman, I wouldn't sit back and let him get away with it, I can tell you that."

"Katy understands."

"Humph. What a woman understands and what she'll put up with is two different things."

It was nearly five that evening by the time Galen was ready to head out again. Ila had suggested he'd do better to get a few hours of sleep and set out fresh the next morning. "The sheets has already cooled off now. A few more hours won't make no difference."

"They will to me."

So he'd bribed Pam to stand by to take him back as soon as he'd talked to Charlie and Buck, to the police, and met at the bank with Bellfort to sign over his shares. If he thought he could flap his arms and fly to Pea Island, he'd have tried it. As it was, he'd try and catch a few hours' sleep on the way down sound, because he had no intention of wasting time sleeping once he had Katy back in his arms again.

Ila was there on the wharf to see him off. "What do you want me to tell that poor girl if you and that old man fetch up on a shoal and drown trying to swim ashore?"

"Pam could sail these waters blindfolded."

"Yes, well . . . don't you go taking no more chances.

There's too much traffic on the water these days, if you ask me."

As it happened, there was a motor launch plowing full chisel through the narrows at that very moment, belching steam and cinders. With a woman standing in the bow. A woman who looked remarkably like . . .

"Katy?" Galen squinted his eyes against the glare.

The launch pulled in astern of the *Queen,* and without waiting for assistance, Katy scrambled up onto the wharf on her hands and knees. By the time she was on her feet, dusting off her hands, Galen was standing before her, a look of amazement on his face.

"Where is she?" Katy demanded grimly.

"Woman, are you *crazy*?"

"Not as crazy as you take me for, if you think I'm going to let her have you. You're *my* husband, Galen McKnight. Marrying me was your decision—nobody talked you into it. So now, you're stuck with me."

If a bolt of lightning had sliced down from the clear sky and splintered him right wide open, he couldn't have looked any more dumbfounded.

"Well? Where is she? You might as well tell her I'm here to claim what's mine. She had her chance. It's not my fault she was too stupid to take it, but it's too late now."

"You tell 'im, honey," called out a raddled old whore who should have retired years ago. A cheer went up from a handful of waterfront regulars gathered to watch the show.

Galen wouldn't have been surprised to see Katy turn and take a bow. He was torn between wanting to turn her over his knee and tossing her over his shoulder to take her back on board the *Queen,* where they might stand a chance of finding some privacy.

Not that there was much privacy to be found even there, with the evening crowd beginning to arrive. Dammit, when a man's home was also his place of business, there was no place to hide.

"We'll discuss this in my quarters, if you don't mind, madam."

The steam launch operator lifted out Katy's bag and set it on the wharf just as Pam came alongside. "Ready to set out, Cap'n?"

"Look, can you wait—that is, I'm not sure—" Helplessly, he looked at Katy. She was beating a fast tattoo with one foot. Arms crossed over her bosom, she was pale but determined not to give an inch. "How about tomorrow morning? No—make that the day after. Oh, hell, can you pick us up here on your regular run?"

"Shore can. Rate I'm a-goin', I'll make me a fortune, runnin' mail, freight, and crazy folk up an' down the Banks."

Now that she was actually here, Katy was finding it almost impossible to hang on to her courage. Ever since she'd first set out, not two hours after Galen had left with Margaret, she'd been juggling doubts and anger. If it hadn't been so hard trying to talk over the monstrous noise, she might have told the boy to take her back, because she'd changed her mind.

Instead, she'd huddled miserably in the open launch while sparks and smoke escaped from the fire box and steam belched noisily from the single stack on the boiler. Juggling hope and regret, she'd thought about a row of graves on a certain hillside an ocean away. Feeling lost and lonely, she wondered what on earth she would do if Galen no longer wanted her.

Go on the way she had always done. What choice did she have?

Shortly after they crossed the inlet the pilot shouted, "Roanoke Sound! Over yonder's Nags Head!"

Where she'd spent her wedding night.

The pilot was young, scarcely out of his teens from the looks of him. Evidently he considered himself something of a guide. "Point Harbor," was his next designation. He'd waved an arm toward a smudge of shoreline off to the right, and later on he'd informed her at the top of his voice that they were now entering the Albemarle Sound.

It had all looked the same to Katy. By the time they'd entered the mouth of the Pasquotank River, she'd been sick with fatigue, and even sicker with doubts.

Now, without another word, Galen led her up to his private quarters and ushered her inside, ignoring curious stares and hastily stifled questions. He locked the door, looking every bit as grim as she was feeling, if nowhere near as lost.

Glancing around, Katy tried to tell herself she didn't care.

"If you're looking for Margaret, she's not here. She's never been here."

Katy shrugged, as if it really didn't matter. Inside, she was dying. The outburst of anger, indignation, and possessiveness that had launched her hasty flight had drained away before they'd even lost sight of Merriweather's Landing.

Ana had tried to assure her that Margaret meant nothing at all to Galen, and that their leaving together had been mere coincidence, but Katy had been beyond consolation.

It was Brand who'd said, "Let her go, honey. Let her do whatever she thinks best." And then he'd gone out and waved in one of the small motor launches and bribed the operator to take her all the way to Elizabeth City—paid him rather a lot, she was afraid, but that was the least of her worries now.

"Oh—here's this. Brand told me to give it to you." She dug a rumpled envelope from her purse.

They were both standing. A mere five feet of carpet separated them, but it felt more like five miles of barren desert. Katy had never felt so alone in her life.

Galen ripped open the sealed envelope, scanned the few lines, and she watched in amazement as his face crinkled into a smile.

Her heart was breaking, and he was *smiling*?

"Here, read it," he said, and handed her the note. Katy

shot him a suspicious look, then took out her glasses, slid them on, and did her best to decipher what was written there.

"Accept delivery? Merchandise nonreturnable? What merchandise?"

"My brother's idea of a joke. Katy, Margaret's halfway to Atlanta by now. She didn't even hang around long enough to cast a shadow. Do you honestly think I wanted to leave you?" Judging from the stricken look on her face, she obviously had. "Sweetheart, I explained why I had to leave."

"With Margaret," she reminded him.

"I told you, she was only along for the ride. Margaret only went along to help Ana with the baby, but she's used to much fancier watering holes. Believe me, she'd had quite enough of Merriweather's Landing even before we got there."

He saw her gaze shift to his bookshelf and remembered the pair of photographs he'd set out when he'd first moved aboard. They happened to be the only pictures he had to remind him of home. A picture of the horse barn, or his father's old farm manager, would have meant as much. More, in fact.

Someday he would have to tell her about all that, but not now. Right now, all in the world he wanted to do was hold her in his arms until neither one of them could think beyond the moment.

He opened his arms.

She took a step back.

It wasn't going to be quite that simple. "All right, suppose we start at the beginning," he said with a sigh. "Sit down, this might take a while."

He started with the longstanding competition between the *Pasquotank Queen* and the *Albemarle Belle,* and Aster's determination to see Jack Bellfort's every bet and raise him. From there he went on to Bellfort's unexpected offer to buy his share of the *Queen.* He even threw in his own suspicion that Bellfort had something a bit more personal in mind than a simple, straightforward business deal, but that was their business, not his.

And then he went on to tell her what he knew about the crime that had led to their marriage. Not that he put it in those terms. He might not be the world's greatest diplomat, but he did know that much.

"So that's where we stand at the moment. I was on my way back to The Landing when you showed up."

Katy bit her lip. Galen stared at the place where her white tooth sunk into the soft pink flesh. His groin tightened. It took every bit of self-control he possessed not to let his actions speak for him, but she was still skittish. He didn't know quite how to convince her, and was afraid of saying the wrong thing.

"Is that it?"

"Is that what? I've told you all I know, Katy. The police are on the way to putting the murderer behind bars. They don't have a high tolerance around here for that sort of thing. Buck and Charlie will have to put in some time behind bars, but as Charlie's a first-time offender—oh, he's been in a few scrapes before, but nothing serious—he'll be out in time for Sal's big event. Now, does that about cover everything?"

She looked as if she wanted more. Not for the first time, Galen wished he hadn't relied so heavily on the fact that women seemed to like him without any effort on his part. He hadn't developed a lick of skill when it came to dealing with them outside the bedroom.

Of course, they weren't outside the bedroom. As it happened, there was a perfectly good bed going to waste.

Uh-uh. He wasn't going to take the easy way out, not this time. He had too much riding on this one.

"Dammit, Katy, I—"

"I love you."

"I don't know what—*what did you say*?"

"I'm not asking you to love me back, but you might as

well know I'll not be stepping aside for Margaret or any
other woman."

Becalmed. Dead in the water. The wind went out of his
sails so fast he couldn't find breath to speak, even if he'd
known what to say.

She was looking straight at him, as unflinching as gran-
ite. Not for the first time Galen told himself there ought
to be a law against eyes that clear and direct. He couldn't
think, much less dissemble, even if he'd wanted to.

She was waiting for him to say it. To say either that he
did or he didn't.

He did. The certainty of it damn near floored him. All
this time it had been growing inside him—this feeling of tenderness, of protectiveness, of pride and possessiveness—
this thing that made him feel as if she were as much a part
of him as his own heart—it was love.

Hesitantly at first, stumbling over his words, and then
with growing assurance, he told her so.

A long while later, they got around to talking again. That
is, to talking about something other than the miracle that
had brought them together against all odds, that had captured them both and bound them inextricably together for
all time.

They talked about the house on the other side of the river.
Katy wanted yellow. Galen would have agreed to paint it
purple with lime green stripes if she'd asked him to.

Katy insisted she still intended to open her own business,
and telling himself he might as well take the giant step into
the twentieth century, when women were probably going to
rule the world, anyway, he said he'd back her in whatever
she chose to do.

They talked about Tara, and the fact that she was growing up, and Galen figured he might as well get in some
practice at being a father. Although, God help him if any of

his children showed signs of inheriting what Katy called the Sight.

The Sight. Was it really just humbug?

He thought about green tables and gold, and about a few more of Tara's hit-or-miss prophecies. He didn't know if there was anything to it or not, but something had brought Katy to him. That was miracle enough to last him a lifetime.

BRONWYN WILLIAMS

"Simply wonderful! Don't miss this novel or you'll be unfulfilled!"
—Catherine Coulter, for **SLOW SURRENDER**

"A terrific read. I loved it!"—Pamela Morsi, for **SEASPELL**

"Filled with sexual tension and humor."
—*Romantic Times*, for **HALFWAY HOME**

□**ENTWINED**	(407512—$5.99)
□**SEASPELL**	(407504—$5.99)
□**HALFWAY HOME**	(406982—$5.99)
□**SLOW SURRENDER**	(406435—$5.50)
□**BEHOLDEN**	(407490—$5.99)

Prices slightly higher in Canada

Payable in U.S. funds only. No cash/COD accepted. Postage & handling: U.S./CAN. $2.75 for one book, $1.00 for each additional, not to exceed $6.75; Int'l $5.00 for one book, $1.00 each additional. We accept Visa, Amex, MC ($10.00 min.), checks ($15.00 fee for returned checks) and money orders. Call 800-788-6262 or 201-933-9292, fax 201-896-8569; refer to ad #TOPHR4

Penguin Putnam Inc.   Bill my: □Visa □MasterCard □Amex_____(expires)
P.O. Box 12289, Dept. B   Card#_____
Newark, NJ 07101-5289   Signature_____
Please allow 4-6 weeks for delivery.
Foreign and Canadian delivery 6-8 weeks.

Bill to:
Name_____
Address_____City_____
State/ZIP_____
Daytime Phone #_____

Ship to:
Name_____ Book Total $_____
Address_____ Applicable Sales Tax $_____
City_____ Postage & Handling $_____
State/ZIP_____ Total Amount Due $_____

This offer subject to change without notice.

SUSAN KING

☐ LAIRD OF THE WIND   0-451-40768-7/$5.99

In medieval Scotland, the warrior known as Border Hawk seizes the castle belonging to the father of the beautiful Isabel Scott, famous throughout the Lowlands for her gift of prophecy. During the battle, Isabel is injured while fighting alongside her men, and placed under Border Hawk's protection. As the border wars rage on, the warrior and prophetess engage in a more intimate conflict, discovering their love for the Scottish borderlands is surpassed only by their love for each other.

Also available:

☐ THE ANGEL KNIGHT	0-451-40662-1/$5.50
☐ THE BLACK THORNE'S ROSE	0-451-40544-7/$4.99
☐ LADY MIRACLE	0-451-40766-0/$5.99
☐ THE RAVEN'S MOON	0-451-18868-3/$5.99
☐ THE RAVEN'S WISH	0-451-40545-5/$4.99

Prices slightly higher in Canada

Payable in U.S. funds only. No cash/COD accepted. Postage & handling: U.S./CAN. $2.75 for one book, $1.00 for each additional, not to exceed $6.75; Int'l $5.00 for one book, $1.00 each additional. We accept Visa, Amex, MC ($10.00 min.), checks ($15.00 fee for returned checks) and money orders. Call 800-788-6262 or 201-933-9292, fax 201-896-8569; refer to ad #TOPHR1

Penguin Putnam Inc.

P.O. Box 12289, Dept. B

Newark, NJ 07101-5289

Please allow 4-6 weeks for delivery.

Foreign and Canadian delivery 6-8 weeks.

Bill my: ☐ Visa ☐ MasterCard ☐ Amex _____ (expires)

Card#_____

Signature_____

Bill to:

Name_____

Address_____ City_____

State/ZIP_____

Daytime Phone #_____

Ship to:

Name_____ Book Total $_____

Address_____ Applicable Sales Tax $_____

City_____ Postage & Handling $_____

State/ZIP_____ Total Amount Due $_____

This offer subject to change without notice.

ROMANTIC ESCAPES